SHE'S HIDDEN HER
MAGIC FOR TOO LONG

SEP   2022

**Books by Mara Rutherford
available from Inkyard Press**

The Poison Season
Luminous

Crown of Coral and Pearl Series

Crown of Coral and Pearl
Kingdom of Sea and Stone

LUMINOUS

MARA RUTHERFORD

inkyard
PRESS

If you purchased this book without a cover you should be aware
that this book is stolen property. It was reported as "unsold and
destroyed" to the publisher, and neither the author nor the
publisher has received any payment for this "stripped book."

Recycling programs
for this product may
not exist in your area.

ISBN-13: 978-1-335-42685-7

Luminous

First published in 2021. This edition published in 2022.

Copyright © 2021 by Mara Rutherford

All rights reserved. No part of this book may be used or reproduced in any manner
whatsoever without written permission except in the case of brief quotations
embodied in critical articles and reviews.

This is a work of fiction. Names, characters, places and incidents are either the
product of the author's imagination or are used fictitiously. Any resemblance to
actual persons, living or dead, businesses, companies, events or locales is entirely
coincidental.

For questions and comments about the quality of this book, please contact us
at CustomerService@Harlequin.com.

Inkyard Press
22 Adelaide St. West, 41st Floor
Toronto, Ontario M5H 4E3, Canada
www.InkyardPress.com

Printed in U.S.A.

I wish I could show you, when you are lonely or in darkness, the astonishing light of your own being.
—Hafez

IVERNA

HANDER

CRAVEN

CORONE

Liora's house

Sylvan

TEZHIA

ANTALLA

N

TREMELLE

BELASAVA

Vaile River

MAP ILLUSTRATION: MARISA HOPKINS

Keep watch, my dear, for the Evening Star,
She warns when night is falling.
Make haste, fair maidens, into bed,
'Fore Belle Sabine comes calling.

ONE

My father once described magic as an invisible beast, an unseen enemy that could snatch our lives away at any moment. As a small, impressionable child, I had imagined a lupine creature lurking outside among the whispering pines, breathing over my shoulder in our garden. For years, I didn't even leave the house; it was magic that had killed my mother, after all.

I was old enough now to understand that magic didn't work that way. But as I hurried down the dark road, past the woods that had become my haven during daylight hours, my childhood fears didn't feel so foolish. I glanced behind me, sure I'd find Belle Sabine, the fabled witch of every young woman's nightmares, swooping down as silent as an owl, ready to steal my youth and leave an empty husk behind.

To my relief, there was nothing there. My only traveling companion was the wind nipping at my heels, spurring me forward. But in my brief distraction, I tripped over a rock in the road, falling hard onto my knees. Cursing myself for my clumsiness and superstition, I dusted off my hands, wincing as a sharp pebble dislodged from my palm. I couldn't afford this kind of delay. It was close to midnight, and there was no moon to speak of, which made my situation even more precarious; my exposed skin glowed so brightly that moths circled me like a flame. But my little sister, Mina, was missing. I had to tell Father.

As I rose, I heard the sound of footsteps up the road. I glanced around for a place to hide, but there was no time. A moment later, a figure loomed at the margins of my glow.

Some said Belle Sabine had died, others that she was biding her time until the townspeople became complacent once again. But I was convinced she had come to kill me on the one night I had dared to venture past our threshold.

I shrank back as skirts and slippered feet came into view, followed by a woman's arms cradling a basket, and finally, the face of Margana, the weaver who lived next door. Not here to kill me, then. But a witch, nevertheless. And one arguably as dangerous as Belle Sabine, given who she worked for.

"What are you doing on the road, Liora? It's the middle of the night."

"Mina is gone," I said. "Father is still at work, and I didn't know what else to do."

Margana scrutinized me for a moment. "You're a witch."

A chill that had nothing to do with the cool night air crept over my scalp. No one had ever called me a witch to my face before, though of course I knew what I was. My entire life revolved around my glowing skin and the fear that the kingdom's most powerful warlock would discover it. Lord Darius was employed by the king himself, gathering mages and torturing them if they didn't do his bidding.

I pulled Father's cloak tighter around myself, but it was fu-
tile. She already knew. I had wasted too much time getting up
the nerve to leave the house after I found Mina's bed empty,
wringing my hands at the window, wondering if she'd been
kidnapped by drifters or lured into the forest by a ghost lantern. Then, once I was on the road, I had foolishly stopped
to look at the devil's footprints, little white mushrooms that
grew in pairs of two, resembling the cloven hooves of a demon.
I'd seen them in daylight plenty of times, but never at night.
They had caught my eye because their glow was so similar
to my own.

Oddly, Margana's basket was full of the mushrooms. Her
cornflower-blue eyes and auburn hair were pale and other-
worldly in their light. As if sensing my curiosity, she shifted
the basket to her other hip. Margana was one of the few people
who lived outside the gates of the ancient village of Sylvan,
like us. She was also my best friend Evran's mother—and the
only other witch I knew.

"I always wondered why your father moved you girls out
here after your mother died," she said. "Now it all makes
sense. But something tells me your father wouldn't be pleased
to know you're outside, exposing yourself." She grabbed one
of my hands and turned it over, examining it like a bruised
apple at market. Against Margana's dull skin, mine looked
false, as if I wasn't a real person at all.

I pulled my hand free as politely as possible. "I should go."

She sighed. "Keep your head down, and pray you don't meet
anyone on the road. Darius's spies are everywhere."

My eyes widened in fear, and she chuckled to herself. "Not
me, silly girl."

I swallowed audibly. If there really were spies in Sylvan,
Margana was the most likely suspect. After all, she did work

for Lord Darius. She might not be his servant by choice, but he was dangerous enough that no mage dared cross him. No mage who had lived to tell about it, anyway.

I was about to step around her when my eyes drifted to the basket once again. "I thought the devil's footprints were poisonous."

Her lips curved in a smile that didn't reach her eyes. "Oh, they are. Highly. Fortunately, I don't plan on eating them. Good luck, Liora."

I nodded and hurried to the stone steps leading down to Sylvan, which was tucked away in a gorge, hidden from the roving eyes of river pirates. Above me, a heavy iron chain was suspended between the cliffs. As far as I knew, Sylvan was the only village in Antalla—maybe the world—that could boast having attracted not one, but two falling stars. A fragment of the first had been melted into the shape of a five-pointed star and hung from the chain. At night, it was only a glimmer overhead.

The second star—*my* star—had disintegrated amid the flames when it landed.

I wound my way silently through Sylvan's narrow streets, toward Father's shop. He and Adelle, my older, more responsible sister, were likely the only ones working at this hour. Just as I quickened my pace, I heard a high-pitched shriek from somewhere above me. I looked up to where a lamp winked on in an apartment window, illuminating two silhouettes, then down to the shop on my left. The tailor's shop.

Mina.

Without thinking, I grabbed the cast-iron boot scraper sitting by the front door of the shop and hurled it through the window. Glass shattered, leaving a jagged hole that gaped like a mouth midscream.

Heart racing, I flattened myself against the alcove by the door as a man shouted and a window screeched open. The tailor, a young man nearly as alluring as the fabrics he sold, poked his head out for a moment, then disappeared, likely heading downstairs to look for the culprit. I scurried to the nook in front of the butcher's, hoping my light would be hidden there.

"Get behind me," Luc said from somewhere inside the shop. "The thief could still be out there."

"You're so brave."

I sighed in relief at the sound of Mina's voice, before fury shot through me like an arrow. I should have known she would come to the tailor's; she had flirted with Luc relentlessly today, which was how we'd acquired four yards of the champagne-colored silk she wanted for the dress I'd spent all evening working on.

A moment later, they emerged onto the street, Mina clutching at Luc's sleeve as he lifted his lamp and peered into the darkness.

He tossed his black hair out of his eyes and frowned. "It doesn't look like they stole anything. Just vandals, I suppose."

"Or someone trying to send you a message," Mina breathed, dramatic as ever. "Do you have any nemeses?"

When he turned his dark gaze on her, something tugged at my heart. She was wearing a dress I'd made for myself when I was her age. It hung loose on her thin frame, but the hem grazed her calves, a sure sign she had altered it. She had nothing but a shawl pulled around her shoulders, and from where I stood, it was painfully clear that the tailor was not interested in her the way she no doubt hoped.

"I have to find a member of the night guard and report this. You shouldn't be here. If your father catches you, he'll have me hanged. You're a sweet girl, Mina, but this is inappropriate."

"But the silk…"

"That was for your sister. Now, please, go home."

Mina caught her lip in her teeth to keep from crying. With a nod, she hurried away, tears already streaming down her cheeks. I waited for Luc to start up the street before I ran out of the alcove to catch her.

She squealed in alarm when I placed my hand on her shoulder, and I quickly clapped my other hand over her mouth.

"It's me," I whispered, lowering my hand slowly when I was confident she wouldn't scream.

She swiped at her tears. "Liora? What are you doing out? What if someone sees you?"

My anger softened at her concern, until I remembered that she was the reason I was out in the first place. "I might ask you the same questions. If Father had come home and found you missing, he'd have killed you."

"And what if he goes home and finds both of us missing? Have you considered that?"

I opened my mouth to scold her, but she was right. "You can explain what you were doing once we get back," I said.

In typical Mina fashion, she stuck her tongue out at me, then turned and ran toward home.

We were indeed lucky. We made it home not long before Father and Adelle. By the time he came to our room to check on us, we were both in bed. I waved sleepily at him and Mina let out an emphatic snore, but once the door was closed, I threw back my covers and leaped out of bed.

"I hope you have a good explanation for this," I hissed.

Her voice was muffled by the thick blanket pulled up to her nose, but I could hear the tremor in it when she said, "I thought Luc liked me."

"And I thought you were dead!" I whisper-shouted, then stalked to the window ledge to keep myself from throttling her. I plucked a pendant from the collar of my nightgown, running my fingers over the five points on the star charm to calm myself. Evran had given it to me, years ago, and its contours were as familiar to me now as the feel of his hand in mine as he pulled me through the Sylvan woods toward home at twilight. Perhaps I was being too hard on Mina. I would risk a lot of things for Evran.

"Luc told me he was having a party tonight," she said. "I didn't realize how late it was when I got there. Everyone else had already left."

I was surprised that the thought of her getting ready for a party, the excitement she must have felt as she sneaked into Sylvan to meet a handsome young man, made me more envious than angry. "I heard you cry out."

The whites of her eyes flashed in the dark.

"Don't you dare roll your eyes at me," I snapped.

"I'm just stretching them, Ora." The world-weary tone was classic Mina: so eager to be a grown-up, ever since she was little. "A moth got tangled in my hair. Anyway, Luc was a perfect gentleman. And as it turns out, it's not me he wants."

The silk was for me. The last of my anger waned as I imagined how sure Mina must have been of Luc to do something so foolish, only to find she'd made a huge mistake. This was his fault as much as it was hers. "He was just being kind because I spend so much money in his shop."

She snorted. "He spoke about you the entire time. He asked why you hadn't come to the party, and what you liked to do in your free time, and why he never saw you out in town."

"What did you tell him?" I dropped the pendant into my

collar and pulled back the edge of the curtain just a bit to gaze at the real stars.

"I told him you were making me a dress, that that's what you're doing most of the time."

I sighed and let the curtain fall. For a girl with glowing skin, I sounded unbearably dull. But it was the truth. If I wasn't sewing, I was cooking, cleaning, or rereading one of our few books.

Father trusted me enough to let me go out on sunny days now. *The smallest stars don't shine at noon*, he said, and my glow could be kept dim as long as I stayed in control of my emotions. But the downside of having even just a little bit of freedom was that it came with responsibilities. Father had only given me permission to go to town for errands, never to dawdle, which made taking Mina along particularly frustrating. She had made an art form out of window-shopping. I missed my afternoons in the woods with Evran, those glorious days when I could sneak out unnoticed while Father was working and my sisters were in their lessons.

I climbed back into bed and pulled the covers up, a wave of guilt washing over me. Had I really believed Mina was in mortal peril? Because if not, there was no excuse for my own behavior. What if some part of me had risked going out tonight because I wanted to prove to myself, finally, that my magic wasn't as dangerous as Father feared?

If that was the case, I had failed spectacularly. It had only taken a few minutes for me to undo all our years of hard work, and I couldn't blame my sister for that.

"Promise me you won't sneak out again, Mina. I don't know what I'd do if something happened to you."

She twisted onto her side to face me. "I'm sorry. I should never have put you at risk like that. I won't do it again."

"It's all right. Get some sleep now."

Mina responded a moment later with a very genuine snore.

I smiled and tried to fall asleep myself, but I lay awake for hours, thinking about Margana. Would she tell Darius about me, potentially destroying not just my life but those of everyone I loved? I thought of Father and wondered if all this time it hadn't been me he was protecting, but them.

Because as much as I had wanted to believe that the invisible beast was *out there*, that if I simply hid myself away like a secret, we would be safe, I had known for quite some time that the beast Father feared most lived inside of me.

TWO

The next morning, I waited until my father and Adelle went to the shop and Mina was studying with her very old, very nearsighted tutor, then hurried across the road to the woods in search of Evran. He had become oddly reclusive in the past few months, but I needed to know if his mother was going to keep my secret or if our family should start looking for somewhere else to live.

It hadn't always been this dangerous for mages. But with Lord Darius hunting them down, most people didn't want to associate with anyone capable of wielding magic. It put them at risk, too. Public sentiment had slowly soured over time, until most people were prejudiced against mages. It had never just been Darius I was hiding my magic from—it was the world.

I found Evran in our blackberry glade, the secret meeting spot we'd discovered as children. No one else was foolish enough to brave the thorns to get to the little clearing in the middle, but Evran had pruned back the hedges in one spot to create a hidden tunnel. I had to get on hands and knees to use it now; either I had grown more than I realized, or lack of use had given the hedges an opportunity to run riot. Whatever the case, I emerged scratched and filthy, and more than a little annoyed.

"There you are," I huffed, straightening and brushing myself off. "I've been looking all over for you."

He was sitting cross-legged in the center of the glade, his face turned up to the sunlight filtering through the trees. At the sound of my voice, he lowered his chin and opened his eyes. He smiled, and for a moment I caught a familiar glint of mischief in his expression. "Why? Did you miss me?"

I tried to scowl as I sat down on the sparse grass, but my mouth twisted into an involuntary grin at his teasing. "Hardly. I had a bit of an emergency. I could have used your help."

Until last night, Evran had been the only person outside of our family who knew about my magic. I was six or seven the first time Adelle noticed him watching our house from the edge of the woods. Mina, who was cheeky even as a toddler, stuck her tongue out at him. When he stuck his out, too, I liked him instantly. He found me in our yard the next day, while Father was working, Mina was napping, and Adelle was hanging up the wash.

He had crept into the yard so quietly Adelle didn't hear him. As I watched him make his way carefully toward me, I tried to cover my hands in the folds of my skirt. But Evran took them in his own, staring like they were the most beautiful thing he'd ever seen. I should have been horrified— I was never ashamed of my magic, though I took Father's warnings seriously—but I trusted Evran from the start.

I couldn't pinpoint exactly when I'd fallen in love with him. It hadn't been the kind of whirlwind romance Mina dreamed of, or even the smart, sensible love that Adelle would no doubt find. It had been slow and gradual, like a season changing, and then all at once, a revelation. Like the moment you noticed that the barren branches of winter were suddenly heavy with blossoms.

It was clear to me now that he'd never so much as hinted at my secret to Margana. Not that I had ever doubted him.

I recounted the story of Mina's escapade and my run-in with his mother, though I left out the part about Luc and the silk. Evran didn't like Luc, and he'd been distant enough lately as it was.

By the time I was finished, his initial concern had faded to amusement. "Sounds like you handled things pretty well on your own," he said with a laugh. "I can't believe you broke the tailor's window."

"It's not funny." I punched him lightly on the shoulder. "What if I'd been discovered?"

He caught my hand, swiping at a scratch with his thumb. I felt my glow pulse brighter and blushed, wondering if he noticed.

"I'm sorry I wasn't there. I've been a bit distracted lately, I know."

Distracted was putting it mildly. He was as elusive as a fox during the day, and if there was any question of me join-ing him on his nocturnal escapades, I had firmly answered it last night. I glanced up into his eyes and noticed that the whites seemed red and irritated. It made the green of his irises even more brilliant.

"What's the matter?" I asked, momentarily setting aside my fear about his mother. "Maybe I can help."

I could read his expressions well enough to know that his smile was forced. "Not this time, I'm afraid. But I'll sort it out. Don't worry."

So something *was* troubling him. It was a relief that I wasn't imagining things, but it pained me to know I couldn't help. We sat in silence for a while, me absently braiding strands of dried grass while Evran soaked up what little sunshine he could. There were so many things I wanted to say to him, but I'd never been good at expressing my feelings. How could I be, when I'd spent most of my life trying to repress them?

"Do you think your mother will tell Darius about me?" I asked finally.

"Of course not. Mother despises him. And your magic isn't likely to interest him, anyway."

The words should have comforted me, but I had always been morbidly curious about magic, particularly my own. On some level, I might have even hoped there *was* more to me than glowing skin.

But it was a foolish notion. Far better to be boring than tortured, I reminded myself.

"I should get back. We're going to the farmers market this afternoon. I don't suppose you want to come?" Evran rarely strayed far from the woods, so I knew it was unlikely he'd say yes. But I couldn't help imagining the two of us out together, holding hands, drawing no more attention than any young couple.

When he shook his head, the sunlight turned the lightest strands of his auburn hair to gold. "I wish I could, but Mother needs my help with a loom. Try not to get into any more trouble, would you? Otherwise I'll have to start being the responsible one."

"No promises," I said with a smile, but we both knew there was nothing to worry about. Liora Duval didn't get into trouble.

My sisters and I walked along the side of the road toward town, Mina stopping every now and then to pluck a wild-flower and drop it into her basket. Underneath her blouse and skirt was the dress I'd made for her from Luc's silk, so lustrous it reflected golden light onto her skin. It was exactly the kind of fabric I was drawn to; dull cloth like wool or linen contrasted too harshly with my "condition," as Father called it.

The townspeople thought we were snobs, using the interest we earned off of their unpaid debts for our own vanity. I couldn't very well wear silk and satin while my sisters wore homespun—that would call more attention to my magic, not less—so we suffered the whispered insults of the townspeople: *Those Duval sisters, always buying tailor-made. Think they're too good for ready-made like the rest of us.*

The only person who didn't seem offended was Luc, since we spent more money in his shop than anyone else in town. But we couldn't live on satin and velvet; we needed food.

The farmers market was crowded today. Autumn was coming and the late-summer offerings were on display: plump red tomatoes, sweet corn, ripe melons. Money was tight, as always—Father teasingly lamented having three beautiful daughters to clothe, but pawnbroking was not a wealthy man's profession. Still, the ever-frugal Adelle had saved enough for us each to get a one-penny shaved ice, something cool for our walk home.

"Now this is a rare sight indeed," a familiar voice said behind me.

Mina went rigid, pretending to find her cherry ice infinitely fascinating, but Adelle, who knew nothing of our adventure last night, turned to smile at Luc.

"Good day, Mr. Moreau." She inclined her head politely. "How are you today?"

Father often remarked that Luc was suspiciously well-dressed for a village tailor, as if he must have some other, more nefarious source of income. But no one could deny Luc had excellent taste. "Better, now. I can't say I've seen all three Duval sisters together for at least a year. You look like a bouquet of spring flowers. Miss Liora," he added, tipping his hat. "You're looking especially well."

I bobbed a curtsy, wishing I had worn a hat instead of a kerchief today. I kept my dark hair hidden when I went out—otherwise, my glow radiated off it like a halo—but I had nothing to shade my flaming cheeks.

"Did you get the silk?" he asked me.

My eyes darted involuntarily to Mina's. "Yes, thank you." He knew we couldn't have afforded enough to make a dress, and he also knew that I wouldn't have accepted such a gift. Even Evran wouldn't have given me something so extravagant. It was wrong of Luc to use Mina like that, even if he had never seen her as anything more than my little sister.

Clearly oblivious to my true feelings about the gift, he leaned in conspiratorially and grinned. "I'm sure you've heard about our special visitor today."

I shook my head. "I'm afraid not. We rarely hear anything outside the Sylvan gates."

"Ah, then allow me the pleasure. Lord Darius was just in town."

I tensed at his words, and Mina placed a cold hand on

my arm, causing goose bumps to erupt on my skin. "Lord Darius is here, in Sylvan?"

"I imagine he's left by now. It's a shame you missed him. He has a new acquisition."

"A mage?" Adelle asked, her brow furrowed in concern.

"No. Three black sight hounds."

I gave a small internal sigh of relief, but when none of us responded, Luc cleared his throat. "*Magic* sight hounds," he continued. "They say they're not like normal dogs. Their muzzles are too pointy, their legs too long. And they don't hunt rabbits or squirrels."

Mina bounced on the balls of her feet with anticipation, revealing herself for the girl she was, not the woman she wanted to be. "What, then?"

Luc dropped his voice an octave. "They hunt mages."

Mina gasped, and I felt my own knees grow weak.

The tailor went on, apparently encouraged by our reactions. I couldn't imagine he truly enjoyed running into Darius, but he was a natural storyteller, and Mina made the perfect audience. "Just last week, they tore a witch to ribbons when she tried to flee." He tugged on the tail of a bow in Mina's hair for emphasis. "There wasn't enough left of her to bury when the hounds were through."

My stomach was already churning, but I had to know more if I hoped to protect myself. "What did she do?"

He shrugged, unconcerned. "I'm not sure that particularly mattered to the hounds."

I had always consoled myself with the fact that I was likely below Darius's notice, as Evran said. But could the same be said of the hounds? Sweat prickled my back, but I kept my expression vague. Sometimes my reputation as a snob worked to my advantage. Let Luc think I was above his gossip, rather than terrified for my own life.

"I'm surprised you didn't hear. I believe the weaver made them. Doesn't she live just down the road from your family, Miss Duval?" His dark eyes gleamed beneath his thick lashes.

"We have to go." Adelle was never rude or sharp-tongued, and her tone startled all of us. "I'm sorry. Good day, Mr. Moreau."

He frowned. "So soon?"

"I'm afraid so." She turned to leave, and I followed without a backward glance. "We must get back to the house, or we'll risk meeting Lord Darius on the road," Adelle said when we were out of earshot.

Mina clutched at my arm, spilling the remnants of my shaved ice.

Laden with our heavy baskets, the best we could manage was a brisk walk up the stone steps to the road. The sun was hot on our backs, and my silk blouse clung to me like a second skin. Tendrils of dark hair had managed to work their way free of my scarf, but there was no time to adjust it. We were just cresting the rise of the hill before our house when I heard the barking.

"He must be visiting Margana." My heart was racing now, and I could barely catch my breath. "What do we do?"

"Quickly." Adelle pointed to the woods. "We can hide there until he's gone."

We stumbled into the thick undergrowth of the forest, where at least it was cooler than on the road. Adelle led the charge and I followed, with Mina bringing up the rear. I could hear Adelle's heavy breaths and the occasional curse from Mina as we wound between the trees and stepped over fallen logs. I tried not to picture the witch who had been torn limb from limb, but as I passed a patch of devil's foot-prints, I shivered involuntarily.

Our house was the last one on the road out of Sylvan, be-yond Margana's. We would have to cross the open road to get to it. Through the trees, I could make out three horses grazing on the brambles in front of the weaver's house. Three dark shapes slithered around their hooves, sleek and sinuous as eels.

"We should go farther into the forest," I whispered.

Adelle shook her head. "There could be drifters."

"Or monsters," Mina breathed, her eyes going so wide I could see the whites all the way around. "What if there are Lusiri in the woods?"

"Honestly, Mina! Now isn't the time for one of your flights of fancy." Adelle peered through the trees toward home, then glanced at me. "I can't imagine the hounds will smell you from this far away."

"Do they smell the magic or see it?" I asked. "They're sight hounds. Who knows how close they need to be?"

We gasped in unison as a man plodded through the un-dergrowth behind us. He was wearing the black-and-white uniform of a palace guard. Adelle stepped in front of me, blocking me from view.

The guard stopped and straightened his tunic at the sight of us. "My sincerest apologies, ladies. I didn't mean to frighten you."

We curtsied as best we could under the weight of our bas-kets. "Good day, sir. We're sorry to have interrupted your... stroll." Adelle looked disheveled in the best possible way, her cheeks flushed the same pink as her blouse, her thick fishtail braid unraveling down her back.

The guard smiled at his own good fortune to encounter

such a lovely young woman in the forest. "You have nothing to fear, you know. Lord Darius is only here for the witch."

He couldn't possibly understand the irony of his words.

"Our house is just there," Adelle replied, pointing. "We don't want to disturb anyone."

"I assure you, it's no problem. Please, let me help you with those baskets." He took Adelle's in one hand and threaded his other arm through hers, leaving Mina and me to make do on our own. Even in her fear, Mina didn't spare him a hearty roll of her eyes, and I tried to take a deep breath. Maybe with an escort they knew, the dogs would leave us alone.

We had just broken out of the woods when Margana's front door opened. She stepped outside, scowling at the hounds and shooing them away from her. A moment later she noticed the guard and the three of us. Our eyes locked, and she started to mouth something to me.

Before she could finish, a man stepped out from behind her, and even though I'd never seen him before, I recognized him instantly.

I had done everything I could to avoid trouble my entire life, and now, it seemed, it had finally caught up with me.

THREE

My sisters and I froze. There was no time to cover my hair or make a run for the house. My heart pounded as Lord Darius took us in, three withered flowers strewn across a dusty road.

"Girls!" Margana shouted, running forward. "You look like you could use some help."

The hounds chased her, bounding with excitement. She reached me just before they did, pushing me behind her as the lead dog caught up.

Luc was right. There was something wrong with the black creatures, who looked like the elongated late-afternoon shadows of normal dogs. They circled us, their cold, wet noses pressing against our hands and legs, sniffing rapidly before letting out short, sharp exhalations. Their coats were as smooth and glossy as black satin stretched over their thin, muscular bodies. I struggled to subdue my glow, but it was hopeless. I was terrified.

"I see you've met my hounds."

I nudged one of the dogs away with my knee, carefully avoiding its dagger-sharp teeth, and looked up to find Lord Darius standing just a few feet from us. Adelle dropped into a graceful curtsy next to me, and Mina and I did our best imitations, though I was trembling like a cornered rabbit.

Margana only moved half a step to the side. "Lord Darius, I'd like you to meet the Duval sisters: Adelle, Liora, and Mina."

He bowed deeply. "It's a pleasure to meet you, ladies. I believe I knew your father, once. Is he at home?"

"I'm afraid he's in Sylvan working, my lord." Adelle's voice remained remarkably calm given how scared she must be.

Since the hounds hadn't torn me to pieces yet, I allowed myself a steadying breath. Darius looked younger than I'd expected, around Luc's age, although that would be the result of his magic. He must be over a century old by now. Dressed in riding attire, he had removed his dark jacket and rolled up his shirtsleeves. I considered myself an expert in color, but his hair and eye color were strangely difficult to pinpoint. Even looking at him I wasn't sure how to describe them: was his hair the color of wheat, or autumn leaves? Were his eyes hazel or bronze?

At some point in the last minute, all three dogs had converged on Margana and me. I gingerly kicked them away with my slippered feet, but they would not give up their sniffing and circling.

"My hounds like you." Darius's eyes met mine for the first time. They were the color of newly fallen acorns, I decided.

"I'm sure it's my magic they're interested in," Margana said. "Stupid creatures."

"On the contrary, they're quite intelligent. You should be

proud of them, Margana. You wove them, after all." Darius
knelt down, scratching one of the hounds behind the ears, but
his gaze never left mine. There wasn't a cloud in sight, and yet
I felt like my skin was glowing brighter than ever under his
scrutiny. "Have you heard of my hounds? What they can do?"

Adelle responded before I could, which was fortunate because my mouth had gone completely dry. "I beg your pardon,
my lord, but we should really get these baskets into the house.
We wouldn't want the cheese and milk to spoil."

"Oh no, we wouldn't want that." Darius rose and stepped
closer to Mina. "I must say, your garments are quite lovely.
I haven't seen such excellent craftsmanship in years. Did you
buy them in Sylvan? Or were they imported from Corone,
perhaps?"

Mina looked at me helplessly.

Somehow, I smoothed my features into a mask of calm. "I
made them," I said, willing my voice not to break. "I make
all our clothing."

His eyes flicked to mine again. They were the color of
moth's wings. I was sure of it. "Your talents are clearly being
wasted here. Come to the palace next week. I'm sure I can
find a position for you."

I stared at him, my mind a total blank now that all my worst
fears were coming true. What could I possibly say to such a
request? No, thank you, I'd rather not? Sometime in the past
minute, he'd called the hounds to his side with a flick of his
hand. They sat in a line next to him, their long pink tongues
lolling from the sides of their mouths, dripping with saliva.
When Darius took a step closer to me, their velvet ears perked
as they licked their muzzles. He stayed them with his flattened
palm, but their tails whipped back and forth against the dirt
like writhing snakes.

"I must say, Miss Duval, you look rather pale. Are you ill?"

My fingers traced the outline of the star pendant, just below the hollow at the base of my throat, where I could feel my pulse pounding. Was Evran inside the house? Was he watching this from the window? I wanted to believe he would come out to help us if he could. "No, my lord."

"It's strange. I've come to Sylvan many times over the years, but I don't recall ever seeing you."

I edged closer to Margana. "I don't leave home often, my lord. My lungs were weakened in the fire that killed our mother." This was the lie we had concocted years ago, if anyone asked why I rarely ventured out, particularly in the winter months when the days were gray and the glow from my skin was more obvious.

He tsked in sympathy. "I hadn't realized your mother was gone. A fire, you say? How tragic. Perhaps one of my mages can do something about your lungs at the palace."

My mages. As if he owned them. Despite my fear, my face grew hot with anger. But when he placed a hand on my upper arm, the strangest sensation came over me. My sisters, Margana, the hounds, and the road seemed to fade away, and all I felt was the warmth of Darius's hand through my sleeve. I looked into his eyes and realized I was no longer worried about being discovered. I wasn't worried about anything.

"I—"

"I'm afraid that's impossible." Margana's voice cut through the haze like a knife.

Darius removed his hand, and all the fear that had evaporated only a moment ago came rushing back in, causing me to stumble against Margana.

"And why is that?" Darius asked.

"Because…" Margana hesitated, and it was my own voice that filled the silence, shocking all of us.

"Because I work for Margana." As soon as the words left my mouth, I realized I wished they were true. Margana may be as prickly as a hedgehog, but who better to keep me safe from Darius than a mage he knew and trusted? And what better way to learn about my own magic than from a powerful witch?

Darius's lips flattened into a line. "Is that so?"

To my immense relief, Margana nodded. "It is. She's the finest seamstress in all of Sylvan. I need help with my work, and she's the only person I trust to do it."

He narrowed his eyes. "I see. And you?" he asked, turning to Mina. "Can you sew?"

She hesitated before giving a small nod. "But not as well as Liora."

"Then she can train you. I'll return in two weeks to collect you."

"Mina is just fifteen." Adelle wrapped a protective arm around Mina's shoulders. "My lord," she added with a deferential curtsy.

"The perfect age to learn a trade." He turned on his heels and walked back to his horse. The hounds hesitated, their black eyes still fixed on Margana and me. "Come!" he commanded, and with a final whimper, the dogs obeyed.

When Darius and his attendants had disappeared down the road in a cloud of dust, Margana herded us all into our house. I followed on legs as wobbly as a newborn foal's. Adelle still held a sobbing Mina, but her own expression was blank. Like me, she seemed unable to process what had just happened.

Margana took the basket from Mina and began to put our groceries away, as if she'd lived in our house for years, though we'd hardly interacted when I was young. As a child, Evran was often banished from the house so his mother could work, which was why we'd met in the forest. That, and because I wasn't allowed to talk to strangers.

"I'm sorry about Mina, but this is for the best," she said. "Unless you'd rather go yourself, Liora. Of course, if you go, I doubt it will be as a seamstress. It's only a matter of time before someone discovers what you are."

I searched Margana's face. Aside from a few faint creases around her eyes and mouth, her skin was as smooth as Adelle's. Rumors that she was ancient swirled in her wake, but she appeared no older than thirty. I'd heard that the more powerful a mage was, the slower they aged, which helped explain Darius's deceptively youthful appearance. "You shielded me from the hounds, didn't you?"

Margana pursed her lips. "I tried. The hounds aren't able to distinguish one magical 'scent' from another. Darius, however, is not easily fooled."

Adelle shot me a frightened glance. "How does she know?"

The weaver answered for me. "I saw her on the road, the night she went to find your sister."

Mina ducked behind me as Adelle's expression shifted to shock, then anger.

"I hadn't told them yet," I muttered.

"If I may make a suggestion, don't keep secrets from each other anymore. If you want to keep Liora safe, you'll all need to work together."

"Am I really in danger, then?" Father had always insisted I was, but I never fully understood why. As far as I could tell, the only advantage to glowing skin was that I never had to fumble around in the dark looking for the privy, like my sisters. And I was pretty sure Darius had other ways around that.

"All mages are in danger when it comes to Darius. He

doesn't like things he can't control. He keeps track of us all, whether he has a use for us or not."

"But why?"

"He has made mistakes in the past, overlooking mages who ended up being far more powerful than they first appeared. While none have proven stronger than Darius himself, he will do anything to protect his position. So now, if a mage comes across his path, he tests them, to be sure."

Adelle folded her arms across her chest. "And by test, you mean torture?"

Margana avoided my eyes as she replied, "If he discovers that a witch has been hiding in Sylvan all these years without his knowledge, he'll be displeased, to say the least."

"What do I do?" I asked Adelle. She was the closest thing I had to a mother, and I trusted her judgment, perhaps more than Father's.

"Margana is right. We can't send you. We'll find a reason that Mina can't go."

Margana scoffed. "Oh she'll go, willingly or by force."

Mina burst into a fresh bout of sobs. For once in her life, she wasn't overreacting. Everything we'd worked so hard to prevent was happening.

"This is all my fault," I whispered, my own eyes filling with tears.

"Don't go feeling sorry for yourself, now." Margana had put the kettle on the fire and was rummaging in the cupboards for tea. "The palace isn't a bad place to work if you're not in Darius's service. And it will pay well. Adelle will be marrying in the next year or two, I imagine, and your father won't be able to work forever. Now you'll have two additional incomes."

I blinked in confusion. "Two?"

She set the teacups down on the countertop and turned to

face me. "You told Darius you were my apprentice. I imagine that idea came to you for a reason?"

I hesitated. Even if Father agreed to the apprenticeship, associating with a known witch would only further ostracize our family from the community. Yes, the money would be welcome, but not at the expense of Adelle's future happiness.

Despite my reservations, I found myself nodding. "I would like to work for you, yes. But I can't do what you do."

"Of course not. But you can organize thread, dye yarn, and help around the house. You'll begin as soon as Mina has gone to Corone. In the meantime, you'd better start teaching your sister how to sew." She poured the tea into three cups. "Liora, walk me back to my house."

It wasn't a request. I glanced at Adelle, who nodded for me to go.

"I know you have questions," Margana said once we were outside.

I had so many I wasn't sure where to begin. Mina had been trying to get a glimpse of Margana's tapestries since she was a child, peering through the curtains of ivy that Margana had allowed to enshroud her house, and though I admonished Mina's nosiness, I couldn't deny that I thought of Margana often. Magic—especially the kind people wielded deliberately—was as much of a mystery to me as the world outside Sylvan.

But my immediate concern was Mina, leaving home for the first time in her life to go to the palace, of all places. "Will Mina really be safe in Corone?"

"I believe so."

A little of the tension left my shoulders. "Then Darius isn't as bad as people say?"

Margana laughed wryly. "Oh no, he's far worse."

"But he hasn't hurt you."

She turned on me, her blue eyes fierce. "And what do you know of my life? You have no idea the things I have done for that man."

I shook my head. "I'm sorry. I didn't mean…"

She took a deep breath. "I forgot. He touched you."

"What does that have to do with anything?"

"Let me guess. You felt as light as a feather with his hand on you. All your troubles melted away like butter. You've never been so carefree in your life." She made an expansive gesture, her tone belying her words.

I remembered the warmth of his hand on my arm, the enveloping fog and the steadiness of his gaze. "Magic."

"Of course. Darius is one of the most powerful warlocks in Antalla. How do you think he ended up working for the king in the first place?"

I flushed at my own ignorance. I knew what Darius was—tales of his cruelty and ruthlessness had served as bedtime stories in my house. What had I been expecting him to look like? A literal monster? Still, no one had ever explicitly told me what he was capable of. "What is his power?"

"His power is absence, child. Absence of pain, of worry, of sickness, of hunger. He is the void between waking and dreams, the fleeting moments in your life when you feel nothing. His touch has destroyed our king, turning him into a shell of a man, one too far gone to rule effectively or even comprehend Darius's actions. Your father had good reason to hide you. You do not want to know what life in his service is like."

A chill crept down my spine, even though it was still warm outside. We stopped at the low wall in front of Margana's house. "But what's so terrible about nothingness?"

"It's not the feeling of nothingness that's dangerous, at least not for a moment or two. But things that are empty want to be filled, and Darius is no exception. That's why he takes all the mages and uses them up. He hides behind the king and hollow words about the 'good of the people,' but Darius will search until the emptiness inside of him is filled. And I fear such a thing is impossible."

"But…he hasn't used you up, has he?" I asked, unsure what that even meant.

Her hard features softened for a moment. "Not yet. Now I suggest you get home and start working with your sister. She's still a child in many ways, and she'll need her wits about her if she's going to make it at the palace." She saw the worry flicker across my face and shook her head. "I don't mean Darius. I mean the other girls, mostly. They can be ruthless. And the young men are trouble of a different sort."

Mina managed to get into enough trouble in Sylvan, a sleepy village compared to Corone. Adelle and I would need to educate her in more ways than one. Two weeks wasn't much time, and while I had no doubt Mina could sew, the question was whether she'd sit still long enough to learn.

"Thank you, for what you did today," I said.

She paused with her hand on the gate, and I thought I saw a shadow of regret pass over her eyes. But then her forehead smoothed, and the edges of her lips twitched in a faint smile. "You're welcome, Liora. I'll see you in two weeks."

FOUR

"Damn it!" Father slammed his hands down on the dining table, rattling our empty plates. He was generally a soft-spoken, introspective man, and his anger was alarming. "How could you do such a thing, Liora? After everything we've sacrificed?"

I dropped my gaze, ashamed. Father had been the king's treasurer, once upon a time. He'd seen firsthand how Darius, the king's most trusted advisor, used mages as instruments of profit and power. But the king seemed oblivious to the evil in Darius, so when Adelle was just a baby, my father resigned as treasurer and moved his young family to Sylvan. He knew he'd made the right decision when my magic emerged. Working as a moneylender and pawnbroker was not nearly as prestigious, but anything was better than handing over a daughter to Darius.

"It was my fault," Mina insisted. "If I'd never run out, Liora wouldn't have been exposed."

"Darius would have seen us anyway." Adelle placed a gentle hand on Father's shoulder. "This is no one's fault."

He lowered his head, revealing how thin his hair had grown since Mother died. "I have always feared for the day we would lose Liora, and now my Mina, too…"

"We're not losing either of them, Father. Mina will just be a day's journey away in Corone. And Liora will be home with us."

"I don't trust Margana. I don't trust anyone with ma—" He cut himself off, but it was too late. He glanced at me and sighed. "I'm sorry. I know you're not like them. But the more a mage gives in to his powers, the less human he becomes. Lord Darius was an abomination twenty years ago. I can't imagine what he's like now."

"Margana saved me from him, Father. She didn't have to do that."

"Who knows what her motives are? I'll find a way to get you out of the apprenticeship. And from now on, Adelle will do the shopping. I was a fool to ever relax your restrictions."

His words were a reminder of how badly I wanted the apprenticeship, how desperate I was to learn the truth about my magic. "Father, please—"

"Do I need to remind you of the girl who cried diamond tears?" he shouted, silencing me. "Of the things Darius did to produce them? How he forced me to count them, every night?"

I shook my head and shrank back in my chair. "No, Father. Of course not."

"And what about me?" Mina asked. Her eyes were red from crying. All the scrappiness and sarcasm, the longed-for adventures and wishes to see the world outside of Sylvan, had vanished at the prospect of moving to Corone.

"Other Sylvan girls have gone to work at the palace before," Adelle said. "The Leroy girl?"

I nodded. "She's a cook there."

"She had no other prospects." Mina crossed her arms petulantly. "She has a face like a plum pudding."

Adelle frowned. "That's unkind."

"So is Liora letting me be sent off to Corone when she's the one Darius wanted!"

Never before had a room full of Duvals been so quiet. I could feel Father and Adelle's eyes flitting back and forth between Mina and me. I stared at my little sister, my heart filled with equal parts guilt and hurt. She was right. It was my magic that had created this situation. I should be the one to go to Corone, not Mina.

Father's gaze settled on mine as though he could read my thoughts. "You are not going, Liora. That's my final say on the matter."

I'd never seen Father so determined, but then, Darius hadn't known about me before. This was why Father had left Corone, I reminded myself. This was why we lived outside of Sylvan, why Mina didn't go to school, why we never went to parties. If I had only stayed home today, this never would have happened.

Mina ran from the room, the front door slamming behind her a moment later. Father and Adelle started to rise, but I stopped them.

"Let me go. Please."

"It's dark outside," Father said. "Margana—"

"Margana already knows."

For a moment I thought he might forbid it, but finally he relented. "Be careful."

Mina hadn't gone far. I found her standing by the tree outside of Margana's house, gazing at the five-, six-, and eight-pointed copper stars and tin crescent moon that hung from strings in the branches. They had been a tenth birthday gift from Evran, who spent so many nights in the forest that he knew all the constellations by heart.

Now you can look at the stars all day long, Liora, he'd said, knowing I'd only ever seen them from my window.

"Leave me alone," Mina murmured without turning.

"I'm so sorry. I would go in your place if I could."

She lifted a hand to her cheek. "It's not just that."

"Then tell me. What can I do?"

She turned her head far enough that I could see the tears on her skin glistening in the moonlight. "I'm afraid. I don't know how to live without you and Adelle."

"Oh, Mina." I pulled her against me. "I don't know how to live without you either."

"Who's going to take care of me at the palace? Who's going to make sure I eat my vegetables and dress appropriately?"

I smiled through my tears. "I'll only send you with sensible clothing. And if you skip your vegetables every now and then, no one will notice."

"I can't sew like you can, Ora. What if the king is disappointed in my work?"

"I'm going to teach you everything I know. And if he's disappointed, I imagine the worst he'll do is send you home."

She sniffled and dabbed her cheeks with her sleeve. "In that case, don't teach me *too* well."

I laughed and hugged her tighter. "I won't."

Mina cried herself to sleep that night, but I was still awake when I heard a light tap on our window. I pulled the curtain aside, revealing Evran's face. He motioned for me to join him.

"What are you doing?" I whispered as I gingerly lifted the window, afraid of waking Mina.

"I heard about what happened with Darius." He reached for my hand. "Come on."

"I can't go out now," I said. "Look what happened the last time I did."

"There's no one around. I'll help you."

I knew how angry Father would be, but I also knew I might not have many opportunities to see Evran, now that I was being confined to the house. I climbed out of the window and let him lower me to the ground, glad I had put on my slippers and robe. Evran was still dressed in his tunic and breeches, as if he'd been out all night.

"Where were you this afternoon?" I asked as we crossed the road and slipped into the woods.

"My mother sent me on an errand outside of Sylvan."

"I thought you said you were helping her with a loom."

He held a branch aside so I could pass. "I was. She needed a special part for it, though, so I went out to buy it."

"Oh." I wasn't sure where we were going, but Evran was still pulling on my hand. "You heard about Mina, then? And my apprenticeship?"

He nodded. "I know you must be feeling overwhelmed and frightened right now, but I think the apprenticeship will be good for you, Liora. You've been curious about your magic for a long time."

I squeezed his hand unconsciously. "Yes, but I'm scared, Evran. Lord Darius is…"

Finally, he stopped and turned to face me. "Don't worry. Mother will protect you."

I lowered my eyes. I had hoped he would say he would protect me himself, even if it wasn't possible. "I'm cold," I lied, attempting to cover up the hurt that surely showed on my face. "We should get back."

He nodded, but he made no move to leave. He was staring at me in a way that made me pull my robe tighter around myself.

"What is it?"

"Liora." He reached for my hand, which was glowing alarmingly bright.

"I'm sorry." Embarrassed, I began to tug at the sleeves of my robe. But Evran didn't let me. He brought the back of my hand to his mouth, where he brushed his lips lightly against my skin. I trembled, and he stepped closer to me. The air around us felt charged, like a lightning storm was coming, though the sky was clear.

"There's something I need to tell you." He smoothed my hair back from my face with his other hand, then let his palm rest against my cheek for a moment. I leaned into the pressure, wishing I was brave enough to tell him how I felt about him, that I loved him as so much more than a friend.

"What is it?" I asked gently, hoping he could say the words that I couldn't. The robe slipped from my shoulders, and I let it fall. The cold was worth it just to see Evran's eyes light up, absinthe bright, in my glow.

He leaned closer, and I automatically followed; Evran might think of me as a star, but the truth was, I had been caught in his orbit since the moment we met. I had been wishing he would kiss me for months now. I just needed him to take the first leap.

Instead, he straightened, and the cold I had ignored before was suddenly sharp and cutting. I followed his gaze to our clasped hands. My glow was flickering strangely, like a candle in a breeze. When I raised my eyes back to his, he was staring

at my hand, not in awe but in horror. He dropped it abruptly
and stepped back.

"I'm so sorry," he said, running his hands through his hair.
"I didn't mean…"

"What's wrong?" I asked as a horrible hollow feeling spread
through my chest.

He shook his head. "You're right. It's late. We should go."
He turned away and headed back toward the road without me.

The two weeks passed quickly, any free time I might once
have spent in the woods with Evran now occupied by training
Mina. In some ways, I was grateful for the excuse not to see
him. I could pretend it was simply because I was busy, rather
than him deliberately avoiding me.

And if every now and then my thoughts betrayed me and
turned to Evran and our last encounter—what I'd done wrong,
what I should have done differently—I steered them instead to
my upcoming apprenticeship. Maybe a small part of me had
hoped that getting to know his mother better would somehow
bring me closer to Evran, but I'd genuinely wondered what
Margana's tapestries were like, how she turned something
woven from yarn into something real. Not just the hounds,
but gold for the king's coffers. Some even said she had woven
the queen herself. *That* was true magic.

The morning of her departure, Mina's packed trunk sat
by the front door like a black cat just waiting for us to cross
its path.

Father ate his breakfast quickly and grabbed his cloak, surprising all of us. "I should get to the shop."

"Don't you want to see Mina off?" Adelle asked.

He could barely meet our eyes. "Lord Darius and I parted
on bad terms. I'm afraid if he sees me again, it will bring up old

feelings of animosity. You're better off without me. I'll come to Corone for a visit as soon as I can." He embraced Mina and kissed her forehead, then hurried away without another word.

We watched him go, and for the first time I had the feeling there was far more to Father's time at the palace than he'd told us. I knew he was afraid of Darius and had left suddenly, but not that there had ever been a falling-out. According to Father, he'd told Darius that he wanted more room and fresh air for his growing family.

When the knock finally came, I peered out through the window with Mina. Darius's golden gaze found mine like a falcon narrowing in on its prey, and my heart beat frantically in my chest, like a silly little bird about to be eaten.

Adelle took a deep breath before opening the door. "Lord Darius," she said. "Welcome back."

"Good day, Adelle. Liora. Mina."

As we curtsied, I peered around him to the front of the house. A small cart for two people was waiting with a single horse. There was no sign of the palace guards, or the hounds, I noticed with relief.

Darius glanced over his shoulder to see what had caught my attention. "I traveled alone today, since this trip will be brief. Adelle, would you mind going next door and fetching Margana? I'd like a word with her before we depart."

Adelle's eyes darted to mine. I knew she didn't want to leave me alone with Darius, but she also couldn't refuse him. I nodded, and she hurried out, leaving me to lead him into our parlor. He wiped his brow with a handkerchief, though he didn't appear to be sweating. "I'd love some cold water before we set off again, if it's not too much trouble."

"I'll have to fetch it from the well." I was grateful for the excuse to escape his presence. "Mina, can you get a pitcher from the kitchen?"

She was quieter than I'd ever seen her, her large eyes fixed on the floor. She nodded and hurried away.

Rather than wait in the parlor, Darius followed me into the yard. I glanced around, as if there were someone here who could help me, but we were alone. Reluctantly, I turned my back to him to get the water.

"Try not to worry too much about your sister, Liora."

I leaned over to fetch the pail, willing my shaking hands to cooperate. All it would take was one push from Darius, and I'd plummet headfirst into the well.

"She'll be taken care of at the palace," he continued. "I promise to keep an eye out for her."

I tied off the rope and turned toward him. "You will? Why?"

"I'm the one bringing her to the palace. Surely that makes me responsible for her."

I stared at him, once again trying to reconcile this young man who appeared no older than Luc with the monster I knew him to be.

I thought once more of the girl who cried diamonds, how Father said Darius tortured her to produce her valuable tears. At the shop, Adelle had overheard customers retell stories of his evil deeds. He'd once discovered a boy whose voice was so pure and beautiful, it could make people forget all their worries. The boy had been put in a giant birdcage in the palace, forced to perform for the king for the rest of his days.

While I might not have magic Darius could use, that didn't mean I could be complacent around him. I could only hope he never discovered I had magic at all.

I was so busy studying his face for some sign of malice that

I didn't realize he was reaching out to touch my shoulder until it was too late.

Suddenly the fear I felt for Mina, even my fear of Darius himself, vanished. The bright day became dim and fuzzy; the brilliant sapphire of his coat was now black, and the pale blue of my dress morphed to a soft gray. Darius was smiling, but it was a kind and reassuring smile, and I believed that he would keep an eye out for Mina, that she would be safe at the palace.

When he removed his hand, the colors of reality came back to me in a rush. As quickly as the emptiness had swept in, it was sucked back out, like a tide, leaving me breathless. I would have stumbled if I hadn't been holding on to the well. My head spun with anger, confusion, and, as wrong as it was, longing for the freedom of another moment without fear.

I scrambled away from him, eliciting a crooked smile.

"You're flushed." He pulled the ladle out of the pail and handed it to me. "Please, take a drink."

I shook my head, still struggling for words, and he shrugged. "Suit yourself." He drank deeply, his eyes never leaving mine. "Thank you. I feel much better now."

There was something about the way he looked at me, so unruffled despite my obvious terror, that made my skin crawl. I could see it now, how he used his handsome face and soothing words to draw people in, as dangerously deceptive as a poisonous flower. It was an insidious disguise, but a brilliant one. If he were the horror I'd imagined in my head, he'd never get close enough to anyone to hurt them.

Margana's words echoed in my head: *That's why he takes all the mages and uses them up. He will search until the emptiness inside of him is filled.*

I gritted my teeth and backed away from him toward the

house, vowing to never let him touch me again. My magic may be worthless, but at least it was mine.

When we went back inside, my emotions felt raw and exposed, like I might laugh or cry at any moment, and I struggled to suppress my glow along with my feelings. Margana was waiting with Adelle and Mina in the parlor, and her eyes flicked to mine as we entered the room.

"Ladies, why don't you help Mina load her trunk into the cart," Darius said. "I'll just be a moment."

When we were finished, we came back to the parlor, stopping outside the door at the sharp tone of Margana's voice.

"You don't need to see it. I promised it will be ready, and it will be."

Darius sounded just as angry. "You have a month. Do you understand?"

"Have I ever missed a deadline before?"

"No, but this is different," Darius said. "There's far more at stake."

"No one is more aware of that than I am."

"Good. And the baby?"

"When would you like it?" she asked, her voice strained.

"Within the fortnight."

"Very well."

"It won't cut into your other work too much?"

She sighed. "I already told you it would be done."

There was a pause. "Your apprentice is unusually talented, Margana. I hope you're keeping a close eye on her."

"If you're referring to her sewing abilities, yes, she is remarkable. And of course I'm keeping an eye on her."

Despite the harmless topic of conversation, the entire exchange was curiously tense. My blood pulsed loudly in my ears as the silence dragged on. I imagined the two of them, locked in their silent battle. And somehow, I was at the middle of it.

There was a rustle as someone rose. "Well, then. I suppose I'll be on my way. You can bring the beast along with the baby." When he spoke again, his voice was a low growl. "And remember, Margana, I've gone easy on you all these years. I can make things much more painful, should you cross me."

She grunted in acknowledgment, and my sisters and I stumbled backward just as Darius entered the hall. He stared at us for a long, uncomfortable stretch. "Take a moment and say your goodbyes, please. I'll wait outside."

We stood there blinking, as if we somehow hadn't believed it would really come to this. Finally, Adelle held out her arms, and we all embraced, a tangle of limbs and tear-streaked faces.

"You're going to do wonderfully in Corone." Adelle straightened, tucking Mina's chin-length hair behind her ear. "Just be your delightful self and everyone will love you."

"Write to us," I said. "At least once a week. I promise we'll write back every time."

Mina sniffled. "I'll be sure to learn all the latest styles in the city and sketch them for you, Ora. Maybe you can start selling your own clothing in Sylvan."

I smiled, proud of her bravery.

"Tell Father that I love him," she added.

"We will."

We walked out to the cart, where Darius waited. He helped her up onto the bench, then turned to bow to us.

"Farewell, ladies. I do hope we'll see more of each other soon." He climbed up beside Mina, who waved to us over her shoulder as Darius slapped the reins against the horses' haunches.

I had never said goodbye to my sister before, and for a moment I was overcome with the feeling that I would never see her again. Adelle gripped my hand as though she was having the same thought.

When they had disappeared over the crest of a hill, Margana led us back inside. Adelle wept silently next to me, and I did my best to soothe her, though all the fears that had evaporated at Darius's touch clung to me now, as thick and suffocating as wood smoke.

Adelle and I sat together in the parlor while Margana made tea. "Are you feeling all right?" my sister asked me. "You look a bit...odd."

"I'm fine," I replied, only because I had no words to describe how I truly felt.

Margana gave us our tea and sat down in the worn yellow armchair across from our sofa. She was quiet for a few minutes, sipping her tea, but I couldn't help noticing the way she stared at me.

"What is it?" I asked, unnerved.

She set her cup down on a side table. "He knows."

"Who knows what?"

"Darius, you foolish girl. He knows you're a witch."

An icy chill crept over me, and Adelle's tea nearly spilled onto her lap. "How? The hounds weren't with him today."

"He touched her, twice if I had to guess. He can feel magic as easily as the hounds can sense it."

A flush of anger bloomed above Adelle's collar and began to creep up her neck. "If he knows, then why did he take Mina?"

Margana leaned back in the chair. "All I can think is that Liora's magic is too weak for him to bother with, at least for now."

My eyebrows lifted. *For now* implied that magic could change. That *my* magic could change.

"My guess is that he's holding on to Mina just in case."

Adelle rose from the sofa. "Just in case what?"

"Just in case there's more to Liora than meets the eye."

"So Mina is collateral?" Adelle asked, horrified.

"Essentially."

Guilt pressed onto my shoulders like heavy hands. Here I was, hoping that my magic meant something, when I'd just sent my little sister off with a man who tortured children for profit.

"Did you know about this?" Adelle sounded more vicious than I'd thought possible.

"I can't say I didn't expect it, but my duty was to protect Liora."

"And why are you so interested in protecting Liora? What's in it for you?"

Margana rose to her feet. She was taller than Adelle, but my sister didn't flinch. "There's nothing in it for me, other than a skilled seamstress and the desire to help a fellow witch."

"And Mina?" Adelle spat. "What about protecting her?"

"Mina is an ordinary girl, and a very pretty one by Sylvan standards. She would have gotten herself into nothing but trouble at home. At least in Corone she'll learn a trade and some street smarts."

Adelle threw up her hands, exasperated. "So now our fifteen-year-old sister is a pawn in Darius's game, and Liora isn't safe either."

"Liora will be fine," Margana said. "If there's more to her magic, I'll find it before Darius does."

"And no doubt use it for your own gain," Adelle said, echoing Father's accusation.

"What gain could that possibly be?"

Adelle only glared at Margana until she looked away, reminding me of the hushed argument between Margana and Darius. Darius had told Margana to keep an eye on me, and she had essentially agreed to. It was a firm reminder that I couldn't trust her, or anyone else in Sylvan.

But if Darius already knew I had magic, then the most important thing was that I come to understand it fully before he did. He knew I wouldn't run as long as he had my sister, but if I could learn how to hide my magic and convince him it was useless, he might let Mina go. And if there *was* more to me than there seemed, I might be able to use my powers to free my sister, or at the very least to protect myself. Somehow, I had to undo years of repressing my magic and instead learn how to wield it. And in order to do that, I needed a teacher.

I was taking that apprenticeship, I decided. Whether Father liked it or not.

FIVE

Father did not, in fact, like it. But with him and Adelle at work every day, and me being far too old and resourceful to be locked in the house, there was little he could do about it. The realization was oddly freeing, even if I still had to be cautious. Hiding had kept me safe for over a decade, but it was no longer enough. I couldn't know my limits without finally testing them.

I arrived at Margana's house shortly after dawn, as instructed. She immediately escorted me to the yard behind her house, to a row of cooking pots filled with colored liquid. She put me to work dying yarn, and by midday my hands were stained purple and I reeked of wet wool. I was only allowed inside the house briefly for lunch, at which point she showed me several of her looms, from a crude hand loom a child could use to a foot-treadle floor loom that took up half the workroom she kept it in.

"So you've never woven before," Margana said as she

handed me a cup of tea. She'd been a patient teacher today, considering how my ignorance was impeding her own work.

"No," I admitted, trying not to grimace at the smell of my hands as I sipped my tea. "I've always purchased cloth at the tailor's."

"Who taught you to sew?"

"I taught myself."

"Not Adelle?"

"She was only six when our mother died. She hadn't learned yet."

There was a long, uncomfortable silence, which I spent praying she wouldn't bring up my mother's death. She had died saving me, and I hated reliving those last terrible moments.

"Evran has always had a fondness for Adelle," she said finally, absently stirring her tea.

My cup rattled as I returned it to the saucer. "He does?"

"Oh yes. He used to come home from school and talk about 'Miss Duval' until I sent him outside to play. I don't think she spoke more than five words to him, mind you. Once, he made me promise that if she never loved him back, I was to weave him a girl just like her when he was old enough to marry." Her eyes sparkled at the memory. "He was a very serious little boy. I think that's why he liked Adelle so much."

It was as if she were talking about a different Evran from the one I knew. His adventurous spirit, his freedom, his utter fearlessness—when I was afraid of *everything*—were what had drawn me to him. This was the boy who, when I was nine, convinced me a stream was only knee-deep by standing on a rock. While I spluttered and splashed in a panicked circle, he laughed so hard he slipped and fell in himself. Another time he had placed a dead beetle on my chest while I slept, then waited outside all night so he could hear my screams when I woke.

After he discovered the hard way that I did not take kindly to insects, no matter how dead, Evran's mischief turned to teasing and eventually flirtation, before it became something more. If he had ever wished for the love of a "Miss Duval," it could only be me.

"And now?" I asked as casually as I could.

"Oh, it's hard to say. He hasn't mentioned anyone in quite a while. He has other things occupying his mind these days."

My heart sank, but if I hoped to find out why Evran was pulling away from me, this was my chance. "Such as?"

Her expression clouded over, her eyes darting briefly toward the ceiling. But she shrugged a moment later, her tone nonchalant as she said, "His future." She took my empty teacup, and I followed her to the kitchen. "What about you, Liora?"

"What about me?"

"It must be difficult to meet anyone when you never leave the house. Don't you want to get married?"

Her words stung, especially after learning Evran had never mentioned me by name. "I imagine I'll spend my life alone." I raised my chin. "Like you."

She dried her hands on a towel and led me back outside, apparently not offended by my comment. "I wasn't always alone. Don't forget, I had a child."

Margana's frankness always caught me off guard. But if she was going to speak freely, so would I. "Can I ask what happened to Evran's father?"

"We never married, if that's what you mean. He was a low-level mage working with a traveling magic show. They stayed in Sylvan for a few weeks while they performed here and in other nearby towns. Then they moved on."

"People do that?"

"What, have dalliances?"

She seemed determined to make me blush. "No, travel as performers. Warlocks, I mean."

"And witches, too."

"Darius doesn't imprison them?"

"There are very few traveling shows left in Antalla. Most have moved to more welcoming kingdoms, and those that remain are wise enough to relocate frequently to avoid Darius's attention. And as I said, Evran's father was a low-level warlock."

And I'm a low-level witch, I thought. Was it possible I could do something like that? If I were to join a magic troupe, I could leave Antalla, earn a living on my own, and meet other people like me. In another kingdom, my glow might not even be considered worthy of notice. I could open my own dress shop if I wanted. I could be with Evran, publicly. After the way he'd looked at my glow the other night, I had started to wonder if it was my magic creating the distance between us, a fear I'd never had before. But maybe it was the secrecy rather than the magic itself. My heart surged at all the possibilities I hadn't known existed.

Of course, if Father had his way, I'd never leave the house again.

At the end of the day, Margana took me upstairs to her bedroom to show me what she was currently working on. Inside was a tall freestanding loom with a nearly complete tapestry suspended in the frame.

"What is it?" I asked, cocking my head from side to side to try to make sense of it.

"It's a creature dreamed up by the king."

"What?" I stepped forward, bringing my face within a few inches of the intricate weaving. The animal had a body like a horse, a long slender neck, and a head shaped like a deer's, with

spiraling black horns. The thread Margana used had an iridescent sheen to it, like the feathers on a hummingbird's chest.

"The king literally dreamed this *thing* up. He drew it for
me and commanded me to weave it."

"Why?"

"For his personal menagerie. He does this from time to
time. He likes to show his creatures off to visiting dignitaries."

"*This* is what the king does with your magic?"

She sighed and sat down on a velvet wingback chair in the
corner. Her room was spare on furniture, but there were unusual knickknacks on almost every available surface. A funny
little lamp shaped like a teapot sat on the nightstand. A green
glass ball rested on a gold pedestal in the corner. At the back
of the room was a heavy black curtain embroidered with silver stars, which went from floor to ceiling and wall to wall.

"The king's requests are generally useless and absurd," Margana said. "Darius's commissions are different."

"Like the hounds?"

"The hounds, yes. But also gold, weaponry, creatures of his
own design whose purposes are far less benign than the king's."

"Have you ever refused a commission?" I asked, running
my fingers over the beast's woven horns.

Her blue eyes darted away from mine. "No."

Sensing she wanted to change the subject, I asked her more
questions about her process. She explained that when she finished weaving, the tapestry would be removed from the loom,
though the final knot had not been tied. Once it was tied, the
beast would come to life, and it was important the tapestry
was already in the menagerie at that time. Though the weaving was no taller than a man, the king envisioned the creature as ten feet tall, and Margana had imbued this notion into
the tapestry. A weaving might show a pile of gold containing

one hundred coins, but once finished, a far larger pile would remain in its place.

"When will you take the weaving to Corone?" I asked as I helped her untangle a pile of yarn.

"In two weeks."

I had never really considered the possibility of visiting Corone myself, though it wasn't far from Sylvan. Father never spoke of it, but Mother had told Adelle about it before she died, about the beautiful palace, vibrant markets, and visitors from all over the world. Unexpectedly, I now had a means of getting there—and an opportunity to make sure Mina was safe.

"Can I come with you?" I asked hesitantly.

She stared at me for a moment. "You're not afraid of seeing Darius again?"

I was definitely afraid of Darius. The memory of his touch made my skin crawl. But if I couldn't venture as far as Corone, how could I possibly hope to survive out in the world? "I am," I confessed. "But I'm also scared for Mina."

Margana sighed heavily. She pushed herself to her feet and waved a hand at me. "If your father allows it, you may join me. Come, it's getting dark."

As I followed her downstairs, one question continued to nag at me. "Margana, why haven't you woven yourself a pile of gold and left Antalla? You could do so much more with your magic than weave beasts for the king."

She stopped at the threshold, leaning against the doorframe. "If I had my way, I'd never weave anything again. Well, perhaps a scarf," she added in an uncharacteristic moment of dry humor. "But I have something else keeping me here. Good night, Liora."

I wanted to ask where Evran was. I was eager to share with him all the things I'd learned, but it was clear Margana was finished with me. My arms prickled with goose bumps at the hollow chiming sound of the copper stars in the tree. Whatever was happening between us now, he *had* loved me. I believed that with all my heart. I remembered him leading me into the blackberry glade for the first time, his green eyes wide with wonder at the glow from my skin. *Are you a star, Liora?*

The *thunk* of a knife on a wooden board snapped me out of my reverie as I pushed through the front door of our house. Adelle looked up from the shredded cabbage, her nose wrinkled in disgust. "Good heavens, Liora. You smell like a wet dog."

I stepped closer to her and grinned. "Wet sheep, technically."

"Just take a bath, please, before Father comes home."

I plucked a ribbon of cabbage from the chopping board and headed down the hall. The cabbage was almost the same color as my hands.

I soaked until the water grew cold, but though the stench had faded, the dye hadn't. The glow from my arms was even brighter against the purple of my hands. Tomorrow I would purchase leather workman's gloves to spare myself in the future.

I recounted my day to Father and Adelle over dinner, but a part of my mind wandered to thoughts of Mina, of her new life in Corone. Just entering the weaver's house had opened my eyes to a new world of possibilities; what must it be like to live in the palace with powerful mages? What wonders would Mina see there? The king's menagerie? A magic show?

Adelle kicked me under the table and jerked her head toward Father. He was watching me expectantly.

"I'm sorry, Father. Did you ask me something?"

"I was telling you that Mr. Moreau came by the shop today.

He said he'd like to speak with you, alone. I told him I would discuss it with you."

I glanced at Adelle, who smiled hopefully. I knew she only wanted to see me happy, and as far as my family was concerned, I had no prospects for marriage. My sisters thought that Evran and I were just friends, because unless he reciprocated my feelings, that was all we were. Luc was a successful businessman and well-liked in the community. If Evran truly didn't love me anymore, perhaps I would be a fool to turn down someone like Luc.

But this particular fool wasn't interested in marrying for the sake of comfort or convenience. "I'll consider it," I lied.

Father nodded. "Good. Remember, Liora. Most witches have to settle for a life alone, like Margana. Or worse, marriage to a warlock. Luc might be willing to overlook your condition, given how much you have in common. Consider it a safety net, for all of us."

I swallowed down the bile rising in my throat. The only thing Luc and I had in common was a fondness for clothing, and that wasn't exactly a foundation for a successful relationship. While marriage to Luc might sound like a safety net to Father, it sounded eerily like the tightening of a noose to me.

SIX

As the days passed, I was more grateful for the apprenticeship than I could have imagined. It allowed me to take my mind off what I could only suppose was Luc's impending proposal, as well as Evran's continued avoidance of me. He was never home when I went to Margana's house, and while I knew he preferred to be out of doors, it seemed impossible we wouldn't have at least run into each other by now.

Margana told me I could come late today, as she had work to do and wouldn't have time to supervise me. I found a note on her door instructing me to let myself in and check the dye pots. The wool would be ready when it was a deep plum. I found a stick propped against the fence and used it to pull the wool out of the liquid. Steering clear of Luc meant I still hadn't purchased myself a pair of gloves.

After I'd checked all the yarn, I went into the kitchen to make tea. A cuckoo clock on the wall told me it was nearly lunchtime. I almost dropped the kettle when it struck twelve and a real bird flew out of the clock. "Cuckoo," it called, in an eerily human voice. Twelve chimes later it flew back into the hole at the top of the clock and the little door clicked shut behind it.

Margana's home appeared to be filled with these kinds of oddities. I wasn't sure if she'd woven them herself or purchased them from other mages. We had nothing like them in our house. Magical objects were costly, and I had always suspected Father avoided bringing home anything magic from the shop. It seemed to me now that he'd spent the past thirteen years pretending my magic didn't exist. By hiding me from Darius, my father had also hidden me from himself.

I waited a quarter of an hour, but Margana didn't come down. Perhaps she couldn't hear the clock upstairs. I walked as loudly as I could so she wouldn't think I was snooping and stomped up the stairs. All of the bedrooms were empty, including hers.

A sudden clatter sounded on the other side of the black curtain. I'd assumed it was being used to shade windows, but now that I thought about it, I remembered seeing an attic window from outside the house. The stairs leading to it must be behind the curtain.

"Margana?" There was no answer, but I could hear a muffled voice. Had Evran been in the house all day? If we could just talk, I knew we could work things out.

I called twice more, but there was still no response. Carefully, I pulled back the edge of the curtain. As I suspected, a narrow staircase was just on the other side of it, the top shrouded in shadow.

If my magic was good for anything, it was this. I cautiously loosened my tight grip on my emotions, allowing my genuine fear to rise to the surface. My skin brightened in response, revealing a door at the top of the stairs.

A voice inside told me to turn around. I had no business in Margana's bedroom, and there was no reason to suspect she was in any sort of trouble. But curiosity compelled me forward. I was halfway up the stairs when I heard a creak and looked up.

"Liora?" Margana stood at the top of the staircase, all the more imposing than when we were on even footing. "What are you doing?"

I tried to rein in my glow, but calling it back was not nearly as easy as summoning it. "I'm sorry for intruding. I heard something behind the curtain."

"You shouldn't be back here."

I knew instantly that whatever special project Darius had been referring to was there, in the attic. "I'm sorry."

"Let's get back to the dye pots. The wool should be ready by now."

Margana didn't seem any more annoyed with me than usual, but my heart was still stuttering in my chest as she pulled the wool out of the pot and hung it up to dry.

"What will you use it for?" I asked.

"I'm not sure yet. Probably some beast for the king, eventually."

"How long do you have to complete each tapestry?"

She finished hanging the yarn and washed her hands in a basin. With a bit of rough scrubbing and soap, most of the dye came off her hands, though they were still tinged lavender. "It depends. Sometimes I'm ordered to complete a small project in a week. Other tapestries I'm given a year. The beasts for the king don't have firm deadlines. Darius's tasks take precedent."

"What's the longest you've ever worked on a tapestry?"

She glanced at me over her shoulder. "Nearly twenty years."

"Twenty years! It must be massive. What was it?"

Instead of answering, she looked up at the sky. The first star winked overhead, as though it had just woken from its daylong slumber. Was that the tapestry she kept hidden in the attic? What could be so large or intricate that it took twenty years to create, and why the secrecy?

The look in Margana's eyes told me the conversation was finished. "We can start skeining yarn on the spinner's weasel tomorrow. Thank you for your help today."

That night, I went to bed early, hoping to avoid Father's questioning looks. The more I thought about marrying Luc, the more stark the possibilities for my future seemed: remain in Sylvan forever, married to a man I didn't love, while providing safety and comfort for my family; or leave and discover what I was capable of—not just as a mage, but as a person in the world. The second option was unquestionably more dangerous, but it elicited a spark of excitement and possibility I'd never felt before.

Sighing, I picked up one of my favorite books, about a maid sent to work in a haunted castle who falls in love with a handsome ghost. When I got to the part where the maid touches the ghost for the first time, I clapped the book closed and set it aside, wanting to savor the anticipation a little longer. I climbed out of bed and went to the window, opening it just enough to let in the cool night breeze.

Voices drifted over from the parlor, where Adelle and Father had also opened the front windows. I had left Adelle embroidering flowers on a pillowcase while Father prepared collection slips for customers who had failed to make their payments. He kept the goods offered for collateral and sold them in the shop when people couldn't afford to pay him back, but the money was almost always worth more than the objects since there was no guarantee they would sell.

"You look like your mother, sitting there with your hair down," Father said.

I opened the window wider to hear Adelle's response. I had always thought Adelle looked very similar to the portrait Father had commissioned of Mother at a fair before I was born, but I'd never heard him say as much.

"What would Mother have made of Mina going to Corone?" Adelle asked. She rarely spoke about our mother, even though she was the only one of us who could remember her. When she was little, Mina would ask Adelle all kinds of questions. Did she look like Mother? Had Mother been very beautiful? What had been Mother's favorite flower? Adelle would answer in as few words as possible: yes, yes, poppies. Mina had been obsessed with poppies for a while after that, asking me to embroider them on all of her clothing.

There was a long pause, and I was afraid Father had left the room. But finally he cleared his throat and said, "She would be heartbroken. I was the one who insisted we leave Corone, but she wanted to leave Antalla altogether. I should have listened."

Adelle sounded as surprised as I felt. "Mother wanted to leave Antalla? I thought you left Corone because of Darius."

"We did. He had taken too much of an interest in your mother, truth be told."

Adelle and I gasped in unison. "Why?" she asked. "What could he have wanted with her?"

"She was beautiful. And…she was special."

Special how? I wanted to shout, but I pressed my lips together to keep from talking. Something told me Father would not have had this conversation in front of me; he knew how much guilt I carried for Mother's death.

"It was naive of me, perhaps, but after your mother passed, I thought I was rid of that man. I didn't know about Margana when we moved out of town, you see. But with Liora always at home, and Darius rarely venturing to Sylvan himself, we seemed safe. We *were* safe."

"And now?" Adelle asked.

I was leaning so far out the window I had to brace myself on the sill to keep from tumbling out into the garden.

"Now he knows I have a daughter I've kept hidden away for years. He might not have felt Liora's magic at first, but he's no fool. He knew right away that there was a reason he'd never seen her before. So he took my Mina…" He broke off in tears, and the guilt I'd felt when Mina first left came roaring back.

"But he didn't take Liora, Father. And he has no reason to harm Mina."

He was quiet for a long time. "There is more to Liora's magic than you know. More than any of us know. I never wanted to frighten her, but her power is far more sinister than it seems. I had hoped we could keep it in check if she never had reason to use it. But now that she's spending time with the weaver, who has a direct link to Darius, I fear we are all in very real danger."

I could imagine Adelle shaking her head in disbelief the same way I was. "There is nothing sinister about Liora, Father."

He didn't seem to hear her. "Perhaps we can contrive a reason to bring Mina home and leave Sylvan quietly before Darius notices. Though where we would go and how we would keep Liora hidden are things I've never been able to reconcile."

My heart was beating so loudly I could hardly make out Adelle's response. "Father, I don't want to move."

His tone was gentle when he asked, "Because of Kylian?"

Kylian? The name was familiar, but it took me a moment to place it. He was the son of the hotelier. Father and Adelle sometimes had lunch at The Evening Star when they were working. Kylian was the chef. But I'd had no reason to think Adelle had any kind of relationship with him.

Adelle must have nodded, but Father's next question still took me by surprise. "Has he asked for your hand?"

"Not yet," Adelle murmured. "But I think he will."

Father was silent for a while. "He should make his intentions clear. If Darius thinks he's seen something he can use in Liora, it will not go well for any of us."

"What do you mean?"

"I mean that the people of Sylvan will no longer trust us. My business will suffer, and your reputation will be tarnished, if not altogether ruined. But if you are married to a man of good standing, the people of this town might be more forgiving. The same goes for your sister."

A long silence followed, and I quietly closed the window and crept back to my bed. What had Father meant about Mother being special? Had Darius had romantic feelings for her? If so, it was no wonder Mother wanted to move farther from Corone than Sylvan.

And what did he mean about my magic being sinister? While I had certainly hoped for more than glowing skin, I had never envisioned my magic being capable of evil. Was learning to wield it a mistake? What if I hurt my family by accident? What if I hurt Evran?

In that moment, I started to wonder if leaving Sylvan wasn't just the best option for me, but for everyone I loved. If what Father had said was true, my very existence was putting all of them in danger.

Father had apparently convinced himself I needed to consider all my options right away, because he invited Luc to our house the following afternoon, though I'd never given him a final answer. I was tempted to feign illness, but given Father's concerns for my safety, I knew I should at least hear Luc out. Perhaps he would be willing to leave Sylvan, possibly even Antalla. Luc had far more money than I could hope to make as Margana's apprentice, and realistically, it would take me months to afford passage to another kingdom, not to mention to find some means of supporting myself wherever I went.

Still, my dread grew as the minutes ticked down to Luc's arrival. Father and Adelle were at work, leaving me on my own to deal with him. I darted around the parlor, lighting candles and lamps and, though it was warm outside, a fire in the hearth for good measure. Perhaps he'd get so hot he'd leave of his own accord.

When the knock finally came, I put a kettle on and stopped at the hall mirror to make sure I wasn't too exposed. I was wearing a blouse and long skirt, my typical attire, but my head was uncovered. Grabbing a kerchief from the coat rack, I hastily tied it around my head, took a deep breath, and opened the door.

"Good afternoon, Mr. Moreau," I said, curtsying before leading the way into the parlor and gesturing for him to sit in one of our armchairs. "I'll just fetch the tea."

"There's no rush, Liora," he replied, crossing his long legs. Something about his posture, his gleaming white teeth and dark hair, reminded me momentarily of Darius's hounds. I shuddered despite the heat.

"The water is already boiling," I said, then hurried away. In the kitchen, I made sure to let the tea steep a little too long so Luc wouldn't ask for a second cup.

When I returned, Luc was standing, examining the portrait of my mother over the mantel. "She was quite beautiful, wasn't she?" he asked over his shoulder, then picked up a candlestick and inspected it before wiping his finger along the mantel.

I loudly prepared a cup of tea for Luc, setting the teapot down heavily on its tray and allowing the cup to rattle in its saucer, and held it out for him.

"Ah, thank you." He took the cup, but instead of returning to his armchair, he settled himself next to me on the sofa. "I must say, you keep a lovely home. So neat and tidy."

My eyes narrowed involuntarily. "Well, I can't take all the credit. Adelle does a lot of the housework, too."

"Of course. Your father is lucky to have such dutiful daughters." He dabbed at a bead of sweat on his forehead. "Warm in here, isn't it?" He glanced pointedly at the fire.

Adelle had always believed that Luc liked me, but now I wondered whether he was looking for a wife or a maid. I didn't move toward the fire, as he no doubt expected me to, and instead took a delicate sip of tea.

He forced a smile and tried his own tea, then grimaced at the bitterness. "Lovely," he rasped, setting his cup back in the saucer.

I grinned into my tea.

I felt him adjust his body so he was angled toward me, forcing me to look up. "Liora, I suppose you have intuited my reasons for coming to see you today."

I swallowed. For a marriage proposal, his tone was strangely ominous.

I hadn't been looking forward to a flowery speech or a forced declaration of love, but I was surprised at his directness. No buildup, no attempt to gauge my feelings. He wasn't even going to ask me a few perfunctory questions about myself before asking me to be his wife? "I—"

We both startled at a loud knock on the front door. My

family never had visitors, let alone two at once. I excused myself and went to see who it was, grateful for the excuse to leave Luc's side.

Evran stood in front of me, a bemused look on his face.

I was so caught off guard by the sight of him that I didn't know whether to be relieved he had finally come to see me or angry he'd kept me worrying for so long.

"Why are you wearing a kerchief in the house? You should never cover yourself up."

I pushed it back from my face. "I forgot I was wearing it," I said absently.

Evran was at my house. He was talking to me as if everything was fine between us, and my family was out. This was the perfect opportunity to discuss our future, if there was still any hope of one.

Or it should have been. I frowned and looked behind me.

"Is someone here?" Without waiting for an answer, Evran stepped past me into the house and stopped short when he saw Luc sitting on the sofa, a smirk playing on his full lips.

Evran turned back to me. "I didn't realize you had company. I'll go."

"Don't trouble yourself. I need to get home anyway." Luc rose and walked past Evran to the front door, pausing with his hand on the doorknob. "We'll speak further soon," he said to me, his tone far too intimate. "And Evran is right. Someone as special as you should never cover up."

He was already down the walkway when I found my voice. "Thank you for stopping by," I called weakly, then turned back to Evran.

"Where's Adelle?" he asked. "You shouldn't have a man here when you're home alone."

"*You're* here," I shot back, my cheeks burning.

"Are you really comparing me to…" He trailed off, waving his hand in the general direction of the front door.

"I'm sorry. Father insisted I meet with him. What was I supposed to say?"

"*No* would have been a good start."

I folded my arms over my chest and went back to the parlor to dump ashes on the fire. It was already far too hot before Evran arrived.

"Why do you dislike him so much, anyway?" I asked over my shoulder. "He's never done anything to you."

"He's arrogant," Evran retorted. "And I don't like the way he looks at you."

I straightened and turned to face him. Evran was breathing hard, as if he'd just run a mile. Was it possible he was jealous of Luc? The idea was ridiculous. He must know the tailor meant nothing to me.

I took a step closer to Evran, emboldened. If he was jealous, that meant he still cared. "How does he look at me?"

His green eyes glittered in the light of the dying embers. "Like you're a bolt of beautiful fabric he wants to drape and pin until it's just as he desires. Like you're something to own, rather than someone to love."

I placed my hand on his chest, felt the steady *thump-thump* of his heart beating below my fingertips. "Where have you been?" I asked softly. "I was afraid I wasn't going to see you again."

His brow furrowed in what looked like genuine remorse. "I'm sorry. I needed some time to think."

"About what?"

His gaze flicked down to where my hand rested on his chest. I was doing an admirable job of keeping my emotions in check, I thought. My glow was bright but not out of control. "About what happened the other night."

"When? In the forest? It's just my stupid magic." Father had to be wrong about it. I would never hurt someone, especially not Evran. I just needed to keep myself in check. "If being in your arms meant I never glowed again, I'd happily stay there forever."

He smiled, but it was strained. "Don't say that. Your glow is part of who you are."

"*You* are part of who I am, Evran."

His hands remained at his sides, but he leaned forward and pressed a soft kiss to my forehead. "If anything about you has to change to be with me, then it isn't worth it."

"What are you talking about? Nothing is changing. It's you and me, Evran. Just like it always has been."

He blinked several times, and I thought I saw his pupils dilating and constricting rapidly. He backed away from me and I let my hand fall. "It's not. Not anymore."

"Please don't say that. I'll figure out how to control my magic. Or we can leave Antalla. There's nothing stopping us from going on *real* adventures, the kind we've only dreamed about. Your mother said—"

He sighed. "Liora."

"Just…please. Don't leave me." I hated how pathetic I sounded, but I couldn't help it. My heart was breaking, and Evran didn't even care. "I'm so sorry. I don't know what's wrong with me."

"There is nothing wrong with you, Liora. Promise me that whatever happens, you'll remember that."

I shook my head. "What do you mean, 'whatever happens'? Nothing is going to happen."

Evran had backed up until he stood on the threshold, silhouetted by the setting sun. "I think it would be best if I kept my distance from you, at least for now."

A lump rose in my throat, making it difficult to swallow. "If you don't want to see me anymore, just admit it," I ground out. "But don't tell me it's what's best for me."

"You can't see it now," he said. "But it's true."

"Evran—"

"I have a few things I have to take care of, Liora. We'll talk when I get back."

I came to stand before him, my entire body trembling with anger and hurt. "What is there to talk about? You've made it perfectly clear that you don't want to be with me. Just tell me you don't love me so I can move on." I almost added that Luc wanted to marry me if he didn't, but I was terrified Evran would tell me I should accept Luc.

He leaned ever so slightly toward me, and for a moment I thought he might kiss me. But instead he took another step back. "Goodbye, Liora."

I didn't call after him. It hurt too much. It wasn't until he'd disappeared into the darkness that I closed the door and fell against it, too empty even to cry.

SEVEN

"This new tapestry must remain a secret," Margana told me as she led me up to her bedroom several days later. "It's absolutely vital that you not discuss it with anyone, not even your sisters."

"I promise," I said, my palms growing clammy as she sat down in front of a loom a few feet high. I hadn't heard from Evran, and when I'd asked about him, Margana simply told me he'd gone on another errand. It was difficult to function with a broken heart—I had no appetite, and I couldn't sleep for more than a few hours at a time, haunted as I was by dreams of Evran—but at least the apprenticeship forced me to get up, put clothing on, and leave our house.

Margana would be weaving this tapestry from a pile of ivory and peach silk skeins nestled in a basket near her feet. She positioned herself on a bench in front of the loom and gestured for me to sit in a chair next to her. "We are weaving the king and queen a baby."

I nearly missed the chair and had to right myself with a hand on her shoulder. "Excuse me?"

"The queen is barren, and the king needs an heir. I have been asked to create one."

I stared at the pile of what I now realized was meant to be flesh-colored silk thread. "You're going to weave a human child?"

"That's right."

I took a deep breath and sank slowly into the chair. "I grew up hearing rumors that you'd woven the queen, but I never believed them until now."

She pursed her lips as if she'd tasted something sour. "She wasn't my finest creation, I admit. But to be fair, the king's specifications didn't include the words *intelligent* or *fertile.* 'Make her beautiful,' he'd told me, 'with hair like flax and skin like warm honey, and eyes of the palest blue.' Honestly, it was as if he were describing a palomino mare, not a woman. But as the king asks, so it must be. At least I put some kindness into her. She's not a bad woman, just a bit vapid."

"But why would the king want a woven wife? Surely there were plenty of beautiful *real* women to choose from."

"Oh, he had a real wife, once. Things didn't end well for Salome."

I had no idea the king had been married before. Father had certainly never mentioned it. "What happened?"

Margana passed me some loose thread to skein while she spoke. "Darius happened."

It took me a moment to understand what she meant. "The king's wife was a witch?"

She nodded. "From a neighboring kingdom. She was a relatively weak witch, only capable of telling truth from lies. Handy for card games, mostly. But it concerned Darius. He couldn't have someone around who might tip the king off to his ill intentions."

I stared at her, horrified. "Did Darius *kill* the queen?"

Margana gave a small huff of laughter. "No, no. The marriage was declared invalid and the queen was sent away to a convent, supposedly for madness. Their daughter went with her, for the same reason. She was only a little girl, and Darius had the nerve to call her mad."

I sat there blinking for a moment, trying to process what I'd just learned. No wonder Mother had wanted to leave Antalla. I could only imagine what he'd do to a woman who spurned him if he was brazen enough to banish a queen.

"Is that why you wove the king a wife?" I asked. "So Darius could control her?"

She nodded and began to weave the thread onto the loom. "And naturally he wants an heir he can control, as well. Which is what we're here to work on today."

"Does that mean you weave character into your creations, not just a physical appearance?"

She nodded. "I say a spell before I begin each weaving and repeat it every day I work. There's a separate spell for finishing the tapestry."

"What did the king ask for?"

Margana arched an eyebrow. "A baby boy, naturally. A living extension of his own ego. He wants him to be strong, healthy, a natural leader. Fortunately, the queen had some input, and she asked for him to be kind and gentle, too. I've put all those things into this particular spell. And this time I'm adding intelligence, since we're talking about our future king. I can't give him magic, unfortunately... Darius would know the instant he held the child."

"Have you already written the spell?" I asked, shifting

closer. Although troubled, I was also fascinated. She was going to weave a human baby out of silk. What magic could be more powerful than the ability to create life?

She nodded and began to sing as she picked up a skein of pale pink thread.

"Child sweet, child strong,
Child made of words and song.
Child male, child kind,
Child pure of heart and mind.
He shall be wise and fair to all,
He shall lead and never fall.
Child woven, child sewn,
Child made of blood and bone.
Magic mine, hear this prayer,
Make him good, make him fair.
Guide my hands upon this thread,
To weave the image in my head."

She continued to hum as she worked, carefully warping the frame.

"How long will it take?" I murmured, transfixed by her words.

"A day or two. Far less time than a traditional baby, but you can go home if you like. I'll be busy with this and won't have time to train you while I work." She picked up a small lock of hair tied with a pale blue ribbon.

"What's that?"

"Hair from the king's first haircut. It helps to have some token of the thing you're trying to create when you weave. It gives the finished product an authenticity that it would otherwise lack."

My scalp prickled as I imagined what a power like this could do in the wrong hands. The thought of Darius's special project just a flight of stairs away made my pulse quicken with fear. The hounds, though awful in their own way, were surely not the worst things Darius could commission.

Through Margana, I was beginning to see how magic could be a force of creation and destruction, of good and evil. I knew of very few magicians and their powers: Margana, Darius, the girl who cried the diamond tears. And me. So far, my magic had brought me nothing but loneliness and secrets. If my magic really was evil, maybe Father was right, and I was better off not knowing.

"Can I ask you something, Margana?"

She let out a quiet "hmm" that I took as a yes.

"Did you know my mother?"

"Not well. Your family lived in town back then, and as you know, I don't spend a lot of time socializing."

"But do you know why they moved from Corone?"

She glanced at me from the corner of her eye. "Your father never told you?"

"I always just assumed it was because he was afraid of Darius."

"Oh, I imagine your father was quite afraid of Darius."

"I know. And for good reason, clearly. But I overheard him talking to Adelle the other night. He said Darius had taken an interest in our mother, that she was 'special.'" I chewed my lip for a moment, wondering just how much Margana would reveal. But I supposed there could be no harm in asking. "Was Darius in love with my mother?"

Margana stopped working and leveled me with that cold blue gaze. "Listen to me, Liora. Darius is not capable of love.

Whatever interest he had in your mother, I can assure you it had nothing to do with *feelings*."

I shrank a little at her tone and she sighed. "You're young and inexperienced. Perhaps I need to put it more plainly. There is some magic that is harmless, and some that can be harmful in the wrong hands. But the most dangerous magic of all is the kind that uses mages as vessels, that feeds like a parasite and grows beyond the capability of the wielder to control it."

"And that's the kind of magic Darius has?"

"Darius doesn't just have magic, child. Darius *is* the magic. Or the magic is Darius. There is nothing of the man he may have been left, no humanity to appeal to. And the sooner you understand that, the better."

I nodded, feeling foolish for my question but also angry, because it wasn't my fault I had never learned any of this.

Margana resumed her work and began to hum again, and I took that as my invitation to leave. Just as I reached the door, she held up a hand. "Oh, and one more thing, Liora. You may want to start packing. We leave for Corone in two days."

I sat across from Margana as the carriage rattled down the road, the rolled tapestry on the floor between us. Father had begged me not to go, but I insisted that someone needed to make sure Mina was all right, and he finally relented. It had been weeks and we'd had no word from her, not even a way to reach her. With Evran's feelings for me now painfully clear, it was time I prioritize the safety of my family. And once I knew Mina was all right, I was determined to leave Sylvan for good. Luc had never officially proposed, but surely those were his intentions. When I returned home, I would agree to marry him, if he agreed to move far, far away from Corone.

Darius had sent the carriage to collect us, and it felt strange to be heading into the den of the very beast I'd been avoiding my entire life in such comfort. Margana didn't think we would have much contact with Darius, and she assured me I'd never be alone with him. But there was still a knot in the pit of my stomach at the prospect of seeing him again.

Corone was Antalla's capital and largest city. As we drew nearer over the course of the day, past fields of lavender that stretched to the horizon, the villages and towns grew in size, putting into perspective just how small Sylvan was.

When the city finally came into view, I gasped despite myself. The jutting spire of the palace rose above the landscape, seven progressively smaller arches piled on top of one another like a tiered cake, each decorated with a glass sunburst. The white marble gleamed in the setting sun.

It looks like me, I thought. The whole palace was glowing.

Soon we rode through the tall white walls surrounding Corone, along with all the other carriages and wagons coming for commerce or pleasure. Margana pulled me away from the window and closed the curtains. "Best we keep you hidden. Darius has people searching for mages for his collection at all times. He may already know of your abilities, but the last thing we need is some money-hungry amateur witchhunter harassing us."

I stared at her in bewilderment, trying to make sense of her words. "What?"

"The hounds are a recent commission, imagined after a hunting trip with the king. But he relies on his spies, mostly. He offers large enough rewards that they don't always bother to ask questions first. Best to avoid them if we can. To be honest, I'm surprised no one in Sylvan has discovered you yet."

Margana had mentioned spies the night she found me on the road, but I still had a hard time believing that our quaint,

quiet little town, filled with people going about their perfectly ordinary lives, harbored such dangerous secrets. If she
was right, anyone I knew might be a spy.

"I'm constantly amazed at how sheltered your father kept
you," she continued. After a few moments of silence, she
sighed and pulled the curtain back just enough for me to see
out.

People in all manner of dress filled the streets, more than
I'd ever seen in my life. I wished I'd brought a sketchbook to
record all the wonders. As we passed a massive square house set
back from the road by a vibrant green lawn and a long rectangular pool, I glanced back at Margana with raised eyebrows.

"Lord Darius's home. Many of the most prominent mages
lived in houses like these in generations past. These days they
call the palace dungeon home."

"How many mages does Darius keep prisoner?"

"Around a dozen at any one time. Others he dispatches.
Only a few powerful mages are permitted to live alone, like
me, providing they comply with Darius's orders. But the threat
of imprisonment or death is always there, and Darius never
misses an opportunity to remind me."

A chill crept over my scalp as we rolled past the house. Two
bronze statues flanked either side of the path leading up to
the front door. As I watched, they slowly began to shift their
positions. So slowly that at first I thought I was imagining it.

I glanced at Margana again, wide-eyed, and she gave a little nod of acknowledgment. "He keeps several mage artists
on hand at all times, mostly for aesthetic purposes. Darius is
a collector, after all."

We rounded the corner onto a street twice as broad as the
one we'd been on. The palace's spire was so tall I had to crane
my neck back to see the top from this close. It really did seem

to glow in the sunlight, a brilliant facade of white marble with silver, gold, and black accents.

"It's beautiful," I breathed.

"It was built by one of the most renowned witches of all time, long before you were born, of course. She had a power similar to mine, though it was her paintings that came to life, not tapestries."

How ironic, I thought bitterly. A king who allowed mages to be tortured was content to live in a palace built by one. "Does a lot of magic work that way?" I asked, taking in the wide white-and-black checkerboard tiles of the courtyard behind the iron gates. Topiaries in the shapes of various mythical beasts studded the grounds, further evidence of the king's fondness for strange creatures.

"Only one strand of magic. There are many different kinds of magic, too many to name."

I turned back to Margana. "Are you considered a powerful witch?"

"Powerful enough to be useful to Darius, but not so powerful that he considers me a threat."

"What about the king? Doesn't he have any say in the matter?"

She leveled me with her piercing blue eyes. "Darius *is* the king, as far as any of us are concerned. And you'd be wise to remember it. Come. He'll be expecting us."

EIGHT

The sun was just dipping behind the great spire, casting its long shadow across the checkerboard courtyard. A guard helped us out of the carriage, escorting us through an archway and down a covered walk into a garden.

"You'll have tonight free, with your sister," Margana said. "Tomorrow I'll need you with me. I want you to pay close attention to everything I do."

"You mean I'll be in the room with you when the prince is…born?"

She cast me a flat look. "Yes, of course. You're my apprentice."

I knew that I was useful to Margana insofar as I could sort and dye wool and buy materials, but I hadn't expected to be included in the birth. Margana had seemed hesitant to even bring me. Presumably I would be meeting the king and queen, or at least be in their presence, and I hoped the dress I had packed would be suitable. "Thank you. And thank you for tonight. It will be nice to spend some time with Mina."

Instead of acknowledging my thanks, she narrowed her eyes at me. "I hope I can trust you two to stay out of trouble."

"Of course," I replied quietly as another guard approached us.

"The king wishes to see you, witch." The guard frowned at me, as if unsure how I should be addressed. "You can wait here. Someone will be along to get you shortly."

Margana hesitated, clearly not thrilled with the idea of leaving me on my own, but the guard shoved her forward. "I'll see you in the morning," she called to me. "Remember what I said about hunters."

Witch-hunters, she meant. I shivered and stepped out from under the shaded walk to warm myself. Suddenly, I was in the most beautiful garden I'd ever seen. In our small yard at home, the grass was long and wiry, varying in hue from pale yellow to forest green. But this grass was the same emerald green as Darius's lawn, perfectly manicured, without a single blade out of place. How could anyone achieve such perfection?

The answer came to me immediately: magic.

I wasn't used to standing in the sun for long periods, and since it didn't seem like anyone was in a hurry to get me, I headed for a small stand of trees. As I drew closer, I realized that the leaves and fruits weren't matte like they should be. They were iridescent and nearly transparent, like colored jewels. I was reaching up to touch an apple when I heard someone clear his throat behind me.

I whirled around to find Darius watching me. So much for not being alone with him, I thought with a shudder, wondering if I should make a run for it. But the idea of bolting across the palace grounds like a flushed pheasant was ridiculous. I backed up against the tree instead, eliciting a wry chuckle from Darius.

He wore an exquisitely tailored coat of fawn-colored velvet, and his hair was neatly combed, unlike the first two times I'd seen him, when he'd been disheveled from traveling.

For a moment, I was relieved that the hounds weren't with him, but it was a false sense of security. He couldn't rip me apart with his teeth, perhaps, but he had other ways of destroying people. I dropped into a hasty curtsy. "Good afternoon, Lord Darius."

He bowed his head as he approached. "Liora."

"I'm sorry for taking the liberty of exploring. The guard told me to wait, but my curiosity got the better of me."

He stopped a few feet from me, just out of arm's reach, and I willed him not to come any closer. "Ah yes, you don't get out much, as you said."

I didn't know what to say to that, so I let my eyes wander around the garden to avoid his gaze. "It really is beautiful."

"I'll tell the groundskeeper you think so." He reached up, and I shrank back involuntarily, realizing a moment too late he wasn't aiming for me. Instead, he plucked a perfect ruby orb with a cut emerald leaf from the branch above me.

"Just a word of caution," he said as he held it out to me. "They'll chip your teeth. And they taste terrible."

"Is it real?" Fascinated despite my fear, I took it gingerly, careful to avoid his fingers. The apple was cold and hard in my hand, not at all like fruit.

"A real gemstone? Yes. The pears are peridot. The lemons are citrine. There are amethyst grapes on the wall over there."

"How?" I asked, still marveling at the apple.

"One of my mages has a green thumb, you could say. I discovered him way out in the desert, tending to the saddest little cactus garden you've ever seen."

"Do you sell them?" I ran my fingers through the cool

leaves of a nearby hedge, which tinkled faintly as they brushed against each other.

"Sell them?" He grinned, clearly amused by my ignorance.

I flushed and looked away. "I imagine they must be valuable."

"In monetary terms, I suppose they are. But there is value in beauty, too, isn't there? Take your clothing, for example. A simple tunic and trousers would serve you well enough. But you chose to adorn your dress with beads and embroidery. Sometimes an object's value lies purely in the pleasure it gives the beholder."

"It just seems like most magic has a purpose. At least, the little I know of it."

"The most powerful magic, perhaps."

There was so much I didn't understand, and something told me that if I asked Darius a straightforward question, he would give me a straightforward answer. But I also knew just being with him was dangerous. I started to hand the apple back to him, but he shook his head. "Keep it. A souvenir of your visit."

I placed the apple in my pocket. Father wouldn't want it in the house, but this could help pay for my travels. "Thank you. I should probably go see Mina."

"She's almost finished with her work for the day. I thought you might like a tour of the grounds."

I studied him for a moment, trying to make sense of his game and failing. I knew he acted kind in order to lure people in, but I still didn't understand what he could possibly want with someone like me. He wasn't even human anymore, according to Margana. What did a man with no soul desire, other than power?

"I'm sure you have far more important things to do," I said finally.

He waved a hand dismissively and started walking, clearly intending for me to follow. I glanced back at the palace, wondering where Margana was and how she would react if she knew I was with Darius. What else could I do but follow?

He led me around the garden, pointing out neat little beds of jeweled pansies and rows of crystalline dahlias as wide as my head, until we reached a small stream. The cultivated part of the garden ended at the water's edge. Beyond it, a field of wildflowers stretched to the forest outside the palace grounds.

Darius seemed amused by my wonder, and he made no more attempts to touch me. It was difficult to keep my guard up when everything seemed so pleasant and cordial, but then I would remember Margana's warnings and move as far away from him as I could without being obvious.

As we walked back, Darius leaned down near the base of a tree and plucked a delicate stalk of lily of the valley from the ground, twisting it between his fingers. The white jeweled buds glistened in the fading light, which filtered through the leaves above and danced on our skin like a thousand tiny opals.

"Moonstone," he said as he held the flower out for me. "Prized for the way it seems to glow from within."

The intensity of his gaze and the pointedness of his words unnerved me. I suddenly felt completely exposed, despite the fact that most of my skin was covered. I wished someone would come and take me to my sister. "It's very beautiful."

When he saw I wasn't going to take the flower—it was so small that avoiding his touch would be almost impossible—he held it to his nose, though I'd noticed none of the flowers or fruits had a scent. "I agree. It pleases me to look at it, regardless of its value." He tucked the lily of the valley into a buttonhole on his coat. "Come, let me show you to your room."

As I followed him through the halls of the palace, I thought back to every encounter and conversation we'd had. He was assessing me, clearly. But for what, I had no idea. I was struck with the sudden thought that perhaps he simply wanted to study me, like a piece of jeweled fruit, useless but mildly amusing. Margana's words echoed in my head. *Darius is a collector, after all.*

He opened a door to a chamber and held it open for me. I'd barely stepped inside when I heard a squeal.

"Ora!"

A moment later, I was nearly knocked to the floor by a blur of green silk and black hair. Behind me, Darius chuckled.

"I've missed you so much," Mina cried, pulling me into an embrace. She'd only been gone a couple of weeks, but she already looked older, more mature. Her hair had grown since she left, her normally blunt-cut bangs swept to the side with a silver clip. She wore a dress I'd never seen before—one made of dark green silk, with a collared neck and long sleeves. It was much more modest than I'd have expected. She could have passed for nineteen or twenty, rather than fifteen. Maybe that was the point.

"I've missed you more," I whispered against the top of her head. "I can't wait to hear all about…" My voice trailed off when I realized Darius was still standing in the doorway.

"Thank you," I said to him. "Clearly my sister is doing well."

He bowed his head. "It's the least I can do, after separating the two of you."

"I love it here," Mina proclaimed. "Coming to Corone is the best thing that's ever happened to me."

I was glad Mina was happy, but the fact that she didn't seem uneasy in Darius's presence worried me. Had she somehow forgotten what he was?

Then I remembered that Mina wasn't aware of any of the things I'd learned since she left. She didn't know what Darius was capable of, or even that he knew I was a witch.

"Mina, would you mind waiting for us outside? I need to speak with Lord Darius for a moment."

When she rolled her eyes, I felt a surge of affection at the familiar gesture despite my concern. "Fine. I have something to give you anyway. I'll be back in a few minutes."

As soon as she was gone, I turned to Darius. "My sister seems quite comfortable here."

He glanced around the room. "I can't say her quarters are as fine as yours, but she wants for nothing, I assure you."

I tried to keep my tone deferential, but there was a strain in my voice when I said, "No, I meant she seems comfortable around *you*."

His brow furrowed in confusion for a moment, then relaxed as he lifted his chin in realization. "Ah. That explains why you've been keeping an entire horse length between us since you arrived. Margana told you about my power."

"She did."

"I promise you, I have had no contact with your sister since I deposited her in the maid's quarters when we arrived here. Though you should know, my power wouldn't have nearly the same effect on her as it does on you."

I flushed with a mixture of embarrassment and anger.

He had the nerve to laugh. "I mean because she's not a mage. It works differently on non-mages. With you..."

He moved toward me, and on instinct I reached for the closest weapon I could find, a poker next to the fireplace.

"What are you doing?" he asked, but his tone was patronizing, as if the idea of me harming anyone was ridiculous.

All of Father's and Margana's warnings were ringing in my

head, and I didn't have time to take stock of the fact that I was brandishing an admittedly feeble weapon at the most powerful mage in the kingdom. "Don't come any closer."

He clucked his tongue and reached out, grabbing hold of the poker just below the point. I knew instantly that his grip was far stronger than mine, and the fact that I had no way to defend myself should have terrified me.

Instead, a surge of anger surfaced from somewhere deep inside me. It flared like kindling catching fire, burning with an intensity I almost didn't recognize. I was used to the light that poured out of me when I was with Evran, like a physical manifestation of my love for him. But this was something different entirely.

Darius hissed and dropped the poker. I glanced down and saw that the tip was glowing, red-hot. My hand opened on instinct, though I realized after the poker had clattered to the floor that I hadn't been burned. My eyes shot to Darius's, expecting to find fury there.

But he only looked at me and cocked his head, blinking as if he was seeing me for the first time. Then he turned his palms toward his face and shook his head slowly from side to side. "I knew it."

"Knew what?" Mina asked, stepping into the doorway. "What did I miss?" She glanced between us innocently, a cloak draped over her arms.

I realized that I'd been staring at Darius and shook my head a little, forcing a smile. "It's nothing," I said, before Darius could respond. "Lord Darius was just leaving."

He lowered his hands, the expression of wonder on his face replaced with a mask of indifference. "Indeed. There is work to be done in preparation for tomorrow." He bowed with exaggerated grace, his gaze holding mine the way it always did, steadily, without a hint of self-consciousness. "Enjoy your evening, ladies."

I watched him go, residual heat still coursing through me.

Mina approached me cautiously. "Are you all right, Ora? You look...*glowier* than usual."

"I'm fine," I lied. I was the furthest from fine I'd ever been. But it wasn't just fury making me tremble. It was shock, and maybe even elation. I wasn't just a girl with glowing skin. There *was* more to me.

And Darius knew it. I remembered his words then, how the most powerful magic had purpose. Did that mean *I* was powerful? Was this the reason he'd spent time with me, why he'd vowed to look after my sister? Was this what Father was afraid of?

Concern tamped down the last of my anger. If Darius threatening me caused this kind of reaction, what would I do if he actually hurt Mina? I hadn't fully understood what Margana meant when she told me Darius was holding on to my sister "just in case." As collateral, Adelle had phrased it. But I was beginning to see just how dangerous it was for Mina to be at the palace. I needed to talk to Margana, as soon as possible. She might have the answers I sought, now that I knew what to ask.

I turned to my sister, trying to shake off my fear. "What did you bring?"

She held up a rich cloak of midnight blue velvet. "I made it just for you, with some of the cloth Luc brought. What do you think?"

I managed a genuine smile. "It's beautiful. Truly. But that's an evening cloak. You know we'll have to stay here after nightfall."

She smirked. "That's what the cloak is for."

"Why? Where are we going?"

The smirk broadened into a grin. "To a magic show. Now hurry, or we'll be late."

NINE

Mina dragged me down the sidewalk outside the palace, the midnight cloak thrown over my shoulders, my face mostly hidden by the deep hood.

"If we hurry, we'll have time for a drink with my friends before the show starts," she explained. "They're all so excited you're coming."

I lifted my eyes to the sky. The sun was well below the spire of the palace now, and it would be fully dark in less than an hour. "Mina—"

She waved her hand at me and dragged me down a narrow alleyway, around a corner, through several more alleys, and finally stopped in front of the seediest establishment we'd come across. It had a narrow wooden door and shabby dust-brown curtains in the single high window.

I folded my arms across my chest. "All right, enough. I'm not going to take another step until you tell me where we're going."

"It's just through here. I wish you'd trust me. I would never get you into trouble."

I looked at her with enough ire to remind her of the night at Luc's shop.

"Fine, fine." She glanced over her shoulder to make sure the alley was empty. "There's a bit of an underground in Corone."

"An underground what?"

"An *underground*." She closed her eyes to keep from rolling them. "You know, people who don't want to be part of the system. Activities the palace doesn't know about."

"You can't be serious, Mina. You've been in Corone less than a month. How have you managed to get yourself entangled in this so quickly?"

"I'm hardly *entangled*. Really, Liora, you can be so dramatic. Now please, follow me before someone sees us. I promise you'll understand once we're inside."

Before I could respond, the door cracked open and a single bloodshot eye appeared. "You girls coming in or what?" a man asked, his voice full of gravel. "You know you're not supposed to loiter outside."

"Come on," Mina urged, yanking me by the arm through the narrow doorway.

I was not encouraged by what I saw. The pub was just as unpleasant on the inside as it was the outside. Mismatched tables and chairs were scattered around the room, with a few unsavory characters playing cards or drinking. One man had either fallen asleep in his plate of greasy food, or he was dead.

But Mina didn't let go of my arm. "This way," she said, dragging me past a wooden bar stained with condensation rings. She pulled aside a curtain and led me through another door. On the other side was a stairway leading straight down.

I dug my heels into the floor. "Wait a minute. When you

said 'underground,' I didn't know you meant *literally* underground."

"Yes, it's underground. My friends are already going to wonder what's happened to us. I promised Helen we wouldn't be late." With a final yank, she pulled me down the stairway. We descended for what felt like ages, though it was probably closer to a few minutes. Finally, we emerged in a dank tunnel. Something scurried past us in the darkness.

"Mina!"

"Almost there," she chirped.

The tunnel was lit every now and then with a dim lantern, but for the most part it was dark inside. We passed several people who acknowledged us with silent nods.

"Does Lord Darius know about this?" I asked, my worry mounting with every step.

She dropped her voice to a hiss. "He doesn't, and he can't find out either. I only brought you because I know you're as discreet as a lord's mistress."

"Where did you learn that lovely turn of phrase?" I scowled in disgust, but Mina continued to speak over me.

"Look, some of my friends would be in a lot of trouble if Darius knew where to find them."

"Exactly. So why are we here? He has *spies*, Mina."

That seemed to catch her attention. "What?"

"Margana told me. He has people everywhere looking for mages. You could be leading them right to your friends."

She chewed her lip for a moment before finally shaking her head. "I've been careful. I'd have noticed if someone was following me."

I doubted Mina noticed much beyond the tip of her pert nose. "I need you to listen to me. There are things about him you don't know. His touch—"

"Ew," she said, pretending to gag.

I sighed, not sure whether to shake her or hug her. I couldn't explain everything to her here, and maybe it was better if she didn't know. There was no use in her worrying about our family when she seemed genuinely happy. "I just need you to promise me you'll stay away from him. And I would really appreciate it if you would find another way to spend your free time. I'm sure the palace has a wonderful library…"

She threw her head back in frustration. "Come on, Liora! We've spent most of our lives in hiding. I thought you'd be excited to meet other people like you."

"It's not that I don't want to meet other mages, Mina. It's that I don't want to put them in danger."

"And you won't. The underground scene is a place for warlocks and witches to get together safely, without the judgment of the non-mages."

"Aren't you a 'non-mage'?"

"Well sure, but I'm a supporter. Don't you dare roll your eyes at me, Liora Duval."

"I'm just stretching them," I said wryly.

"Please do this for me, Ora. Consider it an early birthday present."

Mina's birthday wasn't for another seven months, but I could see the eagerness in her wide eyes, the earnest desire to share something she loved with me. I'd always had a hard time saying no when it came to Mina. "All right, then. Lead the way."

She squealed with joy and skipped ahead, until we finally came to a part of the tunnel that was brightly lit and vermin-free. The dirt floor had given way to cobblestones, and the smell of cooking food wafted toward us. Mina gestured to a door in the side of the tunnel. A sign carved with the words The Crystal Gazer hung above it.

"Here we are." Mina smiled and took my hand. "You can remove your cloak now."

Part tavern, part theater, the space was far more beautiful than I would have imagined from the outside. Everything from the light sconces to the ceiling was carefully crafted, echoing the motifs I'd seen at the palace: chevrons, scallops, sunbursts, and stars. Here the colors were less austere: warm peaches, pale greens, peacock blues, and metallic hues decorated every surface.

My sister watched me with a knowing grin. "I knew you'd like it."

A man wearing a tall hat and an exaggerated pinstriped suit walked toward us, twirling a cane tipped with a crystal sphere in his left hand. "Welcome, ladies. The show is about to start. Do you have your tickets?"

Mina handed him two slips of paper.

He bowed with a flourish. "Enjoy the show."

"That's Gerard, the owner," Mina explained as he disappeared into the crowd. "He's a warlock. Oh look, I see our friends over there." She waved and led me across the room to a booth at the edge of the theater space. A girl with short red curls held in place by a sequined headband thrust her hand out to me.

"I'm Helen. You must be Liora. I've heard so much about you."

"Pipe down, Lenny," a young man said. "The show's about to start."

Mina reached for my cloak, and I shrank back. "What are you doing?"

"It's all right, Ora. Everyone at The Crystal Gazer is either a mage or a supporter. You have nothing to worry about."

Nothing to worry about. In a way, I envied her blithe spirit.

She was having the grand adventure she'd always longed for. I had never known what it was like to be carefree. "I don't mind wearing it, Mina," I murmured.

She shook her head and undid the clasp, causing the hood to slip away from my hair. Despite her words, everyone turned to stare at my exposed skin. I waited for gasps or muttered insults, but after studying me briefly, each of the patrons returned their attention to their friends. No one tutted in disgust or hurried over to arrest me. I was just another person to them.

Still, I worried my light would distract people during the show. I mumbled an apology as I scooted into the booth next to Mina.

"Hey, don't apologize," another young man replied. "I think it's beautiful."

Mina beamed next to me. "I told you."

"So what else can you do?" a girl asked. She was the last member of the party.

I glanced around to be sure she was speaking to me. "Excuse me?"

"I mean, do you just glow, or can you…do things?"

I remembered the way Darius had looked at me back at the palace. *I knew it.* But how could he have known more about my powers than I did? "I—"

"Leave her alone," Mina said, placing a protective hand on my shoulder. "The show's about to start."

The theater dimmed, and just as I expected, the area around us remained lit with soft white light. But if anyone was bothered by it, they didn't say. The man who had taken our tickets, Gerard, walked onto the stage, and the room fell silent.

"Good evening, ladies and gentlemen, and welcome to The Crystal Gazer. We have a few new performances this evening, which I know you're going to love. Please keep in mind that everything you see is true magic, not razzle-dazzle like you'll find elsewhere in Corone. Please also remember that our performers work at great peril to themselves, should their identities be known. Your discretion, as always, is not only appreciated, but vital."

I looked at Mina, my eyebrows raised in question, but she ignored me.

"And now, without further ado, I give you our very own crystal gazer, Cherie!"

The guests clapped politely as the velvet curtain was swept back, revealing a stage set with a small round table, on top of which sat a large crystal ball. A woman wearing a dress that seemed to be missing about three yards of fabric stepped onto the stage, and the applause increased in volume and enthusiasm. The young men at the table seemed particularly rapt.

"Cherie is Gerard's wife," Mina whispered. "She's a seer."

I cast her a glance from the side of my eye. "Can she tell me how long we have until the palace guards burst in and arrest us?"

"Shhh, I'm trying to watch."

Cherie strode to the other side of the stage on long legs and stopped before the crystal ball. As she rubbed the smooth surface, a mist slowly formed inside the ball, rolling and twisting like a whirlwind. The applause ceased.

"A vision comes to me," she said, her eyes rolling back in her head in a very convincing display. "Yes, I can see it now. It's about tonight's performance. It's going to be…marvelous." She opened her eyes and smiled at the audience, who laughed and cheered. "First up we have everybody's favorite fire starter, Felix. Ladies in the front, you may want to sit back. Women tend to get a little flushed when Felix comes around."

Felix strode onto the stage, a tall man wearing nearly as

little as Cherie. But I quickly forgot about his naked torso, because Felix didn't just create flames—he created art. From a tiny spark to a blast of fire that heated the entire room, he wielded his fire the way a dancer wields their own body. I was entranced by the grace of it.

The next act featured a woman who could create illusions so real everyone in the audience found themselves reaching out to touch the butterflies drifting overhead. Food appeared on our table, but when we tried to pick it up, our hands passed through it like smoke. After her came a young girl who could imitate any voice, including Gerard's.

Several more acts followed, each as interesting as the last, until my head was swimming with wonder. Where had all these mages come from? How was it possible that until recently I hadn't met anyone else like me? Were there others in Sylvan, also in hiding, also afraid that Darius would take them away? I'd always thought of Corone as a dangerous place that was to be avoided at all costs, but now it felt like what I'd really avoided was the truth: I was not alone, and not everyone was as ashamed of my magic as Father.

Still, I was surprised these mages were brave enough to perform. Their magic didn't seem low to me; an illusionist and a seer could surely come in handy. And unlike the traveling shows Margana had described, these people remained in Corone, right under Darius's nose.

The last performer was a handsome young man wearing a simple white shirt and black trousers. His dark hair was slicked back from his face, his eyes a clear crystal blue against his porcelain skin. The moment he stepped onto the stage, Mina straightened in her seat. From the corner of my eye I saw her patting her hair self-consciously, and suddenly everything started to make sense.

When he called for a volunteer, her arm shot up so fast she almost smacked me in the head. The young man, Cyril, smiled in her direction, and I climbed out of the booth to allow her to slide out. She walked onto the stage confidently, as though she'd done this before.

From the way the young man continued to smile at her, it was clear that she had.

"For my first trick," Cyril began, "I'm going to make this stunning creature disappear. I know, I know, it seems a waste. But I promise it will be worth it."

He placed his hand on Mina, uttered a few words in a language I'd never heard, and just like that, Mina was gone. The audience applauded their approval, Mina's friends loudest of all. I glanced at Helen, who winked at me.

"Just wait for it," she said.

Cyril went on to make various items disappear from the audience: a woman's drink, a man's bowler hat. People seemed too delighted by the tricks to wonder if they'd get their belongings back.

"Now, what happened to that lovely volunteer of mine? Oh yes, I seem to recall making her disappear. Do you miss her?" Cyril asked finally. "Is it time to bring her back?"

"Bring her back! Bring her back!" the audience chanted.

Just as quickly as she'd disappeared, Mina reappeared holding Cyril's hand. Her simple dark green dress had been replaced with the champagne silk one I'd made her before she left. She raised her hands in the air and did a twirl. Women clapped, men whistled, and Mina clasped hands with Cyril and bowed. A moment later the curtain dropped. By the time it lifted, Mina and Cyril were gone, and Cherie and her crystal ball were back.

"Well, folks, what did I tell you? Was the show marvelous or was it marvelous?"

"Marvelous!" Mina's friends shouted.

"We thank you for your patronage, and we hope we'll see you all again next week. As always, we promise a show like no other. Good night!" Gerard walked onto the stage and dipped his wife low, kissing her on the mouth for everyone to see, just before the curtain fell for good.

"What did you think?" Helen asked, leaning across the booth to me. "Amazing, isn't it? Mina has been dying to bring you since the first time I took her. Of course, I had no idea she'd become a part of the show, but she seems made for it, doesn't she?"

"She's stunning," one of the young men said. "A natural."

I rose and pulled the cloak around my shoulders, suddenly cold. "Where is she? We need to get back to the palace."

"She's waiting backstage," Helen replied, looking somewhat crestfallen. "Don't be cross. Mina was really excited to bring you here."

Helen was just as naive as my sister, I realized. I looked around at the other people and wondered what they were thinking. Maybe they had gotten used to the constant threat of Darius hanging over their heads, or maybe they simply didn't care. But seeing Mina *in* the show had eclipsed the sense of wonder I'd felt just minutes ago. I would never get used to the threat of Darius, and I cared far too much about my sister to do nothing.

I mumbled a goodbye and walked toward a door to the left of the stage. I let myself in without knocking, but it wouldn't have mattered. Everyone was changing and chattering, completely oblivious to who came and went. I spotted Mina to-

ward the back of the room, sitting on Cyril's lap with an
enormous bouquet of roses.

"Liora!" She jumped to her feet and smiled. "What did
you think? Wasn't it fabulous?" She still wore the gold dress,
though at least she'd wrapped a fringed shawl around her
shoulders. Cyril stood next to her, his clear eyes watching me,
waiting to see what I would do next.

I forced a tight smile. "We can discuss it back at the palace."

A few heads turned toward us at the word *palace*.

"Can you get changed, please?" I said in a low voice.

She handed the roses to another girl and pulled me forward. "Cyril, this is my sister, Liora. She's a witch, as you can
see." She smiled eagerly as she tossed the cloak away from my
shoulders, revealing my hands and neck.

"Lovely to meet you, Liora," Cyril said. "Mina has told me
a lot about you."

"She's made many new friends in such a short time. Unfortunately, we really do need to get back."

Mina laughed. "We're not going home yet, silly. It's still
early, and Darius told us we could have the night to ourselves."

I knew that Mina wanted me to throw caution to the wind
and have a good time for once, but what she needed right now
was someone who understood the very real consequences of
our actions. "*Lord* Darius didn't mean for us to stay out all
night. And I have work to do tomorrow, I'm afraid."

Mina looked at me with daggers in her eyes. This wasn't
what she'd wanted, and while I understood that, I couldn't
afford to humor her tonight. Not only for our sake, but for
everyone else's as well.

"Let's just get a quick bite to eat, Ora. We can't go all night
without eating."

"We can have something brought up to my room at the palace. I've had a long day of travel. Please come with me."

Cyril placed his hand on her arm. "It's all right. I'll see you soon."

"Go change, Mina," I said. "I'll wait outside."

"But—"

I leaned toward her, lowering my voice. "Now, or I'll tell Father all about your new career on the stage."

When her eyes widened in understanding, I left the room and hurried past Mina's friends. Helen followed me out of the club, where it took a moment for me to get my bearings. I'd forgotten we were underground.

"What's the matter?" Helen asked, pulling on the edge of my cloak. "Didn't you like the show?"

"The show was lovely, thank you. I'd just like to get back to the palace."

"Cyril is a nice boy. He really likes Mina."

"I can see that."

"She—"

"I can take it from here." Mina emerged from the door, clearly furious but at least clad in her green dress. "Tell the others I'll come alone next time, okay? See you later."

They embraced, and Helen let herself back inside, while Mina began stomping down the tunnel away from me. I walked at a comfortable pace behind her. I'd take the cold shoulder over a tantrum any day.

But she couldn't hold her tongue forever. After we exited the tunnel and were back on the streets of Corone, she rounded on me. "What's the matter with you? I thought you'd be excited to meet other people like you."

"You *thought* you could show me off to all your friends and impress Cyril by showing how 'supportive' you are to mages."

"What are you talking about?"

I forced myself to take a deep breath and lower my voice. "I know everything must seem fun and exciting and new, and Cyril is certainly handsome. But this is dangerous, Mina."

A group of young men came around the corner just then, weaving and stumbling, clearly intoxicated. "Look here, lads," one of them called to his friends. "A streetlamp in the middle of the street!"

It took me a moment to realize they were talking about me. In my agitation, the hood of my cloak had slipped back, and my face and hands glowed brightly in the dark.

"Hullo," another one slurred, sidling up to Mina. "What's a pretty girl like you doing with a witch?"

She shrugged him off. "That's my sister you're talking about. Go back to your drinking and leave us alone."

The boys laughed as she took my hand and led me away. "She's probably a witch, too," one of them said.

"I bet she has scales under her dress," another replied.

"Or a tail!" They laughed so hard someone snorted.

Mina shot a disgusted look over her shoulder. "Just ignore them, Ora. Some people are so ignorant." I got the impression she'd experienced this kind of thing before.

"Just because you want the world to be as accepting as you are, doesn't mean it is," I said gently. "The world of The Crystal Gazer is not the rest of the world, and you need to remember that."

"I do," she insisted.

We walked on, away from the boys. After a few minutes, I felt some of the tension between us subside. Mina needed to take Darius and his spies seriously, but I needed to remember that my reality in Sylvan was not the same as it was for people in Corone. These mages had to know about Darius's hounds, about the girl with the diamond tears and all the other mages he tortured, and still they were willing to risk their lives by gathering and performing. They could have run away like Father. But for some reason, they didn't.

I nudged Mina with my shoulder. "So how did Cyril pull off that trick, anyway? He can make other people and things invisible, but how did he change your dress?"

"He doesn't make things disappear. He moves them. Instantly. He transports me backstage, where I change into my costume, and then he brings me back. Same with the audience's belongings. He just moves things around so fast they seem to disappear. He has to be holding an object to transport it, but he comes back so quickly your eyes don't register the movement."

I suddenly had a very disturbing image in my head of Cyril transporting himself into Mina's room at night. Thank goodness she shared it with several other girls. "That seems like powerful magic, Mina."

"It is. Cyril has been running from Darius since he was a child. Fortunately, he's always managed to transport himself in time. But I'm terrified he'll be caught one day."

So maybe some of them took Darius more seriously than others. Judging by the genuine fear in her eyes, this wasn't just one of Mina's crushes. She had real feelings for Cyril. "Why doesn't he leave Corone? He'll never be safe as long as Darius is after him."

I could see the blush rising in her cheeks. "He was going to leave. He's been working at the show for months to earn the money. He had everything planned." She raised one shoulder. "Then he met me."

"Oh, Mina. Are you in love with him?"

She nodded, her brown eyes wet with tears. "I am."

"But you're so young. And you only just got here."

She laughed, swiping away her tears with the back of her hand. "What difference does that make?"

I shouldn't have been surprised. I'd always known Mina would fall hard and fast when she met the right boy. She had the kind of heart that was open to falling and had enough buoyancy to survive the landing.

I had believed that what Evran and I had was special, not the sort of puppy love young people experienced every day. But though Cyril had a very good reason to run away, he had chosen to stay, for Mina. I pulled her to my chest in front of the wide courtyard of the palace. "Just promise me you'll be careful."

She nodded against my chin, and I squeezed her tighter. I didn't know how I would get her away from Corone. Darius would never allow it, and it was clear to me she wouldn't willingly leave Cyril. But there was no doubt in my mind she was in danger. As long as Darius thought he had a use for me, she was the perfect bargaining chip.

I said goodbye to my sister reluctantly, watching her disappear down the hallway to her room with a growing sense of doom. I didn't even know when I'd see her again.

Margana had gone off to repair a few tapestries, leaving me alone in an unfamiliar room. After I changed into my nightgown, I perched on the windowsill, looking out over a hedge maze in a part of the gardens I hadn't seen. Dark clouds passed slowly in front of the moon, the reflection of my pale face in the smooth glass a sorry substitute. Through a break in the clouds, I could make out the constellation Exeriel, the ghost ship. Pria, one of the brightest stars in the sky, was its figurehead.

In mythology, Pria was the daughter of a demigod who

caused great storms at sea whenever he was in a foul mood. To secure safe passage across the ocean, a pirate kidnapped her and tied her to the front of his ship, knowing the demigod wouldn't harm her. But the pirate fell in love with Pria, who later gave birth to triplets. Their constellation was just below their mother's, but it was covered in shadow tonight.

I'd always felt a little sorry for the stars, static sentries watching over the planets, lighting the way without ever experiencing the journey. Maybe I identified with them more than I wanted to admit. For the past thirteen years, I'd lived in fear that life would pass me by and all I could do was watch. But something felt different tonight. I had something Darius— the man who Margana claimed ruled the kingdom—wanted. Whatever it was, whatever I'd done to Darius, it hadn't come from my skin. It came from somewhere deep inside of me.

And it was time to find out where.

TEN

Birth by tapestry turned out to be far less dramatic than I imagined real childbirth to be. Mina had come so quickly the midwife hadn't made it to our house, and Father had delivered her himself. I was too young to remember it, but Adelle had assured me it was a loud, messy endeavor. In comparison, tying off the last row of a weaving was simple, painless, and neat.

"I want you to pay close attention to everything I do," Margana had said as we walked to the queen's chambers in the morning. "Not only the words I sing, but also the knot I use. It's a special knot that I don't use for anything else."

I nodded, but I was confused. "What difference does it make if I know how to do the knot? Weaving isn't part of my magic."

"Maybe not, but you're my apprentice, and someone else should know how it's done."

The only other people in attendance of the birth were the

king and queen, along with a nurse and the queen's closest lady-in-waiting. I was relieved, and a little surprised, to see that Darius wasn't coming.

A servant rolled out the tapestry on the floor of the queen's chambers. Blankets and hot water were on hand, and the queen lay in her bed as if she really were giving birth. The king paced anxiously as Margana took up the final thread and began to sing.

"The work is done, my purpose true,
By caring hands this weaving grew.
I finish now in peace, not strife
And bring this tapestry to life."

On the final note, she tied an intricate knot, weaving the thread around her finger, through the middle, around again, until she was left with a ball of thread. The knot—and the rest of the weaving—disappeared almost as soon as it was completed. Where there had once been a tapestry of a human child, there was now a real newborn baby.

We all gathered close as the queen held her infant, who blinked in wonder at everything around him, not making a sound. For a moment I was worried he'd been born without a voice, but eventually he cooed at the nurse and everyone clapped in delight.

"He's perfect!" King Clement declared. For some reason, I had imagined him as weak and elderly. After all, he was allowing another man to essentially rule in his stead. But the king was close to Father's age, tall and well-built, with dark hair and a beard streaked with silver at the corners of his mouth.

Neither the king nor the queen acknowledged my presence,

which suited me fine. I had never been taught how to address royalty, and though I had been proud of my periwinkle silk dress when I'd made it, it felt like the wrong choice for attending the birth of a royal.

The king thanked Margana over and over, handing her a large sack of what I assumed were gold coins.

"It's an honor," she replied, curtsying deeply. "And the beast? Should I complete it now?"

"Ah yes, my new pet. I'd nearly forgotten in all the excitement. You may go to the menagerie after you've rested from your endeavors."

She inclined her head and motioned for me to follow. But just as we reached the door, Darius entered the chamber. He walked past us, heading straight for the baby, who was sleeping on his mother's chest.

"A healthy prince," he exclaimed, smiling. "Congratulations, your majesty." He bowed to the king. "And to you, Queen Juliana."

"Thank you, Lord Darius, for working so tirelessly on the king's behalf," the queen said. "We owe everything to you."

The queen was indeed beautiful, with her flowing flaxen hair and bright blue eyes. But there was something vacant in her expression, and a hollow ring to her words, as though they'd been scripted for her.

"I live to serve." Darius bent into an even deeper bow. He left the room as we did, but I made sure to keep Margana between us.

"Will you be joining us?" Margana asked him. "I would think you've seen enough of the menagerie by now."

He wore a pleasant smile, so at odds with his true nature. I almost wished he would scowl more. It would be much easier to tell who the villains were if their appearances reflected their intentions. "On the contrary. I rarely get to spend time there."

Too busy torturing mages, no doubt, I thought with a sideways glance. We had left the palace and were passing through the jeweled orchard. A high white wall stood on the far side of the garden.

"The menagerie is through here," Margana said to me as we walked through a guarded gate.

Servants had already delivered the tapestry, which lay on the floor of a large enclosure; now it was simply a matter of tying the knot. The other enclosures contained an array of creatures, some real, some imagined by the king, and I found myself openmouthed in wonder, the way I'd felt the first time I entered the jeweled garden. I caught myself, but not before Darius noticed.

"Come with me." Margana took my arm and led me into the enclosure with the tapestry. "I want you to observe closely again, but be prepared to run for the gate. I wove this creature to be gentle, but the king wanted it to be ten feet tall."

Before I could express my concern, Margana bent to her task, singing the same words she'd performed for the newborn prince. I watched carefully as she repeated the knot. I would need to practice at home to get it right, but I thought I had the general idea.

The moment she finished, the tapestry vanished, replaced by a looming beast. Fortunately, it didn't try to move, and I was able to scramble backward toward the gate. It was enormous, its chest thick with muscle to support the long neck, which reached all the way to the top of the wall. The horns were black and formidable, but the creature had a sweet face, with large brown eyes surrounded by thick lashes, reminding me of Mina in a way. When the sun caught its coat, a rainbow of hues appeared, from rich greens to deep teal to fuchsia. Margana and I stood by the gate watching it slowly walk the perimeter of its enclosure. Even she looked impressed.

"Not bad," Darius said from the other side of the gate, startling me. "The king has quite the imagination."

"It's useless." Margana opened the gate and closed it carefully behind us. "But even I will admit that this is one of his better creations."

As we began to walk back to our waiting carriage, I found myself next to him and took a hasty step away so he couldn't reach me.

He chuckled. "Don't worry, I received the message loud and clear last night. I'm not going to touch you."

Margana shot me a horrified look, but before I could respond, Darius spoke again.

"Oh, and, Margana, I almost forgot. I've decided to come to Sylvan tomorrow to check on the special project."

She blanched noticeably. "You said I had another two weeks. It won't be finished tomorrow."

"Nevertheless, I'd like to see your progress for myself." He wore that pleasant, crooked smile, but there was something in his eyes that made my blood run cold.

"Everything is on track, I assure you. It would be a wasted journey."

"Tomorrow," was the stony reply.

Finally, Margana nodded. "Very well. Tomorrow, then." She climbed into the carriage and waited for me to join her.

Just as I placed my foot on the step, Darius withdrew a long wood-and-brass object from inside his coat. "This is for you, Liora."

I made no move to take it. "What is it?"

"It's a telescope." He pulled on one end, nearly doubling its length. "You look through this end," he explained, bringing it to his eye, "and you can see the stars as if they were thirty times closer than they are."

I set my foot back on the ground. "It's magical."

He laughed. "No, it's not magic. It's science. Cleverly placed lenses and a lot of trial and error. Go on." He held it out to me. I noticed the flesh on the pad of his thumb was pink and shiny, like it had been burned. Had I done that?

I could feel Margana's eyes on me through the window of the carriage. She must have come to our room very late last night because I went to sleep before she arrived. When I woke up, there hadn't been time to tell her about my confrontation with Darius or attending the magic show.

"Why are you giving me this?" I asked Darius.

He lowered his voice so only I could hear him. "I saw you at the window last night."

Anger coursed through me, heating my veins. "You were spying on me?"

"I was taking a stroll through the gardens. It's not my fault you were glowing like a full moon up there." He lifted his chin toward the palace. "Anyway, I thought perhaps you had an interest in the stars."

I did, now more than ever. And I hated that he knew it. Slowly, I reached out my hand and Darius lowered the telescope into it.

"Do you...have an interest in the stars, Lord Darius?" I asked, unsure if he'd take my meaning. Only one other person had ever called me a star, and he had meant it as if my glow was something precious. Not as if he wanted something from me.

Darius's mouth softened into a smile, but his eyes glim-

mered, darkening from gold to burnished bronze, and I knew
he understood. "Only one."

My palm began to sweat around the cool metal of the telescope. I swallowed the lump in my throat. "Why?"

"Let's just say you remind me of someone. Good day, Miss
Duval." He turned on his heel and departed before I could
ask him if he meant my mother.

I climbed into the carriage, more confused than ever. Margana was silent for several minutes, but she turned to me as
we passed Darius's manor. "So, Liora. What do you think?"

I didn't like the tone in her voice. "Of what?"

"Everything."

I pulled the curtain closed. "I think there is a lot in this
world that I don't know. Too much."

"You prefer to lead your sheltered existence in Sylvan,
then?"

I bristled for a moment, but I knew she was right. I hadn't
just sheltered my powers from other people; I had sheltered
myself. "There is a part of me that's full of curiosity and questions, that wants to know how magic works and what my options are, what the world beyond Sylvan is like. But another
part of me is afraid."

"Being frightened isn't always a bad thing. It's a defense
mechanism sometimes, a means of protecting ourselves."

"But if fear sometimes protects me and other times holds
me back, how will I know when to listen?"

Her focus shifted slightly, and I knew that she no longer saw
me. She saw whatever prompted her response. "You'll know,
Liora, when you are not willing to give up the thing you're
afraid of."

★ ★ ★

That night I told Adelle everything I'd seen and done on my trip to Corone. Margana had said not to tell anyone about the prince, but I trusted Adelle, and I needed to confide in someone, especially about my concerns for Mina. Father was a different story. I told him only the most benign details about the birth, the beast, and my visit with Mina. Adelle agreed it was better if he didn't know about the underground club and Mina's new beau. He would only fret, and as long as Mina was there and we were in Sylvan, there was nothing he could do for her.

"I can't believe Margana wove a baby," Adelle said. We had our own rooms now, but she was sleeping in Mina's bed tonight so we could talk. "It sounds like evil magic to me, Liora."

"Evil? It was a baby, the plumpest, healthiest baby you've ever seen. There was nothing evil in it, I assure you."

"But if she can create life, imagine what else she can do. What's to stop her from weaving someone's death?"

That gave me pause. I didn't know if Margana could weave an event into reality. I had no idea what the limits of her power were. But this was Evran's mother we were talking about. "Margana would never do that. She's only doing what the king commands."

"You mean what Lord Darius commands."

"She doesn't do *everything* he commands," I insisted, feeling strangely defensive of Margana. "She allowed me to be her apprentice when she could have easily left me to deal with Darius on my own." I ignored the little voice reminding me she'd never refused a commission. Whatever the "special project" in the attic was, I still didn't believe Margana was capable of murder.

"I just wish none of this had ever happened." Adelle sighed. "I miss Mina, and I miss you when you're at Margana's house. It's not the same anymore."

"No, it isn't."

Later that night, when my sister was asleep, I found myself tossing and turning, unable to find a comfortable position. I was worried for Mina, who seemed to be skipping merrily toward the edge of a cliff. I was afraid for Adelle, whose marriage prospects hinged entirely on my reputation. And while Corone had been a good distraction from Evran, here in Sylvan, everything reminded me of him: the chain tangled around my neck, the call of night birds from the forest, and the faint chiming from my copper stars. I hated Darius for what he'd done to my family, for creating a world in which I could never be free.

But it was as if I had walked through a door that only opened one way. I couldn't go back to living a life contained within these same four walls, not after what I'd seen. Not now, when I knew it could be different.

I took the telescope to the window, cracking it open just enough to squeeze the end through. Hesitantly, I pressed my eye to the smaller end.

I pulled it away immediately, convinced Darius had lied to me. The moon looked enormous, and its surface, normally smooth and white, was rough and pitted. How could the contraption *not* be magic?

I took a deep breath. Darius had said it was just carefully placed lenses, and I didn't *feel* any different. I braced myself and looked again. And again.

The moon was so much more than a flat disc in the sky. It had depth and contours, mysterious shadows and unexpected colors: silver, platinum, and shimmering white. It was the most beautiful thing I'd ever seen.

I didn't stop looking until dawn.

ELEVEN

When I went to Margana's house the next morning, she answered the door still wearing her dressing gown. Her long auburn hair was in a messy knot at the back of her head, rather than the loose waves she usually wore.

"What is it?" she demanded, her voice strangely hoarse.

"I'm here for work." I didn't want to be rude, but something was clearly wrong. "Are you ill?"

"Didn't I give you the day off?" She glanced over her shoulder like she was looking for someone. Had Lord Darius already arrived?

"No, but I can go, if that's preferable."

She stared at me for a moment, like I'd grown a third eye. "Just wait a moment," she said before closing the door in my face.

I turned to look at the elm tree, where my stars and moon hung. Before, they had always brought me solace. Now they reminded me of the last time I'd seen Evran, how badly he'd hurt me. And yet, as painful as the memory was, I would have given anything to see him just then. "Where are you, Evran?" I whispered.

The door opened behind me. "Well, are you coming in or not?" Margana asked, more harried than I'd ever seen her. She had dressed and combed her hair, but her eyes darted past me to the road.

I murmured an apology and went into the parlor, where the curtains were closed and the air was warm and stale.

"Lord Darius will be arriving soon," Margana said. "I'm just finishing something up. Will you let him in when he comes?"

I nodded, wondering what had her so flustered. I found some skeins of yarn that needed to be wound and set to work while I waited. But several minutes later, the quiet was broken by the sound of shattering glass and an angry shout. I froze.

Silence followed. Even the birds outside had gone quiet. After a moment, I rose and walked to the base of the stairs. "Margana?" I called.

There was no response. Quietly, I made my way up to Margana's bedroom. The curtains were drawn here, too. I increased my glow slightly so I could see in the gloom, rubbing at the back of my neck. I had the strange feeling that someone was watching me.

That was when I realized the black curtain hiding the stairwell to the attic was open.

Margana had told me quite clearly I didn't belong back there, but the sound I'd heard could only have come from the attic. If she was hurt, wasn't it my moral imperative to check on her safety?

I approached the stairs and walked up them slowly, my ears straining for the sound of Darius at the door or Margana struggling in the attic. There was no denying my fear. I'd seen what Margana was capable of creating, what Darius was capable of commissioning. I thought of what Adelle had said, about weaving someone's death, and a pit formed in my stomach. Literally anything could be on the other side of this door.

I turned the handle and stepped through the doorway.

Margana and Evran stood at the far end of the room, staring at the single round window. No, I realized. They were staring at the hole Evran had punched into it. His hand was at his side, dripping blood onto the wooden floor. In his other hand was a long knife. They both turned as I stepped into the room, their faces pale with what I assumed was shock. The sound of the knife hitting the floor was a million miles away.

The only object in the attic was an enormous wooden frame, running nearly the length of the room and all the way up to the gabled roof. Margana must have used a special loom to weave such a massive tapestry.

But the strangest part was the tapestry itself. At first I thought it was pure black, but the color was so saturated it was difficult to focus. It was darker than black, if such a thing were possible.

Eerie as the tapestry was, it was also intriguing, and without thinking I reached out my hand to touch it.

"Stop."

Evran's voice was so sharp I froze immediately.

"What is this?" I asked, still not understanding the fear in his eyes.

"It's the tapestry Darius commissioned," Margana said.

That much was obvious. "But what is it?"

Evran tore a strip of cloth from his tunic and wrapped it around his bloodied hand. "All you need to know is that it has to be destroyed, immediately." It struck me then that whatever this monstrosity was, Evran had probably known about it for a long time. What else had he been keeping from me?

Margana shook her head. "You know I can't do that."

"Wise decision."

We all turned at the sound of Darius's voice. He must have let himself in, though it seemed unlikely Margana would have left her front door unlocked.

"So it is finished," Darius said as he entered the room. He was clad in black today, though against the darkness of the tapestry, his fine clothing looked almost drab. "Tsk tsk, Margana."

"I was up all night working."

Darius laughed softly. "I imagine it's been done for quite some time. Well, I suppose I did give you twenty years to complete it. I should have known you'd use up every last day if I allowed it."

Margana scowled. "I had hoped you might change your mind. Surely even you can see what a terrible idea this tapestry was."

Darius stopped in front of it, his arms folded across his chest, and studied the tapestry as if it were a work of art. "It's breathtaking."

I looked at the weaving again, trying to see what Darius could possibly admire in it. But staring at it too long made me dizzy. I shuddered and looked away. "It's horrible."

He turned toward me. "Why should you of all people fear the darkness?"

"I didn't say I was afraid."

"You should be," Margana warned. "We all should be."

Evran came to stand beside me. Normally his presence was a comfort, but right now I just felt confused. If this tapestry was what was causing him so much distress, why hadn't he told me?

"Go home, Liora," Evran said. "Please."

I touched his forearm. "Evran—"

"The boy is right." Darius's gaze traveled over Evran like he was something stuck to the bottom of his boot. "You don't need to be here, Liora. Margana is going to roll this up for me and bring it to the palace, where she's going to finish it. Isn't that right, Margana?"

Margana and Evran exchanged a look I couldn't read.

"Go on," Darius insisted, stepping toward me, and that was all the threat I needed. I squeezed Evran's hand and walked to the door, stopping just outside it to listen.

Margana spoke a moment later. "If you force me to complete this tapestry, it will destroy everything."

"That's what you've never understood," Darius said, his voice oddly soft. "It's not destruction. It's the opposite."

I was surprised by the forcefulness in Evran's reply. "She's not going to finish it. And if you think that by threatening either one of us, you'll get her to comply, then you overestimate how much we value our lives."

"Is that so?" I could hear the cold detachment in Darius's voice, far more terrifying than if he had yelled. There was a long silence, followed by a brief scuffle and a scream.

I threw a hand over my mouth to muffle my gasp.

"What have you done?" It was Margana, and the utter anguish in her voice frightened me more than anything. I was about to reenter the room when I heard Darius's heavy footsteps on the floorboards.

"Now I've given you a reason to finish. You have until Saturday, Margana. Five days. How long do you think Evran will last?"

I stepped into the doorway and nearly collided with Darius, who stared down at me with those terrible, empty eyes. "Tell me, Liora. Are you afraid now?"

I waited until the front door had closed behind him before returning to the attic. Margana was on the floor weeping, and I held my breath, bracing myself for the sight of Evran's wounded body.

But Evran was gone.

"What happened?" I asked, rushing to Margana's side. "Where is Evran?"

Seeing Margana cry was deeply unsettling. She had rarely betrayed more than a hint of emotion before, and I realized there had been something reassuring in her stoicism. If she wasn't afraid of Darius, then I could at least try not to be. But whatever he had done had unmoored her.

"He pushed him."

"Evran?" I glanced out the window stupidly. There was no way he could have fit through it. "Where?"

Silently, she raised her hand and pointed toward the tapestry.

"What?" I turned to face it. There was no tear in the tapestry to indicate Evran had fallen through it. And there was no design in the weaving, nothing there that could have come out and taken Evran, even if it were finished. It was a bottomless chasm, an abyss.

"That's impossible," I whispered. Behind me, Margana had risen to her feet. Her cheeks were still wet with tears, but she had stopped crying.

"Haven't you learned by now? Nothing is impossible."

"But it's a thing, not a place." I thought I felt something brush my ankle, but I was so absorbed in the tapestry that I ignored it. When I finally looked back again, Margana was staring at me, her eyes full of wonder.

"You're still glowing," she breathed.

I let out a nervous laugh. "Of course I'm still glowing. What is it?"

She took a step toward me. "Forgive me, child. I have no choice." Then she shoved me so hard that I stumbled backward, bracing myself for impact with the tapestry.

But it never came.

I continued falling backward, my arms windmilling uselessly until I landed hard on my backside, bruising my tailbone. But it wasn't the pain that made me cry out. For the first time in my life, I was in the dark.

I was surrounded by it. Beyond the reach of my arms, everything was utter blackness. The glow from my skin revealed nothing more than me.

"Margana!" I screamed, fear rushing in to replace my confusion. She had pushed me *into* the tapestry. "Help me!"

A muffled sound came from somewhere, but it was impossible to orient myself. I rose and spun in a circle, afraid to leave the spot where I stood because I'd never find my way back. I screamed again, this time wordlessly, a scream of pure terror.

There had been times in my life when I'd wanted nothing more than to experience darkness, simply because I knew I never could. Now I understood why small children were afraid of the dark. Anything could be out there. Something could be right behind me, reaching out with claws like daggers, and I wouldn't know. I spun again, my breath hitching as I struggled to subdue my fear.

Don't panic, I told myself as I plucked my star pendant from my collar and clenched it in my fist. *Evran.* He was in here, too.

"Evran!" I screamed into the darkness.

There was nothing, not even an echo. I'd always imagined

darkness as a feeling of crushing closeness, something that swallowed my light by pressing in. But this place felt vast and empty, more like I was dissolving in it than being suffocated. I stared down at my hands just to make sure they were still there, that I wasn't dead.

Help us.

I jumped backward at what sounded very much like a human voice nearby. Had it been me? Was I losing my senses already, or had I been in the tapestry longer than I realized? I wanted to scream, but what if there was something out there? What if swarms of creatures from my nightmares were even now converging on me?

A moment later something tugged at my foot. I shrieked and struggled, but the tugging didn't cease. I dropped down into a crouch, half expecting to find a monster's talons wrapped around my ankle.

Rope. Someone had tied a rope to my leg. A sound that was half-hiccup, half-sob burst out of me, and I grabbed ahold of the thick cord, pulling it up so that I could stand while holding it. The tugging continued, and I let myself move toward it. Margana must have slipped the rope around my ankle while I was looking at the tapestry. There was a final yank, and then I was falling forward until I hit the wooden floor of the attic with a smack.

I recovered quickly, righting myself and bolting immediately for the door. But I hadn't gone more than five feet before the rope on my foot pulled taut and I crashed back down to the floor, this time landing on my hip. I yelled in pain and fear, my eyes finding Margana's as I attempted to scramble backward out of the room.

"Please calm down, Liora."

My eyes followed the rope to where it had been tied to a

wooden support beam in a complicated knot. She had shoved me in, but at least she hadn't abandoned me in there. "What is that thing?" I demanded, gesturing toward the tapestry. "What did you do?"

Margana slid down the wall, looking exhausted. "Evran calls it the Shadow Tapestry, though as you can see, it's far worse than any shadow. It's meant to be an empty place, a physical manifestation of Darius himself. Oblivion. It's woven from the hair of the Lusiri."

The Lusiri, the Hollow Ones. As far as I knew, they were fairy-tale monsters used by desperate parents to threaten their children into compliance. *Get to bed, or the Lusiri will eat your innards first, followed by your eyes, your tongue, and then your soul.* "The Hollow Ones are real?"

"They were. They've been extinct since long before I was born. This hair was collected from all the stuffed and mounted Lusiri Darius could gather from around the kingdom. He paid people incomprehensible sums of money for their tails."

I shook my head in confusion. "Their tails?"

"Imagine a hideous beast with a body resembling an ox, a massive, boxy head with two forward-curving horns, and a tail like a horse. Their entire body, from horn to tail, is the same color as that tapestry, as dark as a sky without stars. But they're far worse on the inside—black holes devouring anything unfortunate enough to cross their paths. In the old days, Lusiri hunters were powerful mages revered by the people. The bodies of the beasts were normally destroyed, but every now and then an individual would get greedy and sell one illegally. Their carcasses fetched enough money to last a lifetime."

I stared at her in shock. "But *why* does Darius want the Shadow Tapestry? What does he plan to do with it?"

She released a heavy sigh. "You've seen what happens when I complete a tapestry."

"It becomes real."

"Exactly. This isn't just a tapestry. It's a place, and once it's finished, it will spread like a wave, swallowing everything in its path."

My stomach churned as I imagined that infinite darkness spreading across Sylvan, Corone, and all of Antalla. But it wasn't a void, the nothingness that Darius hoped it would be. When he touched me, I was freed of emotion. In the tapestry, I'd felt all of the worst emotions at once. Now I understood why Margana had refused to finish it.

"I've spent countless hours trying to find a way to stop Darius," Margana continued, "or at the very least a light source that can't be swallowed by the tapestry. That's why you saw me with the devil's footprints. I had hoped there was some way around Darius's plan. He had asked me to create horrible things before, but I'd always been able to find some small way to thwart him." She closed her eyes. "And then I had a child."

"He threatened to hurt Evran?"

She wrapped her arms around herself and nodded. "Darius said he'd kill my son if I didn't finish this tapestry. But I knew that if I did complete it, we were all as good as dead anyway." She took a deep breath. "I finally told Evran the truth. Together, I thought we might be able to end this."

"Is that what's been distracting him?" Once again, I wondered how he'd managed to keep this a secret for so long.

She nodded. "It was pointless, of course. He searched for a mage who might have the power to destroy the tapestry, but he was met with dead end after dead end. He was so desperate he attempted to cut it apart with a knife just before you came in. As if it could possibly be that simple. His hand and the knife went right through the tapestry."

"So what do we do now?" I asked, refusing to believe it was over.

Margana reached for my hand, but instead of taking it, she held it up in front of my face.

Realization crawled over my skin like a thousand spiders. *You're still glowing.* I started to back away, the rope digging into my ankle. "This is why you allowed me to be your apprentice, why you protected me from Darius? Because I can see inside the tapestry?"

"I won't lie to you and say I didn't have selfish reasons for keeping you close these past few weeks, but I hope you can see that we're all in grave danger. And now that Evran is trapped inside... Darius is a smart man. He knew I'd have to finish the tapestry to have any chance of freeing Evran."

I groaned in horror, covering my face with my hands as I began to cry. Evran was trapped in there. And just as Darius had used Evran against Margana, now she had me completely at her mercy. There was nothing I wouldn't do to save Evran, even if he would never love me like I loved him.

She crouched down in front of me, her furrowed brow smoothing. "*You* were his Miss Duval."

Grief was building in my chest, closing up my throat, but I managed a nod.

"Oh, child, I'm so sorry." She pulled me against her and held me like I really was a child, and the anger I felt toward her slowly faded as I released some of the pain I'd been carrying. "Shhh," she whispered, stroking my hair. Though it wasn't a true memory, a part of me knew that my mother had held me like this once, when I was very small.

We sat that way for several minutes, until my tears had

subsided enough for me to speak. "It's black as pitch in there, Margana. I could hardly see. And Evran doesn't have any light source. How would I possibly find him?"

She was quiet for a long moment. "I spent most of Evran's childhood working on the tapestry, while he played in the forest and helped with the housework. But one day, when the tapestry was about half finished, I caught him standing in front of it, staring.

"After that, something changed in Evran. I found him lurking in the dark, sticking to shadows. He would go into the woods in the morning and sometimes not come out for the entire day. He even took to sleeping in the forest. I was concerned, of course, but I had to finish the tapestry. The sooner it was completed, the sooner Darius would release me from his service. I planned to take Evran as far away from Corone as I could, perhaps even out of Antalla."

I touched my star pendant as she spoke. All this time, Evran had been dealing with something I knew nothing about. Why hadn't he confided in me? Didn't he trust me to keep a secret, especially when he'd kept mine for so long?

"I didn't fully understand what it was until three years ago, when our little dog, Pippin, disappeared. Evran spent days searching for him. I didn't have the heart to tell him what had happened."

I remembered Pippin's disappearance, vaguely. He was a small brown terrier that accompanied Evran everywhere when we were young, but he'd stayed home more as he got older. "What happened?"

Margana winced at the memory. "I came upstairs the day Pippin disappeared and found that the attic door was open, just enough for a small dog to squeeze through. The latch hadn't caught, and he must have nudged his way in."

"Pippin went into the tapestry?"

She nodded. "It was the only explanation, though it seemed impossible." She touched the knot on my ankle as she spoke, and the rope fell away instantly. "I'd been ordered to weave it from the Lusiri's hair, to create something as large as I could. That was the only information Darius gave me. He didn't tell me what it was for, and he didn't ask me to weave any intention into it. I suppose I could have, inadvertently. I certainly had no idea that even unfinished, something could disappear into it.

"I knew at that point I couldn't finish the tapestry. Even if Evran and I did escape Darius, there would be no escaping the tapestry itself. I sent Evran to Corone to speak to other mages, but those who were willing to talk to him had nothing useful to say." She gave a small, sad smile. "Now I understand why he never told me about your magic. He was protecting you."

Guilt coursed through me. I thought Evran was trying to push me away because he didn't love me, but he knew what his mother would do if she discovered my magic. He'd been protecting me all along.

"That doesn't explain how you think I can find him," I said. "If it truly is a void, it could be infinite. And Darius will be here on Saturday." Somehow, it was already the afternoon, which meant we had less than five days to find Evran.

She glanced down at her hands. "Liora, I don't think it's just the tapestry that has been distracting Evran."

"What do you mean?"

"He's been struggling with something. I don't know exactly what, but I believe it drew him to that tapestry, even as a child. If anyone can survive in there, it's Evran."

It sounded like reasoning based in a mother's love, not rationality. I didn't know if I could save him. I didn't know if we could stop Darius even if I did find Evran. But Margana wasn't the only one who loved Evran.

"All right," I said, rising to my feet. "What do I have to do?"

TWELVE

I paced around Margana's parlor, the closest I was willing to be to the tapestry, trying to steel myself for what I had agreed to.

"And what if I can't find him?" I asked. "What will you do when Darius comes?"

"I'll destroy it." Her eyes were hard and resolved again, to my relief. I was glad I'd gotten to see how much Margana loved Evran, but right now, I needed her calm and logical. Because I wasn't sure I could be.

"Even if Evran is still inside?" I asked.

She nodded. "The only thing that's kept me from doing it all this time is my son. And I know that he would rather die than let me complete that atrocity."

I had no idea how I was going to go into the tapestry and come back out with my sanity intact. I'd only been inside for a few minutes, and I could still feel the boundless terror every time I closed my eyes. A day would kill me. And what did that mean for Evran? Even if by some miracle he survived, the experience would be extremely traumatic.

But the thought of Evran alone in there, trapped and hopeless, brought fresh tears to my eyes. I stopped and sat down next to her on the sofa. "And if I don't go?"

Her eyes were full of the same pain I felt in my heart. "I can't destroy it, Liora. Not without trying."

"What makes you so sure you *can* destroy it?" I pressed.

"Everything I weave can be unraveled, at least until the final knot is tied. Once that happens and the spell is cast, it becomes real. Then there's nothing I can do to stop it."

"Are you sure Darius intends for you to complete it now? Why bother gathering mages or working for the king if his plan is to destroy the entire world?" Why bother with *me*?

"He doesn't want me to tie it off until we're at the palace, but I have to assume that he wishes it to be completed."

I rose again and resumed my pacing. If I refused to go back in, if I did nothing, Margana would complete the tapestry and we'd all be taken by the darkness anyway. Not just Evran and me, but my father and sisters, everyone in Sylvan, Corone, and beyond, according to Margana. How could I not at least try?

There was something I had to do first, however. "I need to speak to my family. I can't just go in there and disappear."

She nodded. "I understand. Take a few hours to think about it."

I stared at her openmouthed. "A few *hours*?"

"Darius comes in five days. It could take you that long to find Evran, and we're going to need time to destroy the tapestry and get as far away from Sylvan as possible."

I twisted my braid around my fingers as hard as I could, wishing the pain would wake me up from this nightmare. But I was awake, and it wouldn't matter how many days I took to consider returning to the tapestry. I would always conclude that I didn't want to, and I would always conclude that I must.

I promised Margana that I would return as soon as possible. She walked me to the door, clutching my shoulder just as I reached for the handle.

"He loves you," she said, her gaze burning into me. "And I believe you love him as much as I do. You'll do the right thing. I know it."

I should have gone directly back to the house. Adelle was expecting me, and it would be easier to talk to her first and approach Father together. But instead I found myself heading to the blackberry glade in the woods.

I hadn't been back since the day we encountered Darius. It was Evran's and my place, and if there was no us, what was the point in going? But as I pushed through the undergrowth that was already beginning to obscure the path, I remembered another time I'd met him there, when I was thirteen. It was a bitterly cold December day, and the blackberry bushes were bare brown snarls around me. Evran had found me crying.

The mayor had recently taken down the star above Sylvan to be cleaned, and that night it would be hoisted back up into its place above the city. The town librarian was going to tell the story of Sylvan's founding and the origin of the star for all the children. Father had agreed to take Mina, while Adelle would stay behind to care for me. I'd insisted I didn't need a nursemaid, preferring to wallow in my misery alone. Sweet Adelle had stayed anyway, doing her best to comfort me. But I didn't want comfort. Instead, I ran away to the forest.

"What's the matter, Ora?" Evran had asked, placing a gentle hand on my shoulder.

"What do you think?" I muttered, still feeling petulant and sorry for myself.

His hair was longer then, hanging nearly to his shoulders. He constantly had to brush it out of his eyes, a habit he'd held on to even after he cut it shorter. "I went to your house to find you. Adelle said you were upset about the star ceremony."

"Of course I'm upset. I never get to see anything." He handed me a handkerchief so I could wipe away my tears. "What are you doing here, anyway? Don't miss the ceremony on my account."

"Why would I want to see some silly star strung up on a chain when I have you?" He had smiled, tucking a finger under my chin, but I pulled away.

He always did that, called me a star, like there was something truly special about me. "What good are stars, Evran? So they shine. So what?"

He held my gaze, and in that moment, something changed between us. We weren't adults, but we weren't children either. "Stars don't just shine, Liora. Never forget that."

He'd brought me one of his mother's cloaks, and together we crept to the edge of the cliffs to watch the star ceremony from above. When he took my hand, I felt it in every nerve in my body. That was the night I began to see Evran as more than a friend.

Now, I approached our glade and squeezed my star pendant in my fist. It was a commemorative trinket they'd sold at the star ceremony, and Evran had spent all of his pocket money to buy it for me. Most girls my age had probably outgrown or lost theirs, but I never removed mine. Right now, it was all I had left of Evran.

Shhhh!

I glanced up into the tree above me and nearly screamed. A

girl dressed in dirty gray rags was perched there like an owl, one finger pressed to her lips.

She pointed toward the glade. *Lord Darius is here. He's hunting for mages.*

It took me a moment to realize she wasn't speaking out loud. Her voice was in my head.

I had no idea how to respond.

Don't say anything, she said, apparently able to read my thoughts. Before my trip to Corone, I might have been more frightened, but she was smaller than me and clearly afraid. *Go back the way you came, quickly.*

But it was too late. I heard a long, mournful howl, then a man's shout.

Run!

I wanted to, desperately. My entire body was poised for flight. But if I ran, the hounds would surely find the girl in the tree. They knew me. If I held my ground, I might be able to shield her the way Margana had shielded me.

I took a deep breath and released a little of my control over my glow. It wasn't hard; my emotions were a jumbled mess just below the surface, and soon light was pouring out of my skin. I took a few steps toward the blackberry glade, away from the girl in the tree.

The hounds burst through the undergrowth a moment later. They yipped and hopped on their front legs, but they didn't bark or growl. It took all my courage to continue walking forward, farther away from the girl.

I almost sighed with relief when Darius appeared. I was fairly confident he wouldn't let the hounds eat me.

He shielded his eyes against my glow. "Liora?"

"It's me," I said, doing my best to tamp down my fear so my light would dim with it.

"What are you doing in the forest at night? I thought I told you to go home."

I glanced up at the sky and noticed the stars for the first time. I had been so lost in thought I hadn't realized night had fallen. My hair was uncovered, my braid unraveling, and I had no jacket or shawl. I shivered and wrapped my arms around myself.

"I know what you did to Evran. He was my friend. I'm... concerned for him." I didn't want Darius to know how much I cared about Evran. It would just give him one more thing to use against me.

"And what about concern for yourself? There were reports of a drifter camp in the woods. My hounds got to one of them before I could." He waved behind him, toward the glade. "I believe there's another one still out here. It's not safe."

"Not safe for whom?" I started forward, but he stepped to the side to stop me. I froze before our bodies made contact. "Why would the hounds attack a drifter?"

"Drifters are mages, Liora. You must know that."

I shook my head in confusion. Father had always told us that drifters were vagabonds, people who had no permanent homes and occasionally robbed a coach or traveler for money. We were told to stay out of the woods in case we should stumble upon one of their camps, though in all my wanderings with Evran, we'd never met anyone.

But it made perfect sense that drifters were mages: warlocks and witches driven from their homes because of Darius and his spies. I trembled as I pictured what the hounds had done to this person. I started forward again, and he held out an arm.

"Don't. Please. It's not something you want to see."

Bile burned the back of my throat. "How could you?"

He ignored my question. "Come, I'll take you home."

I shook my head and stepped farther away from him. *Someday*, I thought bitterly, I would gain enough control of my magic that he wouldn't dare come near me or anyone I loved. "I can get home by myself."

"Maybe, but I'll feel better if I escort you. You shouldn't be on your own. Does your father know about this?"

Father. It was early enough that he might not be home yet, but what if he was? Father clearly wanted nothing to do with Darius. "He's in Sylvan," I said, hoping it was true. "Adelle is expecting me."

He glanced over my shoulder, toward the tree where the girl was hiding. One of the hounds had slipped away and was standing stock-still, watching.

I turned to leave and heard Darius sigh behind me. He whistled to the hounds, who immediately sprang toward him.

While he attached leads to their collars, I continued away from the girl in the tree. *I live at the end of the road out of Sylvan*, I thought to her, having no idea if she'd be able to hear me. *Come find me when it's safe. I can help you.*

We walked in silence for a while, until I couldn't take it anymore. "You said I reminded you of someone," I began, not really sure what I was hoping for. More information about my mother, perhaps.

He grunted in acknowledgment.

I took a deep breath. "Did you mean my mother?"

I could sense his posture change. "What would make you think that?"

I hesitated. I didn't want him to know the full extent of my ignorance or inadvertently reveal something about Father he was trying to hide. "I don't really remember her. I just thought perhaps..."

"I hardly knew your mother." Darius's tone was so flat I

couldn't tell if he was being sincere. "Or your father, for that matter."

I chewed my lip for a moment. We were nearly at the house; this might be my only opportunity. "Then who do I remind you of?"

He paused with his hand on our front gate, studying me, seemingly unsure if he should answer me or not. Finally, he straightened. "Me."

My jaw dropped, but I couldn't find my voice. Just then, the front door opened, spilling light onto the walkway.

"Where have you been?" Adelle cried. "I've been worried sick about you!" She peered over my shoulder and gasped. "Lord Darius. What brings you here at this hour?"

"Good evening, Miss Duval. I was just escorting your sister home. She got herself lost in the woods."

I shot him a furious look, but he busied himself with tying the dogs' leads to the gate.

Adelle grabbed my wrist and yanked me through the house to the kitchen. "What's going on? Why is Lord Darius in Sylvan?"

"It's a long story. I'll explain as soon as he leaves. Is Father home?"

"Not yet. But he could arrive any minute."

Father being out was the only small mercy we'd been spared today. "Then we need to get rid of Darius as quickly as possible."

The moment she heard his footsteps in the hall, she straightened my dress and wiped a smudge off my cheek with her apron hem, then plastered a smile on her face and walked into the parlor. I trailed after her, unsure what to do with myself.

"Can I ask what brings you to Sylvan tonight?" Adelle sat

down on the sofa and gestured for Darius to take a seat in the yellow armchair. I perched next to her, my entire body tense.

Darius was watching me from the corner of his eye. "Drifters in the woods. We had reports from someone in Sylvan that there was a camp of them. I came to check for myself."

That was a lie. He had come for the tapestry. The drifters were just a convenient excuse.

"Then I suppose we should thank you," Adelle said, as ignorant as I had been. "We don't always feel safe outside the gates, especially so close to the forest."

"Completely understandable." He flashed a smile that didn't reach his eyes. "I don't suppose you have any of that delicious cold well water on hand."

She glanced quickly at me, the fear of refusing him clear in her eyes. "No, but I will get you some, my lord."

As soon as she was gone, the false smile dissolved, his whole face hardening, until I could see a muscle in his jaw twitch. "What were you doing out there, Liora?"

I forced myself to hold his gaze. This was the man who had commissioned that horrible tapestry, who had forced Margana to create the hounds, who had thrown Evran into the tapestry like he was refuse. I thought of the girl in the tree, of how terrified she had been. Darius thrived on fear, and I wouldn't give him the satisfaction of mine.

"Exactly what I said. Worrying about my friend. Trying to understand why you would create something so evil."

Adelle returned with a glass of water and handed it to Darius before he could respond. He drank it quickly and rose, finally dragging his gaze away from me to my sister. "I should be going. It's late, and I imagine your father will be home soon. Send him my regards."

"Are you planning to travel back to Corone at this hour?" Adelle asked.

He cocked his head, seemingly perplexed by the question. "Why wouldn't I? I have no reason to fear the night."

No, I thought bitterly. You *are the thing that people fear.*

Adelle laughed nervously. "I suppose not. Only young women are warned never to risk meeting Belle Sabine on the road."

Darius's tone was soft when he replied, "You have nothing to fear from Belle Sabine. Not because you aren't beautiful, but because she's long dead."

"How do you know?" I asked, my eyes darting away from my blushing sister as I followed him to the front door.

He paused on the threshold, amber eyes boring into me. "Because, silly girl, I killed her myself."

I shuddered and closed the door behind him, making sure to lock it. But my relief at Darius's departure was short-lived. Now I had to tell Adelle and Father that I was going into the tapestry. As far as they knew, Evran and I were friends and nothing more.

How could I explain to them that I was in love with Evran? That it hadn't happened in one pivotal moment but in hundreds of them. That it wasn't every kind gesture, show of faith, knowing laugh, and sun-gilded afternoon. It was the moments in between that added up to loving Evran enough to risk everything for him. Mina might be able to fall in love in a matter of days, but my heart wasn't as free as hers. And only Evran had taken the time and care to coax me out of my cage, to earn my trust, to prove to me over and over again that he would not betray me.

Even if Adelle and Father did believe me, they would try to talk me out of going. They'd insist we leave Sylvan immediately, fetch Mina, and go. They would tell me there was no way Evran had survived in there, and a part of me would fear they were right.

But Evran was not like other people. He traveled through the forest like a fox, able to pick out troublesome roots and soft spots I couldn't see even in my light. He could go all day with no food and little water. He was content to spend hours alone, as if he needed solitude as much as Mina needed human contact. If anyone could survive in the tapestry, it was Evran.

From next door, the tin stars chimed, softly at first, then louder, more insistent.

Come find me, they seemed to say.

"I'm coming," I whispered back.

THIRTEEN

It was close to midnight when Father finally returned. He rushed into the room, still wearing his coat and boots.

"Are you both all right?" he asked.

"We're fine," I assured him. "How did you—"

A girl stepped into the parlor behind him, her dress so loose it was slipping off one slender shoulder. I hadn't gotten a good look at her before, but I knew it was the girl hiding in the tree. Everything about her seemed dishwater gray, from her wide eyes to her filthy hair, but she looked no older than Mina.

"This is Jean." Father gently urged her forward. "She met me on the road and told me Darius was here. She was separated from her parents. She needs a change of clothing and something to eat."

"Of course," Adelle said, rising quickly to her feet. "Liora, come help me in the kitchen."

Adelle assembled two plates for Father and Jean while I put the kettle on. "Who do you think she is?" she whispered.

"I met her in the woods just before I ran into Darius. He was hunting mages with his hounds."

"What were *you* doing in the woods? I was worried sick."

These were not the ideal circumstances to discuss something serious with Adelle. But then, when was a good time to tell your sister you were disappearing into a tapestry tomorrow, possibly forever? "I'm sorry. I'll find something for Jean to change into, and then I'll tell you everything. I promise."

We gathered around the table a little while later. Adelle had helped wash Jean, who I could now see had ash-blond hair that hung to just above her shoulders. I had given her one of Mina's dresses to wear, but it was still loose on her. I wondered when Jean last had a proper meal.

Once I'd described her magical abilities to Adelle, Jean began to tell her story around mouthfuls of stew. "My parents aren't mages," she explained, shrugging sheepishly as she spooned a carrot into her mouth. "We fled Corone after we learned of Darius's hounds. That was weeks ago. We've been in the woods hiding ever since.

"Then last night, a man stumbled into our camp. He promised he wouldn't tell Darius about us, but I read his thoughts, and he was far more interested in the reward he'd get from Darius than in protecting us. We tried to run, but we got separated when the hounds caught up with us. They got to an old man we'd been traveling with…" She broke off, her voice thick with unshed tears.

"And your parents?" Adelle asked, placing a hand over Jean's.

She bowed her head, letting her hair cover her face. "I don't know what happened to my parents."

Adelle's eyes darted to mine, full of concern. "We'll help

you find them tomorrow. Try not to worry. If they're not mages, Darius has no reason to go after them."

Father couldn't be happy about having another mage in the house, especially one being hunted by Darius, but I knew he wouldn't send a girl back out into the woods at night.

Jean looked up at me suddenly, her large gray eyes studying me. "When are you going to tell them why *you* were in the woods?"

I could feel Father and Adelle looking at me, and I sent Jean a mildly sarcastic *Thank you for the help*. But she was right. I needed to tell them about the tapestry now if I was going to leave tomorrow. There was no reason to keep any of this from Jean, who could read my thoughts if she wanted to. And it seemed she already had.

"Let me make some tea first," I said with a sigh. "It's a long story."

Adelle and Father were horrified when I told them about the tapestry, and it took a long time for them to see that I really was in love with Evran and was going in no matter what. Eventually, they seemed to understand how desperate the situation was, or they were just too tired to keep arguing with me. I went to bed and fell into a deep, dreamless sleep.

I went to Margana's in the morning to tell her about my encounter with Darius and to let her know that I would be back at noon to begin the search for Evran. In the meantime, Father went to the shop to settle overdue accounts, and Adelle began to pack up our belongings. If I was successful in finding Evran, we would need to leave as soon as the tapestry was destroyed.

But someone had to fetch Mina first.

Going to Luc had been Adelle's idea. Considering we hadn't

spoken since our last awkward encounter, I thought it rather presumptuous to ask him for such a large favor. Adelle argued that if he cared enough about me to marry me, he would be happy to help. But he had never actually proposed, and even if he had, I knew now I couldn't marry him. Whether or not Evran wanted to be with me, I wouldn't commit my life to someone out of convenience. It wouldn't be fair to either of us.

Still, someone had to get Mina, and I had no one else to ask.

I could see Luc through the window of his shop when I arrived, bent over a piece of fabric at the counter. He was dressed in his usual pinstriped trousers and vest, his sleeves rolled up to the elbows. He lifted his head when I knocked on the door.

"Liora." His smile was easy, confident. "To what do I owe the pleasure?"

I had to force myself to stop fidgeting. "I'm sorry to disturb you so early. I was wondering if I could speak with you for a moment. I have a favor to ask of you."

"Of course," he said, opening the door wider. "I'm always happy to help you."

"I'm happy to hear you say that. It's Adelle. She's taken ill."

"Oh dear. Not seriously, I hope."

I swallowed nervously. I'd never been good at lying, and I was uneasy around Luc under the best of circumstances. "Not too seriously, no, but she's heartsick for Mina. I was hoping you might be able to go to Corone in the next day or two and fetch her. I think it would help Adelle recover to have both of her sisters nearby. Father would go, but we have no horse, and he'd hate to leave Adelle right now."

Luc touched my arm in sympathy. "Of course. I'll go tomorrow. But will Lord Darius mind?"

I cocked my head. "Why would Lord Darius mind?"

"Oh, no, I didn't mean it like that. I just wasn't sure if she's allowed to come and go at will."

I smiled to cover the uneasy feeling in my stomach. "She's a seamstress, not a prisoner. I'm sure Lord Darius has far more important things to worry about." The truth was, I didn't know for certain if Mina would be allowed to leave. But it disturbed me that Luc was questioning it, too. People in Sylvan knew Darius had asked Mina to work at the palace, but they didn't know the true reason why.

"I'm sure you're right." His lips curled in a tight smile. "Oh, I just got some fabric in I thought you might like. A silver-and-lilac brocade with the most beautiful sheen to it." He was still standing in the doorway, waiting for me to enter. "Or perhaps you need some new trimmings for your hats?" He stepped to a display and strummed the array of hanging ribbons like a harp.

"Thank you, but I really should get home. Adelle needs me. Goodbye, Mr. Moreau." I turned when I felt his fingers close around my wrist. My eyes flew up to his.

Instead of releasing me, he looked down at where his skin met mine. There was no denying the light coming off of my exposed hand. I waited for him to say something, but he only swallowed and relaxed his grip until I was able to slip free.

"Special, indeed," he murmured. "Don't worry. I'll bring Mina back safely."

I managed to smile and thank him, but I could feel his eyes on my back until I rounded a corner. I ran the rest of the way home.

Breathlessly, I changed into a white tunic and a pair of riding trousers I'd sewn for Mina once at her insistence. She'd never gone riding, of course, but I'd enjoyed the challenge, and she'd paraded around the house in them for days. My heart ached at the memory. I could only pray Luc would be true to his word and I'd be reunited with my sister soon.

Adelle rebraided my hair twice, fretting the entire time about how she wished I would reconsider and how she couldn't believe she was letting me do something so foolish. But she must have sensed my resolve because she didn't try to talk me out of going.

"Luc should be bringing Mina home in the next day or two," I said to Father as we embraced. "As soon as I'm out of the tapestry, we'll go."

He held out a small parcel wrapped in a handkerchief, his hand trembling slightly. "It's your grandfather's pocket watch. I thought it might help you to keep track of time while you're there. Three days isn't so long."

Three days might not seem long, but in the tapestry? It would feel like an eternity. And yet I had no confidence I'd be able to find Evran by Friday. Any longer, though, and there wouldn't be time to get away from Sylvan. I clenched my teeth to keep from crying.

I was about to turn when something stopped me. I might die in the tapestry without ever knowing the truth about my mother or myself. I had to at least ask. "I overheard you the other night, Father. When you and Adelle were talking. You said my magic was dangerous. What did you mean?"

Father covered his mouth with his hand, a look of profound sorrow on his face. "I'm so sorry, Liora. You shouldn't have had to find out that way."

"No, I shouldn't. You should have told me. But I'm asking you now—what do you know about my magic?"

I could see him warring with himself. He was afraid, I realized. Not of me, but for me. "I don't know everything," he said finally. "I do know you aren't like most mages—"

He was deflecting again, like always. "How do you know that? Maybe I'm exactly like them."

He shook his head, unable to meet my eyes. "No. You aren't selfish like the others."

I realized then that it had comforted him to believe I was different, that while other mages were inherently evil, he could make me the exception by keeping magic from me. By keeping *my* magic from me. But what if the line separating someone like me from someone like Darius was far thinner than we imagined? What if, in discovering what I was capable of, I was going to become someone else?

"What if you're wrong?" I whispered.

His eyes were damp when he finally looked up at me. "You're a good person, Liora," he said. "When the time comes, you'll do the right thing. I know it in my heart."

I sighed, unsatisfied but resigned. He hadn't answered my question, but I wasn't sure he was even capable of being honest with me. Not if it meant being honest with himself.

Jean, who had been quiet all morning, rose and took my hand. "You're very brave," she said. "I know you don't believe it, but you are."

"Come on." Adelle wrapped her arm through mine. "I'll take you to Margana's."

She was waiting on the porch for us when we arrived, her red hair falling around her like a mane. "Come along. I have your supplies ready." She led us upstairs to her room, where a pile of food was set out on a low wooden table. She picked up a small ivory-handled pocketknife and held it out to me. "It's not much, but I'm afraid you'll injure yourself trying to wield anything larger."

I slipped it into my pocket next to the watch. "I'm not going to need it, though, am I?"

"As far as I know, the Shadow Tapestry is a void. That's what Darius commissioned, and that's what the Hollow Ones are—empty. But I can't say anything for certain, and I don't want you going in unprepared. I've never woven a place before, Liora. I don't even know how time operates inside."

Dread washed over me at her words. What if time moved faster, and I didn't have enough of it to search for Evran? Worse, what if it moved slowly, and three days felt like a year?

"I've packed enough food for several days," Margana continued. "Plus a canteen I wove that never runs out of water."

As I filled my satchel, she glanced over at Adelle. "What did you decide to do about Mina? Evran and I will need to leave as soon as possible. We won't have time to wait for you."

"Liora asked Luc to get her. He thinks I've taken ill."

"The tailor would go all the way to Corone for you?" she asked me, one eyebrow raised. "A witch and a non-mage are almost always a poor match, you know."

I rolled my eyes in a fair imitation of Mina. "Don't I have a tapestry to climb into?"

Margana snorted and led us up to the attic. There were coils of rope everywhere, starting near the tapestry. "What is this?" Adelle asked, bending down to touch the rope.

"It's a rope that never ends. Liora will fasten it around her waist, and when the three days are up, we will pull her out if she hasn't returned. We won't lose you, Liora," Margana said, addressing me. "I promise."

She lifted the rope from the ground and fastened it around my waist with a clasp. I'd expected it to be heavy, but it appeared to be made from some kind of lightweight silk, almost like a thousand strands of spiderweb woven together.

I adjusted the satchel over my shoulder and Adelle fastened my cloak on top. As I turned to face the tapestry, my heart began to pound against my rib cage, filling my ears with a bloody drumbeat. The blackness was so intense that if I stared at it too long, I felt like I was falling in. I looked away to steady myself.

I turned back to Adelle, clasping my hands in front of me to keep them from trembling. "I'm scared."

She pulled me into an embrace, and the smell of her—lavender from the little sachets she kept in her dresser, honey from baking bread—was so comforting and familiar I almost broke into tears. What if I never got to see my sisters or my father again? What if all Margana brought back on the end of the rope was a corpse, or worse, nothing at all? The thought that I could become lost forever was even more terrifying than death.

But I couldn't think about that now. I forced my fear deep down inside of me, to the place where I thought my light might come from, a dark lump of coal to fuel a fire. "I love you."

"I'll be right here, waiting for you," she said, squeezing me tight.

When we finally separated, Margana was watching us, her own eyes wet with unshed tears. "I know what a sacrifice this is. It won't be in vain, child."

I did not believe her, but I would hold on to her faith that Evran was alive, that I could rescue him, when my hope faltered. "I'm ready." I turned back toward the tapestry, facing the wall of pure midnight.

I closed my eyes and took a deep breath. *One, two, three.*

FOURTEEN

The darkness swallowed me, as thick and impenetrable as ink. It was worse than I remembered, so still and quiet. The only thing reminding me I was alive was the blood surging in my ears. I gripped the rope in one hand, my lifeline, my tether to the real world. Part of me was tempted to turn back now, just to see if I would be able to get out, but it had worked last time. I wouldn't think about being trapped for three days. I would focus on finding Evran, on placing one foot in front of the other.

I took a cautious step forward. With so much of my body covered in clothing, I could only see down to my waist, as if my lower half was submerged in water. I knelt down to touch the floor. It had a rough woven feel to it, like I was walking on a tapestry. But not being able to see where I was placing my feet made my steps too tentative. It felt as if any moment I could step into an abyss. I untied my leather boots and stuffed them into my satchel along with my stockings. The light from my feet was minimal, but it gave me a little bit of visibility. Until I knew that I really was safe in here, I didn't want to call too much attention to myself by releasing more light.

With one hand holding the rope and my other gripping the satchel, I walked in what I could only hope was a straight line. I had entered the tapestry at noon and vowed to walk until I couldn't keep my eyes open any longer. The thought of sleeping in this place made my skin crawl. I might never wake up, and if I did, would I be able to tell the difference between waking and sleep?

Less than an hour into my journey, I could already feel something akin to madness creeping into my consciousness, like frost forming on the edge of a windowpane. The hair on the back of my neck prickled as a voice, so faint it was only a shadow of a whisper, drifted past my ear. *Help us.*

I began to sing in my head to pass the time and drown out the whispers, which I was almost positive I was imagining. I walked until midnight, my thoughts straying from what I would do if I found Evran to what would happen when we destroyed the tapestry. When I used to daydream about my future, I had always imagined Evran by my side. Now, without even the assuredness of his love to hold on to, I couldn't envision anything beyond the darkness.

I stopped to take a sip of water, and for the first time I realized the ground under my feet had changed. The texture was now smooth and hard, like marble. I bent down close to my feet and touched the ground. It was wet, though the film of liquid was so thin it was barely noticeable. I lifted my fingertips to my face and rubbed them together. The liquid was clear and odorless, but I didn't taste it. I could only hope this meant there was drinkable water here. I had enough in

my canteen to last forever, according to Margana, but Evran
didn't have that luxury.

I wondered if I should put my boots on, in case the liquid
was in any way harmful to my skin. But I was more afraid of
not being able to see any other changes in the ground. Margana had said the void was empty, but the very presence of
this liquid meant that it wasn't completely empty after all.

A chill crept over my skin, and I pulled the cloak tighter. I
definitely wouldn't be able to sleep on wet ground. I tucked
the canteen back into my satchel and pressed on.

I made a game out of seeing how long I could go without glancing at the pocket watch. The longest I made it was
two hours, which felt more like twelve. I wasn't hungry, but
I chewed on a piece of dried meat just to distract myself. It
worked so well that I forgot to keep my eyes on my feet and
only stopped myself from walking headfirst into something
when I brought my hand up to my mouth for another bite.
My elbow took the brunt of the impact.

Grimacing, I followed the object up to eye level, then up
until the darkness swallowed everything. I tucked the meat
back into my bag and reached out with trembling fingers.
The surface was smooth and hard, like the floor, but as my
hands ran outward it began to curve, like a giant tree trunk.
I stepped back for a moment, wishing I could see more than
three feet in any direction. I walked around the object, which
appeared to be some kind of column, taking care to walk back
the way I had come so the rope didn't get caught.

What was this thing, and why was it here? Margana had
definitely been wrong. The tapestry was not an empty void.
Whatever *this* was may be harmless, but it existed. I tried to
climb, but it was as slick as polished stone. There was nothing to grab hold of, no possible way to get a purchase. My

only option was to keep walking. Cautiously, so I didn't run into anything.

Finally, when the sun would have been rising in the world outside the tapestry, the ground changed back to the rough woven texture I'd felt when I first entered. I'd passed half a dozen more of the "trees" throughout the night, at least that I could see. I could only imagine there were many more of them out there. They were all the same: giant black pillars stretching toward forever. Part of me was afraid I'd walked in a giant circle and come back to where I started, but there was simply no way of knowing.

For the first time I allowed myself to rest. I sat on the ground and ate a small hunk of bread and the remaining strip of dried meat from last night to keep up my strength. I wasn't worried about running out of food, so long as Margana really did pull me out after three days. In the meantime, fear seemed to have robbed me of my appetite.

My eyes were so heavy they started to flutter closed on their own, but a whisper so real I felt it ruffle the hair near my ears startled me awake. A dream, of course, but vivid enough that I no longer felt tired. Fear would carry me farther, at least for now.

I stopped trying to mince my steps, though every now and then I'd imagine something horrible just beyond the edge of my vision and catch myself. But for the most part, my mind wandered and I simply walked. The pace became so automatic that I sometimes started to wonder if I was still moving forward at all. The ground was perfectly flat, so there was never any strain of going up or downhill. The air was so still it would have been suffocating if it were hotter, but the temperature was just cool enough that I never broke out in a sweat. I tried not to let myself think about eternity or the idea that I could be in the tapestry, walking, forever.

I paused to take another drink of water in the late morning. I had survived nearly an entire day and night, and so far I wasn't too much worse for the wear.

"You can do this," I said out loud, startling myself. It was the first audible noise I'd made since reentering the tapestry, and my voice rang out sharper and clearer than I expected. Was that how I sounded to other people? I laughed a little to myself, which felt good, and kept walking.

For a second, no longer than a blink, I thought I saw two small green lights flash ahead of me. I froze and held my breath, the lightheartedness I'd felt before gone in an instant. My hand slipped into my pocket, searching for the little knife Margana had given me.

There's nothing here, Liora. Nothing but you and the strange trees.

I waited for a minute, just to make sure, and finally exhaled when the light didn't reappear. It had been a trick of my mind; lack of sleep and fear could do that to a person. Perhaps this was a sign that I should rest now. I didn't feel sleepy, but I had been awake for more than a day. At least the ground was dry. I wished there were a tree nearby so I could have my back to something, but other than that, this spot seemed as good as any. I dropped to the ground, spread my cloak on the rough floor, and curled into a tight ball.

I closed my eyes and tried to imagine I was home in my bed, but now that I'd stopped moving, my muscles were beginning to cramp. I stretched and tried to find a more comfortable position, using my satchel as a lumpy pillow. I was just closing my eyes when I saw it again: two tiny green lights, though they seemed a bit larger than the first time.

It was just a flash, but I was sure I'd seen it. It almost looked like the eye shine of an animal at night in the woods. I'd never seen one of the creatures up close, but sometimes from my window I would spot them, high up in a tree or down below in the undergrowth. Raccoons and badgers, Father had said. Perhaps a fox or two.

But something told me there weren't badgers in the void. Margana may have underestimated this place, but I highly doubted she'd imagined assorted woodland creatures while weaving. I needed sleep, before I started conjuring up something worse, like spiders.

"Go to sleep, Liora." This time, just as I was closing my eyes, there were four lights instead of two. They winked on and off in perfect unison, one set on top of the other. I wasn't imagining this.

Run. The whispered word echoed in my head, but it wasn't coming from me. I stood up and threw the satchel and cloak over my shoulders, grabbed the pocketknife, and obeyed the voice.

I ran for what felt like ages, though I doubted it was more than a mile, if distances even mattered in this place. With each step, I was afraid I'd run face-first into a tree, or worse, whatever it was creating the lights. I finally stopped when the burning in my lungs and legs surpassed my fear.

There was nothing behind me, not that I could see. The lights had disappeared as soon as I fled. It would be easy to convince myself I'd imagined them, but I knew in my heart I hadn't, and I didn't want to fool myself any longer. The tapestry was not what Margana had said. She either didn't know or had lied to lure me in. There was a scream building in my chest, but the sound of my voice had brought the lights out. I couldn't make any more noise.

I shouted his name in my head instead, wishing I had Jean's ability to communicate silently. *Evraaaaaaan!*

I wiped the tears away from my cheeks and took a few deep, ragged breaths. If I was calling for him, maybe I was starting to believe that Evran was really alive. Or I was just so desperate I was trying to convince myself I wasn't alone.

It was late afternoon now. I'd made it through nearly a third of my time. No more talking, no more rests. I would keep walking until I collapsed.

I chewed on the dried meat, working my jaw until it softened between my teeth. If there had been an animal back there, it was small, judging by the size and distance between the eyes. Unless it really was a spider, with tiny eyes clustered close together.

Stop it, Liora. Imagining the worst wouldn't do any good. But maybe there was a more efficient way to do this. I couldn't call out for Evran, but so far I had seen no other light here other than my own. My presence didn't seem to be attracting the creatures, just the sound. If Evran couldn't hear me, perhaps he could see me.

I removed the cloak from my shoulders and stuffed it into the satchel. Rolling up my sleeves and pant legs released considerably more light, and I felt less encumbered without the cloak. As I walked on, I noticed trees in the gloom at the edge of my light. Sure enough, the ground was wet again, almost as if the trees grew in some kind of marsh, though the floor here was as solid as ever.

Soon, there were more trees, far more than I'd seen before. They slowed my pace, as I had to watch carefully where I stepped. I weaved in and out of them, holding firmly to the rope, afraid I'd become tangled and would have to retrace my steps. So far the infinite length of rope and the never-empty canteen were working, at least. Margana may have been wrong about the inside of the tapestry, but she hadn't sent me in completely unaided.

I started to sing in my head, a song about a falling star Evran had made up for me when we were children.

Plucked from night by an unseen hand,
The star searches for a place to land.
Shining, falling, burning bright.
She bathes us all in purest light.
Where darkest shadows stretch and grow,
She keeps us safe within with her glow.

Almost directly in front of me, six green lights appeared. I stopped cold, clapping a hand to my mouth. Had I sung the words out loud?

To my left, four more lights winked at me. Another eight on my right. Slowly, terrified, I looked up. The expanse of darkness above me was filled with the little green lights. I couldn't hold back the whimper that clawed its way out of my throat.

The thing in front of me was now within range of my glow. I inched forward just enough to bring it into focus. Surely whatever I was imagining could not be as bad as the reality.

A little sigh of relief escaped me when I saw the creature. It was small, not much larger than a squirrel, though it did indeed have four eyes. Maybe more. They blinked at me curiously in the fuzzy face. Two sharp, tufted ears sprouted from its head. It crawled down the trunk just a bit farther, bringing more of its body into view.

That was when I realized it wasn't the size of a squirrel at all. It had a long, segmented body, with small legs on either side, at least twenty pairs. It was like some hideous combination of rodent and centipede, like something the king would have woven, only far worse. It made a faint chittering sound as it poked its head forward, sniffing.

I was frozen in place, but I risked a quick glance over my shoulder. I was surrounded on all sides by these things. One might not be large enough to harm me, but hundreds of them? What if they hunted in packs? What if they were hunting *me*?

I cursed Margana in my head, every terrible word I'd heard throughout my life. She was a witch in the harshest sense, and she had sacrificed me to this place, for what? For a son who had surely been nibbled down to the bones? The thought of Evran surrounded by these disgusting creatures sent a spark of anger through me, heating my skin.

A breeze so faint I wouldn't have noticed it if it weren't for the perfect stillness here passed over my neck. From the corner of my eye, something dark streaked past, something much larger than the squirrels.

I gripped the rope with one hand, the pocketknife in the other, the tiny blade glinting in my glow. Why had I taken my cloak off? Did I dare move enough to put it back on? I felt something sharp on my toe and looked down. One of the squirrels had sneaked up in the dark and bitten me. Two dots of red blood welled on the top of my big toe. The creature darted forward again and lapped at the blood with its small black tongue.

I opened my mouth to scream.

Something closed around my mouth and waist at the same time.

"Don't make a sound," a raspy voice breathed in my ear. "Run."

FIFTEEN

The hand fell away from my mouth, but I was grateful for the one around my waist. It was strong enough to practically lift me from the ground, so that my feet were just skimming the floor. I was sure that without it I would have collapsed in fear.

Trees streaked past us in flashes, and above us the little green lights seemed to leap from trunk to trunk, following us. I had no idea how we'd outrun them or if we were even getting out of the forest. As we ran, the arm around my waist slipped a little, and I regained enough strength to propel myself over the ground, though I clung to the arm anyway. I had never been so grateful for human touch in my life. At least, I assumed it was human.

"Evran?"

"Shhh!" He ran on with purpose, as though he had a destination in mind, but he couldn't possibly know where he was going. Still, my thoughts were clear enough that I could take comfort in one thing: he was alive. Somehow, he had survived this long. And maybe, together, we could make it out.

As my muscles began to ache, I started to wonder how much longer I could keep this up. Even with his arm around me, I was slowing. The temporary surge in strength had started to fade, and now a million questions were rising up in its place. My foot ached where the creature had bitten me, and the toll of no sleep, little food and water, and walking for nearly twenty-four hours was catching up with me.

"Please," I whimpered.

"Almost there."

I risked another glance behind me. I couldn't see any more green lights or trees. The ground was dry again. We'd made it out of the forest.

Finally, Evran slowed to a jog. He brushed a finger against my cheek so I would look at him, then pointed ahead. I couldn't see anything, but a warm rush of relief coursed through me. A moment later, he dropped to his knees, motioning for me to follow. Now I could see the entrance to some kind of hole. Evran lowered himself into it, then waved for me to come in after him. The drop was short, just above my head, but Evran caught me by the waist and motioned for me to get on my hands and knees. We were in some kind of a tunnel. Here, in this cramped space, my light wasn't swallowed as easily as it was outside. We crawled for a minute before Evran emerged into a small rounded enclosure.

As I followed him inside, he pulled something over the entrance to the tunnel, sealing it off. We were in a kind of burrow, made of the same rough, textured material as the floor of the tapestry. The ceiling was too low for us to stand, but we could sit comfortably enough.

"You can talk," he said. "Just a whisper, and only as much as necessary. No more singing."

It had been out loud, then. I must have been even more delirious than I'd realized. "I'm so sorry."

"It's all right. If you hadn't sung, I might have let the squirrels eat you."

I punched him on the arm out of habit, but I wasn't in a playful mood. I stretched out as much as I could in the small space to keep my muscles from cramping and jumped when my fingers brushed against something furry. "What is that?"

"Shhh. It's a squirrel pelt. I made a blanket out of them."

I shuddered and scooted away from the fur. "Those aren't really squirrels, you know."

When he smiled, my heart felt like it was being clenched in a fist. *His* fist. I took a moment to examine him. His sharp jawline was softened by several days' worth of reddish-brown stubble, but even his thick lashes couldn't soften the look in his green eyes.

"I can't believe you followed me, Liora."

I frowned at him. "Of course I did."

"I've been horrible to you lately. I'm so sorry."

I wanted to tell him that even if he'd stopped loving me, I hadn't stopped loving him. I never would. But I shrugged instead. "I couldn't just let you die in here, not without at least trying to find you."

He reached for my hand, but I turned away. I didn't want to hear more of the same excuses he'd given me before, that I was better off without him. A second later, I felt a tug on the rope at my waist as Evran pulled me toward him. "Liora, look at me."

Reluctantly, I forced my eyes to his. I had long ago memorized the color of his irises, a rich forest hue that would always be my favorite shade of green. "Why did you avoid me, Evran? What did I do wrong?"

He dropped the rope and moved his hand to my face. "*Nothing.* You haven't done anything wrong. I can't believe you don't know that."

I shook my head. "How would I know that?"

"That day at your house… You looked right into my eyes. You had to have seen."

I placed my hand over his. "I did. And I'm so sorry I did that to you."

He shook his head. "No, you don't understand."

I waited for him to explain, but he was quiet for a few minutes.

I flinched when something brushed the top of my foot.

"Don't worry about the bite," he said, pressing gently on the skin near the wound. "The squirrels have sharp teeth, but they're not venomous."

I hadn't even considered that possibility and shuddered again at the thought.

"We need to get you home. Your family must be worried sick."

"They are. But I have supplies." I remembered the canteen and brought it out of my satchel. "I should have offered you some right away. You must be so thirsty. And hungry."

He took the canteen and drank while I pulled out some of the remaining food.

"What have you been drinking all this time?" I asked.

"The water on the forest floor is pure, fortunately." He gestured to the rope around my waist. "Did my mother make that?"

"Yes."

"How did you know you'd be able to see here?"

"Your mother figured it out. She forced me in here—"

His eyes widened. "She what?"

I swallowed down the memory of those horrible initial minutes, the disorientation I'd felt experiencing darkness for the first time. "She pushed me in to see if my glow would be extinguished by the tapestry. Darius is coming back soon, and she wasn't going to destroy it without at least trying to save you."

He sighed and pulled me against him. "I'm so sorry. That must have been terrifying for you."

I sat back a bit. "And yet *you* don't seem terrified."

He inhaled and released his breath slowly. "I think... I think I belong here. Alone, where I can't hurt anyone. Where I can't hurt *you*."

I shook my head in confusion. "What are you talking about?"

"My magic, Liora. I'm talking about my magic."

"Your *what*?" The last word came out so loud that Evran threw his hand over my mouth. He held his breath, listening. After a minute, he moved his hand away, but his posture remained rigid.

"What are we hiding from?" I whispered.

"It's better if you don't know. You should go, now. Before we're found."

"*I* should go now? I'm not leaving here without you!"

He tapped his pointer finger against his lips. "Please, be quiet. I promise I'll explain everything. I just need you to stay calm."

I scooted as far away from him as I could, which wasn't more than two feet. "I'm calm. Now explain. And quickly."

He folded his legs, not making any attempt to touch me. "I think I first realized I might have some kind of magic when I was little. Mother would scold me for staying out in the woods after dark, and I would have no idea what she was talking about. I could still see, even when the sun had set. Here in the tapestry, I can see roughly ten feet in every direction, but I can't see much beyond that. Everything is black and white in the dark."

All this time, Evran had had magic. I sat with the weight of that for a minute. It helped explain why he had befriended me that day in my garden. "But if you knew you had magic, why didn't you tell me?" I asked. "I wouldn't have had to be alone. Neither of us would."

"I was afraid of my magic."

It struck me then that I had never been afraid of *my* magic as a child, that I had never even thought to be. Magic in general, yes. Father had made sure of that. But I'd never feared I would hurt myself or someone else until recently. "Why?" I asked gently.

He avoided my gaze, clearly ashamed. "I have some kind of shadow magic. Power that comes from darkness. Not light, like yours. When I first came across the tapestry, I saw forests and rivers and animals, a whole world within the fibers. Not the pure darkness my mother described."

I couldn't imagine seeing anything in the tapestry. It was so dark it had hurt to look at it. "Did you tell her?"

"No. I was afraid she would hate me, that she'd turn me out."

My heart hurt for him. He seemed to believe that darkness was inherently evil, and while I'd admittedly never felt more lost and alone than when I first came into the tapestry, I knew that wasn't true. Darkness meant rest, a time when the day world went still and the night world came alive. It was a reprieve from the heat of the day and a chance to wonder at the cosmos. It was beautiful.

Besides, light was not always good either. It was a star that had killed my mother.

I scooted closer and placed a tentative hand on his arm. "She wouldn't have done that, Evran. She loves you."

"I know she does, in her own way. But I wouldn't blame her if she didn't."

There was something in his tone that made it clear he didn't think he was worthy of love, when nothing could be further from the truth. *Tell him*, I thought fervently. *Tell him you love him*. But just because he hadn't been mad at me all this time didn't mean he loved me back. And I wasn't ready to take the risk of telling him when his rejection still weighed so heavily on my heart.

"Your mother loves you," I repeated instead.

He nodded without conviction.

My eyelids were growing heavy despite myself, and I made a feeble attempt to stifle a yawn.

"Have you slept since you got here?" Evran asked.

"No, I was too afraid."

He touched my hand, a brief but reassuring gesture. "You're safe here. You should get some rest now."

"What about you?"

"I've had plenty of sleep here, believe me."

I handed him my grandfather's pocket watch. "Don't let me sleep more than an hour or two. I want to make sure we get back in time to destroy the tapestry and get out of Sylvan."

He was quiet for a moment, his lips pressed together in a thin line.

"You do *not* belong here, Evran. Promise me we'll leave, together."

He finally nodded. "I promise."

I pulled my cloak out of my satchel and folded it into a

pillow, careful to avoid the squirrel pelt blanket, and curled onto my side.

He brushed my hair back from my face and kissed my cheek. "You're safe now. Get some sleep, Liora."

I woke to someone shaking me roughly by the arm.

"Wake up," a man hissed against my ear. "Please."

I sat up and rubbed my eyes, grimacing at the aches in my joints and muscles. My head felt like it was stuffed with cotton batting. "What's happening?"

"Shhh!"

The realization that I was inside the tapestry with Evran came back to me in a rush, and I sprang into a crouch, my satchel already in my hand. "What's going on?"

"You were screaming in your sleep." He pressed a finger to his lips. "Listen."

For a moment all I heard was the silence of the tapestry, but then it came, a *whoofing* noise, like a large animal puffing air out of its nostrils. The burrow shuddered as something massive moved above us, followed by another *whoof.*

What is it? I mouthed.

Oo-ee-ee, he mouthed back.

I squinted in confusion. *What?*

He made the same shapes with his mouth, and then, in a whisper so soft it sent chills over my skin: "Hollow Ones."

"Lusiri?" I whispered back, horrified.

He nodded and pressed his finger to his lips again. I shrank against him and was grateful when he wrapped an arm around my shoulders and pulled me closer.

A few moments later, when the sounds above us stopped, he released his breath. "I think it's gone."

"I don't understand. The Lusiri are supposed to be extinct. How can there possibly be one in here?"

"Not just one. I've seen three together before. I'm sure there are more." He moved over to a corner of the burrow and appeared to be gathering a few small belongings. But we couldn't leave as long as the Lusiri was out there.

"How did it get inside the tapestry?" I asked.

"Mother probably explained to you that the properties of the material she weaves can imbue the tapestry with its own characteristics. The Shadow Tapestry was made from the hair of the Lusiri. Somehow that brought them back to life, at least in here."

I pulled my cloak on. "So there are the squirrels and the Hollow Ones. What else?"

"I don't know. I managed to climb one of the trees. I saw creatures flying up there. Bats, or something similar, I imagine."

"How?"

"I made picks out of bones and used them to climb. The trees are hard, but they're hollow inside. I found one that had fallen and used it to make the tunnel."

I couldn't imagine how difficult that must have been, in the dark, not knowing what was out there. "Where did you get the bones from?"

He paused his packing and looked at me, his green eyes so intense I knew I'd asked the wrong question. "I found Pippin's skeleton."

I bit back a gasp. "I'm so sorry, Evran."

He was facing away from me, but I could sense the sorrow in the slope of his shoulders. "We should get going. They could return."

"I'm ready," I said, though the thought of going back out

there, knowing what we might encounter, was almost worse than coming into the tapestry had been. "Do we have a plan?"

"Follow the rope and try to make as little noise as possible. We'll need to cover you with the cloak, too. Most of the creatures here rely on senses other than sight, but the squirrels have some limited vision. They don't open their eyes often because the eye shine attracts other predators, but they'll use it to confirm that what they're detecting is prey."

I yanked on my boots. "I should have known better."

"I may have heard your singing, but it was your light that led me to you." He smiled. "It always has."

When I smiled back, I felt the glow from my skin pulse brighter for a moment. It took all my effort to tamp it back down. I redid the now-fuzzy plait in my hair and pulled the hood of the cloak over my head. "I'm afraid there's not much I can do about my face."

He traced my jaw gently with his fingers. "I wouldn't want you to cover it even if you could."

SIXTEEN

Evran gathered his few belongings and removed what I now realized was some kind of pelt from the entrance of the tunnel. He held up a hand as he crouched there for a moment, listening. Satisfied, he began to crawl out of the tunnel, but a sudden thought struck me and I grabbed on to his foot.

What? he mouthed.

I unfastened the rope around my waist and gathered enough of it to tie around his waist, then refastened it around mine. I couldn't risk losing him out there in the dark.

He nodded and began crawling again.

When we reached the end of the tunnel, he wedged himself into the vertical shaft and shimmied up easily, then turned around to pull me up.

I immediately missed the cozy confines of his burrow. Out here, the darkness extended on infinitely, like a night with no moon or stars. It was easy to believe this place really was devoid of anything, but I knew now that it wasn't empty at all.

The only thing that held me together was the length of rope connecting Evran's waist to mine.

He took up the rope in his hands and began to follow it, hand over hand, striding confidently back the way we had come. Following my tracks meant we'd have to return to the forest where he'd found me, but I tried not to think about the squirrels or the Lusiri. I pulled the cloak tighter around myself. It meant I had far less visibility, with only my face providing light, but I could see Evran's back in the glow, and I wasn't sure I wanted to see anything beyond that.

I had imagined it would take ages to get back to the forest, since it felt like we'd run forever yesterday, but we were walking at a good clip and reached the forest within an hour. It was approaching dawn of the third day, which meant we only had one more day to make it back. But if Evran was right and we kept up a good pace, we should be out of the tapestry in plenty of time.

I wished we could talk here. It would have distracted me from my bleak thoughts. I had tried to project confidence to Evran, but even if we did make it out of here alive, there was plenty of danger waiting for us once we got out.

We wove through the trees, following the rope, and I forced myself not to look up or glance behind me more than once every minute or so. If Evran wasn't worried, then I shouldn't be. But I kept the pocketknife in one hand anyway, the other on the rope. Now more than ever, it felt like a lifeline. Once or twice I saw a pair of eyes winking in the dark, but they were never very close. Perhaps the squirrels recognized Evran as the one who had killed some of their brethren. Or maybe they weren't prepared to take on two people at the same time. I'd probably seemed like an easy target before, and I'd been glowing like a torch.

I smiled to myself at the irony. I'd come here to save Evran, but he had saved me instead. Tentatively, I placed my hand on his shoulder. He whipped around, but I shook my head, indicating that I was fine. A moment later, he laid his head against my hand, embracing me without arms, and walked on. I kept my hand on his shoulder.

As we made our way, my thoughts began to wander. If the pillars really were some kind of tree, then perhaps there were other plants here, though certainly nothing green, given the lack of sunlight. I wondered how long Evran could have survived on nothing but water and squirrel meat. He didn't seem to be suffering. Maybe his magic allowed him to live without sunlight. Maybe, like me, he didn't understand his magic at all.

We stopped to rest in the late afternoon. I had plenty of meat and cheese left, though what remained of the bread was hard as a rock. Evran didn't seem bothered by it, though. He ate perfunctorily. I stretched out a bit on the woven ground, wishing I could remove my cloak but only daring to push the hood back slightly from my face. I moved closer to him, knowing it was dangerous to speak but too curious to maintain the silence any longer.

"How did you make your burrow?" I whispered against his ear.

In answer, he placed his hand on the floor and began to scrape with his finger. It took time, but eventually he managed to pull up one of the fibers. "Once I realized it was possible, I made a knife out of bone and carved the tunnel, then the burrow. I slept inside the tree I felled until I finished."

It didn't seem possible he could have accomplished that in just a few days, and I thought again how time might operate differently in the tapestry. His whiskers brushed against my cheek as he whispered in my ear, sending small shivers over my skin. A moment later, he sat up abruptly, hearing something I couldn't no matter how hard I strained. "Pull your cloak up. We need to keep moving."

I didn't argue, even when he started to jog. What was behind us now? We'd made so little noise, I couldn't imagine the Lusiri had found us in all this darkness. But a few minutes later, Evran stopped so suddenly I crashed into him.

"What?"

He motioned me forward, and I peered over his shoulder. There was something lying on the path ahead, on top of the rope.

Evran removed what looked like a sharp piece of bone from somewhere near his waist and crept forward. Whatever it was didn't move. At first glance I thought it was a skeleton, but as we drew closer, I realized that its skin had been pulled taut over its bones. It was disturbingly human-like in shape, though shorter and squatter. Large canine teeth protruded from its open jaw.

"What is that?"

He shook his head. "I don't know. But the Lusiri got to it. This creature must have found the rope and followed us."

If this thing was following us, what else might be? Had the Lusiri fed on it yesterday or within the past couple of hours? We couldn't go around the corpse because it was lying directly on top of the rope, and it was large enough that I knew Evran would need help moving it. I steeled myself and went to the creature's feet, trying to ignore the way the skin felt tight and leathery under my hands.

He nodded, and we both knelt down to get a better purchase. It was lighter than it looked, probably because it was empty inside. There was no blood, at least. Just a carcass that had been sucked dry.

We didn't stop again until late into the evening. We now had one night and part of a day remaining. We had to be close to the exit.

"Should we rest or keep going?" Evran asked me as he handed me the canteen.

"Let's rest just for a few minutes. We can sleep on the other side." *In beds.* I unscrewed the lid of the canteen. We had to stand close to whisper to each other, and my skin tingled at his nearness. Once, we had known each other so well that I would never have hesitated to pry into his thoughts, but things were different now. "Can I ask you something?"

"Of course."

"Do you really think you could have lived here forever?"

He continued to chew on his piece of dried meat, but I could tell he was considering. "I don't know. I know I would have missed a lot of things."

"Like real food?" I examined the hard bread I was gnawing on. "I'm not sure I could live knowing I'd never have a slice of chocolate torte again."

He smiled. "I've never cared that much about food. I eat to survive. No, I would have missed the important things. Like laughter and color and stars."

I nodded, still not meeting his gaze. "Those are all good things. Well, stars are good as long as they stay in the sky, I suppose."

He made a sympathetic noise in his throat. "I never really thought about how hard it must have been for you."

I looked up finally. "What?"

"Knowing that your magic caused... Well, you know."

My hand froze with the canteen halfway to my mouth. "No, I don't know. What are you talking about?"

He turned away, but not before I saw him wince. "Never mind. We should go."

I grabbed his arm, willing him to face me. "Evran, tell me. I've been kept away from anything having to do with magic my entire life. I'm tired of being ignorant to my own nature."

For a moment I was afraid he wouldn't respond. His eyes dragged slowly back to mine, his pupils dilated wide to compensate for the darkness. "Your magic attracted the falling star that killed your mother, Liora."

Cold crept over my scalp and seeped into my stomach.

Seeing the shock on my face, he hurried on. "You didn't cause the star to fall, of course, but the dormant magic inside of you called to it, in a way. Didn't you ever wonder why the day a star fell on your house, you started to glow?"

I dropped his arm and clutched at the front of my tunic, as if that could keep the pain in my heart from spreading. "I thought it was *because* the star fell on my house."

"Magic doesn't work that way. Otherwise your sisters would have it, too. Magic was inside of us, waiting for a trigger. For you, it was the star. For me, it was the tapestry."

"So what are you saying? If the star hadn't fallen and if you hadn't seen the tapestry, we wouldn't be mages?"

"I don't know."

My chest was growing tight, and I forced myself to take a deep breath. "So you're saying I killed my mother."

"No, that's not what I'm saying." He gripped me by the shoulders. "Liora, you didn't kill her. I swear it."

I drew in another shaky breath. "Maybe not directly, but if it wasn't for me, the star may have landed somewhere else. My mother would still be alive."

"You can't think of it that way."

"What other way is there?" I gasped as another terrible thought struck me. "Does my father know?"

"Know what?"

"How magic operates? That it's my fault?"

"Maybe. I'm not sure." He chewed on his lower lip, clearly wishing he'd never said anything. "Liora." He reached for me, but when I didn't move closer, he dropped his hands.

"We should go." I wasn't sure if I wanted him to apologize or stop speaking altogether, but he chose the latter, so I started walking. It wasn't long before the ground changed from dry to wet.

"This is the first forest I encountered," I whispered over his shoulder. "That means we're less than twelve hours away." Probably a lot less, given how much faster we were moving than I had.

He nodded in acknowledgment. I stared at his back, trying to reconcile what he'd just told me with what I'd believed my entire life. It had been a horrible accident, my father told me. He'd been downstairs with my sisters when the star hit our roof. I'd been upstairs with Mother, taking a cool bath because I had a fever that wouldn't come down.

The room had gone up in flames so quickly, Father said. He'd taken Adelle and Mina outside and come back in for Mother and me, but the smoke was too thick to breathe or see. Later, they discovered me in the undergrowth at the edge of the forest, naked, unconscious, and glowing white. I'd found my own way out of the house and somehow made it through the gates and into the woods, they said, though how I'd escaped without a single burn was unknown. A result of my magic, the doctor said. The flames had been so hot they'd never even found Mother's body.

But now I knew the truth. Father must have known I was the one who brought the star down on us. I was the one who had killed Mother. And he'd kept that from me, probably to protect me. But he'd also done everything he could to deny the very existence of my magic. He must despise it. Maybe he even despised me on some level. Evran was convinced that he needed to stay away from other people, but *he* hadn't hurt anyone with his magic. *I* was the one who needed to go.

Turn around! The whispered voice I heard yesterday, the one that had commanded me to run, was back. Evran must have heard it, too, because he turned to face me, his brow furrowed with concern.

"Who is that, Evran?"

"I'm not sure, but I believe they're the souls of the people killed by the Lusiri used to make the tapestry. I've tried talking to them, but they never respond. They beg me to help them, and sometimes they warn me of danger."

"Then we'd better turn—"

A sudden, tremendous pull on the rope yanked us forward. I slammed hard into Evran's back as he regained his footing.

"What was that?" I shouted, forgetting in my panic to whisper.

"I don't—"

He was cut off by another yank on the rope, and this time we both ended up on the ground, being dragged through the water by something incredibly strong.

"What do we do?" I screamed.

"Grab on to a tree!"

I floundered in the dark, moving too fast over the slippery forest floor. When my hand finally brushed against one, there was no chance to gain a purchase. The trees were nearly as slick as the ground.

Evran grunted as his leg hit a tree, and I scooted myself to the side just in time for the rope to catch on the tree between us. He swung around and grabbed a hold of the trunk while I braced my feet against it, but whatever had a hold of the rope was too strong. My waist felt like it was going to tear in half.

"Do you think there's any chance it's Margana?" I asked through gritted teeth.

"No. This isn't human strength."

I knew he was right, but I didn't want to think about what that meant.

"We've got to cut the rope," he cried. His face was contorted with pain and effort. "I can't reach my knife."

"You can't be serious! We'll be trapped in here without the rope!"

"And we're going to die if we don't cut it."

Something roared in the darkness. Sound carried strangely here, but it was loud enough that I would have covered my ears if my hands had been free. I reached for my pocketknife. If I cut the rope between us, I'd be sending Evran to his death. But if he let go of the tree, we'd both be dragged off. How was I supposed to cut the rope on the other side of him?

"What do I do?" I cried.

"Let go of the tree and grab on to me. When I let go, I'll cut the rope." He grunted as the thing that had us pulled even harder. "I'll get you out of here. I promise. But you have to cut the rope."

He didn't understand. There would be no way out without the rope, no matter what promises he made. Margana would pull that rope back and find it severed. She'd know something terrible had happened to me, but not that I'd found her son. She would unravel the tapestry tomorrow, and what would become of us? Would we simply disappear? Or would we be torn apart piece by piece as well?

"Liora!" Evran screamed.

I sent a silent prayer to my sisters and father, and then I let go.

SEVENTEEN

I grabbed on to Evran's waist as tight as I could. The added weight immediately pushed him off the trunk and sent us racing across the ground again.

We were flying faster than ever now. If we hit a tree, we'd likely break our legs, or worse. I had the knife in my hand, the blade still folded, but I was terrified I'd drop it. Fortunately, Evran could see better than I could. He took the knife from me with a steady hand, flipped it open, and sliced.

Nothing happened.

"What is this rope made of?" he yelled.

"I don't know!"

"Your knife will never cut it. I've got to get mine."

We had to be nearly through the forest by now. Whatever had us was undoubtedly on the other side. "Where is it?"

"There, at my waist. Near your hands." He wrapped his arms around me so I could free mine, and I fumbled at the leather belt at his waist until my fingers found the bone handle. "Be careful."

There was no time to be careful. I leaned forward and brought my arm down with all my strength. Again and again I struck, until, finally, the rope snapped. We skidded to a stop as the end of the rope disappeared in the darkness. It was another minute before we heard the roar.

"Now what?" I hissed as he hauled me to my feet.

"We run." He grabbed my right hand in his and took off. I had no idea which direction we were headed, only that it seemed to be away from where the rope had gone.

My sodden cloak was so heavy it felt like a person was hanging on my neck. I was still holding Evran's knife, so I let go of his hand and undid the clasp, immediately feeling lighter as it fell away. Mina could make me another one if we ever made it out of here. Without the cloak, the light from my arms, neck, and face was too bright, but there was nothing I could do about that now. I ran harder than I'd ever run before, my boots splashing in the shallow water, my free arm pumping with all my strength.

Another roar erupted behind us.

"It's chasing us," Evran said. "We'll never outrun it."

"What is it?"

"A Lusiri."

A sob tore free on my next exhale. My lungs burned with effort, and my limbs felt leaden.

"Don't slow down, Liora. We have to keep running."

"What's the point? There's no way out. We'll never find your burrow. My light will attract every hungry monster in this place." I let go of his hand, but the rope was still connecting us. "I have to cut you loose, before it's too late."

He stopped beside me and took my face roughly in his hands. "You can't give up."

"Your mother is going to destroy the tapestry in one day, Evran!" Hoofbeats sounded on the ground behind us. "Just go, please. I can't have your death on my hands, too."

Before I could cut the rope, he leaned forward, his hands still gripping my face so I couldn't look away even if I'd wanted to. In his eyes, I saw that he truly loved me, that he had never meant to hurt me. For one moment, the terror and exhaustion disappeared as he pressed his lips to mine, tender and urgent at the same time. Too quickly, it was over.

"Stars don't just shine, Liora," he said, taking the bone knife from my hand and stepping in front of me to face the beast.

He'd said it to me once before, but I didn't understand what he meant now any more than I had then. A moment later there was a sound somewhere between a roar and a whinny, and the Lusiri came into view.

It balked at the edge of my light, its massive hooves pawing at the ground. I could only see bits of it, an enormous square head leading to shoulders rippled with muscle, sloping hind-quarters and a tail that ended with long hair, like a horse's mane. The entire creature was as black as pitch. Its eyes were pure black, too, not even a crescent of white at the edges, but I could see them glimmering as they rolled in its head.

"What's it doing?" I asked, my own pathetic knife held out in front of me.

"It's the light. I think it's afraid to come closer."

The beast roared again, clearly frustrated. But then it planted its hooves at the edge of my light, shifted its weight backward, and began to inhale. The large equine nostrils flattened, then flared as it exhaled, then flattened again.

In horror, I realized that Evran was being sucked forward.

I grabbed him around the waist and pulled, but I was being drawn in, too.

"What's it doing?" I cried.

"Feeding!"

My stomach twisted in horror. I tried to brace my feet against the floor, but it was no use. The pressure was too strong. My clothes were flattened against my back, as if a wind was forcing me forward from behind and pulling me from the front. "Is there a way to stop them?" I shouted.

The silence that followed was answer enough.

Suddenly I felt myself pulled sharply to the right, and I looked to see another Lusiri standing at the perimeter of my light, inhaling. I lost my grip on Evran and grabbed on to the rope still connecting us at the waist, but it was no use. I watched the first fiber of the rope snap, then another.

"Evran!"

"Liora!"

We reached for each other at the same time, but just as our fingers brushed, the rope snapped. He disappeared into the darkness as I was pulled backward. The last thing I saw was the glowing green of his eyes. I hadn't noticed it before in my own light, but he had an eye shine just like the animals of the forest.

Fear was replaced by fury as I came to a stop inches from the Lusiri. It exhaled sharply, blowing my hair back from my face. Beneath my skin, it felt like my blood was beginning to boil, the way it had when Darius tried to touch me back at the palace. It wasn't possible that I'd come this far only to fail now. I may not have courage and strength like Evran, but he was right. As long as there was breath in me, I couldn't give up.

I forced my arms in front of me, one palm out, the other wrapped around my knife, and the Lusiri tossed its head back as the light flashed directly in its eyes. I heard a human scream behind me, and the anger seething inside of me intensified.

The Lusiri pawed at the air in front of it and tossed its massive head. It inhaled again, trying to pull me forward, but I imagined that my feet were roots, that I was as unmovable as an oak. I thought of Darius's face when my skin seemed to burn him through the fire poker. *I knew it*. But what did he know? What was there about me that he hadn't been willing to let go of?

Stars don't just shine, Liora.

A memory of the night my mother died came to me in a sudden flash. The two of us, standing at the window as the bath filled. My mother's outstretched arm pointing to a light in the sky. The light growing and growing, until it was no longer a star but a giant ball of flame heading straight toward us. My mother's scream. The boom as the star struck the roof and the entire house shook. The fire raining down on us from above.

Stars don't just shine, Liora.

They burn.

I reached for the place inside of me where my light came from, pushing past my fear and ordering it to show itself now, before it was too late.

To my shock, it responded. My head thrust backward, and my arms flew wide open as my entire body erupted in white light. I barely heard the screams of the Lusiri, hardly noticed the searing heat encompassing every part of me, burning away my clothing, burning away the darkness all around me.

The smallest stars don't shine at noon, Father said. But I had looked at the stars through Darius's device, and they weren't small. Far away, perhaps, but just as bright and brilliant as our own sun. I had kept my own light hidden deep inside of me for so long.

Not anymore.

★ ★ ★

The next thing I remembered was a cool embrace.

I was lying on the floor, my eyes closed, naked and shivering. I felt something slip away, like a shadow passing over me, and opened my eyes.

The floor beneath me was bare wood. That was all I saw before the morning light streaming in the window seared my sensitive eyes and I had to close them again. I was not dead. I was no longer in the tapestry. This was Margana's attic.

I sat up, cracking my eyes open just enough to see. "Where's Evran?"

"I'm here."

Someone laid a blanket over my shoulders. I gathered the soft wool around myself and opened my eyes a little more.

Evran was crouched a few feet away from me. "How do you feel?" he asked gently.

"Sore," I said, taking stock of all my limbs. "And confused. What happened?"

"You burned your way out of the tapestry." Margana stood above me. She was as imposing as ever, her arms crossed over her chest, her fiery hair flowing over her shoulders. "You would have burned yourself along with it if it weren't for Evran."

I turned back to him. "What is she talking about?"

"I'll explain later," he said gently. "The important thing is that you're all right."

I pushed to my feet and turned to see Adelle standing behind me. She held her arms out to me as tears streamed down her cheeks, and I walked into her embrace, knowing she was too overwhelmed to speak. Somehow, her vulnerability gave me strength. "I'm okay, Adelle. Really."

She shook against me as she sobbed. "When the rope

came back, and you weren't there, I thought you were gone. I thought I'd never see you again."

"But I'm here now. We're okay. It's over."

"It is not over," Margana said, with a sigh too full of regret for a woman who'd just been reunited with her son.

"Mother." Evran went to stand beside her, squinting against the bright light. I could see him now, all of him. He looked like a drifter with his tangled hair and rumpled clothing, not like the gentle young man who called me a star. I blushed at the memory of the kiss we'd just shared in the tapestry. My first kiss.

The tapestry was behind them, or what was left of it anyway. It hung in tatters, a gaping hole burned right through the center. It looked ruined beyond repair. I had done the hard work for Margana, twice now. So why did she look so miserable?

"You let Lusiri into our world," she said. "Two of them. For all we know they were a male and a female."

The heat had left me by now, and even with the blanket a chill ran over my skin. "What do you mean? How did I—"

"They came through the hole you made, right after Evran and you." I followed her gaze across the room. There were holes punched into the wooden floorboards. The attic door was hanging by one hinge.

"They came through here?"

"They tore out of the house like demons and fled into the woods. Who knows how far they've gone?"

"There are two Lusiri loose in Sylvan?" I asked, my voice rising. "We have to stop them!"

"You're not going anywhere," Margana replied. "Not until we know you're really all right. And I'm not letting Evran out of my sight, despite what he thinks."

He folded his arms across his chest and glared at her, and for a moment they were simply a feuding mother and son. "The longer we wait, the farther they'll get."

"That's the best we can hope for. The Lusiri hate the light. They come from the north, and we must hope they return there."

"People will die," he growled.

"Not as many as would have if the tapestry was completed."

"Liora needs to eat and rest before we leave," Adelle cut in. "I'm taking her home." She pulled me under her arm and began to lead me toward the door.

"Wait," Evran said. I turned to face him, and when our eyes met, the rest of his appearance faded away. He needed to eat and rest even more than I did, but he hadn't mentioned his own needs at all. "I wanted to thank you, for doing what I could not."

My cheeks heated as he placed his hands on my shoulders. "I couldn't have done it without you."

Margana stood behind him, silent, observant as ever. Perhaps the shadows he feared clung to him more than I realized and he had changed in ways I couldn't yet understand. Only time would tell.

But Darius was coming to Sylvan tomorrow, and I had just destroyed his precious tapestry. Time was not on our side.

EIGHTEEN

That night, I perched on the window ledge, staring at the sky, feeling more grateful for the moon and stars than I'd ever been before. I never wanted to experience pure darkness again.

"Are you all right?" Jean asked from Mina's bed. She, Adelle, and Father had taken turns waiting for me outside the tapestry with Margana. Our belongings were all packed, and Father had settled as many accounts as he could. We would leave at first light, if all went according to plan.

I was sore all over but too anxious to sleep. "I'm worried about Mina," I said as I twisted my star pendant in my fingers. "She should be here by now."

"You don't trust the tailor, do you?" she asked.

I shook my head.

"You should always listen to your inner voice, Liora. It speaks to you for a reason."

Before I could respond, there was a heavy pounding on the

front door. Maybe it was Margana or Evran. But one look at Jean confirmed my biggest fear.

"Run," I said. "Through the window. Get Evran and go to the woods."

"I can't leave all of you!"

"You have to, Jean. I'll stall Darius as long as I can."

She nodded, her wide gray eyes glimmering in the dark, and slipped out through the window. I could hear Adelle and Father rousing from their rooms.

"Open up in the name of the king!" someone shouted, banging their fist against the door with renewed vigor.

The clothes I'd worn into the tapestry were gone. The most practical clothing I had left was a simple muslin dress Mina had made for practice before she left. I pulled it on, along with a woolen sweater of Father's. It was large and rough, but it was warmer than anything else I owned. My leather-soled slippers would have to do. I pulled a knit cap I'd made for Mina over my hair and joined my family in the parlor.

Father and Adelle were still dressed in their nightclothes. "Where's Jean?" Father asked me.

"I sent her to get Evran. What do we do?"

"You have to go," Adelle said. "Darius will know it was you who destroyed the tapestry. He has no use for me and Father."

No use for them, perhaps. But that didn't mean he wouldn't hurt them. "I can't leave you."

Father reached for my hands. "Adelle's right. You should go." I stared down at the knuckles gnarled with age, the careful fingers that had counted coins at the palace once, the strong forearms that had held my sisters and me when we were babies. "Save yourself, and don't worry about us. We'll take care of each other."

I nodded and embraced him briefly, then squeezed Adelle

tight before stepping into the hall. I'd barely made it a few feet when the front door exploded, sending splinters raining down on me.

"Stop right there, or your sister dies."

I spun around, expecting to see Mina with a knife to her throat, but Darius was alone.

"Mina is in the dungeons right now," he said.

I froze in horror as his booted footsteps rang out on our wooden floorboards like a death knell.

"I've already been to Margana's. I've seen what you did to my tapestry. The boy escaped, but my hounds are hunting him right now. He won't get far." As he lifted his hand, I braced myself for his touch, but instead something sharp pressed against my neck. A knife. Adelle screamed.

"Do you have any idea what you've done?" he ground out.

I didn't dare answer. The knife had already broken my skin, and I felt warmth trickling down my neck into my collar. Seeing the blood, he lowered the knife a fraction of an inch.

"I didn't mean to burn it," I whispered, trying to keep my throat from brushing the blade. "Evran was going to die. I had to use my light. And the next thing I knew, I was on fire."

"Ignorant fool. You should never have gone into the tapestry." His breath brushed my cheek, odorless. It was the first time I'd noticed that Darius didn't even have a scent. "I've waited twenty years for it, and now it's gone."

I lifted my eyes to his, steeling my voice. "Good."

His other hand came up to strike me.

"Stop!" Father stood behind Darius, his hands clasped in front of him. "Please, stop hurting her. The tapestry can be repaired. It may take another twenty years, but what is that to someone like you? Nothing."

Darius rounded on Father. "It can't be repaired, you imbe-

cile! The Lusiri are extinct. I gathered every hair in the kingdom, by force when necessary. There is nothing left!"

He didn't know about the escaped Lusiri. My eyes darted to
Father's, silently imploring him not to tell. Having the Hollow Ones back in the world was dangerous, but they weren't
as bad as the Shadow Tapestry. Without the Lusiri, Margana
would never be able to complete it. Perhaps Evran and I could
find a way to destroy the Lusiri on our own. I shook my head
as much as I dared.

Darius turned back to me, his voice deceptively gentle, as if
he'd spent his anger on Father. I didn't believe it for a second.
"What was your plan, then? Destroy the tapestry and run? I
suppose if Moreau hadn't warned me, you might have gotten
away with it. For a time."

My stomach soured at my own poor judgment. "He was
never planning to propose," I said to myself, shaking my head.
Jean was right. I should have trusted my instincts.

"Oh, I wouldn't be so sure about that. It's possible he wanted
you on his arm. A bright, shiny accessory. But a large reward
for valuable information can prove too tempting, even for the
most pure of heart. And we all know Luc is not that."

"Was he the one who told you about the drifters in the forest, too?" I asked. "One of your spies?" Luc was no better than
the hounds, just a pet at his master's beck and call.

He clucked his tongue. "Try not to be too disappointed,
Liora. There will be other suitors, and that boy's morals were
as slippery as silk. To his credit, he waited two days to come to
me. But you had to know I wouldn't let your sister go that easily. You must have been desperate to try something like this."

I searched his eyes for some shred of humanity to appeal to,
but I found nothing. "Mina is innocent in all of this."

"I know that. But sometimes children have to be taught their lessons the hard way."

I jerked forward but was stopped by the pressure of the knife. "What did you do?"

"I burned down that club she loved so much, along with most of her friends. I kept the transporter. His abilities are rare. The rest we're better off without."

A sob burst out of me, driving the blade even deeper into my flesh. Darius pulled it back a moment later, but I deserved the pain. All those innocent people, murdered out of spite. Why hadn't I gone to Corone in Mina's stead? I could have prevented so much suffering. My only consolation was that she was still alive. As long as she was safe, I hadn't failed everyone.

A strange look passed over Darius's face, almost as if my anguish confused him. He gripped my chin in his free hand, forcing me to look at him. It took everything I had to keep the world from fading out at his touch, to not let my power flow into him the way it so desperately wanted. "Where did you think you would run to, Liora?"

A knock sounded on what was left of the door, and Darius leaned back.

I inhaled a full breath, wincing at the pain in my throat as I turned to see a guard in the doorway.

"My lord, I'm sorry to disturb you, but the hounds have found something in the woods."

"And by some*thing*, I hope you mean some*one*."

"Yes, my lord. Two people, in fact."

Whatever emotion Darius had experienced a moment ago was gone. "Come with me," he said, forcing me forward with the knife. I stooped through the ruins of the door and outside.

"Liora." Evran stood beyond our front gate, his hands and

feet bound with rope. He saw the blood at my neck and tried to step toward me, but he could barely move.

Jean stood next to him, similarly bound. "I'm so sorry, Liora. Evran wasn't home when I got there. I couldn't outrun the hounds."

"I heard a scream and came to see who it was," Evran explained. "I thought it was you."

I hadn't known my heart could hurt more, but seeing the people I loved restrained like animals was a different kind of agony. I glanced up at the night sky. The constellations seemed impossibly clear and bright, and I felt a connection to them that I hadn't before. It suddenly seemed as if I could call them all down, if I wanted to.

Someone shouted, and we all turned to see Margana struggling against several guards. "Let him go, Darius!"

He ignored her, turning to the guard who'd knocked on our door. "Who's the girl?"

"She's a mage drifter."

"Ah, you must be the one who escaped me the other night. What's your power, child?"

Jean was silent, but her eyes narrowed in hatred. A moment later Darius laughed.

"Such a filthy mouth for such a young girl. Well, at least I won't have to repeat myself." He took Jean's face in his hands, and her body slumped against him. "Was she alone?" he asked the guard.

He nodded. "The boy came out when he heard the screams. I'm not sure we would have found him otherwise. Even the hounds didn't see him."

He released Jean into the guard's arms and went to examine Evran more closely. "The weaver's boy. Not truly a boy anymore, I suppose. Your powers were always weak. I'm impressed you survived in the tapestry as long as you did. Yet, you couldn't destroy it, could you?" Darius grinned, realizing he'd touched a nerve. "I'd venture to say that you even enjoyed it a bit."

"Leave him alone," I said, stepping forward.

Darius's gaze traveled from me to Evran and back again. I retreated, but it was too late. I'd revealed enough that his eyes narrowed in calculation. "This is quite a ragtag troupe of mages we've assembled, isn't it? The dungeons are going to be quite full until the executions begin."

"What executions?" I lurched toward Darius this time, but one of the guards yanked me back by my shoulders.

Darius gave me a long, cold look and turned to his horse. "Bring the weaver's son and the drifter."

"What about the witch?" the guard holding me asked.

"She's free to go."

"No!" I shouted. "I'm going with them."

Darius didn't even bother to look back at me. I directed some of my heat to my skin, and the guard hissed, releasing me. Another guard kicked Evran forward and grabbed hold of Jean's bindings, yanking her toward the wagon.

"I'll never weave anything for you again, Darius." Margana's voice was as steely as her eyes.

"No, you won't." Darius turned to one of the guards. "Remove her hands."

Adelle gasped, and Jean began to sob. Evran shouldered one of the guards restraining him, but with his feet bound, he could do little more than hop a few feet before another guard grabbed him.

"Wait!" I cried as Darius turned to his horse. Telling him about the escaped Lusiri was a risk, but I was desperate, and this was the only leverage I had.

"What is it now?" Darius asked, one foot already in the stirrup.

"Two Lusiri escaped from the tapestry."

He pulled his foot free and finally looked at me. "What?"

"When I burned the hole in the tapestry, there were two Lusiri. They got free somehow."

"It's true," Margana said. "They ran into the woods, heading north. If we capture them, I may be able to repair the tapestry."

There was a glimmer of hope in Darius's eyes, but it faded quickly. "I'd have to catch the Lusiri first, and there are no hunters left."

"I'll do it," I blurted. "Let everyone else go, and I will do whatever it takes to bring the Hollow Ones to you."

"And how exactly do you plan to do that?" he asked, laughing. "You have less experience in the world than most children."

I lifted my chin and stood as straight as I could. "I defeated the Lusiri and destroyed your tapestry. I'd say I'm better prepared than you think."

One side of his mouth lifted in a smirk. "Fair enough. But you have no idea how to track a wild animal or survive in the forest. It could take weeks."

Margana started to protest before Evran even opened his mouth, but I knew as well as she did what he was about to say.

"I'll go with her."

I turned to him. "No, Evran. You're safer here."

Darius folded his arms and gave Evran a cursory once-over. "And what do you know about tracking?"

Evran maintained his composure admirably. "I've hunted in the woods here my entire life. I survived inside the tapestry, and I have observed the Lusiri more than any living person. If you really want the tapestry completed, Liora and I are your best hope."

Darius considered for a few moments. "Very well. I'll give you a month. Your mother and the remnants of the tapestry will come to the palace, where she'll salvage what she can. Under lock and key, of course. She's had far too much freedom over the years."

"You have to promise not to hurt Margana or Mina while we're gone," I said.

"You're hardly in a position to be making demands. But I won't hurt them, if you bring me the Lusiri within a month."

"And what about me?" Jean asked quietly. "Am I free to go?"

Darius turned, as if he'd forgotten she was there. "No. You may come in handy, scrawny as you are. You'll go with them."

I sent Jean a silent apology. If she had never come to our house, she could have avoided all of this. Evran growled as a guard yanked his arms up behind his back. His gaze was sharp and feral, an animal tracking its prey. He could have escaped Darius, but he'd given himself up, thinking he could help me. Father was right: my magic *was* sinister, all the more so because it had seemed so benign. No wonder Darius said I reminded him of himself.

"What will you do with the Lusiri once you have them?" Margana asked.

"I'll build a special enclosure for them and keep them. The king will be delighted to have the last two Hollow Ones in his menagerie. And I will breed them until I have enough hair to complete the tapestry."

"Why?" Adelle asked suddenly. She had hardly said a word since Darius came.

"Why what?" His tone gentled when he realized it was

Adelle who had spoken. "Ah, why do I want to complete the tapestry?"

She nodded.

He stepped forward and placed his hand on her cheek before I could warn her. Her rigid posture softened, and she leaned her head toward him, emitting a soft sigh. Father began to protest, but Darius was already pulling away. He knelt down in front of her, his eyes meeting hers.

"Do you see now?" he asked.

She nodded again.

"Everyone thinks emptiness is a bad thing, but I know the truth. So do the king, my guards, and even you, Liora," he said over his shoulder. "The tapestry will set everyone free from their fears, their worries, even their desires. When you are no longer ruled by emotion, there can be no more pain."

"You're wrong!" I shouted. "The tapestry is none of those things. It's pure pain and misery, not freedom."

He walked back to me, his voice a grating whisper only I could hear. "Does it matter? Whatever the tapestry is—emptiness, sadness, darkness, madness—it is not *this*." He waved his hand at our surroundings.

All this time, I had believed he wanted absolute power. That was why he controlled the king, why he stole magic from the other mages. But Margana was right. It would never be enough. And if he couldn't fill the void, he'd drag everyone else into it with him. "What happened to you?" I wondered out loud.

Darius's eyes locked with mine, his expression inscrutable. "You should prepare for the journey. The longer the Lusiri are out there, the more people will be hurt."

I knew he didn't care about anyone but himself. But going after the Lusiri would buy me time. I had destroyed the tapestry once. And when I was sure that the people I loved were safe, I would find a way to destroy it again.

"I'll be back tomorrow with horses and supplies. My guards will stay here tonight, in case anyone plans to escape. Jean, you can stay, unless you'd rather ride back to Corone with me." He arched an eyebrow and laughed at whatever Jean said to him in response. "I'll take that as a no. Don't forget about Mina, Liora. She's counting on you." Darius reached into his cloak and pulled out a small parcel, wrapped in paper. "She asked me to give you this."

I stared into his eyes, which momentarily shone rose gold in my glow. But Darius's gaze gave nothing away. I unwrapped the parcel gingerly, afraid of what I might find.

Tears burned the back of my eyes when I saw what it was: a dried and pressed poppy, just like the ones our mother had loved. I imagined Mina in a stone dungeon, with no light, fresh air, or flowers. Without me, she might never see one again.

I looked back up at Darius. Facing the Lusiri had been the most terrifying thing I'd ever done. I never wanted to do it again. But for Mina, for my family, I would be brave.

NINETEEN

My only consolation was that Darius didn't take Father or Adelle with him. He had Mina, who was all the collateral he needed. For now, they would stay in Sylvan, but once the townspeople heard I was a witch, I had no idea what would happen to them. I didn't even know how long we'd be gone. The Lusiri had almost a day's head start. Margana said they came from the north, a land of eternal winter. I'd never been farther than Corone.

I went back to my room, hoping to get at least a few hours of sleep before our journey, but I couldn't quiet my restless mind. I got out of bed and went to the windowsill with the telescope Darius had given me. A storm had rolled in, and the clouds were too dense to see the moon and stars tonight. I was about to turn back to bed when I saw something move at the edge of the woods.

For one terrified moment I was sure it was the Lusiri, but whatever I was looking at was too small. It scurried across the road, a shape even darker than the night, and materialized in front of my window in the form of Evran.

I glanced at the guard standing near our front gate, who paced back and forth but clearly hadn't seen Evran cross the road. This must be part of his magic, I realized. I understood now why he'd been able to spend so many nights in the woods, how he could sneak up on me without so much as a crunched leaf to alert me to his presence. I pushed the window open as quietly as I could and leaned out.

Evran pressed his finger to his lips and held out his hand. Once I was outside, he pulled me to him fiercely, and I inhaled the scent of soap and pine needles.

"I can shield both of us," he whispered.

I nodded, shivering as a cool shadow slowly slipped over us. When we were far enough into the forest to avoid being seen, Evran released me.

"What are you doing?" I asked. "We can't leave. Mina is depending on me."

"I would never endanger Mina, but there's something I need to show you." He held out his hand, and I took it gladly, wishing he would pull me to his side again. I hadn't had time to grab a cloak, and I was shivering in my nightgown. Even my feet were bare.

"It's over here," Evran said finally. "I saw it when I was hiding."

"What is it?" I asked as we broke through the brush and stopped at the edge of a clearing.

He cursed quietly. "It's even bigger than it was before. That rock was feet away from it, and now it's only a few inches."

I peered into the darkness. "What am I looking at, Evran?"

"Look closely. But don't get too close. I don't know what it does."

I walked slowly toward the clearing, until my light was near enough to see that this wasn't a clearing at all. It was an absence, as if the forest floor had been erased and only a blurry smudge was left in its place. Evran pointed to a small, furry, shapeless mass at the base of a nearby tree.

I looked back at Evran. "I don't understand."

"That was a rabbit, Liora. I moved the carcass away from the hole so it wouldn't disappear. I think the Lusiri fed here. And when they did, they didn't just eat the rabbit. They ate everything around it, too."

My scalp prickled as I knelt down. "What do you mean?"

"Here." He picked up the rock and tossed it toward the smudge, where it vanished. "It's a void, I think. Like the tapestry."

"But why would the Lusiri leave a void behind?"

"I don't know. Those Lusiri aren't like any others that have ever existed. They came from inside the void itself. They must have brought a part of its power with them. The fact that the hole is growing confirms my worst fear."

I stepped back, horrified. "What?"

"That the void isn't static. It's expanding. It sucks in everything around it and feeds off it, getting bigger the more it consumes. Just like the tapestry will, if it's completed."

A terrible thought occurred to me. "Does this mean every time the Lusiri feed, they'll leave one of these in their wake?"

"I have to assume so."

I pushed my hair away from my face with numb fingers. "Should we tell Darius?"

"No. If he discovers what the Lusiri are doing, he won't need the tapestry." Evran's eyes flashed in the dark. "He'll let the voids spread and do the work for him."

I hadn't realized I was still moving backward until I bumped into a tree. The solidness was reassuring. "But even if we don't tell him and we hunt the Lusiri, he's going to use them to make the tapestry. And in the meantime, these holes are going to spread."

"Not necessarily. My mother said a void like this, a black hole, wants to be filled."

"Yes, but what can we fill it with?" I asked, afraid to take my eyes off the expanding nothingness.

"Light."

I tore my eyes away from the void just long enough to level them on Evran. "What are you talking about?"

"Your light destroyed the tapestry. A tapestry that was infinite as far as we know. These holes are small. I think if you can fill them now, we can stop them from spreading."

I scoffed. "I think you grossly overestimate my powers."

"I think you underestimate them, Liora."

I released a breath. Maybe he was right. I was certainly capable of more than I'd believed just weeks ago. But I'd also nearly burned myself up in the tapestry. "I'm scared, Evran. Darius said I reminded him of himself. I don't know exactly what that means, but what if using my powers makes me closer to him in some way?"

"You could never be like Darius." He stepped forward, his hand outstretched. "Don't worry. I'll be right here."

I didn't want to get any closer to the void than I was, but Evran was right. I had to try. Otherwise our mission would be over before it had even started. I took his hand, my fingers prickling as his warmth seeped into them. "I don't have good control of my light. The only thing that seems to bring it out is emotion. I glow brighter when I'm happy or embarrassed. The heat comes when I'm angry."

"What about before?" he asked, stepping closer to me. "In

the blackberry glade. You used to hold my hands and glow so bright I thought for sure they'd be able to see the light in Sylvan."

My cheeks warmed, my glow brightening with them. "That was different. It wasn't embarrassment *or* anger."

"Then what was it?" He took my other hand, and I was suddenly very aware of my thin nightgown, of all my exposed skin. On this cloudy night, I was the only light for miles around.

I knew exactly what it was that made my skin glow like this. I was in love with Evran, and it seemed impossible that he could ever feel as strongly for me.

"Evran—"

He cut me off with his lips, pressing them to mine so urgently I would have faltered if I weren't backed against a tree. I couldn't tell if the warmth I felt was from Evran, or my longing, or my light, and I didn't care. When I parted my lips, the sigh that he breathed into me held everything I'd wanted to say to him for so long.

I wasn't ready when he pulled gently away and stood back, our hands still clasped. "Look at you."

I opened my eyes and glanced down. Light had flooded the entire clearing. It radiated from me, spreading along the ground where it met the edge of the void. And as we watched, the void began to shrink.

I dropped Evran's hands and stepped forward, the absence shrinking farther as I walked. When the smudge was only a foot across, I knelt down and pressed my hand against it. For a moment, my light faltered, and I felt a tug against my skin, as if the void was trying to suck my power out of me. But I thought of Evran and the kiss we had just shared, and in a blink, the hole vanished.

When I was sure it wouldn't return, I ran into Evran's open arms and pressed my cheek to his chest, listening to the steady drum of his heartbeat. "Do you think we'll be able to get them all?"

He kissed the top of my head. "I believe in you."

I pushed away just enough to look into his green eyes. They glimmered in the glow from my skin like stained glass. The last time I had glowed like this for Evran, the last time I had tried to show him what he meant to me, he had pulled away. But tonight I had controlled my magic. My skin wasn't hot, and I had managed to reduce the light back to a dim glow.

Evran lowered his face to mine and kissed me again, and for the moment, I forgot to worry about why he hadn't believed in me enough to stay before.

Adelle woke me just as dawn was breaking with a cup of my favorite mint tea, which I took out into our little front garden while she helped Jean prepare. A path had been trampled into the woods directly across from our house. The Lusiri would be easy to track, at least for a while.

Someone approached our front gate, backlit by the sun, and the memory of the kiss Evran and I had shared brought a smile to my lips. But as the figure got closer, I saw that his shoulders were too broad, his stride confident, unhesitating. Darius.

I drew my shawl around myself, avoiding his eyes.

"May I?" He gestured to the wrought iron bench I sat on.

The last thing I wanted was to sit and chat with Darius, but I reminded myself that Mina's safety hinged on his volatile temper. Reluctantly, I scooted over.

"You asked me yesterday what had happened to me."

I glanced at him from the corner of my eye. "I wasn't expecting an answer."

"Perhaps not. But it was a reasonable question. I hope I'll be able to share the answer with you in the days to come."

I stiffened. "What do you mean?"

"Did you think I would send you off into the woods alone? You're just a girl, and a vulnerable one at that, even if you managed to fight off the Lusiri."

I turned to face him, letting the snub about being just a girl slide, because I was more concerned by the word *alone*. "I'll have Evran."

His features softened. "Of course. But he's just a boy. You may as well be alone in his presence."

My eyes searched his face for malice or irony. It was impossible to tell when he was making fun of me or insulting me. In the early morning light, his strangely inconstant irises were the color of copper patina. "I don't need help," I insisted, calling up the memory of what I'd managed last night to strengthen my resolve.

"Perhaps not, but the Lusiri need to be caught as quickly as possible, and I won't leave that responsibility in the hands of children."

Had I wounded his pride? Was that even possible? "Then why not hunt them yourself?"

His lips curled in a soft grin. "Where's the fun in that?"

He couldn't possibly be doing this for *fun*. How would Evran and I hide the voids left behind by the Lusiri now? How would I ever have the time I needed with him, to find out where we stood? The kiss had quieted some of my fears, but there was still so much we hadn't discussed. "Won't you be needed at the palace?"

"I've brought your sister's transporter with me, so I can get back instantly if I need to."

"And Mina?"

"Don't worry. She's in good hands with my guards."

I burned with anger, so hot that Darius could feel it through the iron bench. He chuckled as he rose. "You'd better learn to control that temper of yours, or someone could get hurt."

I knew I had to tread carefully around Darius, but he was deliberately baiting me, only to threaten my family when I reacted. How was I possibly going to spend the next days or even weeks in his presence?

A moment later, I heard Evran's soft footfalls on the path. "Good morning," he said, approaching hesitantly.

I pushed aside my worry and smiled up at him. Neither of us acknowledged Darius, who seemed to sense that our conversation was finished.

"I've brought suitable clothing for all of you. You have a quarter of an hour to prepare." Darius lowered his voice and said to me, "Choose whom you'd like to spend it with wisely."

I ignored him and went to Evran. His hair was trimmed and neatly combed, like a child who'd just had a bath. But with his sharp jawline and lean, muscular frame, there was nothing soft or boyish about him.

He ran his fingers over his chin self-consciously. "I figured I should get a final shave in before we go."

I wanted to tell him it would be more comfortable to kiss him now, but I felt too shy in the light of day. "I should get Jean."

He nodded. "I'll go gather my things. Is everything okay? With Darius?"

I swallowed. He wouldn't be any happier about this than I was. "He's coming with us."

"What?" Evran clenched his fists in anger, but he turned at the sound of a wagon rattling up to the gate.

Two large draft horses stopped in front of our house, bearing the remains of the tapestry in the cart behind them. Margana sat with the wooden loom, her hair gathered into a thick braid at the back of her head. Her expression remained determined, but something about seeing her hair restrained like that made me think of a caged bird.

The rest of the guards were mounted, the gold buttons of their uniforms winking in the sun. I recognized Cyril's dark hair and piercing eyes immediately. He was astride a chestnut gelding, his expression grim. By the look of things, he had not been treated well in prison. I hoped Mina was faring better.

When the time came for goodbyes, I turned to Father and embraced him tightly. "I'm sorry," I whispered against his ear. "For everything." I wished I had Jean's ability. Maybe I could convey my meaning better through my thoughts. More than anything, I was so sorry for Mother's death, but I couldn't say it out loud.

He kissed my forehead. "Goodbye, Liora. I'll take care of Adelle while you're gone."

I caught my sister's eye over his shoulder, and we shared a knowing glance. We had always been the ones to take care of him. Saying goodbye to her was harder, but she was a smart, resourceful young woman. If anyone could handle this, it was Adelle.

"I love you," I said as she folded me into her arms.

"I love you, too. Be careful out there."

"I'll try."

"You're stronger than you think, Liora."

I squeezed her tighter, memorizing her scent before forcing myself to let go.

Evran embraced his mother over the edge of the wagon. Neither of them cried, but Evran whispered something in her ear, and for just a moment, her cheeks rose in a smile.

Jean was already mounted on a roan mare, leaving a tall bay gelding for Evran and a white mare for me. As I reached up to take the reins, Darius stepped behind me, guiding my elbow with his hand.

I flinched instinctively. "I can manage on my own."

"Of course you can. But I'm a gentleman."

A disbelieving snort escaped me, and he had the nerve to laugh. He had apparently forgiven me for destroying his tapestry, or else this was part of some other plan I couldn't fathom.

"Place your hand here, on the pommel of the saddle," he said.

I hesitated, but the truth was, I had no idea what I was doing. I did as he said.

"Good. May I?" He motioned as if he was going to place his hand over mine, and while I hated the idea of him touching me, I also knew that if I accepted his help now, I would be able to do this on my own next time.

I nodded. When his skin met mine, I felt a soft tug at my center that I recognized as Darius's magic, but just like when he touched me yesterday, I seemed to be able to fight it. If he noticed, he didn't say. "Now, put your left foot in the stirrup. I'll help boost you."

He lifted me easily onto the mare, then checked to make sure the stirrups were comfortable. I noticed Evran had mounted himself, but he was listening to Darius, confirming that his own stirrups were the right length. My heart ached at the sight of him, and at the thought of what Darius could do to him if he knew just how much he meant to me.

"It's a pity you won't be able to attend the harvest festival with your young man," Darius said, as though he was the one who could read minds. If I hadn't known Darius to be incapable of feelings, I might have thought him jealous of Evran.

Not because he had any romantic interest in me, but because he sought to control everything around him, from his jeweled fruits to what he called *his* mages. I wondered if he considered me one of his mages now.

Darius sidled his horse up next to mine. "Evran and Jean will lead. Cyril will ride in the middle. Liora and I will follow."

Evran looked at me like there were so many things he wanted to say, and all I could do was give him a tight nod to let him know I understood. Reluctantly, he turned away and started toward the woods with Jean, Cyril trailing silently behind. Cyril wouldn't try to escape, not with Mina in prison. I hoped we'd be able to talk later so I could ask about my sister.

"One last thing," Darius said, pressing so close to my mare that our legs touched. He whistled sharply. My horse startled as the three black hounds darted out from under the wagon.

"Is there no end to your cruelty?" I asked Darius as he kicked his horse forward. My little mare followed obediently.

He grinned. "If there is, I've yet to encounter it. Shall we?"

Together, we entered the forest.

TWENTY

It was easy to follow the Lusiri's tracks in the soft dirt of the forest floor. They were animals, after all, and made no effort to cover their trail. We trotted when we could, but we couldn't move very quickly while weaving in and out of the trees. We would have to hope the Lusiri eventually took to the road, or we'd never make up any distance.

Soon, the undergrowth became so dense we had to walk single file, and at one point we had to dismount and lead the horses through the thick brush when they refused to go on their own. The brambles caught at our hair and clothing, and insects buzzed in my ears. Fortunately, Darius had provided me with a pair of remarkably comfortable breeches, and my riding boots protected my calves from the stinging nettles.

We'd been tromping along for hours when Darius finally called for us to stop.

I sat down next to Evran, Cyril, and Jean on a fallen log furred with pale green moss, making sure there was no room for Darius. He only smiled and removed a hunk of bread and a flask from his saddlebags before leaning against a tree.

"Hungry?" Evran asked, handing me a sandwich from his pack.

"Starved."

Jean bit into her own sandwich, watching me. I knew she could read my thoughts if she wanted to, but I hoped she wasn't. She would not find them encouraging.

"I've never been to the other side of the woods before," Evran said, "but I believe there's another town there. Are we camping tonight?" he asked Darius.

"It would be good to talk to the townspeople and find out when the Lusiri passed. But we won't be sleeping tonight."

A groan escaped my lips. Now that I was sitting, I realized just how exhausted I was.

"We're all tired," Darius said to me, "but we don't have the luxury of time now."

Worse than the lack of sleep was the fact that Evran and I would have no time to search for more voids. I had no idea how often the Lusiri fed, and though we hadn't come across any carcasses yet, I couldn't imagine a single rabbit would last them long.

"We also can't afford for anyone to fall ill," Evran said. "Liora hasn't slept more than a couple of hours in days."

"And why is that? Oh yes, because she was destroying my tapestry. Let's not forget whose fault it is that we're all here."

Evran answered with a snarl.

Darius raised an eyebrow at me. "Do you see what happens when a boy spends his days in the woods? He turns into a beast. I wouldn't be surprised if he licks his hands clean after he finishes eating."

Evran stood abruptly and strode off into the forest.

I gulped down the last bite of my sandwich and hurried after him.

"We're leaving in ten minutes!" Darius called.

I found Evran crouched next to a small stream, washing his hands. "Are you all right?"

He glanced up and smiled. "Of course. I figured walking away would give us a chance to talk."

I knelt down next to him, wincing at the burn in my thighs, and washed my own hands in the cool water. "How are we going to keep an eye out for holes with him here?"

"I'm watching, don't worry. If I spot anything, I'll signal you."

"How?"

"I'll stretch my arms, like this." He raised his arms over his head to demonstrate, his sleeves falling back to reveal his muscular forearms. I had the sudden urge to grab him around the middle and embrace him so tight he couldn't ever leave again. "If that happens, make any excuse you can to dismount. I'll find a way to distract Darius."

"What about Jean and Cyril?"

"We communicated while we were riding. They understand about the holes."

Jean's power was more useful than I would have thought. "Can she get into Darius's mind?"

"Sometimes. He has a mental shield up much of the time, she said. It's a difficult skill to master, something that requires years of practice. But occasionally it drops."

"When?"

He paused for a moment. "When he's talking to you, mostly."

We rose at the same time, and I took his hand before he could step away. "I'm so glad you're here. I'm not sure I could do this without you." I kissed him on the cheek, my lips grazing the smooth skin. "How long do you think it will take?"

"To find the Lusiri? I have no idea. At least a week or two, I assume. If they get to the snow before we do, it could take even longer."

I tried not to picture Mina locked up in a cell with Darius's guards for company.

"We won't let them get that far ahead of us," he assured me.

I wished I shared his optimism. We started back toward the horses, though every inch of me wanted to collapse to the ground. "Evran?"

"Mmm?"

I swallowed the lump in my throat. I wasn't sure I was ready to know the answer, but I didn't know when I'd get another chance to ask the question. "Why are you afraid of your magic?"

He sighed and scrubbed his jaw with his hand. "It's complicated, Liora."

"What isn't lately?" I asked, keeping my voice light.

Just then, one of the hounds burst through the brush in front of us, its ears perked forward as if to say, *There you are!* It yipped once, turned on its heels, and bounded back through the undergrowth, its whiplike tail disappearing into a bush.

"Darius is waiting for us," Evran said. And I knew for now, that was the most I was going to get.

As twilight settled over the forest, we were allowed one more stop to eat. When Cyril, Jean, Evran, and I once again huddled into a small group, excluding Darius, he told us he was going to search the woods with the dogs for a few minutes and would return shortly.

As soon as he was gone, I leaned toward Cyril. "How's Mina?" I asked.

His blue eyes, which had been so focused at The Crystal Gazer, were dim tonight. "She was fine the last time I saw her. I don't think Darius will hurt her, at least not yet."

"I've been probing his mind as much as possible," Jean said. "But he doesn't seem to be concerned about Mina, or even the Lusiri."

I frowned. "Then what is he concerned about?"

Her eyes darted briefly to Evran's before returning to me. "You."

"*Me?* In what way?"

She shook her head. "I'm not sure, exactly. Every time I try to dig deeper into his thoughts, a wall slams down, as if he can feel me searching. It's extremely difficult to build that kind of mental block. He's either had experience with another mentalist, or the walls aren't even conscious. But my money is on the former." She exhaled, blowing her wispy bangs off her forehead. "If I had any money, that is."

"Why can't you just transport Darius to where the Lusiri are now and end this?" Evran asked Cyril.

"Because I don't know exactly where they are," he answered. "And I can't transport to a place I've never been before. Besides, based on what Jean is saying, it doesn't sound like Darius *wants* to end this quickly. Hunting the Lusiri gives him the perfect opportunity to spend time with Liora."

Jean caught the look of disgust on my face. "For what it's worth, his intentions don't appear threatening. It's more like there's some kind of riddle surrounding you that he's trying to solve."

"My powers?"

"Maybe."

I looked at Evran. "We have to be careful. It would be bad enough if he discovered the voids. But if he learns that I know how to fill them, that I'm working in direct opposition to him..."

"He won't," Evran said, settling an arm around my shoulders. As much as I relished his touch, I worried that Darius might see us. He had no qualms about using the people I loved against me, and if he gleaned the depth of my feelings for Evran, who knew what Darius would do to him? When the brush started to rustle, heralding the return of the hounds, I ducked out from under Evran's arm with an apologetic shrug.

Cyril passed out the rest of our fresh food as Darius returned from wherever he'd been. Everything else was dried and would hopefully last us through tomorrow, when we should be able to restock in Craven, the town on the other side of the woods.

Even though it was another moonless night, I didn't feel like we were in danger. The woods were quiet, and I doubted the Lusiri would circle back to hunt us when there was plenty of other prey. It was possible they would hole up during the day to avoid the sunlight, but they hadn't so far. They still seemed to be running in fear, the crescents of their hoofprints cutting deep in the soft earth of the forest. They stayed close together for the most part, only separating when the terrain required it.

We packed up after our meal and went to our horses, who were foraging for grass among the fallen leaves. Winter wouldn't be far off.

"I can't believe he expects us to ride all night," I said to Evran as I tightened my mare's girth the way Darius had taught me. "Did you get any sleep?"

"I tried for a few hours while Mother gathered supplies, and I couldn't. Everything felt wrong—too soft, too bright."

He walked over to help me mount my horse. "I'm not sure I belong in Sylvan anymore."

"It's not that you don't belong," I said, turning to him. "It's just that belonging might look different now than it used to."

"You don't understand, Liora. I'm not the same person I was when I went into the tapestry."

"That's not true."

A shadow passed over his eyes, dimming the green to sage, and I couldn't help wondering about his magic. He seemed to think it was evil in some way, something he needed to keep away from other people. But shadows were harmless, and what evil could there be in the ability to find your way in the dark?

By the time daylight began to appear through the trees, I was close to sliding off the side of my horse, every muscle in my body either cramping, aching, or screaming in pain. Jean, Cyril, and Evran looked just as exhausted as I felt, but Darius was as cool and collected as ever.

Between the light from my skin and Evran's night vision, I was fairly confident we hadn't passed any more holes, but the thought that there could be a void out there, spreading surreptitiously in the forest, sent a shiver down my spine.

My fears turned in a different direction as the trees thinned and we approached Craven. It wasn't in a gorge like Sylvan, but the narrow cobblestone streets and quaint storefronts were eerily similar, a long-lost twin living a separate life nearly identical to the other. If Sylvan had been terrorized by two Lusiri.

Women stood in small groups on the sidewalks, wringing handkerchiefs and sobbing. Two men argued in the middle of the road, seemingly oblivious to our party's approach. They only quieted when Darius's hounds barked and went streaking toward them like three black wraiths.

Murmurs of Darius's name went up in the clusters of people around us.

He stopped in front of a group of young women and dismounted, his eyes settling on one of them. She curtsied awkwardly.

"The Lusiri were here, weren't they?" he asked.

The girl glanced at her friends before nodding. "Yes, my lord. Last night. Two of them."

"Is anyone hurt?"

She caught her lip in her teeth, her eyes welling with tears. "A child, my lord. He was cutting through the wheat field on the way home from visiting his grandmother."

Guilt knifed through me. I had known there would be victims, but the loss of an innocent child was crueler than anything I had imagined. Exhausted as I was, it was difficult to maintain a constant state of urgency in the forest, too easy to get lulled into boredom. But this was a terrible reminder that our search wasn't just about saving Mina. We had to find the Lusiri as quickly as possible.

"Who found him?" Darius asked.

"His father. He went out looking for him when he didn't come home for supper. The Lusiri bolted as soon as he approached. None of us would have believed it if we hadn't seen the body for ourselves."

"Where is the body now?"

The girl's tears spilled over her lashes, and Darius withdrew a handkerchief from his pocket and gave it to her. "I'm sorry, my lord," she said. "He's in his home. With his parents."

"You'll take me to them. Everyone else, there is a curfew in place as of now. Nobody outside after dark until further notice. Spread the word."

I leaned close to him. "But the Lusiri are gone."

He turned to me and lowered his voice to the softest whisper. "And yet their fear is still here, so palpable you can feel it. They're desperate for someone to take charge and tell them what to do. They'd stay in their houses for days if I told them to."

"You're taking advantage of their terror. Why?"

"Because I can."

I stared at him for a moment, horrified. It wasn't that this was a game to him; that would imply some sort of enjoyment. It was more like he was sharpening a blade, keeping it honed for when he might need to use it.

"Fear is a useful tool, Liora. Don't ever forget that." He started to follow the girl down one of the streets to the boy's house, then glanced back over his shoulder. "Evran, you'll stay here with the horses. The rest of you, come with me."

"I was thinking I should go look at the spot where the boy was killed," Evran said.

Darius's nostrils flared in annoyance. "And why is that?"

"Because it will help determine which direction the Lusiri went. If they were here last night, it means we're still half a day behind them or more. We won't catch up to them if we don't hurry."

"Fine. We'll meet you in the wheat field after I've spoken with the boy's family."

As Jean and Cyril stepped forward to follow Darius, I hung back. "I'd like to go with Evran."

Darius frowned, his eyes narrowing slightly. "No."

I was about to argue when Jean cleared her throat. "If I may, my lord. The villagers are suspicious of Liora's light. I don't think the family will be pleased to see her."

"And why not?"

Jean lowered her voice. "Because, the people in this town don't like to associate with mages."

None of us needed to point out whose fault that was.

"I knew you'd come in handy, drifter. Very well. Jean, Cyril, come with me. We'll be back shortly, Liora. Don't even think about running."

I couldn't disguise the disdain in my voice. "You have my sister and a transporter, *my lord.*"

He grunted and followed the girl, who'd been watching our exchange curiously, as had the rest of the townspeople. I wondered what else Jean had picked up from them.

The field was on the far side of town, all of the golden wheat already cut and harvested. Even from the edge of the field, we could see the growing hole near the woods. Surely someone else had noticed it by now.

"Hurry," Evran said, kicking his horse forward. We trotted over to the edge of the void, the horses shying at the perimeter. It was at least ten feet across by now, possibly because this prey had been much larger than the rabbit.

"Here, take my horse." I handed the reins to Evran and rushed to the edge, trying to gather my light. But when I reached for it, it flickered weakly, nothing close to what I'd managed inside the tapestry.

"What's the matter?"

"I can't do it." My frustration grew as I reached again and again for the light. "I'm trying, but there's nothing there." I knew it was my fear holding me back. At this point in my life, I had far more practice repressing my light than summoning it. I thought about the time I had burned Darius and what I'd done in the tapestry. It had been anger that brought forth my heat. But with Evran, in the woods, it had been something very different.

"Kiss me," I blurted.

"What?"

I grasped the front of his tunic. "I'm too frightened to be angry. Darius could be here any minute. I need to feel something other than fear."

For a moment I was afraid he wouldn't do it, but then he grinned. "You don't need to tell me twice." He pulled me to him, his free hand pressed the small of my back, and before our lips even met I felt the knot of fear in my stomach start to melt away.

Evran's hand fisted in the fabric of my linen shirt, urging me closer. I felt a surge of heat so intense I stepped back, afraid I would burn him.

He laughed at the startled expression on my face. "I think that's enough for now. We don't need you setting the wheat field on fire."

I smirked and glanced down at the hole. It was already shrinking, but this time I pressed my hand to it right away, sending it skittering back from my touch. Within seconds, the smudge was gone, with more of the shorn wheat coming into focus. The only sign anything bad had taken place here was a rust-colored stain at the center of where the hole had been.

I stood up and brushed the grass from my knees. "Thank you."

His smile was sheepish as he ran his hand through his hair, and I thought I saw a blush in his cheeks. "Anytime."

"Hopefully it won't always be when we're trying to save the world."

Our laughter was cut off by the sight of the hounds cutting through the field, with Darius and the others following.

"Well, which way did they go?" Darius asked as he pulled his horse to a halt in front of us. I breathed a sigh of relief when his eyes traveled to the bloodstain and immediately back to mine.

"Into the woods." Evran gestured to the broken branches where the Lusiri had clearly entered. "We can take the road and hope that moving faster buys us time, although we risk losing their trail that way."

"No, we'll stick to the woods." Darius motioned for the hounds to go in ahead of us.

I looked at my saddle and grimaced. "And will we get to sleep tonight?"

"The horses need rest as much as we do," Evran added.

"We'll sleep if the Lusiri sleep. Right now we're still far behind, and more children could die in the meantime."

For a moment I thought he was simply being cruel, pointing out once again how it was my fault the Lusiri were here, when he was the one who wanted to unleash the tapestry on the world. But Jean shook her head slightly.

I think seeing the child's body with his own eyes affected him far more than he's letting on. He left a bag of gold for the family, to pay for the funeral.

I considered Darius for a moment as he rode ahead and we fell in line behind him. He had admitted something had happened to him and he hoped to share it with me. It was hard to imagine anything could make me feel sympathy for him, but if Jean believed his emotions to be sincere, I would try to accept that as the truth. For now.

TWENTY-ONE

By nightfall, we had come to a part of the forest punctuated by large rocks and boulders, as if a giant had played a game of marbles and left them behind. A stream that had been winding along nearby flowed into a series of natural stone pools, and when we discovered a small, dry cave, Darius finally decided we could rest. The Lusiri did seem to have slowed down today, and Evran had pointed out a flattened area in the undergrowth where it appeared one of the Lusiri had rested for a few hours.

"These beasts have never experienced anything but the tapestry," he explained as we removed the tack from our horses. "They're used to darkness and surviving on nothing but squirrels and maybe the occasional larger creature, like the one we found on our rope. But now they're here, and they're finding a very hospitable world, aside from the light. Easy, human prey must seem like a gift to them. I imagine they'll let their guard down as they spend more time here."

"But they're still heading north," Cyril pointed out.

"As I assumed they would," Darius said. "Which means we can probably afford to use the roads from now on, since we know generally where they're headed."

Evran and I exchanged a look. If we didn't follow the Lusiri's path, we might not be able to find all the voids they left behind. What we really needed was to get rid of Darius, but he didn't seem to have any intention of leaving.

We laid out our rations, which consisted of little more than hard bread and dried meat at this point. Darius surveyed the spread and shook his head. "This won't do. Cyril, fill the canteens. Jean, you've lived in the woods before. I assume you know which berries are edible."

She nodded. We had talked through our thoughts, but she had spoken very little about her parents. I had the feeling she was glad they were far away, safe without her magic luring Darius to them.

"Good. Evran, you obviously know how to hunt. Take the hounds. I assume the darkness won't be a problem for you."

"No, my lord," he said with a scowl.

"I can help Jean," I offered.

"You'll stay with me and build the fire. If you're not all back within the hour, I'll come looking for you."

Jean and Evran cast me worried glances, but I shook my head. If there was something he wanted to discuss with me, perhaps it was better to get it over with.

When the others were gone, Darius cleared some of the dirt with a branch. "Gather some dried sticks for the fire."

I returned a few minutes later with an armful, which he placed in the center of a ring of stones he'd assembled.

"Have you ever done this before?"

I arched an eyebrow. "Built a fire?"

"With your power, Liora."

"Oh." I shook my head. "No. I didn't even know I could produce heat until that day at the palace."

He rubbed his thumb against the side of his forefinger. "I remember."

We sat on our haunches next to each other, and in the dim light of my glow, with his sleeves rolled up and his hair mussed, he could be mistaken for any young man. I wondered what he was like before he found his powers, if he'd always been cruel.

I didn't want to be here with Darius, but I needed answers. "You said, 'I knew it,' when I burned you. What exactly did you know?"

He glanced at me from the corner of his eye. "I knew what your power was."

"If you knew all along, why did you ever pretend otherwise? Why bring Mina to Corone? You could have just taken me."

He sat down all the way, stretching his legs. I copied his posture, tired from squatting after so many hours in the saddle. "In all my years—and there have been many—I've never seen anyone with their magic as suppressed as yours was. I couldn't be sure if what I felt was merely weak magic or power that had never been given the room to grow. Do you even realize how you've changed, just in the short time we've known each other?"

I didn't answer. I knew I had grown these past few weeks, not just in my powers, but as a person. But I also knew the cost of that growth, the danger I'd put everyone in. And I didn't like the implication that he was in some way responsible for the change in me. Who knew what I could have been if I'd never had to hide in the first place?

"Here," he said. "Let me show you."

I glanced into the woods. It would be easy to let my guard down around Darius for a moment, when I was exhausted and he was doing nothing more than teaching me how to build a fire. But it was entirely possible this was some kind of trap I couldn't see. I sat back into a crouch; the pain would keep my mind focused, and I could run more easily from this position.

"I think you've realized by now that anger brings out your heat. So let it fill you now. Not like in the tapestry, of course— I have no desire to burn down the woods. Just here, in the tip of your finger. Think of some small annoyance."

That was simple enough. I thought about how Darius hadn't let us sleep, focusing my anger into the tip of my right pointer finger. As I watched, the glow emanating from my skin began to concentrate there, and I could feel the flesh getting hot. Within seconds, smoke plumed from the kindling. A moment later, it burst into flame.

"That's excellent for your first time. Have you been practicing?"

I tried not to think about Evran, as if Darius was the one who could read minds. "A little."

"Imagine how good you could be by now if you'd had a teacher, if your father hadn't repressed you like this."

"He did it to protect me," I said as the fire began to crackle. "From you."

He poked at the flames with a stick but didn't respond.

"How do you know so much about my power, anyway?"

He looked at me then, the fire blazing orange in his eyes, and I realized that I'd asked the right question without even knowing it. "I used to be like you, Liora."

A chill passed over the back of my neck and along my arms,

and I sat back all the way, hugging my knees to my chest. "What are you talking about?"

"Who I am now, what I can do... This hasn't always been me."

My stomach churned so violently I was sure I was going to be sick. "Is that what you wanted to tell me? Is that why you're here?"

He started to reach for my hand, but I pushed up to my feet. "I told you not to touch me."

"I'm sorry. I forget sometimes."

I wondered what Jean would hear now if she could listen to his thoughts. "I don't trust you. I don't see how I ever could after what you've done."

He looked up at me. "I don't expect you to."

The very fact that he was agreeing with me confused me further. "I don't understand you. One minute you're throwing my sister in the dungeon, threatening to kill her, and the next you're trying to make me feel sorry for you."

He stood up abruptly, and as much as I wanted to, I refused to shrink back from his height. "Not sorry for me, Liora. Never that. I only want you to understand."

Something moved in the corner of my light, and I turned to find Evran watching us, two dead squirrels hanging from his hands. The hounds sat next to him, panting and licking their muzzles as blood dripped onto the dried leaves.

"Are you all right?" he asked me.

It took me a moment to tamp down my glow, which had intensified along with my anger. "I'm fine. Lord Darius showed me how to start a fire."

"Then I guess it's a good thing I found dinner." He held up the squirrels for emphasis and the dogs whimpered.

"Good work." Darius was his indifferent self again instantly. "I'll skin them if you like."

"I can manage."

Darius shrugged. "Suit yourself. Liora, you should lay out our bedrolls in the cave. I'll go check on Jean."

He disappeared into the trees, though I was pretty sure Evran had also noticed he went the opposite direction from Jean. I would have sworn I'd rattled him somehow, if I didn't believe him to be incapable of it. Perhaps Jean was right and the sight of the boy's body had shaken him. But for someone who claimed to be empty, he certainly seemed to be feeling something.

We rode through the next day and part of the night, but though we never seemed to get farther behind the Lusiri, we also weren't gaining on them. Finally, the trees began to thin, a sign we were approaching a town. The road was a welcome sight, though the presence of people meant the possibility of more deaths; weaving in and out of trees, jumping over fallen logs, and avoiding rocks and stones whenever possible had exhausted the horses as well as us.

I hadn't had a good night's rest since I entered the tapestry. Sleeping on the cold, hard ground was almost worse than not sleeping at all. I trusted my horse enough now that I occasionally let myself doze while I rode, jarring awake whenever I began to slip to the side. But blisters had formed on my palms from gripping the reins, bursting open only to form again, and my backside was chafed raw.

As we neared Hander, the crowds began to thicken, and Darius ordered us to dismount. Although people stared at us as we led our horses through the streets, no one said anything, and there was none of the grief or fear we'd seen in Craven.

"It seems the Lusiri didn't come here," Darius said. "Which means they crossed the road where it met the woods and continued north."

"That's good, isn't it?" I asked.

"Yes and no. I find it hard to believe the Lusiri haven't needed to feed again."

My stomach twisted uneasily. If they had fed, and we had missed it…

"I want to ask the townspeople if anyone is missing, just in case."

"Does that mean we're going to stay the night?"

Darius's eyes traveled over me, assessing. The sight must not have encouraged him because he frowned and glanced at the rest of our company. "We'll stay. Everyone could use a bath and a hot meal before we enter Tezhia."

Tezhia was the kingdom north of Antalla. We were already in the foothills of the Tezhian mountains, which we would need to cross to get to the snowfields where the Lusiri were likely headed. The thought of camping in snow made me want to weep, but the promise of a hot bath and a real bed tonight helped.

Darius stopped a passing man with his hand. "Excuse me, sir."

The man lowered the newspaper he'd been reading like he was ready to start a fight, until he saw who had stopped him. "Lord Darius." He bowed uncertainly. "We haven't seen you in Hander for months." He glanced at the hounds. "Are you here for anyone in particular?"

He rounded up the mages then, Jean said in my head. *He took three and left the ones too weak to be a threat. The townspeople must have thought they were safe from him for a while, at least.*

"We're just passing through." Darius gestured to the rest

of us. "And as you can see, we're in need of a place to eat and sleep. Can you recommend an inn?"

The man seemed as suspicious of Darius's calm demeanor as I was. "Uh, yes, my lord. The Silver Arrow is several blocks from here."

We followed the man's directions to the inn, a white brick building with a black roof and shutters. Evran and Cyril made sure the horses were cared for while Jean and I gathered our belongings. Every step hurt, but I told myself it would all be worth it when I got to take a hot bath. Darius paid for three rooms and told us to meet him for dinner at seven. In the meantime, he was going to find out if anyone had seen the Lusiri.

"Jean, you'll come with me," Darius said. "In case anyone thinks it's a good idea to lie."

She didn't try to hide her annoyance as she followed him back out of the inn without a word. Considering everything she'd been through, she was holding herself together remarkably well, though I heard her crying at night sometimes. Once I'd seen her resting her head on Evran's shoulder while we sat around the campfire. It had ignited a petty spark of jealousy in me, but I told myself to let it go. Jean deserved to find comfort where she could. I may have lost my mother, but I was so young then, and I'd had years to mourn the loss. Jean didn't know if she'd ever see her parents again.

The hot bath waiting in my room felt like one of life's greatest luxuries to my aching muscles and dirt-caked skin, but I didn't linger. I wanted time to speak to Evran before Darius returned. I changed quickly into the one simple dress I'd brought with me, combing out my hair and twisting it up on my head before going to his room.

Cyril answered in only his trousers, still toweling his hair dry from his bath. I'd forgotten what he looked like under all the dirt and grime. "You look nice," he said, as if realizing the same thing about me. "Evran's taking a bath. Should I send him to your room when he's finished?"

"The dining room, if you don't mind. I'm so hungry I'm afraid I might start gnawing on the furniture."

When he smiled, his clear blue eyes lit up. I knew then I'd been too hard on Mina. It was inevitable that she would fall for him. "I'll tell him."

It was four o'clock, not yet time for dinner, so I went to the pub downstairs and asked the barkeep to bring me whatever the kitchen was willing to make. It was all dark wood and heavy curtains inside the pub, making my glow obvious, and several patrons turned to glare at me. But the chicken pie the barkeep brought out was the best thing I'd ever tasted, so I focused all my attention on that, devouring most of it before realizing I should have saved some for Evran. I was starting to wonder if he'd come at all when I saw him winding his way through the tables to the bar where I sat.

"I'm sorry," I said, gesturing to the last few crumbs on my plate as he took a stool next to mine. "I guess I was even hungrier than I realized."

He smiled, but even after his bath, he looked weary. "It's all right. I'll eat at dinner."

"How are you?" We'd had so little time to speak lately. I would have given anything for one of our lazy days in the forest, lying on our backs in the fallen leaves, finding shapes in the clouds.

"I'm... Well, to be honest, I'm worried about you."

I blinked in surprise. "What? Why? I've just had a bath and a delicious meal. I'm with you. All things considered, this is the happiest I've been in weeks." I searched his face, the piercing eyes that made me feel like he could see right through me to the thing that made my light, the hidden heart of everything I was. "You're not talking about my physical wellbeing, are you?"

His brow furrowed, and I knew he didn't want to say what he was thinking.

"Evran?"

He glanced away for a moment, sighing. "It's not you. It's Darius. He's different with you than the rest of us. I've talked to Cyril and Jean. We're all afraid he's manipulating you."

I scoffed. "And you don't think *I'm* worried about that? I'm not a fool. I know what he is. But I also know that he's the only one who can tell me about my powers. As long as he understands them and I don't, I'm even more vulnerable to his games."

"I know. I just... I don't trust him, Liora."

"But do you trust me?" I squeezed his hand, willing him to remember the fact that he was the only person I'd ever voluntarily revealed my powers to, the only person I had given my heart to. If I could trust him with that, surely he could trust me now.

His voice was hoarse when he answered. "Yes."

I swallowed the lump in my throat, wishing I believed him. "Can we go upstairs? I don't know when we'll be alone together again, and I just want to spend time with you while we can."

As I said the last words, a hush fell over the room. I turned to see Darius standing in the doorway to the pub, his eyebrows furrowed above his golden eyes as he scanned the room. For me. His posture softened as soon as our eyes met, though Evran stiffened visibly beside me.

Everyone buried their faces in their mugs or behind menus

as he strode through the pub toward us. Without sitting, he leaned down to my ear. "The prince has taken ill. I must return to Corone immediately."

TWENTY-TWO

Darius was to return to the palace the easy way, via Cyril. Evran had gone with Cyril to help him pack his belongings, and Jean, who hadn't had a chance to bathe or rest earlier, had gone back to our room. Darius had asked me to accompany him to the stables, but his tone made it clear it wasn't a request.

A messenger had ridden for several days to tell Darius the news. I was relieved we'd finally have some time without Darius, but I was genuinely worried about the prince, who had seemed so healthy at his birth. Had Margana somehow failed in her spell? A witch healer was already with the prince, one of several kept in the palace, but the king and queen were as helpless as children without Darius. It was frightening to realize that our kingdom was in their hands, until I remembered what Margana had said: Darius might not be king, but he ruled Antalla regardless.

"You can use our horses while Cyril and I are gone," Darius

said as he searched his saddle bags for something I couldn't see. "You'll need more supplies soon anyway." He pocketed whatever he'd been looking for and walked to his stallion, who was tied up in the aisle of the barn. "I could be gone for a week."

I felt a spark of hope. We could search for voids far easier now, and I'd be guaranteed more time alone with Evran. "What do we do if we catch up to the Lusiri?"

"Track them from a distance. I don't want you getting too close. I trust you and the others won't run off in my absence?"

I gave him an incredulous look. "You've got Mina and Margana locked up at the palace, and Jean has nowhere to go, since you separated her from her parents."

"The hounds did that."

I knew I should bite my tongue, but I couldn't hold myself back anymore. "*Your* hounds! You can stop all of this. You could capture the Lusiri, destroy them, and let mages live freely. You can do anything you want!" I realized I was shouting and forced myself to lower my voice. "I don't care what you say. You and I are *nothing* alike."

He leaned back against his horse's side and folded his arms over his chest. "Have you never asked yourself why the other star fell in Sylvan?"

"I—what?"

"The star that hangs over Sylvan, the first one to fall. That was *my* star."

For a moment I couldn't catch my breath. That star had fallen a hundred years ago, at least. I'd never gotten to hear the story of how it first came to be there, refusing to let Mina tell me when she came back from the ceremony that night, but I'd never imagined it was because another mage was involved. And certainly not *this* mage.

My stomach plummeted. This was why I reminded Darius of himself. And this was what Father had known about me, why he said my magic was dangerous. No wonder Father hadn't wanted me to feel anything—he thought I could become a monster, too.

Darius lifted a hand as if he was going to touch me, then dropped it. "I'm sorry. I imagine you must have felt very alone. I know I did."

"But you don't glow," I said, still unable to accept what I was hearing.

He looked down at his hands. There was no light there at all, just sun-kissed skin. "I did."

"What happened?"

He breathed a heavy sigh. "I burned out."

I stared at him, unable to form a response. I tried to imagine myself without my light, but it was like trying to imagine myself without my sisters; I wouldn't be me anymore.

"I'll tell you more when we meet in Iverna, the last city before Tezhia. If you haven't caught the Lusiri by then, that is."

I blinked, trying to make the mental shift from what he'd just told me to our current reality. "You won't be joining us until then?"

"Iverna is the only city north of here that Cyril has been to." He dropped his gaze. "Tell me something before I go. If I'd never come to Sylvan and discovered you, what would you be doing right this minute?"

"Wh-what?" It was the second time he'd caught me off guard in as many minutes.

"You're convinced your life is worse because of me, but what had you really done with it before I came along?"

I was so taken aback I struggled for words. Yes, I was grateful my magic was out in the open, that I didn't have to hide anymore. But he didn't get to take credit for that. All Darius did was cause grief and pain.

"*You* are the reason I was hiding in the first place," I ground out. "Maybe I never would have considered leaving Sylvan before you discovered me. But I'll also never know what my life would have been like if you didn't exist. So don't expect me to thank you. Ever."

He was silent for so long I started to walk away.

"What about Evran?"

I turned to face him. "What *about* Evran?"

"I've heard him talking to Cyril and Jean. Did you know he doesn't want to stay in Sylvan?"

I hadn't known he'd been talking to the others about it, but then, I also hadn't told him that I planned to leave. "He thinks he'll harm people if he stays. But he's wrong."

"What if he's not? Perhaps he knows something you don't."

"What are you talking about?" I was so flustered I didn't move to stop him when he took my hands. My anger was already coursing through me, but it balked at his touch. I didn't feel the pull of his magic now. It was just like holding anyone's hands. Only it wasn't just anyone.

"I don't have to take from people, Liora."

I ripped my hands free. "Oh, so you just do that for fun?"

His lips twitched in a grin. "Sarcasm suits you."

"Why are you pretending to be nice to me? I know the things you've done. What you're going to do to Mina if we don't catch the Lusiri. What you did to the girl with the diamond tears."

That at least seemed to catch his attention. "I did nothing to that girl, Liora."

I shook my head. Father would never have made up something so horrible, even if it was just a tactic to keep me safe.

"You ordered your guards to cut off Margana's hands in front of me. You freely admitted you burned down The Crystal Gazer. You've shown yourself capable of immense cruelty. Why bother pretending you have any compassion?"

"I won't deny that I've done things I'm ashamed of. Terrible things. But I have never lied to you."

I didn't know what to believe anymore, if I could trust anyone now. I didn't want Darius to see how much his words upset me. Not just about himself or the girl with the diamond tears, but about Evran, about what he might be capable of. Something had convinced him he should stay in the tapestry, and now something was telling him to leave.

"I'll see you in Tezhia," Darius called as I walked away. "Be safe."

That night, it was just Jean, Evran, and me. None of us had an appetite after the events of the day, but we weren't tired either, so we decided to go for a walk along the river that bordered Hander. The streets were quiet; Darius hadn't ordered a curfew the way he had in Craven, but everyone knew he was in town.

"Were you able to read his thoughts?" I asked Jean after I told them what he'd said to me. "Does he seem worried about the prince?"

"I don't know." Her brow was furrowed in concern, and I wondered what it must be like for a person so used to being able to glean people's thoughts to deal with someone like Darius. She walked between Evran and me, forcing me to crane my neck forward to see Evran's face. He'd been quiet all afternoon, and I had the horrible feeling he was going to disappear on me again, simply walk into the forest without a trace. "He does seem worried, but his thoughts are scattered."

"And my powers?" I told Jean about the star as Evran watched on, clearly concerned. "Did you catch any of his thoughts about that?"

She shook her head. "I told you, my access is very limited. But there is something in his past that drives him, something so terrible that it has become part of who is."

"Do you think there's any chance he can change?" I asked.

Evran broke in. "You mean become good?"

"Maybe not good," I said quickly. "But human?"

I was too afraid to voice my fear out loud—that if Darius had once been like me, then there was a chance *I* could become like *him*. Because if Darius was irredeemable, what did that mean for me?

"Oh, he's definitely still human," Jean said. "I may not be able to read his thoughts, and there is something empty or blank in him when I try to feel him out. But I've reached into the consciousness of things that are not human—animals, the woven hounds—I've even tried to reach out to the Lusiri. It's very different."

That was some comfort, at least. Maybe there was a chance we could convince Darius not to complete the tapestry by appealing to the part of him that was still human. But on the other hand, if he really did have some humanity left, that meant he simply didn't care about how many people he harmed.

As we turned onto a stone bridge, our shadows stretched out in front of us on the stones, the sinking sun warm on our backs.

"This is my favorite time of day," Evran said quietly.

"Twilight?" I asked.

"Mmm. It's the time when the shadows and the light seem to be teasing one another. But in a playful way, you know?"

I waved a hand, my shadow waving back at us. "I'd say the shadows are winning."

"For now, maybe. But then the morning comes, and the light chases away the shadows. It's like a game of tag."

"Then why do you like sunset more than dawn?"

He cast me a sideways grin. "What can I say, I like it better when the shadows win."

I sighed. "Twilight was always bittersweet for me. It meant 'hurry up, get home before someone sees you.'" As if to prove my point, the glow in my skin brightened in the fading light.

Jean laughed a little, and I looked at her questioningly. "Sorry, I was just remembering something. My mom said when she was a girl, her mother gave her a hideous mask to wear whenever she had to leave the house in the evenings. It had a hooked nose with a hairy wart on the end."

Evran smiled. "What for?"

"To protect her from Belle Sabine. She only killed the most beautiful girls, so she could take their beauty." Her smile faded. "I wish we'd had something to protect us from Darius."

I put a hand out to comfort her, but she shrugged me off. "I'm all right. I just want to be alone for a few minutes."

Evran took my hand, slowing me so Jean could walk on ahead. "Let her go."

Together, we made our way to the side of the bridge. Evran found a pebble on the stone wall and tossed it into the water. "I wish…"

"What?" I asked, searching his eyes.

"I wish we were just a boy and a girl walking on a bridge. Just for one night."

"Just for one night, we are."

He wrapped his arm around my waist, and I felt the warm ember of desire ignite at his touch. There was a part of him that I'd never been able to access before, and now I knew it was the part that felt a connection to the tapestry, that believed his magic was evil in some way. If I could just get him to confide in me, I knew we could find a way through all this, together.

The colors of the sunset rippled in the water below us like spilled paint. "I know that all this time you were searching for a way to destroy the tapestry," I began. "But I don't know what happened between us, when my light flickered and your eyes changed. That wasn't about the tapestry, was it? It was about me."

He studied me for a moment, his face so close I could see the faint constellation of freckles across his nose. I'd drawn it in the dirt one day, asking him to identify it. He'd said it looked like Vulpecula, the little fox, and he'd promised to show it to me some night, as if he'd truly believed we'd get the chance. "I saw something when we touched. A vision or a dream, I don't know what it was. And I believed that if I stayed, I would only hurt you."

I leaned back. "What do you mean, a vision?"

"I can't explain it, really. It was like you were a candle, and I snuffed you out."

I lifted a hand to his cheek, touching the soft spot where his jaw met his ear. "That's ridiculous. You would never hurt me."

"I know. But—"

We were so close I only had to rise onto my toes to kiss him. A tear slipped free of my lashes when I closed my eyes and pulled him closer, pressing myself against him to remind him that I wasn't a girl anymore but a young woman who would no longer be pushed aside or left behind. He hadn't given me the chance to show him how much I loved him, all of him, even the parts he feared. He needed to believe that I would never betray him, no matter what lies Darius told me.

When I lowered myself back onto my heels, I opened my eyes. His were still closed, his thick lashes resting on his cheeks. They fluttered open slowly, green as forests. I may not have convinced him yet, but I saw him for who he was, and I loved him for it.

"You know, it's nice being just a boy and a girl on a bridge," he said, smiling. "We should make a habit of it."

"Deal." I was about to kiss him again when Jean's voice cut into my thoughts so loudly I knew if she were speaking, she'd be screaming.

TWENTY-THREE

Evran and I raced across the bridge to Jean. The body of a girl, or what was left of her, lay sprawled facedown, as if she'd been crawling away from something. The hole, or void, or *nothingness* the Lusiri left behind was so close to her one of her feet was being drawn in. Without thinking, I ran to her and took hold of her withered hands, dragging her empty shell away before she could be consumed.

"So the Lusiri *were* here." Evran peered at the woods on the other side of the field where we stood.

"How have none of the townspeople noticed this?" I asked.

Jean shook her head. "A lot of them are so afraid of Darius that they haven't left their homes since he arrived."

"Let's just be grateful we found it now," Evran said.

I shuddered, thinking of the holes that could still be out there that we might not find until it was too late. I glanced at the girl again, the way her dress fit her shriveled body as loosely as if she were a child wearing her mother's clothes.

The light rose up in me with only a little effort, as I leaned down and pressed my hand to the slowly growing absence. It was the largest we'd encountered yet, which meant the Lusiri had probably fed here more than twelve hours ago. But it still shrank away from my touch. I was getting stronger, at least.

When the void was gone, I rose to my feet and dusted my hands off, trying not to look at the girl's body. "Now what?"

"I don't think we should stay here tonight," Evran said. "We can't afford to let the Lusiri get farther ahead of us."

Jean nodded. "Agreed."

"Do we bury her? It seems wrong to just leave her like this."

Evran chewed on his knuckle for a moment, considering. "We can't bury her. If we do, her family won't know what happened to her. I know it feels wrong, but I think it's for the best."

"We should go back to the inn and fetch our horses. At least we know which way the Lusiri went." Still north, still in the forest. There would be no easy riding on the roads for the next week. No bed or hot meal. But there was Evran, and for now, that was enough.

We found the bodies of two deer and one wolf over the next three days. Why the Lusiri should be getting hungrier, I didn't know, but the holes left behind were smaller, and the carcasses were an easy trail to follow. With our own horses' loads lightened thanks to the extra packhorses, we made better time, though once we hit the snowline, I wasn't sure how fast we'd be able to travel.

The nights were cold, even with a fire, but I had gained enough control of my power to warm myself while I slept, with Evran and Jean close to me on either side. We talked during the day, about our childhoods, about Darius, about what we'd do when we found the Lusiri. But while Jean told us stories of a country called Belasava, where mages were among the elite and made up more than half of the governing council, Evran never talked about the future.

We were just two days from Iverna when it began to snow, lightly at first, then enough to stick. It unnerved us all. We'd been told it wouldn't snow on this side of the Tezhian mountains, especially not in autumn. But we were grateful for the snow for one reason: it revealed a fresh set of tracks.

It wasn't the Lusiri, whose hoofprints were twice the size of a horse's. This was another horse, and its tracks followed the Lusiri's closely. Someone was hunting them, someone other than us.

When we came upon a steaming pile of droppings, we knew we were close. The question was whether or not we wanted to catch up to this person.

"Do you think Darius sent someone else?" I asked.

"It's certainly possible he doesn't trust us," Jean replied. "But how would they have gotten ahead of us?"

"He could have dispatched them in Hander before we left." Evran rose from where he knelt by the droppings. "But the fact that we're catching up makes me think this isn't an experienced hunter. We haven't been going fast enough."

"So do we try to catch up or stay behind?"

Jean spun around a moment before we heard the branch crack.

A giant of a man dressed all in black stood amid the trees. "Looks like the decision has been made for you."

"Who are you?" Evran demanded, putting a protective arm out to shield me. "What are you doing here?"

"The same thing you are, by the look of things."

"Hunting the Lusiri? Why?"

"Is that what they are?" He glanced at me. There was a

scar across one side of his face, all the way from his ear to his nose, which appeared to have been broken more than once. "I know you."

"What?"

"We've met before," he said. "In Corone."

I thought back to my trips to the city, trying to recall when I might possibly have seen him. But his was a face I would remember. "I don't recognize you."

"You wouldn't," Jean said. "That's not his real form. Or *her* real form, I should say."

The man raised his lip in a silent snarl.

Jean didn't seem impressed. "You're a shape-shifter."

He folded his arms across his broad chest. "And you're a mentalist."

"I am. So there's no sense in hiding your true form. We're not going to harm you."

The man scowled. "And why should I trust you? You're working for Lord Darius."

"Not by choice."

He looked around for a moment. "Where is Darius now?"

"Back in Corone." Evran lowered his arm slowly. "The prince is ill."

The man continued to watch us, considering, and finally shrugged. "Oh, very well." In the blink of an eye, he was gone, replaced by a girl with red curls and a mischievous grin, still clad all in black.

It took me a moment to realize where I'd seen her before. *"Helen?"*

Evran turned to look at me. "You know her?"

"She was Mina's roommate in Corone. What are you doing here, Helen? And why are you all alone?"

She folded her arms again. "Why are *you* here? Working

for Darius, of all people. Did you know he burned down The Crystal Gazer? Cherie was killed in the fire. So were several other performers. He collapsed the tunnel so no one could go back and recover anything."

Fresh guilt and horror twisted my stomach. "I'm so sorry for your loss. And I'm so sorry for any role I may have had in it. But please believe me when I say that we are not working for Darius." I took a step toward her. "Do you know what happened to Mina? Have you seen her?"

"Not since she was taken to the dungeon. I took another form when I found out what Darius had done to the club and left. I've been following him ever since."

"But he went back to Corone days ago."

"I knew he had gone, but I figured if I couldn't get to him, I could at least get to the thing he was chasing. I knew it had to be valuable."

Evran glanced at me, then back to Helen. "It's also deadly. You should go home."

She barked a dry laugh. "I'd love to. Got one I can borrow?"

Jean lowered her voice and said quietly, "She's a drifter, like me."

Helen's lip curled in annoyance. "Get out of my thoughts, kid."

Jean was petite for her age, but she raised her chin in challenge. "I'm not a kid. Reveal your true form."

My jaw dropped open. "What?"

"Let's set up camp for the night," Evran suggested. "It seems like we all have some explaining to do."

Evran went first, filling Helen in on the most important details. When it was her turn, she took a seat on her bedroll, clearing her throat as if she was about to give a speech.

"I suppose I should start from the beginning."

Jean, who was sitting next to her, sighed. "Can you please use your true form? This is distracting."

"I never use my real form," Helen answered. "It's too risky."

"Why?" I asked.

"Because Darius has seen it before."

There was far more to Helen than I could have imagined. Clearly, she wasn't as naive as she'd let on after the magic show. I wondered how much of her past Mina really knew. "Darius won't meet back up with us until we get to Iverna. You're safe for now."

Helen looked skeptical, but finally she shrugged, and between the time it took for her shoulders to rise and fall, she was in a different form. Now a girl close to my age sat in front of us. She had black hair cut short on the sides and left long on top, thick brows, and dark eyes. Slender but muscular under her tight-fitting black clothing, she looked like she might actually stand a chance of killing Darius.

"That's better," Jean said with a satisfied nod.

Helen leaned back on her bedroll, eyeing Jean, who blushed under her scrutiny. "So how exactly did you get mixed up with these two?"

"Darius's hounds hunted us down in the woods outside of Sylvan. I got separated from my parents. I don't know where they are now."

Helen was quiet for a moment, then touched Jean on the shoulder. "Well, chin up. At least they're alive. You'll find them again."

One side of Jean's mouth tugged into a smile. "I hope so. What happened to your family?" I wasn't sure if she was just being polite or if she already knew the truth.

"My mother died a year ago when a plague went through

our convent. I never knew my father. I just know Darius ruined our lives, like so many other mages', and if I wanted ven-
geance I needed to go to Corone. My mother warned me to
never let Darius discover my power. She said he'd find some
way to use it. Or kill me."

Jean and I exchanged a glance as she read my thoughts.

"What was your mother's name?" I asked Helen. It was
probably just a coincidence, but a woman raising her daughter in a convent, their lives ruined by Darius, sounded suspiciously familiar.

"Salome," Helen replied. "A witch, like me."

A chill ran over me. Salome wasn't a rare name, but it
couldn't be a coincidence. Helen was the former queen's
daughter. From the way she mentioned her mother, it didn't
sound like she had any idea she was a princess and potentially
the rightful heir to the throne. If that was the case, she was in
even greater danger than she realized. Darius wouldn't send
her away again to die in obscurity; he would kill her.

Jean and I shared a look as I mentally explained my theory.

"And you were working at the palace, right under Darius's nose?" If Evran had made the connection between Helen
and the queen, he didn't show it. "How did you keep from
being discovered?"

"With this." She pulled a leather cord out of her collar, revealing a flat disk of turquoise with a hole through the middle. "My mother gave it to me. It shields my magic so Darius
can't detect me. Neither can his hounds."

"May I?" Evran held his hand out for the amulet, turning
it over in his fingers carefully for a moment before giving it
back. "I've never seen anything like it. I don't suppose you
know where we could get more?"

She shook her head and cast me a sideways glance. "I have

to say, I was surprised to find you here. From what Mina told me, you rarely leave the house, and you seemed so uncomfortable at The Crystal Gazer."

My memories of that night were so vivid—not just the performances, but my own fear and eventual wonderment. It was becoming increasingly difficult to imagine caring what strangers thought of my magic. "I wasn't raised to embrace my powers, or even to understand them. But I would do anything for my sister."

"And I'll do anything to avenge my family and friends. Which is why I have to get the Lusiri."

I admired her determination, but she couldn't possibly understand what she was saying. "Darius will never allow you to take them. He'll kill anyone who gets in his way."

"If the Lusiri don't kill you first," Evran added. "You have no idea what you're facing."

She stretched her long legs in front of her and leaned over, easily reaching past her toes. She was catlike in her grace and agility, but there was something lethal in her eyes. "You're right. I saw what they'd done to some poor animal, and I knew I didn't stand a chance on my own. I was hoping you'd be willing to work with me."

I shook my head. "We understand your motives, Helen. Better than anyone. But if Darius could be easily killed, I'm quite certain someone would have done it by now."

"So, what? You're just going to give him the Lusiri? And then what happens?"

"We don't know," Jean said. "But Darius has Mina and Evran's mother. He made it clear he'd imprison me if I didn't come. We're hoping we'll find a way to stop him. For now, Liora has been filling up the holes left behind by the Lusiri."

Helen sighed. "I'd better show you where the carcass is, then."

Evran rose to his feet and offered me his hand. "And then you'll leave?" he asked Helen. "You won't try to interfere?"

"I'll consider it."

It seemed that was the best we could do for now, so we followed her through the woods on foot for several minutes, until we came to the void. It wasn't as large as the last one, but the body of whatever the Lusiri had killed was gone. It came back into view as the void shrank, something black and furry. A wolf maybe, or a bear.

"What if we've missed some?" I asked Evran as we headed back to our camp.

"We haven't. Try not to worry."

"But Helen's right. We still don't have a plan for how we're going to stop Darius."

Helen settled back onto her bedroll and cleaned her dirty fingernails with a splinter. "The answer seems obvious to me. If the Lusiri are capable of destroying the world, we need to kill them."

"But Mina and Margana—"

"Are just two people. I know that sounds harsh, but are you really willing to sacrifice thousands of lives, maybe millions, for two?"

I was too shocked to speak, but Jean placed her hand on Helen's arm. "If Darius had your mother, you wouldn't be saying that."

She dropped the splinter and folded her arms across her chest. "Maybe not," she conceded. "But I still don't see what choice there is."

Evran squeezed my hand. "I'll think of something."

As much as I wanted to put all of my faith in him, if there

was a solution to our problem, we'd have thought of it by now. And maybe I was being selfish, but I refused to consider Helen's solution. I gripped the star pendant in my palm until it turned white-hot from my anger. My sister needed me, and I would not let her down.

Evran and Helen, who had spent enough time on the road to learn how to hunt, went off to find dinner while Jean and I gathered firewood.

"Can we trust her?" I asked Jean when they were out of earshot.

"As much as we can trust anyone," she said, carefully arranging the fire. "She has serious reasons for hating Darius, too."

"Does she know who she really is?"

Jean shook her head. "No."

"Should we tell her?"

Jean tossed a small twig aside, considering. "On the one hand, I think she has the right to know. But I'm afraid if we tell her, she may act even more rashly if she encounters Darius. And that will be dangerous for everyone involved, including her. I won't pretend to understand how royal succession works, but if she *is* the rightful heir, she needs to be protected. And it's all the more reason for us to somehow find a way to stop Darius."

I nodded and helped Jean place stones around the perimeter of the fire. We had enough on our plates without adding a banished princess to our list.

What I still couldn't understand was how Darius could possibly have gone from being "like me" to like *him*. Could power corrupt a good person to that extent, or did there have to be some innate evil in a person to let it get to that point? And how could my powers of light and heat possibly become like Darius's? He had to be mistaken. Maybe our magic was similar, but I refused to believe he'd ever truly been like me.

"It doesn't mean you'll be like that," Jean said suddenly.

"What?"

"I'm sorry. You just...think loudly sometimes."

I rubbed my arms against the chill. Whenever I felt sad or weak, my heat was nowhere to be found. So far only anger and love worked, and right now I felt neither.

Jean placed the last stick on her neatly assembled pile. "The fire is ready for you."

I knew I'd never be able to summon the heat to light the fire, not with our situation so heavy on my conscience. "*I'm* not ready, unfortunately."

She offered a sympathetic smile. "I can light it the old-fashioned way." She pulled a chunk of flint and steel from her pocket.

I nodded for her to go ahead. "I'm just tired, I think."

"It's more than just being tired, Liora. You've been under a lot of strain. We all have."

I moved closer to the quickly rising flames and wrapped my wool blanket around me. "Do you ever listen to Evran's thoughts?"

"Sometimes. I can't always help it."

"Does he ever think about me?"

She stared at me for a moment, her gray eyes impossible to read.

"I'm sorry. I shouldn't ask that. His private thoughts are his own."

Jean sat back on her haunches. "It's one thing for me to accidentally overhear someone's thoughts. But it's another thing to tell other people what they are."

I looked away, ashamed. "I know."

"So I'm only going to tell you this once, and I hope you won't ask me again."

My eyes darted back to hers. "I won't. I promise."

"Everything Evran does, he does for you. He always has."

I wondered if I could melt from relief. A few snowflakes fell from the sky, evaporating instantly on my skin. Maybe Evran couldn't tell me exactly how he felt, but then, I struggled with the same thing. And Jean had no reason to lie. "Thank you for telling me."

"You're welcome."

A few minutes passed in silence. But as I stared at the flames, I remembered what Evran had seen when we touched before we went into the tapestry: me, a flame, and him snuffing me out. I didn't know if I'd convinced him that his vision was wrong. And I didn't know what he saw when he touched me now.

Jean smiled and placed her hand on my forearm. "He sees the candle coming back to life."

TWENTY-FOUR

We reached Iverna too late.

It was a border town, with a population of permanent residents but more people passing through: fur traders and trappers coming down from the north, farmers coming from the south to sell the fresh produce that couldn't grow here. There was gold in Tezhia, for anyone willing to brave temperatures well below freezing to find it and potentially lose their life to the monsters said to live on the other side of the mountains.

We arrived in the late afternoon, when it should have been bustling with life. But the city seemed almost deserted. We walked through quiet streets lined with houses and shops built from dark wood, their eaves and shutters painted blue, green, or white. Small silver amulets shaped like curved swords hung from many of the door handles. To guard against the evils from the north, Jean explained after listening to someone's thoughts.

But the amulets hadn't protected them from the Lusiri.

They had torn through the town early that morning, killing two people at the edge of a frozen pond. They'd been preparing to fish, according to the innkeeper of the white-trimmed inn we had decided to stay at, not least because it was the first one we found and we were all exhausted.

I stared at the stuffed white fox wearing a velvet waistcoat mounted behind the innkeeper's desk while he checked us in.

"The White Fox," he said, following my gaze. "The inn is named for it."

Helen, who had taken the redheaded form she'd used in Corone, snickered. She had promised to leave first thing tomorrow morning, after she'd had a good night's sleep and a hot meal. Jean said she was telling the truth, but people's truths could change.

"Has a man called Darius been here?" Evran asked as he took the keys to our rooms. "He'd be traveling with a young man with black hair."

"Not that I'm aware of," the innkeeper said. He was short and compact, wearing a waistcoat similar to the fox's. His fluffy white hair even resembled fur.

"Perhaps you can let us know if they come by. In the meantime, can you show us where the bodies were found?"

The man eyed us suspiciously. "I can't leave the inn, but I can tell you it was near the large black willow on the far side of the lake."

We thanked him and took our belongings to our rooms. We'd gotten four: one for Jean and me, one for Helen, one for Evran and Cyril, and another for Darius. Jean and I took turns washing ourselves with the pitcher of hot water the innkeeper provided. It wasn't as good as the bath in Hander, but it was better than nothing.

I met Evran downstairs, and we walked around the lake together. It was our first moment alone since our kiss on the bridge, and despite the morbid task ahead of us, I was grateful for whatever time we could get.

I raised my collar against the cold breeze coming off the lake. "We were lucky Darius wasn't here before us. I don't know what we'll do if we come across one of the holes in his presence."

"We'll get through it, just like we did before Darius went back to Corone. Together."

I reached for his hand, smiling when he took it without hesitation. I kept thinking of what Jean had said, that Evran saw a candle reigniting when we touched now. I knew part of the reason Evran seemed more confident was that Darius wasn't here. Without his looming presence, I had clarity. It was easy to see how evil he was, to believe Jean when she said I wouldn't end up like him. But when he was near, there was a part of me that wanted to believe there was good in him, if only to prove that there was good in *me*.

The black willow tree was easy to spot. It had no leaves on its drooping branches and stood out in stark contrast to the white fields. The snow had come early this year, the innkeeper said, confirming what we already knew. I couldn't help wondering if the Lusiri had something to do with it.

At first, we couldn't find the void. The sun had broken through the clouds, turning everything a glittering white. "Hold on," Evran said.

I watched as his shadow lengthened and stretched, until it was as wide as twenty men. In the shade, we spotted the hole almost immediately.

"How did you do that?" I asked in wonder. I'd seen him obscure himself, but I'd never seen him distort his own shadow.

He flashed a grin that reminded me of the mischievous Evran I'd grown up with. "Magic."

"Very clever," I said with a wry smile. But it *was* clever. I wondered what else he could do with his powers, particularly if he had a teacher, like Darius had said to me.

A chilling thought came to me, then. What if Darius thought *he* was mentoring me? What if his manipulation ran deeper than I realized, and by training me in my powers, he was ensuring I would end up like him?

Somehow, I managed to stifle that horrible thought, closing the void easily despite its size. But while before I'd been proud of myself for mastering my skills, now I had the sinking feeling that every time I did this, I was getting one step closer to Darius.

As if sensing my distress, Evran came to stand behind me, wrapping his arms around my waist. We had dressed in nearly all the clothing we had to keep warm, and I resented the layers between us now. He laid my long braid over one shoulder and pulled my collar aside to kiss my neck, sending a shiver down my spine and my concerns skittering to the recesses of my mind.

With Darius coming, Evran and I might not have another moment alone together. I was going to do everything in my power to stay away from Darius, to not let his presence cloud my judgment. But right now, I needed Evran to know how much he meant to me. I turned to him, holding his hands firmly on my waist.

"You can't put out my light," I insisted. "You helped me control it when I couldn't. But you won't extinguish me."

"Liora—"

"I love you, Evran. So very much. And I trust you, and I need to know that you feel the same way."

"I do," he said, his voice solemn. "I always have."

I pulled back a fraction. "Then tell me."

He smoothed my hair away from my face, his eyes clear and steady as they met mine. "I love you, Liora Duval. I love you, and I trust you."

I had wished on the stars countless times to be like everyone else. I had prayed to be ordinary like my sisters, as content as Adelle and as free from worry as Mina. Every time I walked into Sylvan, I had willed the townspeople to look anywhere but at me. And I had dreamed of a world in which Evran could love me, despite the fact that I was different, despite the fact that I could never live my life freely.

But as our lips collided now, my light still flooding through me, I realized for the first time in my life that I didn't want to be anyone else, even if I still didn't understand my magic. I didn't want to be anywhere else, even if we were standing at the edge of an abyss. Whatever happened next, we had each other, and that had always been more than enough.

We kissed until I felt water seeping into my boot and realized I'd melted a puddle around us. I smiled sheepishly. "Whoops."

Evran laughed and scooped me into his arms, carrying me until we were free of the melted snow. "When this is all over, if everything works out somehow, will you come to Belasava with me?" he asked, gently setting me back on my feet. "I need a fresh start. There are too many bad memories for me in Sylvan."

The fact that he wanted his fresh start to include me was everything I'd hoped for, until I remembered Margana. "But... your mother."

"She can come, if she wants to. But the world is big, and I don't want to spend all of it in one place."

I grinned impishly. "I'd already decided I was going to Bela-sava when this is all over. So I suppose the real question is, will you come with *me*?"

Evran laughed and picked me up again, spinning me around in a circle. It was the happiest I could remember feeling in ages, maybe ever.

We spun and spun, delirious with joy, until I saw a dark figure from the corner of my eye. "Evran," I whispered.

He slowed to a stop, both of us reeling a bit from the spinning.

"Enjoying yourselves?" Darius's hands were thrust deep into the pockets of his fur coat. "How do you think this looks to the townspeople, seeing you two dancing around like fools right where two of their fellow citizens perished?"

Never mind that there was no one else out here. There was too much irony in his words to bother addressing them.

"Come," he said. "I've brought supplies for the last leg of the journey. We need to discuss our strategy."

Evran and I followed, our hands still clasped. Darius knew exactly what we meant to each other now, so there was no point in trying to hide it anymore. The sun had disappeared behind the mountains, and as I glanced up at the sky, I could have sworn I saw the moon and stars pulse brighter. I had burned my way out of an indestructible tapestry. I had called a star down from the heavens. Let Darius try to manipulate me. Let him see exactly what I was capable of.

We met Cyril and Jean in the fire-warmed parlor of The White Fox. Helen was nowhere to be found.

"Can I get you anything?" the innkeeper asked.

"Just be sure no one disturbs us," Darius said as he put his booted feet on the low wooden table. The three hounds, which had returned with their master, were laid out on their sides, panting from the heat of the fire. "And bring us ale."

"Yes, my lord." The innkeeper winked at me as he left.

My eyes darted to Jean's. *Is that...?*

Yes. I asked her to stay away, but she's incorrigible.

Where's the innkeeper?

I told her I didn't want to know.

I shook my head and turned back to Darius. I'd known Helen was trouble from the first time I met her. It was a miracle she hadn't ended up in prison with Mina.

Darius waited until he had all of our attention. "At this point, I think we can afford to lose a little time to the Lusiri. They're in the mountains now, which won't be a quick crossing with all this snow. And once they get to the snowfields north of here, they'll slow down. We'll take tonight to rest and organize. We leave at first light."

The innkeeper returned with a pitcher of ale and five mugs. "Anything else I can get you?"

Darius glared at him with so much ire he squeaked. Knowing it was really Helen made it difficult not to laugh.

"So what's the plan?" Evran asked. "How do we capture the Lusiri without getting killed in the process?"

Darius turned his glare on Evran. "Bait."

"Excuse me?"

"There is no human prey that far north, only wolves and small mammals. If we provide the right bait, they'll come to us."

Evran tensed his jaw. "And just who are you planning to use?"

"Why?" Darius smiled with mock innocence. "Would you like to volunteer?"

"I'll do it," Jean said. "I'm the least important member of

the party at this point, and it's possible I can get into one of their minds. It's worth a shot."

I shook my head. "No. It's too dangerous."

"I already planned on using her." Darius studied Jean with narrowed eyes. "She knows that."

To anyone capable of empathy, it was obvious Jean was just pretending to volunteer to make the rest of us feel better. It was wrong that such a good person was being used in this way, when she had nothing to do with the tapestry. I sent her as much warmth and gratitude as I could.

But Evran's gaze was full of burning hatred. "Leave Jean out of this. Use me instead."

"No." Darius's tone brooked no argument. "We'll need your shadow magic to hide the rest of us. Liora will use her light if things go wrong. And I need Cyril to transport us all to safety, if it comes to that."

"And what will you be doing in all of this?" Evran ground out.

"I'll be harnessing the Lusiri." He pulled what looked like a standard horse halter—albeit a very large one—out of a sack at his feet. "Your mother wove it. It nullifies magic. Once I have it on a Lusiri's head, it will be as docile as a lamb."

"Then why aren't you the bait?" I asked.

"Because I'm the same as the Lusiri. As far as bait goes, I'm worthless."

I released a deep breath through my nose. I didn't believe Darius was as empty as he wanted everyone to think. But at least he was going to be the one to approach the Lusiri. I could only pray he'd be fast enough to save Jean.

TWENTY-FIVE

We replenished our packs with the supplies Cyril and Darius had brought from the palace. Fresh changes of clothing for Jean and me, with fur-lined boots and thicker breeches, plus cloaks made of rabbit fur, were laid out in our room when we returned.

Jean glanced at me as she picked up one of the boots. "What do you make of this?"

I shot her a wry look. "He doesn't want his bait to freeze to death?"

"You're probably right. Although he didn't have to include this." She picked up a glittering object that was tucked under one of the tunics and held out her hand.

I leaned forward and gasped. It was a hair comb made of diamonds in the shape of an eight-pointed star, with a milky blue moonstone in the center. It was beautiful, but I leaned back and shook my head. I still didn't know what Darius's game was, but surely he understood by now I was not the kind of person who could be plied with gifts. "You keep it."

"What? It's clearly intended for you."

"I don't want it. You can use it to pay for your passage to Belasava when this is over, if that's where you decide to go."

She glanced down at the comb again. "Are you sure, Liora? It's probably worth a fortune."

"I'm sure. Just don't mention it to Evran, okay?"

She frowned. "Of course."

"Let's go find the boys. We have a lot to discuss."

We met in Cyril and Evran's room. Helen was in the red-headed girl's body once again, now that the innkeeper had recovered from his "nap," and she rushed to embrace Cyril the moment we entered.

"I'm so glad you're all right." She stepped back to examine him. He looked better than when he'd left, some of the clarity back in his blue eyes. "How's Mina?"

"She's fine. As soon as we got back, Darius moved her out of the dungeon to a cell up in the tower. She's being treated more as a guest than a prisoner now. Except for the fact that she can't leave."

I was surprised to hear about Darius's change of heart, but I didn't trust it. "How is the prince?"

"Still unwell, I'm afraid. The queen doesn't leave his bedside. The king spends most of his time wandering through the gardens and the menagerie. Darius said there was a stack of parchment a mile high piled up in the king's study."

"What did you do the whole week?" Evran asked. "Surely he must have wanted to keep an eye on you, too?"

"He put me in a room similar to Mina's, but a mage black-smith made special shackles that prevented me from transporting. He gave Mina and me an hour together in the garden every day."

Evran looked as skeptical as I was. "I don't understand. None of this fits his behavior."

"It's odd," Cyril admitted. "He seems to have changed since we left Hander."

I could feel Jean's eyes on me. Was there something Cyril wasn't saying? "Changed how?" I asked.

"He's not as cruel. Don't get me wrong, he's still not pleasant. But I thought for sure he'd throw me in the dungeon the moment we got back."

"I'll try to find out what he's thinking," Jean said. "In the meantime, we should eat and get some rest. The mountains will be difficult for all of us."

Helen brushed Jean's shoulder with her own. "I still wish I could come with you."

Jean responded with a shy smile. "I know. But we'd have no way to explain your presence to Darius, and you're better off going to Corone while he's gone and checking on your friends. If we do manage to capture the Lusiri, and Darius really does release Mina and Margana, we can regroup from there. And if things *don't* go well with the Lusiri..." Her voice trailed off as we all imagined the worst.

"How is my mother?" Evran asked Cyril to break the lingering silence. "Is she making progress on the tapestry?"

Cyril frowned apologetically. "I never saw her. I'm sorry. I heard one of the guards say she works day and night, singing strange songs to herself, but that's all I know."

I placed a hand on Evran's shoulder. "She's strong. She'll get through this."

His smile was small and pained. I knew he felt guilty for leaving her, but none of us had a choice in any of this. We were puppets for Darius as much as the king was. At least we were trying to cut our strings.

We all shuffled out of the room and down to the inn's main hall for dinner. There were a handful of other guests, mostly fur traders and trappers. They were a hardy and weathered group, telling loud stories of things they'd seen in the north. I wasn't sure how much of it was true, but I enjoyed listening to them while I sipped my ale. There were beasts I'd never heard of, creatures that made the Lusiri sound downright pleasant. But there were also colorful dancing lights in the night sky, and lakes so clear you could see gemstones sparkling in their depths, though they were far too cold for any person to endure.

The mood changed entirely when Darius entered the room and came to sit at our table. He threw off his dark fur coat and raised a hand, sending a serving boy scuttling away to bring him food and ale. The boy was so frightened his hands trembled when he placed a tray in front of Darius, who barely grunted in acknowledgment.

The traders and trappers eyed him warily. I wasn't sure if anyone knew who he was this far north, but he was an intimidating figure regardless. It didn't help that he had his three hounds with him, waiting eagerly for any scraps he might drop. It was clear to anyone who understood magic that the dogs were not natural creatures. And neither was Darius.

When we'd finished our meals, we all rose to go to our rooms.

"Liora, a word?"

I turned at the sound of Darius's voice. Evran glanced at me questioningly, but I had no idea what Darius could want.

"Should I wait up for you?" Evran whispered.

"I'll be fine," I assured him. "You should get some sleep."

To my relief, Evran nodded and climbed the stairs behind the others. He had promised he trusted me, and this was proof.

I turned back to Darius, too tired to keep the edge from my voice. "What is it? We all need rest before we leave tomorrow."

Without answering, he walked outside, apparently expecting me to follow. I sighed and made my way out into the cold night, releasing my glow to keep myself warm.

He stopped when we were a few yards away from the inn. "Did you receive my gift?"

"*That's* what this is about? You want to know if I like the comb?"

"It's not just a comb, Liora. It's enchanted. It will keep you safe."

I smiled inwardly, glad that I'd given it to Jean. It would protect her from the Lusiri. "Well, then. Yes, I received your gift."

"Good. And you'll wear it once we're in the mountains?"

I nodded without a hint of remorse for lying to him. "Was there anything else, or can I go to bed?"

He studied me for a moment. "You've learned to control your magic quite well since I left. It's freezing out here, and you're not even wearing a coat."

I thought I detected a note of disappointment in his voice. I was learning without his help, and that meant I didn't need him. "I've been practicing."

His eyes narrowed slightly. "You should be careful, Liora. You don't know yet what you're capable of."

"Maybe it's you who doesn't know what I'm capable of," I shot back. "Maybe you're the one who should be afraid of me."

To my annoyance, he laughed. "This is precisely why you need extra protection," he murmured as he walked past me to the inn.

"I don't need anything from you!" I shouted, but the door was already closed.

That night I dreamed I was in a snowfield with one of the Lusiri. Clad in only my nightgown, everything was white except for my loose hair and the beast, who stood opposite me, nostrils flared.

We walked cautiously toward one another, each remembering our last encounter in the tapestry. I reached out toward the massive head, knowing that I could kill the beast now if I wanted to. But if I did, Darius would kill everyone I loved. I awoke just as my fingers brushed the Lusiri's muzzle.

Whether we captured the Lusiri or not, the only way to save the people we loved was to stop Darius himself. I'd learned how to fill up the small voids left behind by the Hollow Ones. I'd even found a way out of the tapestry. But something told me that whatever was inside Darius was more powerful than either the Lusiri or the tapestry. I didn't believe I was strong enough to defeat him yet. But Margana had once said that empty things wanted to be filled. If that was true, I would have to find a way to fill the void.

Helen was already gone by the time I woke up.

Jean glanced up from stuffing her belongings into her bag. "She told me to wish you good luck. And she hopes she'll see you back in Corone."

It was still a little unsettling to have someone reading my thoughts before I was even fully awake. I sat up reluctantly, rubbing my tired eyes. I had slept poorly after the dream about the Lusiri, and I was dreading going back out into the wilderness. "You told her, didn't you?"

Jean went back to her packing, but not before I saw her cheeks flush. "Now who's the mind reader?" She was quiet for a moment. "I've gotten to know her better, and it just felt wrong keeping a secret like that from her."

"I'm glad you did. She has a right to know who she is and

who her parents were. The fact that she agreed to leave anyway means she's not quite as rash as we thought."

"Oh, believe me, she didn't agree without putting up a
fight. She's impulsive and stubborn and—" Jean cut herself off
and touched her flaming cheeks. "At any rate, she did seem
to understand that she had no chance of defeating the Lusiri
on her own. She's counting on us to do it for her. She said
she wants to help rebuild The Crystal Gazer, only 'bigger and
better than before.'"

"Is that a good idea?"

Jean laughed. "Absolutely not."

At first glance, Helen and I couldn't be more different.
While I had repressed all my feelings after my mother's death,
she had encased her pain with anger and vindictiveness until
it was as hard and polished as a pearl around a grain of sand.

But under her tough exterior there was still a girl who had
lost her mother, a girl who had no one left in the world.

"And does she want to be queen, if we do somehow manage to defeat Darius?"

"She doesn't know. She's still coming to terms with the fact
that her father is the king. She also said she'd rather die than
be forced to wear corsets and slippers."

I arched an eyebrow. "And I pity the person who would
even suggest it."

Jean was finished packing, but she turned the diamond
comb over in her hands absently. "So many things were taken
from her, Liora. When all the dust settles, if it ever does, I
think she'd just be happy to have a choice."

I smiled and squeezed her shoulder. "Then I suppose we
can't let her down."

Darius, Evran, and Cyril were already tacking up the horses

when we went outside. I glanced back at The White Fox and said a reluctant farewell to the last bed I'd sleep in for a long time.

Darius's hounds streaked across the frozen pond where the two people had been murdered. I scowled at them, remembering what they had done to the old mage in the woods.

"You don't like them, do you?" Darius asked as he brought his horse up alongside mine.

"Of course not. They're vicious, unnatural."

"They're the product of magic just as much as we are."

I wasn't sure I agreed with his logic; we existed with or without our magic. Besides, they had been designed for only one thing. I kicked my horse forward and caught up with Evran. "We're still using the same signal if we see any holes, right?"

"Yes. But Cyril doesn't think we need to worry too much. He said there's hardly any prey in the mountains."

"Darius mentioned he'd been here before."

Evran nodded. "Cyril is from a village east of here. His parents still live there."

"Does Darius know that?"

"No, thankfully." He glanced over his shoulder to where Jean was riding, alone. Cyril brought up the rear.

I followed his gaze and frowned. "Maybe I should ride with Jean. I got the impression she and Helen had grown close. She's probably lonely without her."

"I'll do it," Evran replied. "If that's all right with you."

I reached out and squeezed his hand. "That's kind of you."

"It's nice being with someone I don't have to explain my feelings to." He immediately shook his head. "I didn't mean it like that."

"It's all right. I know what you mean."

He smiled gratefully and pulled his horse to a stop to allow

Jean to catch up. Which left me with Darius. My mare pinned her ears back when she came up alongside his stallion, as if she shared my feelings toward his rider.

Darius's eyes flicked down briefly, but he didn't seem surprised to see me. "How did you sleep?"

"It was the best night's sleep I've had in ages," I lied, not wanting him to know how much he rattled me. "It's a shame we couldn't spend another night there."

His features were soft and open today, which immediately put me on my guard. "I know this has been a difficult journey."

"It has. But it hasn't been all bad." I turned away at his expression. "Don't look so smug. I don't want to be hunting Lusiri. I didn't want any of this. But—"

"It is difficult to learn who we really are if we never push our boundaries?" he offered. It hadn't been exactly what I was going to say, but he wasn't wrong.

"I suppose so." I checked behind me to see how Evran and Jean were getting along. She was laughing at something, though he didn't appear to be talking. Behind them, Cyril seemed lost in his own thoughts. "When did you first leave Sylvan?" I asked. It was still almost impossible to imagine he had come from the same sleepy village I did.

"I was thirteen when my parents sold me to a warlock."

"What?" It came out so loudly that a crow startled from a tree, sending snow cascading from the branches.

"Quiet." I wasn't sure if he was talking to me or his horse, which had spooked at the sudden outburst.

"I'm sorry. You just surprised me." I waited for him to continue, but in the prolonged silence my curiosity got the better of me. "Who was he?"

"His name was Bastian. He became my mentor. He was

the one who discovered the full scope of my powers, the one who taught me to control them."

Thirteen was only a little younger than Mina. A child. "I don't understand. How could your parents *sell* you?"

"We were very poor. After our house burned down when the star fell, they never recovered financially. My younger brother was nine, and they couldn't afford to feed us both. So when the warlock offered them enough gold to last a year, they sold me. That's what I was led to believe for ten years, anyway."

"It wasn't true?"

"No. I knew early on that Bastian's power was memory manipulation. He could make someone believe that he'd already paid him for a service, for example, or that they'd decided to give him his meal for free. It was small-time stuff, and he was good to me, and he took me all across Antalla with him." He cleared the gravel from his throat. "And I believed my parents didn't want me, so what else was I going to do?"

"He manipulated your mind?" I ducked under a low-hanging branch he held to the side for me. We were climbing steadily up, following a trail into the mountains.

"Yes. But I didn't know that for many years. Slowly, Bastian began to gain more power. He would spend his mornings training me, and then we would travel from town to town, meeting new people, finding out how we could get to Corone and secure better work. I knew he wanted more, but I didn't realize how much more until one day, when I was twenty, we found ourselves having an audience with the king. A former king, anyway."

I raised my eyebrows. "How?"

"Bastian manipulated many people to get us there. Even the guards."

"But what was he hoping to offer the king?"

He looked down at me, his clenched jaw a hard line against the black fur of his collar. "Me."

There was pain in his eyes, and it troubled me, because every time I felt empathy for Darius, I hated him a little less. "I don't understand. To do what?"

The trail narrowed here, forcing our horses closer together. "There is more to your power than just creating light, Liora. The first few times I touched you, you had repressed it too much, though I could sense it far below the surface. It wasn't until that day at the palace that I knew for certain it was there."

I tipped my face up to his again, searching his mutable eyes. "Something beyond my light? What is it?"

"Ask yourself, what is it that stars do?"

"They give light," I said. "And heat." I glanced back at Evran again, who was now riding single file in front of Jean. I remembered what he'd said to me, more than once: stars don't just shine. He'd been afraid of being close to me, because he saw *something* when we touched. A candle being snuffed out. A candle flickering back to life.

Darius nodded, as if he could sense I was close to the answer.

"They…illuminate."

He smiled as though he was proud of me for figuring it out on my own. "That's right. When someone touches you, they see the answer."

"To what?"

"To their question. To *the* question. To the thing that keeps them up at night, that drives everything they do."

I nodded, finally beginning to understand. When Evran touched me, he'd seen himself putting out my light. But what was his question? Whether or not we could be together? What our powers meant?

Thick branches obscured the rest of our party from view. Darius and I were pressed so close together our legs were almost touching. I pulled back on the reins, halting my mare.

Darius yanked on his own reins, wheeling his stallion around to face me. A cold wind picked up, blowing the snow off the trees, blurring everything around us. How far back were the others? Had we lost them somehow? Darius's eyes were like two glowing embers, the only part of his face I could see through the snow.

I didn't want to ask the question, didn't want the answer I was afraid he would give. But I swallowed back my fear. "What do you see when you touch me?"

For a moment, the wind stopped, and the forest went still. Darius's eyes burned into mine, and deep inside, I felt something respond. Something small but unignorable, something that saw itself reflected back.

"I see you, Liora. I see you."

TWENTY-SIX

The storm picked up that afternoon, and by nightfall, we were desperate for shelter. I hadn't spoken to Darius again, Evran and the others having caught up to us just moments later. Since then, I'd talked to Jean about what happened, but I wasn't sure if she'd shared it with the others. Knowing what Darius saw when he touched me, without knowing his question, was no kind of answer. But it was that strange sensation I'd felt inside, like an eye blinking open for the first time, that terrified me most of all.

Finally, Darius spotted a cave a little way from the trail. It was too small for the horses, so we gathered fallen branches and made a rough snow break for them, removed their tack, and crowded into the cave. There was barely enough room for all of us, and the cave floor was hard and pitted. I did my best to fill in the biggest holes with the toes of my boots so we'd have a smoother surface to sleep on while Jean arranged our bedrolls. It would be tight, with all of us pressed up close together, but at least we would be warm.

The hounds had curled up at the back of the cave, but when Darius whistled to them, they joined him near the entrance.

"Where are you going?" Evran called after him.

"To see if there are any signs of the Lusiri nearby. By morning, their tracks will be completely concealed by the snow."

Jean and I shared a glance. If Darius found a void, we were done for.

"I'll go," Evran said. "I have better vision in the dark."

To my surprise, Darius nodded. "Take one of the hounds with you, just in case you find any prey. Otherwise we'll be eating cold meat and bread for dinner."

I set my pack down. "I'll go with him."

"No." Darius's tone was sharp, but he busied himself laying out his own bedroll. "We need you to heat the cave. There's no dry kindling nearby."

Evran went out into the storm while Jean and Cyril dug through their packs, as if by some miracle they might turn up fresh provisions. Darius removed a bottle of amber liquid from his saddlebag and took a long drink.

"Here," he said, passing it to Jean. "It will help warm you."

She eyed him skeptically but took a sip, then passed it to Cyril, who passed it to me.

With the revelations of this afternoon, I was finding it harder to summon my warmth. Or perhaps I was just afraid of what might happen to me if I did. The glow from my skin was enough to light the small cave, and it was certainly warmer than it would be without me, but I took the whiskey anyway. I figured I could use all the help I could get.

The liquor burned its way down my throat, but I forced myself to take another sip, afraid I wouldn't sleep otherwise. Darius had placed his bedroll at the back of the cave, where the two remaining dogs had curled up to sleep, and I found a spot between Evran and Cyril. At any point in my life before now, I wouldn't have even considered sleeping between two men. But now, all I could think of was getting warm.

I passed the whiskey back to Darius, who took another long drink and replaced the lid. I kept my eyes down to avoid his. There was obviously more to his story, but I wasn't sure I wanted to hear it.

Evran returned a short while later without food, his cheeks red from the wind and cold. "It's impossible to see out there," he said, rubbing his arms briskly. "I'm sorry."

"It's all right," I said. "We have enough to eat. Any sign of the Lusiri?"

He shook his head as he crawled onto his bedroll next to me. "No."

The whiskey was warming me already, and I found myself remembering our kiss beneath the willow tree, how happy we'd been in that moment. I wished I could call it back as easily as I could summon my light.

"Where's my hound?" Darius asked suddenly.

"What? I—" Evran glanced toward the mouth of the cave. "It was right behind me."

Darius moved to stand, but Evran shook his head. "The storm has gotten worse. The dog will find its way back when things calm down. He probably took shelter somewhere."

"It's not just a dog," Darius grumbled. The other two hounds raised their heads from their paws and looked at him, lowering their muzzles when he at last resettled onto his bedroll.

We ate our rations in silence, once again passing around the bottle of whiskey as the storm raged outside the cave. I worried for the horses, but there was nothing we could do for them. Hopefully the Lusiri were far ahead of us by now. I doubted even wolves would brave this weather.

We didn't bother to change our clothes as we all settled in to sleep; we would lose too much body heat in the process, and all of our clothing was equally filthy by now anyhow. I watched Evran in the glow from my skin, the soft fringe of dark lashes on his wind-burned cheeks, the rise and fall of his chest. He opened his eyes once and smiled sleepily, and I silently willed him to stay awake, to assure me he loved me again. But then his eyelids dropped, and it felt like a door closing.

At some point I drifted off, too, only to startle awake from another dream about the Lusiri. This time they'd been together, feasting on the body of an animal in the woods nearby.

I crept to the edge of the cave and listened. The wind had died down, and in the glow from my skin I couldn't see any snow falling. One of the horses nickered softly. I pulled on my boots and went around the side of the cave to check on them, only to find them huddled together behind the makeshift hedge, their ears pricked forward, dark eyes watchful. There was definitely something out there.

I pulled my blanket around myself and walked back to the trail, afraid but unable to deny the invisible tug at my feet. I walked slowly, carefully, praying I'd be able make my way back in the dark.

I felt it before I saw it.

The void was by far the largest we'd seen yet. It had crept over the roots of a tree—or where the roots should have been. That horrible nothingness was moving slowly up the trunk. I stepped back a few feet, looking around for signs of whatever the Lusiri had eaten, but it had already been swallowed up by the hole. I thought of the hound and shuddered. It had probably run into the void without seeing it.

The nothingness moved slowly along the ground like an invisible mist, eating everything in its path. And it was heading straight for our cave. If I hadn't woken, what would have happened? How could Evran have missed this?

I gathered my light and aimed it at the void, watching as it slowly shrank. But just when it seemed I'd gained an inch, it swelled and stretched, growing two more. I thought of the beasts the trappers had spoken of; this one must have been enormous to leave such a huge hole behind. But that didn't explain why it was getting harder to close up. Unless the Lusiri were getting stronger.

I had been proud of myself for gaining better control of my power, for not needing to resort to emotions to wield it. But perhaps I needed them now. I closed my eyes and thought of Mina, how frightened she must be; Margana's tears as she told me about the tapestry; Evran's burrow and his knife made from his dog's bone; and Cyril and Helen, who had both lost friends in the fire at The Crystal Gazer.

But try as I might not to think about him, Darius's face was among the people who had suffered because of his magic. Was this the price of power, I wondered, no matter who you were? If it hadn't been Darius, would someone else have done something to hurt the people I loved?

I groaned in frustration. Sympathy wasn't going to close up the void. However Darius had been hurt, whatever regret he felt now over his actions, I could not deny that *he* was at the center of all our pain and loss. He couldn't buy my forgiveness with diamonds or coerce me into feeling sorry for him. I wouldn't let him. My anger rose up in me like a brewing storm, and I let it come, let it build in me until I thought I might burst. I felt more than powerful; I felt deadly.

I opened my eyes, relieved to see the void had shrunk by

half. I took another step forward, and another, mud and decaying leaves appearing at my feet as I melted away the snow. The hole began to shrink faster the smaller it got, until it was only a foot in diameter. It resisted for a moment, and I pushed harder with my light, until at last it let go and vanished.

I kneeled down to be sure the job was finished. On the other side of where the hole had been lay a furry body, the Lusiri's prey. It was indeed massive, even sucked dry, something bearlike but with an impressive set of antlers.

But even closer to me was a much smaller corpse, curled in on itself: the carcass of the hound. I felt a stab of pity for the creature before I remembered what it had done. The world was better off without it. I was turning to leave when I saw something move out of the corner of my eye.

I looked back toward the hound. It was limp and motionless on the damp ground, but it was oddly full, not just a hollow shell like the Lusiri's prey. Suddenly, in one swift, jerky motion, the hound lifted its head and looked directly at me.

I gasped and stumbled backward. The creature had always been grotesque, but now its eyes were vacant black pools, so dark they swallowed even my light. It opened its mouth as it lurched to its feet, its movements strange and unnatural. Long strings of saliva hung suspended between its black fangs. Even its tongue was black.

Just like the Lusiri's.

I tripped over a root and landed in the mud, but I kept my eyes on the hound as it took a step forward. I had wrongly assumed that once something went into the void it was lost forever, but whatever it was, the hound was definitely not dead. I could only hope nothing else had fallen into the voids left behind by the Lusiri and that we hadn't missed any holes.

The hound was getting closer. I rose to my feet, pushing

down my fear as I brought my light back, but the dog moved faster than I could. I was afraid to turn my back on it, but I could see no other choice. Though my legs felt impossibly heavy, I ran.

The dog snarled behind me as I bolted deeper into the woods, knowing I couldn't bring this thing back to the cave.

The blanket was suddenly torn from my shoulders. I risked a quick glance behind me to see the hound shredding the flannel to pieces. Almost immediately, it realized its mistake and resumed the hunt. I could hear it panting behind me. The snow was getting thicker here, slowing us both down, but I would tire far faster.

"Liora!"

I ran in the direction of the voice, my muscles burning as I struggled through the snow that was now knee-deep. I turned just as the hound leaped for me, colliding with my chest and sending me flying back into the snow. I screamed as the hound sank its fangs into the thick sleeve of my wool sweater.

Fear is a useful tool. Darius's voice filled my head, as clearly as if Jean was talking to me. He'd meant other people's fear, not my own, but I had nothing else to use right now. Try as I might, I could not seem to conjure anything resembling anger.

The sharp tips of the hound's fangs broke through my sweater. I screamed again, struggling to shove the hound off of me, but it was pure muscle and sinew, and it pinned me to the ground with its powerful claws. If I died, there would be no one to save Mina, no one to clean up after the Lusiri, no one to stop Darius. If I died, I would never get to know Evran outside of all this mess, never fully experience who I was meant to be. I couldn't die now. I wasn't even close to ready.

I placed my hands on the hound's chest and it yelped in pain, leaping away from me just long enough for me to scramble to my feet and reach for a thick branch on the ground. I hefted it to my shoulder and waited for the dog to attack again.

"Stop!"

I froze, thinking Darius's command was directed at me, but the hound also froze, some part of its mind apparently still under Darius's control.

He strode forward, clad in only his tunic and breeches, a curved saber like the ones hanging from the doors in Iverna in his right hand. I turned away just as he brought the sword down, severing the hound's head from its body.

When I looked back, Darius's chest was heaving as he caught his breath. The hound's blood ran black over the snow, but there was no movement.

Darius lowered the sword and turned to me. "You're hurt."

I followed his gaze to my torn sleeve. "It didn't break the skin."

"We still need to disinfect it." He took a step closer to me. "What happened?"

I sifted through possible explanations. Perhaps now that he'd seen the evidence of what the void did, he wouldn't be so inclined to finish the tapestry. But what if he was undeterred? What if this was what he wanted? I didn't know who he was or how I could possibly trust him.

I settled for a version of the truth. "Something woke me. I came out here to see what it was. I thought the hound was dead, but then it attacked me."

"Were the Lusiri here?"

I shook my head no. "Just the hound."

He swiped at his brow with the back of the hand still holding the sword. Black blood dripped from the blade. "Let me see your arm."

I pushed back the torn wool. There were two red marks on my skin, but there was no blood. "It's all right."

"Let me see it."

I held it out to him hesitantly. "Is Evran here?"

"No." He dropped the saber and took my sleeve, gently pulling my arm toward him.

Foolishly, I had assumed Evran was the one calling my name. But he would have no reason to think I was in danger. "How did you know where I was?"

"The hounds in the cave woke me. They must have realized something was happening to their brother. And then I noticed you were missing." He pressed his fingers gingerly to the skin surrounding the bite marks. "You were lucky. The whiskey will have to do for now. I think there are some clean bandages in one of the saddlebags. We'll need to keep a close eye on it for infection." He scrubbed at his hair. "I just don't understand how this could have happened."

My eyes flicked up to his. His fingers were still pressed to my skin. Part of me wanted to run back to the safety of the cave and forget this night entirely. But I needed to know how his story ended. "Please, tell me what happened. What did you do to become…like you?"

"You want to discuss this here, now?"

My eyes wandered to the snow swirling around us. The storm had subsided a little, but it was still bitterly cold in the wind. "Do you prefer to discuss it in the cave with the others?"

He wiped his sword clean in the snow and offered me his arm. When I didn't take it, he sighed and started to walk back toward camp. I trudged along after him, unconsciously maintaining a safe distance between us.

For a moment I thought he wouldn't answer, but then he began to speak. "I didn't realize it for a long time, but my mentor, Bastian, was using me to answer *his* ultimate question—how could he become as powerful as the king? He eventually manipulated the king into hiring him on as an advisor."

I wondered if he saw the irony in this; it was exactly what Darius would do to King Clement, eventually.

"Once I knew what Bastian was doing, I was torn. My mentor was selfish, but he'd also helped get me to court. I fell in love with a young lady there. I would have done anything for Bastian, if it meant being close to her. But as much as I loved her, it was also difficult for me to open up to her. I couldn't make sense of my past, of how my happy childhood memories conflicted with what my parents had done. One day we kissed, and she saw the answer to her question—what had happened to me to close me off, and would I ever love her completely?"

I winced. I understood all too well how she felt. "And she saw what Bastian had done to your memories?"

He nodded, his brows drawn together. "Yes. I was furious. Angrier than I'd ever been. I went to find him and demanded he tell me the truth. And what he told me was even worse than I'd imagined." He swallowed thickly. "He'd kidnapped me. Taken me from my family in the middle of the night after meeting me in town. All I'd done was shake his hand, and he had seen what I could do for him. So he took me. But worse still, he altered my parents' memories so that they believed I'd run away."

"I'm so sorry." That, at least, wasn't a lie. No one deserved such a horrible fate.

He was silent for a long time, and I feared we would reach the camp without him telling me the end of the story. I needed to know what had become of him, what could become of me. "Finish. Please."

In the darkness of the forest, his eyes were like two smoldering coals. "I tried to find my parents, but they were gone," he said. "They left Sylvan with my little brother, and I never saw them again. I knew I needed to strengthen my mind against Bastian if I was going to get my revenge. So I found another mentalist. She helped me practice, every day for months. Finally, when I was strong enough, I told Bastian to meet me in the woods outside of the city. When mages duel, it's with magic. With my mind steeled against him, I was ready to kill him for what he'd done to my family. And to me.

"But though he had trained me to use my light and heat, he'd never told me the one danger. I'm not even sure he knew. Just like the stars we called down from the sky, our power can be used up. Burn too hot and too bright, and you...well, you become me. I destroyed Bastian that day, but in the process, I also destroyed myself."

I realized I had stopped walking, too stunned to process his words.

"I can't explain what it's like to go from being so full of love and light to being so completely empty," he continued. "I was a shell of who I'd been before. I became a recluse, speaking to no one, not even my lady. I was no longer capable of loving anyone. Then one day the mentalist who had helped train me came to visit. When we embraced, I felt something inside of me shift, a hunger like nothing I'd ever experienced. She tried to pull away, but I couldn't let go. Her magic began to flow into me, and it was the most satisfaction I'd felt since I lost my power. The *only* satisfaction, the first time I'd felt like myself in years. By the time I finally released her, she was dead."

He looked down at his hands as if he didn't recognize them. "I can control it now, as you know. But back then, I couldn't. I felt better for a few weeks, but then the magic began to run out and the hunger rushed back in. And that was how it started. I took from other mages, just a little here and there. And the irony was that whereas before, everyone could see the answers to their questions when they touched me, now I could see what their questions were." A shadow passed over his eyes. "But they found no answer in me."

The words tumbled from my lips before I could stop myself. "What is my question?"

He moved closer to me, so I had to crane my neck to look into his eyes. "How can you be yourself and still be free."

I felt like I was standing at that one-way door again, knowing if I opened it, I could never go back. But I couldn't turn away either. "And what was your question?"

"My question has always been the same, ever since I discovered what Bastian had done to me—how can I stop this terrible hunger? How can I feel complete again?"

Despite the fact that I was using my glow to keep warm, a chill ran down my spine. Because he'd already told me the answer.

Me.

TWENTY-SEVEN

We stood in the forest facing each other, the reality of what he was admitting drifting around us like snow.

Darius needed me, and he'd known it from the first time we met. He may not have understood how or why, but he'd seen enough to want to keep me close. That was why he'd seemed interested in me at the palace, why he hadn't killed me or imprisoned me after I destroyed the tapestry. Perhaps he'd thought he didn't even need the tapestry anymore.

But I knew deep down that he was wrong. I couldn't fix Darius. Not unless he planned on using me up the way he'd done to that mentalist, and I would die before I allowed that to happen.

I folded my arms against my chest, taking comfort in the way my power surged beneath my skin. "It's a mistake."

"What is?" he asked.

"The answer. What you think you see when you touch me. It's wrong."

He shook his head. "It isn't wrong, Liora. I suspected it the moment I saw you, before I even touched you. But I have known for weeks now that it was right."

"If you think I would ever allow you to use me—"

"I don't," he said quickly. "I don't even think that's what the vision means."

"Then what does it mean?"

He glanced toward camp, just a few dozen feet beyond where we stood. "Since I met you, I've felt more like my old self than I have in decades. Since I burned out, in fact. And it has nothing to do with taking your magic. Just being in your presence, with your power near, has been enough."

The hairs on the back of my neck began to prickle as I realized what he was saying. "No."

"Don't you think it's possible that this works both ways? That with powers as strong as ours, we need the force of something in direct opposition to keep us in check? That just maybe I am your answer? Without me, what's to stop you from burning yourself out, too?"

I shook my head, hot tears of anger and confusion pricking my eyes.

As if sensing my weakness, he stepped forward. "Who else could possibly understand you like I can? We are the only two people in the entire world like us. As far as I know, we're the only two mages in the entire world with the same power. Do you think that's a coincidence?"

I was so furious that steam was rising around me. "You're wrong!"

"If you really thought that, you wouldn't care enough to deny it. If you really believed you were nothing like me, you wouldn't have asked me how I became like this."

"No," I said, but it came out as little more than a whisper. He was wrong about everything. He had to be.

I spun on my heels and stalked away, relieved when he didn't come after me. I found my way back to the cave and crawled onto my bedroll as quietly as I could, but Evran blinked as I lowered my head onto my blanket.

"Is everything all right?" he asked.

I nodded, because I couldn't bring myself to lie out loud.

I didn't tell anyone what had happened, though it was possible Jean had gleaned the truth through her powers. Try as I might to contain my thoughts, I couldn't make sense of what Darius had told me. As distressing as his belief that we were somehow connected was the understanding that he had truly once been human. He'd been a child when Bastian came into his life, manipulating Darius into believing his parents had abandoned him and that Bastian was the only person he could trust.

But whether he was aware of it or not, Darius was trying to do the same thing to me. Every time he said we were the same, that only he could understand me, he was attempting to push me away from the people I loved. And as hard as it was to fathom, I knew I was still vulnerable, that the same thing *could* happen to me. If Evran hadn't stopped me when I burned the tapestry, I could have destroyed myself then. And next time, we might not be so lucky.

Whatever Darius believed, the answer to sating his hunger, to filling his emptiness, wasn't truly me. It was my power. And if he was right about my question, then it was possible he was right about my answer, too.

What if being close to Darius really was the only way to keep me from destroying myself?

On this side of the mountains, the entire world was different. The days were so short that we had no choice but to travel in darkness. The snow was knee-deep in most places, slowing the horses and tiring them considerably. And with more snow falling all the time, I wasn't sure how we'd possibly track the Lusiri. I still couldn't understand how Evran had missed such a giant hole. It made me nervous that he wasn't paying close enough attention; even my light wasn't enough to see things clearly in so much snow. I kept to myself, ignoring Darius whenever he tried to ride next to me. Jean and Evran rode together most of the time, though they rarely spoke out loud.

On our third day in Tezhia, one of the two remaining hounds began to whine and yowl, which was out of character for the creatures. They only barked when they found prey.

"What is it?" Darius asked. "Lusiri?"

The hound scented the air and ran off into the trees, returning a moment later to bark even more insistently.

"I smell it, too," Evran said. "Rotting meat."

"It must be the remains of something the Lusiri killed. A good sign we're on the right track." Darius ordered the hound to track down the scent and we followed behind, our horses struggling to keep up with the nimble animal. It went down a small hill into a ravine, barking madly, with the other hound now joining it.

I noticed the small cave under a snowbank at the same time Cyril yelled to Darius to call back his hounds.

"That's not a Lusiri kill!" he shouted.

But he was too late. One moment the closest hound was barking at the entrance of the cave, and the next, something with too many long, articulated legs darted out from the cave and grabbed on to the hound. It disappeared into the darkness with a startled yelp. There was one more anguished howl followed by a wet tearing sound. I covered my ears after that.

"What was that thing?" Evran asked, keeping close to Jean, who looked like she was about to cry.

Cyril's blue eyes were wide with shock. "A tryctus. I'd heard of them before, but I never believed they were real."

Darius was still staring at the hole in stunned silence, the other hound now cowering near his horse.

"They line their burrows with rotting meat," Cyril explained. "It's how they lure prey. I should have realized sooner."

"It's all right," Darius said finally, though he looked as though he might be ill. "We should press on. It will be dark in a couple of hours, and we need to find somewhere to rest."

If there was anything worse than camping, it was snow camping. Cyril showed us how to build a rounded snow fort one night, but we couldn't afford to waste the energy it took to build them every night. I melted the snow down to the frozen ground, but it was rock-hard, and nothing I did could stop the snow from falling on us while we slept. The single remaining hound curled up next to Darius on the far side of the small fire we'd made with the few dry branches we gathered. I was closer to Evran and Jean, who were speaking in hushed tones as the fire died down.

"You must miss them terribly," Evran said. "You're very brave, you know."

Jean's voice was soft, almost bashful. "I don't know about that."

"Well, I do. Which one of your parents is a mage?" he asked. "Or is it both?"

"Neither, actually."

"I thought non-mages couldn't have mage children."

A pocket of air popped in the fire, releasing sparks. "I was adopted when I was just a baby," Jean said. "My parents never talked about my birth parents, but I always assumed they gave me away to try to keep me safe."

Their conversation went on, but my mind had snagged on Evran's words. *Non-mages can't have mage children?* That couldn't be right. I would know if my father was a warlock. And surely he would have told us if Mother had been a witch. Wouldn't he?

I hadn't believed Darius when he said Father was lying about the girl with the diamond tears. But Father had hidden things from me about his relationship with Darius, about our mother, and even about my magic.

Still, allowing me to believe I was the only witch in our family seemed senselessly cruel. It couldn't be explained away as trying to protect me. And Father, though cautious to a fault, wasn't cruel. There had to be another explanation.

I pulled my blanket over my head to muffle their voices. That was what I got for eavesdropping.

The next day, as we rode through the never-ending snow, Jean and Cyril fell a little behind. Darius had gone ahead to scout, his massive stallion able to plow through the snow easier than our smaller steeds, and for the first time in what felt like ages, I had a moment alone with Evran.

I knew I needed to tell him everything I'd learned, but the revelations from the other night were holding me back. I wasn't foolish enough to think things could stay the same between us after he knew the truth about Darius's powers and who he had once been. How could I expect Evran to trust me now, to want to start a new life with me, when any minute

I could become a monster like Darius? How could I possibly put him in that kind of danger?

As my mare sidled up next to his gelding, I smiled, though my stomach was tying itself into complicated knots. "Hello, stranger."

He grinned down at me. "I've been neglecting you, haven't I? I'm sorry."

"It's all right." I bit my lip, unsure how to proceed. "I need to talk to you about something, but I'm frightened of how you'll react." I took a deep breath. "It's about Darius."

He raised his eyebrows. "Frightened? You know you can tell me anything."

"I know, and I want to. But I'm afraid you won't be able to look at me the same way after I tell you."

Evran frowned. "I doubt that's possible. But if you'd feel more comfortable telling Jean…"

"No, no," I assured him. "It has to be you." I told myself I could do this, that it would be easier to share this burden with someone I loved. Evran had been afraid of his own magic, too. He would understand. "Last night, I went out to check on the horses and had the feeling that something was wrong. I found a void, and one of the hounds had fallen into it."

"Go on," he urged, sensing my hesitation.

I tried to steady my hands on the reins, but they were trembling now. "Darius came after me when he realized I was gone. He told me how he became the way he is."

From there, the words spilled out of me almost uncontrollably, as if my body understood that it was too late to turn back. Evran didn't utter a word the entire time, the furrow in his brow the only sign he was even hearing me, and his silence felt like another void I had to fill. I rambled for what felt like ages, until there was nothing left to say.

"What if we go to Belasava together and I'm unable to control my powers?" I asked finally. "What if I hurt you without meaning to? I couldn't live with myself, Evran."

When I'd finished, he remained quiet, his eyes downcast.

I thought I'd feel unburdened once I got the truth out, but Evran's reaction was frightening me. "Say something, please."

He glanced behind him, as if he was waiting for Jean and Cyril to catch up to us. "I... I'm not sure what to say, Liora. I don't think you'd hurt me, certainly not on purpose. You're a good person, and Darius is clearly evil."

"That's the whole point," I said, frustrated. "*He* was good once, too. How do you know I won't become like him?"

"Well, we can't know for sure, can we? I just don't think it's likely."

Tears caught in my throat, making it hard to breathe. "That's all you have to say? That you don't think it's likely?" I realized now I'd been hoping for some kind of assurance, for Evran to pull me into his arms and tell me that it would be all right no matter what. For him to say we'd figure it out, together.

"I'm sorry." He shook his head. "I'm no good at this. You should talk to Jean."

As if she'd heard us, Jean came bouncing up beside us at a trot. "Is everything all right, Liora?"

Horrified that she would read all my thoughts—not just my confusion about what Darius had said, but also my growing doubts about Evran's feelings for me—I swiped my tears away and nodded. I urged my mare into a trot, feeling more alone than ever.

That night, long after the fire had died down and the others had fallen asleep, I crept across the circle to where Darius lay. His eyes opened the second I crouched down next to him.

"What do you want?" I whispered.

He sat up and studied me with his mercurial eyes. "What do you mean?"

"What will it take to make you stop this madness with the tapestry, to leave the king in peace, to stop using up the mages?"

He blinked. "I—I don't know anymore."

"Try."

He sat up and patted the space next to him on his bedroll. I glanced over at Evran's sleeping form. "Please sit," he said. "I know you're tired."

Reluctantly, I joined him.

"I commissioned the tapestry because I was angry and bitter. For many years I had tried to fill this emptiness inside of me, and nothing worked. I resented everyone, and I wanted people to suffer the way I did. Eventually, I came to believe the tapestry was the answer to everything."

"But you don't think the tapestry is the answer anymore?"

"I know it's not."

My stomach twisted. "Because of me."

He nodded.

"Then I'll ask you one more time. What is it that you want?"

"You already know the answer, Liora."

He didn't mean me, I reminded myself. It was my power he wanted, nothing more and nothing less. At the edge of my light, I could just make out Evran's form. My best friend, the only one who had ever loved me for everything I was. Our love was selfless, and that was how I knew it was true. That was also why I couldn't live with the thought that I might hurt him one day.

Our conversation this afternoon had convinced me of one

thing: that Evran would be all right without me. He had friends now, perhaps even the possibility of a relationship with Jean. He could go to Belasava with Jean and Cyril and start a new life. And while I knew he would feel some guilt and sorrow, he could live with those. He could *live*.

Evran had once sacrificed himself for me, and now it was my turn to do the same.

"I will help you kill the Lusiri," I said, trying to keep my voice steady. "Then we will return to Corone and destroy the tapestry, and you will release Margana and Mina and all the other mages you hold prisoner. And in exchange, I will remain in Corone, at the palace." I swallowed the bile in my throat.

For a moment, he only stared at me, as if he wanted us both to absorb the words I'd just spoken. "Are you certain?" he asked finally.

It took everything I had to answer, "Yes."

He took my hand, my skin luminous against his, and shook it. "I accept."

TWENTY-EIGHT

We rode out at daybreak. I hadn't slept at all, but something told me it didn't matter, that things would end today, one way or another. The air was oddly still, the forest silent, without so much as a winter hare padding across the snow.

We hadn't even been riding an hour when my mare reared out of nowhere, sending me tumbling into the snow. I was fortunate it was a soft, if cold, landing.

The Hollow Ones are here.

It was Jean's voice, speaking to all of us. This hadn't been the plan. We were supposed to lure the Lusiri in, not be attacked by them. All I could see in the pale morning light was snow and trees, trees as black as...

Cover yourself, she told me. I spotted one of the Lusiri in the corner of my vision, watching me. I didn't know where the second one was. Slowly, I pulled my cloak around my body, trying not to call attention to myself. My horse was long gone.

The others had clustered together in a circle around me, but Evran was struggling to calm his horse, its pricked ears and tail a sure sign it was ready to bolt. Jean was pressed close to him. Darius and Cyril were more experienced riders, but their horses' ears were flicking back and forth, listening.

I turned my head enough to take in the Lusiri. It was bigger than I remembered, probably because I'd never been able to see it all at once in the tapestry. Now, in the morning light, it was far more monstrous than I'd realized: the great square head, the flared nostrils and shiny black eyes, the hooves as large as dinner plates that pawed at the snow.

"What do we do?" I whispered to Darius.

Silently, he reached down for me with one arm. I stared up at him, remembering the bargain I'd made with him last night. Evran would never understand what I'd done. But I wouldn't regret my decision, so long as the people I loved were safe. I took Darius's hand and let him pull me up behind him onto his horse. By the time I'd wrapped my arms around his waist and peeked over his shoulder, the second Lusiri was there, even larger than the first.

"Can we defeat them here?" I breathed.

He turned his head toward me. "Not without some advantage on our part. Right now, they have it."

"So what do we do?"

"Run!"

At Darius's shout, all the horses took off away from the Lusiri. I gripped Darius's waist tighter, feeling the muscles working beneath his clothes as he spurred his stallion forward. It was the largest horse, but it was also carrying the most weight, and though it churned through the snow with impressive strength, I knew immediately we wouldn't be able to outrun the Lusiri. One glance over my shoulder confirmed it.

Jean had fallen behind. The Lusiri were so close it was only a matter of seconds before they reached her.

"Jean!" Evran screamed, just as she was pulled backward off her horse.

One of the Lusiri went after her mare, while the other approached Jean. She lay curled in the snow, her arms over her head, as if that would somehow save her. Evran had turned around and was galloping back toward her.

"We have to help them!" I screamed at Darius.

"It's too late!"

Horrified, I let go of his waist and tumbled off the horse, tucking into a ball and rolling a few feet before coming to a stop.

"Liora!"

Darius was already riding back to me. I pushed to my feet and sprinted toward Evran and Jean, light and heat building inside of me as I ran past Cyril.

"What are you doing?" he shouted after me.

"Saving them!"

"But you can't kill the Lusiri! What about Mina?"

I ignored him and ran to where Evran and Jean were. One of the Lusiri was finishing off Jean's horse, while the other seemed to hesitate when it saw Evran standing over Jean, as if it remembered him from the tapestry.

"Get away!" he roared at it, waving his arms. I didn't understand why he wasn't using his magic, but perhaps the diamond comb I'd given Jean was working. The Lusiri didn't move any closer.

I stepped in front of Evran, and the monster reared, shrieking. There was no question it remembered me. I poured light into my hands, stretching them out in front of me, preparing to strike. But as I faced the one closest to me, the other bolted for us, knocking Evran to the ground. Jean screamed as I whirled, trying to decide which Lusiri to go for first.

Jean was sobbing behind me. "Please don't be dead," she cried.

I didn't have to summon the heat. It only hurt for a moment; then I couldn't feel anything except a building roar, as if I was going to explode. I could hear the Lusiri screeching, see them trying to flee through the white haze surrounding me. The feeling that had engulfed me in the tapestry, that I would burn anything that dared hurt Evran, was so overwhelming I was sure I was coming apart at the seams.

"Stop!"

I was knocked to the ground by a sudden blow, snow piling onto me as I tried to get back up.

"Cyril, take the second harness!"

I looked up to see Darius holding both Lusiri in place with his outstretched hands, his neck straining as though he had some kind of tenuous hold on them. Darius had said they were "alike" in some way; perhaps that gave him the ability to control them momentarily. As Cyril slipped the harnesses on the creatures, they immediately dropped their heads in submission.

"What are you doing?" I cried. "We need to destroy them."

Darius lowered his arms finally, and the Lusiri sank to their knees. "And destroy you in the process? No, I'll finish them off at the palace."

I crawled to Evran through the snow. My skin still radiated light, but my heat had faded by the time I touched his cheek. He was breathing shallowly, as if the Lusiri had stolen the air from his lungs.

Jean crouched next to me, tears freezing halfway down her cheeks. Cold recognition broke through my own terror and

sorrow for a moment. Jean didn't just have a crush on Evran;
she was in love with him.

"Is she okay?" Jean asked, pulling Evran closer.

She?

I gasped when the round turquoise pendant slipped free
from Evran's collar. "Why does Evran have Helen's pendant?"
I asked, but before the words were out, I realized what I'd
somehow failed to see before.

Helen had disguised herself as Evran. That was why he
hadn't seen the void in the forest, why he hadn't used his
shadow magic. That was why he had spent so much of these
past days with Jean, instead of me. And that was why he hadn't
known what to say when I told him the truth about Darius.

But if Helen was here, where was Evran?

When Darius reached down for me and pulled me up, I was
too tired to stop him. "Why didn't you let me kill them?" I
sobbed. I was weak and exhausted from facing the Lusiri, and
now I didn't even know if Evran was safe.

"You would have ended up like me. I couldn't let that happen."

I turned away to see Evran—Helen, I reminded myself—
sitting up with Jean's help. Pulling free of Darius's grasp, I
stumbled over to my friends and dropped to my knees. "Are
you all right?" I asked Helen.

She looked past me to the Lusiri. "They're still alive."

"Darius is going to kill them at the palace," I assured her.
"Don't worry."

But she didn't look at me. She turned to Jean instead. "This
wasn't the plan."

She shook her head, fresh tears in her eyes. "We tried."

Bewildered, I rose to my feet, cold now that my heat was
draining out of me. *What plan?* I asked Jean desperately.

Before she could respond, Darius was beside me again. "We should get back to the palace now. You need rest."

Helen and Jean exchanged a look. "What did you do?" Helen asked me, her face on the edge of caving in.

"I didn't know." I backed away from them, horror spreading over me. Not only had I foiled some plan I didn't understand, but I had also promised to remain close to Darius, forever. And Evran had no idea about any of it.

Darius reached for me, tucking me under his arm as if I belonged there. "Cyril, take us to the orchard. Then return for the rest. Mina is free as soon as you finish."

Cyril's eyes darted to mine. Whatever Evran, Jean, and Helen had planned, they hadn't told him either. "I'm sorry," I whispered to Cyril, closing my eyes as Darius pulled his black fur coat around both of us.

I knew we were in the jeweled orchard at the palace when I felt the late-autumn sun on my exposed skin.

Darius released me slowly. "Are you all right?" He peered into my face, his eyes searching mine. "You used an immense amount of power back there. I was afraid I was too late."

I stepped back, keeping my gaze downcast. "I'm fine."

"If you're worried about the Lusiri, don't be. I'll take care of them today. You have my word."

"And Mina?"

Darius glanced at Cyril, who stood a little way off. "He may take her home as soon as he's finished."

I nodded and leaned against the nearest tree, where fat jeweled lemons hung from the branches. "What about Evran and Jean?"

"I assume you'll want to say goodbye?"

"No." Helen had already risked her life trying to stop Darius. For all I knew, I'd foiled her plan to take the throne. The very least I could do was give Jean and Helen the opportunity to escape. "He and Jean are free to go, if they want."

"So you noticed it, too, then? Perhaps it's better this way. You won't have to worry if you've made the wrong choice."

"You're right," I said, though inside, my heart was breaking. "I'll stay here until you get back."

I somehow held back the tears until he was gone. He *was* right, I didn't have to worry that I'd made the wrong choice.

I already knew that I had.

I waited for what felt like hours, until a guard came for me at last. "I'm to take you to your room, Miss Duval." He extended a hand to help me up from where I sat in the shade of an apple tree.

I climbed shakily to my feet without his help, though I was exhausted down to my bones. "I was supposed to wait for Lord Darius."

"He told me to tell you he's been detained. There's a hot bath and clean clothing waiting for you in your room. He'll come by as soon as he's able."

I followed him through the winding corridors, and then up so many flights of stairs I knew we had to be climbing the spire. When we reached the top, the guard ushered me into a massive chamber. On the far wall, a glass sunburst window looked out over Corone. I walked toward it, marveling at seeing the world from so high.

The door closed behind me, and I whirled just as the key turned in the lock.

I shouldn't have been surprised. Whatever Evran had done, Darius would have discovered it by now. I had sacrificed everything for nothing. Darius had the Lusiri *and* me. I just prayed that whatever had happened, Mina and Evran were safe.

Numb, I bathed and changed into the clothing Darius had left for me, a black gown with an empire waist and a floor-skimming hem. Once, I had dreamed of being able to dress however I wanted. I had wished to be somewhere I didn't have to hide my magic, to be surrounded by people who understood me.

Now, in this twisted, broken version of the freedom I'd craved, I wanted nothing more than to be back in my own clothing, in my own home, with my family. I braided my hair in a crown on top of my head to pass the time, and when the sun sank below the horizon and Darius hadn't come for me, I climbed onto the large feather mattress and slept.

I startled awake at the sound of the door opening. Darius stood in the doorway, still wearing the clothing he'd worn on our journey. He looked exhausted, his clothing disheveled and his face as close to haggard as I'd seen it.

I sat up, unsure of what to say. How much did he know? How much did he think I knew?

"Your sister was already gone when the guards came to release her," he said, still standing in the open doorway. "This was her room. I assume she's back with your father, though no one can tell me how she escaped."

Darius walked to the fireplace and started a fire, his back toward me. Shadows danced on the walls as the flames roared to life. He rose and closed the door before turning back to me. "I don't know how much of this you were involved in," he said as he approached me. "I don't know how I can trust you after this."

I wanted to hide under the blankets, but instead I patted my hair smooth. "If I had known, I wouldn't have had to make a deal with you, would I?"

Over his shoulder, one of the shadows from the fire grew

larger, stretching and morphing into human form. It took all my willpower not to leap from the bed and run to Evran.

Darius tracked my gaze and began to turn, but I cleared my throat loudly and walked over to a settee. Luckily, Darius followed. By the time he sat down next to me, the shadow had already subsided. I dragged my eyes up to Darius's face reluctantly. "Where are Jean and Evran?"

"The last time I saw them they were heading south on horseback."

"Cyril didn't take them home?"

"They wanted to go to Belasava. I gave them enough money for passage and supplies. I know that must be difficult for you to hear."

I tried to look suitably devastated, but I was glad Jean and Helen were safe, and together. I didn't know if Helen had ever even wanted the throne, but if they were moving on, then perhaps this was the best outcome in the end. "I just want them to be happy."

"I know. The Lusiri are taken care of. Your family is together again. Your lover is gone. I've fulfilled my side of the bargain."

He was making it clear that just because my friends had tried to thwart his plans, I wasn't going to be allowed out of our agreement. My eyes pricked with tears, my stomach souring as the full weight of what I'd sacrificed settled on me. I hadn't thought this through. I hadn't thought about anything beyond ensuring the safety of Evran and my family and friends.

He rose and bowed stiffly. It was clear my emotions unnerved him. "I'll let you get some rest, Liora."

Before he reached the door, I managed to find my voice. "Can I ask you something?"

He turned. "Yes."

"Will I be locked in the dungeon from now on?"

He frowned. "You're not a prisoner, Liora. This will be your room. If it's not suitable, we can find you another one."

Not a prisoner by name, perhaps, but I was trapped, nevertheless. "Thank you, my lord."

He took a step closer to me, landing so close to the spot where Evran was hidden I didn't dare breathe. "It's just Darius from now on."

"Then good night, Darius."

The moment he closed the door behind him, not locking it this time, I sprang from the bed and ran to Evran. He materialized as I reached him, his arms so solid and comforting I immediately burst into tears.

"What's going on?" he asked as he kissed the top of my head. "Why are you here with him?"

Evran's clothes were filthy, his face scruffy with stubble. He had been hiding in the shadows for days, and meanwhile, I was dressed in a gown given to me by our mutual enemy. "I'm so sorry," I sobbed. "I didn't know what was happening out there, in Tezhia. Everything was confusing. I thought you had fallen in love with Jean—"

"*What?*"

I looked up, tears streaming down my cheeks. "Helen and Jean really *did* fall in love. I only realized it was Helen today, when I'd already made that horrible bargain." I broke down again, Evran's arms the only thing keeping me up. I told him everything I thought I'd told him yesterday, about Darius's powers and where they'd come from. "I was so afraid I'd hurt you," I said. "And you had grown distant from me, closer to Jean and Cyril. I thought that meant you'd be all right without me. I thought the only way I could keep you safe was by agreeing to work for Darius." Another sob racked my body. "And now you and I can never be together."

"Oh, Liora," he breathed, finally understanding. He sat down on the bed, scrubbing his hands through his hair. "I told Helen not to do anything stupid. I knew she might have a hard time pretending to be in love with you, but I never thought…"

"Why didn't you tell me what you were doing?" I lowered myself onto the bed next to him, wishing I could go back to sleep and wake up to find this had all been a bad dream. "You said you trusted me."

He closed his eyes and pulled me to him, just as I'd hoped he would when I told him the truth. Poor Helen must have had no idea how to respond. "I hated doing it, Liora, you must know that."

I cried harder at his kindness. "I'm sorry. I'm so, so sorry."

"Not as sorry as I am." He held me for a long time, making gentle noises to calm me. Finally, when I'd run out of tears, he spoke again. "Jean wanted you to know the plan, but I thought it was best to keep it between the three of us. I would have kept it just between Helen and me, but I knew Jean would figure it out."

"But why not tell me?"

"I was still worried about Darius. If he had found out what we'd done, he would have killed all of us."

I lowered my gaze, hurt that he hadn't trusted me. But a part of me couldn't blame him. I had allowed my fear—of losing Evran, of Darius, of myself—to cloud my judgment more than once. Maybe I couldn't be trusted.

When I looked up, Evran's jaw was clenched in frustration.

"I should have told you. I thought if I could free Mina and my mother, Darius wouldn't have anything left to threaten us with, and we could destroy the Lusiri and the tapestry. Cyril brought me to the palace the night before you left The White Fox. I hid in the shadows and stole the guard's keys. It was easy enough to get Mina free. Cyril transported her to a safe house so fast Darius never knew he'd left. By the time the guards noticed in the morning, they had no way of contacting Darius."

At least my sister was safe. "But where is your mother?"

"I haven't been able to find her. I think Darius must have taken her somewhere else. I've searched everywhere and had no luck."

I gripped his arm. "Then my deal wasn't in vain. He's promised to let her go and destroy the tapestry. It was part of the deal."

"You can't stay here, Liora. I'll take you home now and return for my mother. I know I can find her."

I desperately wanted it to be that simple. "He'll just come after us again, Evran. I made a bargain."

"You didn't know what you were agreeing to! He made you terrified you'd end up like him, that *you* would somehow harm the people you love, when this has been his doing all along."

My tears resurfaced, spilling over my lashes and down my cheeks. Darius had manipulated me, just as Evran warned me he would, and I had fallen for it. "I want to go with you to Belasava. I want to live in a world where no one threatens our happiness. But as long as Darius is alive, as long as he thinks that my power is the answer to his problems, he's going to make sure we never have a moment's peace."

Evran buried his head in his hands, looking as hopeless as I felt. "This is all my fault."

"Of course it isn't," I said, pulling his hands away. "You're right. This is Darius's fault and no one else's. Once your mother is free, we'll find a way to fix this." My glow had been weakened by my encounter with the Lusiri, but it lit up the space around us as I leaned in to kiss Evran. Relief that he had forgiven me gave way to a tiny glimmer of hope. As long as we loved each other, there was nothing we couldn't find our way out of.

"Where will you go?" I asked him as we settled back on the pillows together.

"I'll leave the palace and see if I can track down my mother. I'll check in with you as soon as I can."

"Be careful."

"I will."

I felt my eyelids growing heavy, but I didn't want to miss any time with him. I wanted to stay like this, listening to the steady beat of his heart, soothe away the tension in his jaw, and watch the firelight cast dancing shadows over his skin.

"I love you," he whispered, and the soft assuredness of his words was the last thing I heard before I drifted off to sleep.

TWENTY-NINE

Somewhere in Corone, bells were ringing. Not the measured clang marking the hour but the alarm bell that meant something bad had happened. I ran to the sunburst window, scanning the horizon for smoke, but it was barely daylight, and if there was a fire in town I couldn't see it.

I opened the door to my room and poked my head into the hallway. Mine was the only chamber in this part of the tower, and there wasn't so much as a servant passing by. I was still wearing the black dress Darius had picked out for me, so I shoved slippers onto my feet and grabbed a throw from the back of an armchair, wrapping it around myself as I descended the stairs.

Finally, when I was at the main level of the palace, I understood what had happened.

A maid scurried by, tears streaming down her cheeks, and a group of nobles huddled together, speaking in hushed tones.

The queen was surrounded by her ladies in waiting. Everyone was crying. Everyone looked terrified.

"Was it the prince?" I asked a passing guard.

He narrowed his eyes at me. "No, witch. It was the king. I suggest you return to your room. Lord Darius will be looking for you."

I stepped back, shocked by both the news of the king and the way the guard spoke to me. But with nowhere else to go, I did as he said and returned to my chamber. I wanted to change into my old trousers and tunic, but they were gone. I washed my face with the cold water from my bath, fixed my hair, and paced the room. It couldn't be a coincidence that the king had died the night Darius returned. I wished Evran would come back, that someone would tell me what was happening.

Finally, there was a knock on my door. I ran to it, not sure who I was expecting but desperate for information. Darius stood on the other side, clad all in black. He strode past me into the room.

"What happened?" I asked.

"The king is dead."

"How?"

He paced up and down, his hands balled into fists at his side. "One of the Lusiri."

No, no, no. "You said the Lusiri were dead!"

"No, I said they were taken care of. And they were. I put them in an enclosure in the menagerie, with their harnesses on."

I felt the heat rise in me as I grabbed his shoulder and spun him toward me. "You lied to me."

He waved his hand dismissively, as if that wasn't the most pressing concern. "I didn't think the king would be so stupid as to go into the Lusiri enclosure alone. To remove their harnesses. To feed them!"

I started to ask who had discovered him when it hit me: if the Lusiri had fed, they had also created a hole.

Darius nodded. He'd been waiting for me to come to this realization. "So tell me, how many voids did you close up on the journey?"

My first instinct was to lie, but what was the point in lying now? "I don't know. Several."

"And you didn't think this was something worth bringing to my attention?"

"The holes are just like the tapestry. If we had told you, you would have let them take over everything."

He grabbed hold of my shoulders, his features twisted with fury. "You presume to know what I would have done?"

I sent heat to my skin, and he hissed a moment later, releasing me. "Given everything I know about you," I spat, "why would I expect any different? And you saw what happened to the hound..." The edge in my voice faded as a terrible thought struck me. If the Lusiri hadn't fed on the king, but he had instead fallen into the void, he might not actually be dead. "Please tell me you recovered the king's body."

"I did not," he growled. "Which is why you're coming with me." He reached for me again, but I folded my arms and strode past him.

We crossed through the gardens to the menagerie. Guards were clustered at the entrance, keeping a handful of curious nobles out.

"Has anyone seen?" I asked.

"No. And I intend to keep it that way."

"What will you tell them?"

"I haven't worked that out yet." He extended his arm as he passed one of the guards, who handed him a sheathed sword.

I gaped, unsure who the sword was intended for. He stopped outside a high-walled enclosure and turned back to the guards. "Don't let anyone come in here, no matter what you hear. And that includes you."

The guard nodded, his face pale against his black-and-white uniform. "Yes, my lord."

Darius unlocked several large padlocks and opened the gate to the enclosure just enough for us to fit through. He pulled me behind him, closing the gate again so fast he almost clipped my arm. He murmured something, but I was too horrified by what I saw to hear him.

Nearly the entire enclosure had disappeared into nothingness. The Lusiri were still alive, pressed up against the walls of the enclosure, screaming. Whatever they were, whatever had made them, they did not want to return to it. The hole was so large we only had a few feet of room to stand. And it seemed that the larger the holes got, the faster they spread, because in the last minute it had advanced more than an inch toward us.

Without hesitating, I held out my hands, driving the void backward with my light. I advanced steadily, never wavering, my thoughts focused on how Darius had lied to me, how he'd allowed the king to die, how I had been played for a fool and it had cost me everything. I stepped past a body as it came into view. Some part of my brain registered that it wasn't human, but I ignored it, afraid I would lose my concentration. Instead, I continued to the back of the enclosure. Toward the Lusiri.

They shrieked and tried to run, but I spread my arms, and the light spread with it. I had never killed anything in my life, but these creatures should never have been alive in the first place. If Darius would not finish the job, I would do it myself. I raised my arms, my entire body aflame with white light, and let it burst out of me.

The Lusiri exploded. One moment they were there, and the next they were nothing but flecks of black, fluttering to the ground like ashes. But even as I watched them die, I couldn't seem to stop my light. And as I struggled in vain to rein it in, that terrible kernel of nothingness I'd felt when Darius told me his answer awoke again.

Panic rose in me as I felt the distinction between my light and my physical body begin to blur. I was losing myself, I realized. I was losing, and I didn't know if I could bring myself back.

Please! I wasn't even sure what I was pleading for, or who I thought could save me. Darius had stopped me before, in Tezhia, but I couldn't even see him through my light now. I was completely alone.

A wave of horror washed over me at the thought of burning out. Not just because I didn't want to become as empty as Darius, but because I didn't want to lose my power. It was an inextricable part of me. The source of so much loneliness and fear, yes, but I wouldn't be myself without it.

Margana had told me I would know to heed my fears when I wasn't willing to give up the thing I was afraid of. I was terrified of what my power could do, but I would never give it up. Not for Darius, not for anyone.

I would have to save myself.

Reaching deeper than I ever had before, I somehow grasped hold of a tiny thread of my power. With excruciating slowness, I reeled in the thread inch by painful inch. At first, it felt hopeless. There was too much light. Who was I to think I was stronger than Darius, a mage who had wielded his power over decades and had still lost to it?

But it *was* working. The more power I gathered, the more it eagerly returned to me. I realized then that Darius was wrong. I didn't need him to counterbalance me. I could harness my powers without his help.

Finally, when I was finished, I collapsed, my head hitting the dirt so hard I saw stars. Darius was at my side in an instant, wincing as his skin touched mine.

I blinked blearily and sat up, rubbing at the back of my head. Everything hurt, but it was the cold shock of realization that forced my eyes to Darius's. "That's how you burned out, isn't it?" I asked.

He hesitated for a moment before nodding.

I swallowed down bile and let him help me to my feet. I understood now. I knew exactly how Darius had become what he was, how easy it would be to become the same thing. I had beat it, this time. But would I be able to the next?

Several minutes passed with nothing but the sound of our breathing, and then, so quiet I didn't notice it at first, something scratched at the dirt behind us. Our heads turned in unison, though I was the only one who screamed.

It was the king.

It was not the king.

It had pushed itself up onto its hands and knees, every inch of it pitch-black, like the Lusiri. Its head hung down. Aside from the scritching of its claws in the sand, it didn't move.

"Oh no," I breathed. My eyes skittered to the carcass of a goat, then back to the king. "I think... I think the king went into the void, just like your hound."

Realization dawned on Darius's face, but if he was angry with me for leaving out that valuable piece of information, he didn't show it. Without hesitating, Darius removed the sword from its scabbard in one swift movement and approached the king. He stopped just feet away, hefting the sword in his hand.

Slowly at first, and then faster, in the same jerky motion the hound had used, the creature began to turn its head. It continued to turn until the eyes were facing up, its head rotated completely backward. I stifled another scream as the thing that had once been the king opened its mouth, revealing a row of black fangs dripping with saliva.

Darius muttered something under his breath; it could have been a curse or a prayer. Suddenly, the creature began to scuttle across the dirt toward me, so fast it seemed to have far more than four limbs. I tripped over my own feet as I moved backward in terror, but Darius shouted, gaining the creature's attention. As it approached him, he stepped into a fighting stance, his concentration never breaking.

Just as the creature lunged, Darius brought the sword down in one powerful arc, severing its head from its body. It crumpled to the ground a moment later.

As the sword clattered to the dirt, I managed to find the strength to rise. I backed away from the corpse, afraid it would somehow start moving without its head.

Fortunately, the king seemed to be truly dead. "Do you think there are more of these creatures out there?" I asked.

He wiped his forehead with the back of his free hand, his heaving chest the only sign he had just slain a monster. "If there were, I imagine we'd have heard about it by now."

I didn't see Darius for several days. He was busy ruling the kingdom, while I wore down the carpets in my room with my pacing. I wasn't locked in, but aside from wandering the halls looking for Margana—and Evran—there was nothing else I could do. On the fourth day I went to the gardens, where I lay on my back in the perfectly manicured grass and watched the light filter through the jeweled fruits.

"Do you like them?" a man asked.

I blinked and sat up. I'd barely seen anyone since the king died; everyone seemed to want to stay out of Darius's way. The man was middle-aged, with graying hair and a thick mustache. There was dirt caked under his fingernails and into the lines in his hands. "Are you the groundskeeper?"

He nodded and sat down next to me. "You must be Miss Duval."

I was surprised he'd heard of me, but then, news that Darius had a mage who wasn't locked away in the dungeon had probably spread quickly. "Yes."

The man frowned sympathetically. "He told me about you once. It seems like months ago now. Will you be staying at the palace?"

If someone had told me that I would one day agree to work for Darius, I wouldn't have believed them, no matter what the circumstances. "It was a bargain," I said once I'd found my voice again. "I did it to help the people I love."

"Not too many people associate with Darius by choice," he acknowledged with a nod.

"He told me he found you in the desert, tending a cactus garden."

He chuckled. "True enough. I couldn't afford land in Corone—or anywhere else for that matter. So I went to the desert, where no one cared enough to stop me. I could grow whatever I wanted there."

A sad little cactus garden, Darius had called it. But in this man's eyes, I saw the oasis he had created there, the date palms and flowering cactuses, the birds and animals it would have attracted. "What did he offer you in exchange for your talents?"

"Oh, it didn't take much for me. He said I would have a place at court, the opportunity to work for the king. A chance to grow whatever I wanted. I was young and it sounded glamorous, I suppose."

"You gave up your freedom for glamour?"

"Oh, I'm still free enough. Where else would I want to go?"

"Belasava?" I offered. *Literally anywhere Darius isn't?*

His smile was so kind I wondered how he could possibly work for such an evil man. "I'm not a powerful mage, child. Just a gardener. Darius leaves me to my work."

"You're not just a gardener," I said. "Your creations are beautiful." I remembered then how I'd wondered if Darius wanted to keep me in his collection of mages simply because he could. I'd been so foolish. I dropped my eyes. "I have something he wants. That's all it is to him. A transaction."

"I know it's hard to believe, but he isn't all bad. He found a new healer for the prince just this morning."

I turned my face toward him. "He did?"

"Indeed. I reckon he'll rule in the prince's stead for some time, but most of the other mages thought he'd kill the child for sure."

Margana had said Darius wouldn't be able to kill the prince, based on her spell. But that didn't mean he had to heal him. "Can I ask you something?"

He nodded.

"How well do you know the palace?" The groundskeeper was the first person to confide in me at all since I'd been here, and perhaps he could help me find Margana.

"Better than most anyone. I've been here nearly fifty years, since the king himself was a baby."

My eyes widened. "You've known Darius that long?"

He tugged on his mustache. "Yes. I am that old," he added with a wink.

"And has he changed much over the years?"

"There have been difficult times, I won't lie. When he commissioned that tapestry, I feared for all of us."

"You know about the tapestry?"

"Oh yes. But last I heard, he planned to tell the weaver not to finish it."

I was surprised by this news. I had assumed that after everything I'd done to thwart Darius, he wouldn't hold up his end of the bargain, particularly now that the Lusiri were gone. "Do you know where Margana is?"

His bushy eyebrows raised. "You know the weaver witch?"

"She's been my neighbor for most of my life. Her son and I are…close. He's been looking for her."

He leaned toward me and lowered his voice. "Darius has her in a cottage deep in the woods behind the palace. It's spelled. Only someone who knows what to look for can find it."

Finally, I was learning something useful. "Could you… would you take me there?"

"Don't you think you should ask him yourself?"

I chewed my lip, afraid that if I said the wrong thing, I could lose my one chance to save Margana.

He patted my knee knowingly. "I understand. Lord Darius doesn't make himself approachable, and he certainly doesn't grant favors. If I were you, I would stay away from the weaver. Your best bet is to make yourself as unobtrusive as possible around here. You can have a good life, if you're willing to leave your old one behind."

"He doesn't have to know," I said quickly. "You could show me tonight, after midnight." I didn't want to get the grounds-keeper in trouble. He seemed like a genuinely good person.

But we had to find Margana. "I could pay you. I don't know what with, but I'm sure I could come up with something."

He smiled, the corners of his mustache twitching. "I don't need money, my dear. But perhaps you could give me something else."

"I really don't have anything."

"I've heard your power is similar to what Lord Darius's was, before."

How well did this man know Darius? I wondered. "Y-yes."

"May I hold your hand for a moment?"

I breathed a sigh of relief. He could have shaken my hand earlier, and I would never have known what he was doing. Instead, he'd asked my permission, and it cost me nothing to give someone an answer. "Of course."

I turned and adjusted myself until we were on our knees, facing each other, and held out my hands to him. His were warm and calloused from toiling in the dirt for so many years. I closed my eyes, letting my mind go blank, and it was as if my body knew what to do. I thought I saw a flash of memory, of another man with a warm smile holding a jeweled rose and laughing, and a feeling of warmth and rightness spread over me. When I opened my eyes, the gardener had tears streaming down his cheeks.

"Is everything all right?" I asked, releasing his hands.

He nodded. "Thank you. That was all I needed to see." He wiped his eyes on a handkerchief. "I'll meet you here, under the peach tree, at midnight. I'll take you to the weaver woman."

I squeezed his forearm lightly. "I can't thank you enough." As I rose to go, I paused and turned. "Just one more question. Do you know about the girl with the diamond tears?"

His thick brows drew together in a peak, but he nodded.

"Did...did Darius torture her to produce tears?"

He shook his head. "No."

I smiled in relief.

"No, no," he continued with a sigh. "He made that poor treasurer do it for him."

THIRTY

That evening, I stared into the fire in my room, my mind running through every explanation for why the grounds-keeper would believe such a terrible lie. Each time my brain countered with some possible reason it could be true—Father despised Darius and would gladly pin such a terrible act on him; he and Mother had left Corone suddenly, which meant Father could have been leaving to spare the child; my mother was a witch and therefore likely to be similarly tortured if Father didn't comply—I stuffed it back down where it belonged. Father could never have hurt a child. It simply wasn't possible.

When I heard a knock at the door, I wasn't sure if I should be afraid or grateful for the interruption. I was dressed in a nightgown so I wouldn't arouse suspicion if Darius came, and I quickly covered myself with the throw blanket and stood. "Come in."

The door creaked open. I peered into the darkness, waiting.

I nearly screamed when the door closed again.

"Shhh!" Evran hissed, materializing from the shadows.

I sank back down in the chair, a hand against my pounding heart. "Where have you been?"

"Searching. But I heard your conversation this afternoon with the groundskeeper. I'm coming with you." He came to kneel before me, looking even more bedraggled than when I'd last seen him.

"Let me get you some clothes and food," I said. "You must be starving."

"I've been pilfering from the kitchens. No one notices. I'm sorry. I must smell dreadful."

"I spent weeks on the road with you. I'm immune."

He smiled and placed his hands on the arms of the chair, rising up to kiss me.

"What if Darius comes?" I whispered.

"He's in his chambers, signing dozens of decrees. He'll be there all night."

I smiled and leaned in, not caring if he was smelly and dirty. But then I remembered the man's words this afternoon. He was right; I would have to give my old life up to stay here. I couldn't expect Evran to sneak around in the shadows every time we wanted to meet.

"What is it?" Evran asked, sensing my hesitation.

"I just can't bear the thought of losing you." My voice quavered as I dropped my head in despair. "What are we going to do?"

He gripped my shoulders, rising and pulling me to my feet. "You'll never lose me, Liora. I swear it."

"How? How are we ever going to free me? You'll only endanger yourself and your mother by trying. I made this deal to protect you from that very thing."

"Don't you see that I don't want to be anywhere, do anything, if it's without you?" His eyes searched mine. "I was lost, even before the tapestry. I was afraid of myself, of what I might become. And you found me. You were my light in the darkness."

I placed my hands on either side of his face, the glow of my skin turning his eyes into glittering emeralds. "You were mine, too."

He turned his head and pressed a kiss to my palm. "That's where you're wrong, Liora. You were your own light in the darkness. You just needed to believe in yourself."

"Maybe," I said. "Or maybe believing in the good in each other helped us discover the good in ourselves." I was about to kiss him when the first toll of the bell reached us. "We should go," I said, reaching for the throw.

"I'll be with you. In shadow, of course, but I'll be there."

I nodded and led the way out of the chamber and down the many flights of stairs. The palace was quiet, but I made sure to listen carefully before rounding every corner. Just as I was about to step out into the garden, I heard Darius's voice.

"Tell the captain I want someone guarding Miss Duval at all times. If she goes for a walk, I want to know about it. She's extremely valuable. Do you understand?"

I tried to hide as his voice came nearer, but there was no-where to go. I felt it then, like a cool caress; Evran's shadow descended over me, nullifying my glow just as Darius rounded the corner. He walked past me without even a second glance.

Evran kept his shadow over me until we were in the garden. I was still reeling from what Darius had said. Our time was running out even more rapidly than I'd feared. Once I had a guard following me, I'd never be able to see Evran.

Fortunately, the groundskeeper was already there, circling the peach tree anxiously.

He nodded when he saw me and walked toward the woods without a word. I followed, my glow still dimmed by Evran's shadow, but not enough for the man to question it. We passed through the hedge maze, a rose garden, and down a long path I'd never used before. It cut around the menagerie, where Darius's guards were still posted.

"This way," the groundskeeper said as we entered the woods. We walked until the bell marking half-past midnight rang out, when we ducked into an opening in a holly bush I never would have noticed on my own.

"Watch yourself," he said, holding the branches aside to keep the leaves from pricking my skin. His own hands were calloused enough that it didn't seem to bother him. We entered a long tunnel of overgrown hedges, so low the gardener had to stoop. Fog crawled along the tunnel floor. The farther we walked, the closer the hedges felt, as if they were warning us to turn back.

Finally, we emerged through another holly bush into a clearing, where a stone cottage sat like an old man huddled against the cold. The windows were dark, and the absence of even a plume of smoke from the chimney gave the place a feeling of abandonment. Had Margana really been living here this whole time?

I waited for the groundskeeper to lead the way, but he stopped just a few feet from the holly bush.

"I'll leave you here." He glanced behind him, clearly eager to be on his way back. "You'll be able to find the tunnel yourself from this side."

I nodded. "Thank you for showing me. I know it was a risk."

"You showed me what I needed to see. It was only fair that I repay you. Just be careful, my lady. Lord Darius can be..."

"It's all right," I said. "I know."

He nodded and ducked back into the tunnel, disappearing through the leaves of the holly bush. I waited for a moment, and then Evran was beside me, solid and reassuring. He took my hand and squeezed it, but I could feel his fear echoing my own. Together, we approached the front door.

We knocked and waited.

When a minute had passed with no answer, Evran knocked again and tried the knob. It was locked.

"She's probably asleep." I sounded more hopeful than I felt. We walked to the small windows and peered in, but it was too dark to see anything, even with my glow.

"I have a terrible feeling, Ora."

I didn't have it in me to reassure him. If Margana was fine, if she'd been ordered not to finish the tapestry, why was she still here? Shouldn't Darius have released her by now?

"I'm going to try around the back," Evran said.

I stayed close to him, not wanting to be left alone in this eerie place. There was no back door, only another stone wall covered with ivy. We returned to the cottage's sole window, where Evran found a loose stone. He barely tapped the window and it shattered, like the glass was only there for show.

Evran took my throw blanket and wrapped his hand before knocking the jagged shards of glass out of the way. We both knew he couldn't fit through the window. Without a word, I bent my knee so he could hoist me up.

My heart hammered in my chest as I poked my head in through the window. The darkness was so complete it reminded me of the tapestry, but I released my glow until I could just make out a small wooden table and two chairs, a cold fireplace, a narrow bed in one corner. I pulled myself through to my waist, but there was no room to draw my leg up. I extended my arms and fell to the floor, absorbing as much impact as I could before ducking my head and rolling through.

"Everything all right?" Evran called.

My glow cast long shadows around the cottage; the chairs looked tall enough for a giant. On the far wall, the empty frame of a loom cast its rectangular shadow. And below it, in glimmering piles of black, lay the unraveled threads of the tapestry. The ash in the hearth was as black as the remains of the Lusiri when they'd exploded in the enclosure. Margana must have burned what she could; what little remained would never be enough to remake the tapestry.

The question was, how? She had told me once that everything she wove could be unraveled, as long as the final knot wasn't tied. But if she could have unraveled the tapestry all along, why hadn't she done it as soon as she knew what it was? There had been the threat to her life, and Evran's, of course. But both had been willing to die before letting Darius have the tapestry.

"Margana?" I whispered into the dark. I stepped forward, scanning the room, until I heard a creak above me, followed by a strange chittering sound.

"Liora?" Evran called again. "Is everything all right?"

No, I wanted to say. Something was profoundly wrong about this cottage. Slowly, against my better judgment, I looked up.

Margana was above me, staring down. She was suspended from the ceiling like a bat, her head turned in that same horrible way the king's had been. Her black lips pulled back in a snarl, and a strangled sob escaped from my lips.

"Liora!" There was a thud on the door, then another, followed by Evran shouldering his way through. "What's wrong? Are you—"

Margana dropped from the ceiling, scuttling across the floor as my light surged with terror.

"No," Evran groaned. "Oh, Mother, no."

It made no sense. Margana had been here in this cottage, nowhere near the Lusiri and their voids. Had something else come out of the tapestry and attacked her? Had *this* been the cost of destroying one of her creations?

"Mother, it's me," Evran said, his voice breaking. But it was clear from the wild gleam in her black eyes that Margana didn't recognize Evran or me.

I reached for Evran's hand. Margana kept to the shadows, away from my light. I didn't think she'd attack us, but we couldn't let her go. I turned to Evran, my heart already broken for him.

He knew what I was going to say. "There has to be a way to reverse this, Liora. There has to be a way to bring her back."

"There isn't."

We both whirled to face the door, where Darius stood holding a lantern in one hand, a sword in the other.

"Don't go near her!" Evran shouted, placing himself between Darius and his mother.

"She's gone, Evran." Darius's voice was surprisingly gentle. "I know it isn't what you want to hear, but it's the truth. And if she gets loose, she could be just as dangerous as the Lusiri."

Evran only stared at Darius, his face contorted with grief.

"For what it's worth, I didn't mean for this to happen," Darius continued. "I told Margana you had gone away with the mentalist. I told her she was free to go once she destroyed the tapestry. I didn't know you were here, Evran."

"Did you know what destroying the tapestry would do to her?" I demanded. "Did you know what she'd become?"

"How could I have known?"

He could be telling the truth. I wasn't sure if Margana had ever destroyed one of her own creations before, and perhaps no one had understood the cost, not even Margana. The Shadow Tapestry wasn't like any other weaving. It had been a physical manifestation of a place, crafted from the hairs of a magical beast. Besides, Darius still didn't know who Helen was. He thought Evran and Jean were in love, that they'd left Tezhia together. He had not been deceiving Margana when he told her that Evran was gone.

But Darius had to have known the anguish it would cause Margana, to hear that her only son, whom she'd already lost once, had left without saying goodbye. If Margana even suspected that destroying the tapestry would destroy her, too, perhaps she had only been willing to take the risk because she thought Evran had abandoned her.

And yet, maybe it didn't matter why she had done it or what she had known. At least she believed Evran was safe, and perhaps for her, that had been enough.

I was still staring Darius down when I heard that awful chittering sound again, reminding me of the not-squirrels in the tapestry. I spun around to see Evran kneeling in front of his mother, like he was trying to calm a wild animal.

"Mother, it's me." He held his hands out in a gesture of peace. "I'm here. It's going to be al—"

Margana howled and turned toward me. I hadn't realized that my light had been building as I watched in terror. Suddenly, without any warning, she sprang at me. I screamed and fell backward, just as Darius's sword came down on her neck.

I landed on my back, with Margana's severed head landing on top of me. I screamed again as the black blood spilled onto my skirts and looked up, wild-eyed, at Darius. His sword arm had dropped to his side, and with his other hand, he grabbed Margana's head by its black hair and flung it away.

A roar full of anguish and fury tore through the cottage. Evran strode toward Darius, his fists clenched at his sides. Behind him, his shadow began to grow and stretch, morphing into something inhuman, looming so high it engulfed the entire cottage.

I scrambled backward, until my back was against the wall near the remains of the tapestry. *It's only a shadow*, I told myself, but where it brushed my skin, it was so cold it hurt.

Darius held his ground, though he kept the sword at his side. "I'm sorry, Evran. Truly."

It was far too late for sorry. Evran was pure rage and hatred, no rational thought left in his mind. "You did this to her!"

Darius dropped the sword and held his hands up. "I didn't mean to."

"It wasn't just this. You used her powers for evil when all she wanted was to create good. You made her life miserable."

"I saved her."

Evran froze, though his shadow was still a bloated, monstrous thing.

"What are you talking about?" I climbed unsteadily to my feet, trying my best to avoid the black blood staining the ground.

"I found her on the road when she was just a young woman. Belle Sabine had her and was about to suck her dry. I killed the wretched creature to save Margana's life. When I brought her to the palace and offered her work, she discovered an old loom in a storeroom. That's when her gift emerged. She was so grateful she asked to stay."

"You're lying!" Evran's voice came out as a broken, brittle shriek. "She would never have worked for you by choice."

"They all do," Darius said, still eerily calm. "When they realize they can do more with their gifts working for me than they ever could on their own, they practically beg me to let them stay."

I recalled how Margana wished she never had to weave again. She must have regretted ever going to work for Darius, especially once she had a child. But how could she have known what he was capable of?

Darius foolishly went on, as if he didn't see the way Evran's shadow was swelling inch by inch. "Your mother chose her fate. Just as Liora's mother did. And just as Liora herself has."

Stunned, I took a step forward. "My mother?"

Without warning, the shadow behind Evran rushed forward, and the feeling of it passing over me was so horrible I shrank back against the wall. "Evran!" I cried, but he didn't hear me or chose not to.

The shadow swallowed Darius, extinguishing the lantern. My own light sputtered, the way it had when Evran held me before he entered the tapestry. I called his name again, but he was oblivious to everything but Darius. I could barely make him out in the darkness.

Something in the air shifted. Evran stumbled as the shadow began to pull and stretch. Toward Darius's open hand.

It was sucking him forward, the way the Lusiri did, swallowing the shadow as it shrank down, down, until it was twice the size of Evran, until it was a normal shadow. And it didn't stop.

I stared in horror at Darius, whose pupils had expanded to fill all but a crescent of gold. There was no fury on his face, only concentration. Evran stumbled forward again, his shadow gone, until even his body seemed to distort as Darius pulled him in. *This* was what Margana had meant about using mages up.

"Stop!" I screamed. "Darius, please!" I knew even as the words left my lips that he wouldn't stop, that he was as far away from me as Evran was. I closed my eyes, blocking out the sight of the two of them, and reached down deep, to the place where my light had lain dormant for so many years. It came to me without a struggle, and I let it fill me, from the tips of my toes to the top of my scalp. I opened my eyes.

I stepped in front of Evran, who crumpled to the floor behind me.

"Darius, stop," I commanded.

His pupils shrank, just for a moment, as if he was trying to obey. But I felt the void sucking at the edges of my light like a sentient thing, a predator savoring its first drop of blood. It tasted power, and it wanted more.

THIRTY-ONE

We were at a standstill.

Darius's emptiness pulled at my light, like a child in a game of tug-of-war, and I pulled back just as hard.

"Darius," I repeated, hoping that somewhere in there, he could hear me. But the pull only became stronger. Darius was a vacuum looking to be filled.

So I would fill it with the one thing I could: light.

I closed my eyes again and imagined myself in the tapestry, surrounded by darkness. I saw myself glowing, faintly at first, then brighter, brighter, until even with my eyes closed all I saw was white. I blazed like the sun, and then I pushed all that light through my hands and into Darius's chest.

As soon as the light left my body, his void swept in to replace it. I could feel myself tiring, knew that Darius was stronger than me. He'd been honing his powers for years, and I'd only just discovered what mine could do.

His lips curled in a smile that didn't reach his eyes. Whatever was inside Darius, it was both him and not him. I knew that he was not completely empty, that some part of the man he'd once been remained. But right now, there was a war within him, and the emptiness was winning.

I needed to switch tactics. Instead of fighting against him, I surrendered my light. I tried to imagine it sweeping through the vast nothing inside of him, filling it. An image came to me of a golden-haired boy, looking back over his shoulder as a man, woman, and child faded into the distance. Tears streamed from the boy's eyes as the figures grew smaller. Betrayed and abandoned by his own family, his heart was shattering before me. A heavy hand settled on his shoulder, turning the boy away, and the image faded.

Gritting my teeth against Darius's pull, I reached out with my light like fingers, searching the places where Darius tried to hide what was left of himself. And when I found those places, I shone brighter. The shadows fled in my wake.

I was so full of my own triumph that it took a moment to realize something within me was responding to the void, something other than my light. It was the void inside of me, I realized, the small hole that had opened when it recognized itself in Darius. And now, it was yawning wide open, like a fathomless pit. It pulled at me from the inside out, a tidal wave sucking up everything in its path before surging forward. I could sense the infinity of it, understood then that if I surrendered to it, there would be no turning back. Not this time.

My hands were still pressed against Darius's chest. His head was thrust back, his face contorting in agony when our eyes met, as if he finally understood the vision he received when he touched me: I *was* the answer. I could give him everything he wanted.

But in the process, I would destroy myself.

I tried desperately to pull myself back from the edge, but that single thread I'd managed to reel in when I destroyed the Lusiri evaded me. My power didn't want to go back down to where I'd kept it hidden. I wasn't even sure I was big enough to hold it anymore.

Margana had once told me that Darius was his magic, or vice versa, and I finally understood. The emptiness I'd felt when he first touched me swelled within me now, and I knew that if I just let it take me, I would be unstoppable. No one would hurt the people I loved again. Not even Darius. Surrender to the void, and I would never have to hide my light from the world. Become one with my magic, and I would no longer live in fear; people would fear *me*.

But some faraway part of me recognized how wrong that was. I would become what Darius was now, a black hole where a star had once been. Someone who took and took without ever giving. Someone who couldn't love, because love couldn't exist without sacrifice, and empathy, and the terrifying possibility of loss.

Darius said Margana, my mother, and the other mages chose to work for him because they wanted power. But maybe what they really wanted was a life without fear. I couldn't blame them for that; it was an intoxicating promise, one I might have chosen myself just a few weeks ago.

But I couldn't do that now.

Not to Evran, not to my family.

Not to myself.

Darius had been right about one thing: fear was a powerful tool. It reminded us what truly mattered. With the thought of all the people I loved driving me, I pulled my arms back toward my chest as if I was pulling them through a raging fire. Every inch was agony. But slowly, slowly, I felt the light

begin to drain away. Swirling down and down, until everything was black.

When I opened my eyes, I was on the rough floorboards
of the cottage. Evran was holding me, his touch cool and
comforting.

Darius lay on the ground a few feet away. His shirt had
melted away, two blistering burns in the shape of hands
branded on his chest.

I turned my face up to Evran. He looked confused and be-
reft, but he appeared physically unharmed. His shadow was
just a normal shadow again.

"Are you all right?" he asked me, rocking me gently. "Please
say you're all right."

I took stock of myself, not just physically, but mentally. If
I was empty, like Darius, would I even recognize it? With a
wave of relief, I realized that my skin was still glowing. And
where Evran's skin touched mine, I felt no urge to take anything from him. "I'm all right."

Evran released me slowly and crawled over to Darius, pressing two fingers to his neck.

"Is he dead?" I asked, not sure what I hoped the answer
would be.

"Not quite."

I joined Evran at Darius's side. The burns on his chest
were already blistering. There would be scars for the rest of
his life. Unconscious, he looked a little like the boy I'd seen
in my head.

While I couldn't regret where this had ended, I did feel
sorry for Darius. Yes, I had made the choice not to surrender
to my powers, but I had a family, and Evran, and friends who
loved me. I knew deep down that no matter what happened, I
wasn't alone. Bastian had stolen those things from Darius. For

whatever reason, he *had* believed that I was his redeemer, and maybe I was. I could have killed him. I might even have survived. But the part of me that mattered most wouldn't have, and no revenge was worth that cost.

A groan bubbled out of Darius. He blinked and looked up at me. I gasped.

His eyes were no longer that changeable, inconstant gold. They were brown. Just ordinary brown eyes. They searched mine, questioning.

I sighed and took his hand, not for comfort, but to bear witness to the very moment his answer came to him and he understood what I already knew to be true.

"My magic," he said, sounding so lost I couldn't help but pity him. "It's gone."

We tied Darius up with rope, though he didn't put up a fight. It was clear that he was finished. He walked between us back to the castle, a perfectly cooperative prisoner. He hadn't spoken another word.

As soon as we crossed the gardens and entered the castle, we found ourselves surrounded by chaos.

Evran stopped the first guard we encountered. "What happened?"

"The queen," he said, apparently not recognizing Darius. "She...she unraveled. The prince, too. They're both gone."

Evran and I exchanged a horrified look and quickened our pace toward the royal chambers. We heard someone crying in anguish, and maids stood together in corners, whispering.

"When did this happen?" I asked one of them.

"Just now." She exhaled raggedly. "One minute the queen was there, and the next... I can't describe it. You have to see it for yourself."

Evran and I walked to the queen's chambers, shouldering Darius along between us. No one even attempted to stop us. Without Darius giving orders and controlling the king, there was no one left in charge. Inside the queen's room, people I assumed must be healers and advisors stood staring at the queen's bed. There was nothing there but a pile of thread.

"How did this happen?" I had spoken to Evran, but it was Darius who answered.

"They were Margana's creations," he said softly. "When she died, everything she'd ever woven died along with her."

I glanced around at the palace walls. A witch had created this place, but it was still standing, long after her death. "Why?"

"Magic is erratic and unpredictable, Liora. It doesn't like to be taken for granted. Margana destroyed one of her own creations when she demolished the tapestry. And so her magic responded in kind."

We were silent as the full weight of what Darius said settled over us. All the gold Margana had woven would also be gone. The remaining hound. The poor little prince. The entire royal family had just been obliterated in one day.

"Who's going to rule now?" a woman asked the room full of people, who only murmured their own confusion and fear. "There is no rightful heir. There will be chaos!"

"There is an heir," I said, eliciting a wide-eyed look from Darius. "Princess Helen, daughter of Queen Salome."

"She lives?" The same woman's face lit up in wonderment. "Princess Helen is alive?"

"Indeed she is," Cyril replied, materializing out of nowhere. Then he turned to me with the first genuine smile I'd seen from him in weeks. "And she's waiting at your house."

★ ★ ★

It wasn't long before I got to see Helen for myself. Once the guards, who seemed perfectly happy to answer to Evran and me for now, had locked Darius in the dungeon, Cyril took us home.

The moment my foot crossed the threshold, I was nearly bowled over by Mina, who screamed with happiness as she embraced me. "You're okay. I was so worried about you, Ora."

Adelle, teary-eyed and silent, walked over to give me a more reserved, though no less loving, embrace.

When she released me, I took in the company gathered in my living room: Father and Adelle. Cyril and Mina. And Jean and Helen.

Jean's gray eyes were as bright as her smile. "We're so glad you're all right. Cyril came for us, as soon as he felt it was safe."

"But how?" I asked. "I thought you were going to Belasava."

Jean shook her head. "We never would have abandoned you. We let Darius believe we were heading south, but Cyril knew we'd be waiting at The White Fox."

I was almost afraid of the answer, but I had to know. "And your parents?"

Her smile widened. "Safe and sound. They've been hiding in a nearby village since the raid on our camp."

"Kylian found them," Adelle said. "A guest at the inn mentioned an older couple searching for their lost child, and he put two and two together."

Jean took Helen's hand and squeezed it. "I told Helen she could live with my family. But from what I'm gathering from your thoughts, it sounds like she might have a better offer."

Helen's dark eyes darted from Jean to me and back again. "Is Darius dead?"

Evran shook his head. "No. But somehow Liora managed to fill his void without burning herself out. She was amazing," he added, pressing a kiss to my cheek. "Darius lives, but his powers are gone. He will never hurt anyone ever again."

"What does this mean?" Helen's thick brows furrowed as she tried to process Evran's words. "Am I the queen now?"

"Do you want to be?" I asked. "I believe the kingdom will be grateful for your return. But you don't owe anyone anything. Not after what they allowed Darius to do to you."

Helen looked to Jean. "I want mages to be safe. I don't want anyone to have to hide anymore. I want places like The Crystal Gazer to be celebrated, and for people like Cherie to be beloved. But I don't know anything about running a kingdom."

Jean stepped up to Helen and rested her forehead against Helen's chin. "I think you'd be a wonderful queen."

"You're probably right," she said with a smirk. "And I would look stunning in a crown. But I can't do it alone."

Jean glanced up into Helen's eyes. "You wouldn't be."

The sight of Helen blushing made me grin unconsciously. I quickly looked down at my feet before she caught me.

"But what about the tapestry?" Adelle asked. "Aren't we still in danger?"

Evran shook his head. "My mother destroyed it. We don't know how, exactly. But in the process, she...she lost herself. She's gone."

Adelle's eyes flew to mine. I shook my head grimly. I knew Evran wasn't ready to speak about her death, those last horrible moments he spent with her, when she hadn't even recognized him. I just hoped that one day those memories would fade, and he would remember her as she'd truly been, a defiant, powerful woman who loved him more than anything.

My family offered their condolences, and Jean exchanged

a long look with him that I knew held a silent conversation. Whatever consolation she offered seemed to help, because he managed a small smile when it was finished.

"I'd like to get some of my things," he said to me. "Will you come with me?"

I nodded. "Of course."

Together, we walked down to her gate, past the copper stars in the tree. The house was unlocked, the cuckoo clock calling from the kitchen. Inside the parlor, I glanced around at the remaining magical objects. None had been created by Margana, I realized. Otherwise, they would also be piles of thread.

I wondered if Darius really had known what would happen if Margana unraveled the tapestry. If he understood that she'd be destroying not only all of her previous creations, but also herself, then he had willingly given up one of his most powerful mages. By making the bargain with me, he'd chosen the person he used to be—the one who felt, the one who loved— over power. Maybe my presence would have been enough, and he really would have given up his hold on the kingdom. But it would have come at the cost of my freedom, and I wasn't willing to sacrifice my own chance at happiness for his.

Evran sat down on the sofa, next to a small wooden frame. "This was my first loom, you know." He touched the wood with surprising tenderness. "I made a few pieces on it, but I didn't have a knack for weaving."

I settled down next to him, taking one of his hands and pressing a kiss to a scar I hadn't noticed before.

"Do you think my mother really went to work for Darius of her own free will?" he asked. "Do you think he truly did save her from Belle Sabine?"

"I don't know," I said gently. "Would it change anything for you, if it were all true?"

He shrugged. "If she did choose to work for him, then I can't blame him for everything that happened. I would have to blame her, too. And I don't want to believe that she was capable of making that choice."

"Even if she did choose to work for him, that doesn't mean she understood what she was agreeing to. It doesn't mean she was a bad person. If she had no idea about her powers before she met Darius, then she was probably just as lost and scared as we were. It's frightening, knowing you aren't truly in control."

"I suppose I wanted to believe she was too strong to need anyone's help, especially help from someone like Darius."

I thought of my father, how even without magic he seemed lost, desperately trying to hold on to things that were beyond his control. "I think when we're young we all need to believe that our parents have the power to keep us safe. And maybe this is how we know we're growing up—we finally recognize that they're just doing the best they can against impossible odds."

He kissed the top of my head. "Have I ever told you how brilliant you are?"

I snuggled closer to him, grateful when he didn't shrink away. "Why didn't you tell me you were the one who saved me the night the star landed on my house?"

"You finally figured it out."

It had taken nearly burning myself up to recognize the cool embrace I'd felt when I burned the hole in the tapestry, the same one I'd felt the night my mother died. I just hadn't realized it was Evran until I felt how cold his shadow was in the cottage. "I'm sorry it took me so long."

He inhaled, releasing the breath slowly. "I was in the woods the night your house burned down. I saw you lying in the undergrowth, burning like an ember. You were naked and so small. I thought you were dying, so I wrapped you up in my shadows to cool you down. When your color had faded to glowing white and your body temperature was lower, I hid, afraid someone would think I had done that to you. Your father found you not long after."

"Why didn't you say something? All those years... I would have burned to death without you."

"I wanted to. But the more my own powers started to develop, I thought... I thought you would hate me if you knew the truth about what I was. I thought you'd think I was trying to put out your light, when that was the last thing I ever wanted."

It was the same backward thinking that had led me to make the bargain with Darius. "I understand. But you know I never would have thought that, don't you? I love you. I've loved you my whole life."

He held my hands between his, my light emanating from the gaps in our fingers. "Even after what you saw in the cottage? There are times when I can't control my shadows, Liora. They take on a life of their own, and I don't know what they're capable of. What I'm capable of."

"I don't have full control of my powers yet either. We're still learning. All that matters is that I know you would never hurt me."

He kissed me softly, just a brush against the corner of my mouth. "Never."

"I'm so sorry about—"

"I know. I think she must have known all along what would happen if she destroyed the tapestry. She chose to do it anyway. I just wish she could have known a life without Darius in it. She might have found happiness."

"You made her happy," I said gently. "She loved you so

much. And she knew we loved each other. I think it helped her, to know you wouldn't be alone."

"I know it did."

We sat in silence for a while, until Evran finally rose. "I'm going to wash up, change my clothes, and gather my things. I'll come over when I'm finished."

"Are you sure you don't want to stay here tonight? This is your house now."

"I can't stay here, Liora. It's too painful."

"Of course. You know you'll always be welcome at our house." I stood and walked to the door, then hesitated on the threshold. "Evran, is it true that a mage child can't be born to non-mage parents?"

His lips curled down into the smallest frown, as if he'd been expecting this question for some time. "It's true," he said. "I'm sorry."

"That's what I thought."

"Remember what you said, Liora. Our parents are just doing the best they can."

I nodded. "I know. But the least we deserve is the truth."

THIRTY-TWO

While Evran sorted his belongings and Kylian showed Helen, Jean, and Cyril to their rooms at The Evening Star for the night, my family gathered around the table for our first meal together in far too long.

Father sat between Adelle and Mina, thinner than I remembered. Even the house felt smaller, now that I'd been away from it. I smiled wistfully as I glanced around our dear little parlor, where I'd sat sewing with my sisters for hours while Mina dreamed of adventure, Adelle imagined the family she would one day have, and I wished to be something more.

I could try to get Father to admit what I suspected by talking around it or by hinting that I knew. But I was tired of lies, and I was afraid that would be all he had to offer. After we'd eaten the meal Adelle and Mina had prepared, I turned to my father and told him we needed to talk.

By the look in his eyes, I could see that he, too, had been expecting this for quite some time. At least he didn't try to leave.

"Please, Father," I said, taking his hands in mine. "Tell me the truth. Was our mother a witch?"

"What?" Adelle and Mina both blinked in shock, and I knew then that neither of them had ever even suspected it. Why would they, when it had taken me all this time to figure it out myself?

Rather than try to deny it as I'd feared, Father looked almost relieved. "I didn't know what she was when I met her. Her father was a cobbler in Corone. She worked in his shop. I went in for a pair of shoes and walked out with half a heart. She kept the other half, and I was only whole when we were together.

"She told me she was a witch several weeks before our wedding. At that point, I'd already seen what Darius was capable of, and I knew I wanted nothing to do with magic. But it didn't matter. I loved your mother too much to let her go. I told her what Darius was like and made her promise not to practice her magic in Corone. But she was too impulsive, too brave. She wanted to help the little girl with the diamond tears escape."

"Is it true, then?" I asked. "Did you torture her?"

I'd never seen Father look ashamed before. "I didn't torture her, no. But I told her she couldn't go home to her family until we had enough diamonds to fill a chest. The kingdom was struggling at the time, and Darius was forcing anyone with valuable magic to contribute to the coffers. The girl—Capri—wanted to help, but crying was obviously incredibly painful for her. There was nothing I could do other than make her profoundly sad. It is the greatest shame of my life, and part of the reason I wanted nothing to do with magic. All I'd ever seen was how magic could be used against people."

"And Mother?"

"She was different," he admitted. "Magic brought her so much joy. She asked me to take her to the palace, and foolishly, because I would have done anything she asked, I did. She met Darius and some of his other mages. She saw the splendor of the palace and its gardens, and while she knew Darius was not a good man, she was also intrigued by the idea of learning to master her magic. Ironically, the only mages who could wield their powers without fear of discovery were those already working for Darius."

So Darius wasn't lying. Mother had wanted to learn from him. "And that's why you left Corone?"

He nodded. "Darius came to our house to visit when Adelle was born. I saw the way he looked at your mother, then, like she was a puzzle he was trying to solve. I knew he would find a way to use her, and she would agree to help him. It was clear to me that I would lose her to him if we stayed. I was so afraid of what would become of her, of Adelle. So I made your mother promise to never use her magic."

I tried to imagine what I would do if I had to repress my magic now, after I'd learned how to wield it. I wasn't even sure it was possible. "She agreed?"

"Not at first. She wanted to go to Belasava, where she could be a mage and still be with her family. But I was afraid to go that far away from anything we'd ever known, to be a nonmage in a kingdom ruled by them…"

Instead he had forced Mother to be a mage in a kingdom that despised them. If we'd left, perhaps the falling star never would have landed on our house and Mother would still be alive. I released his hands, unable to console him for his own mistakes. "Why didn't you tell me, Father? I had a right to know. We all did."

"I'm sorry. I should have. But once she was gone, it was easier not to. What good would knowing have done?"

"I wouldn't have felt so alone. I wouldn't have felt like I didn't belong in this family."

Adelle turned to me, her eyes reflecting my pain. "Oh, Liora, is that how you felt?"

"Sometimes," I admitted. "Sometimes I felt like I fell out of the sky instead of being born into this family like you were."

I was surprised when Mina spoke, her voice flat, sounding much older than her years. "What was her magic?"

In the same moment I'd remembered Evran saving me as a child, I had remembered that whole night. Not just the fever and the star coming toward the window and waking up in the woods, but everything in between. I had remembered my mother, and what had really happened to her.

"Come here, Ora," Mother had said, folding me into her arms. The roof was falling down around us. There were flames everywhere, licking up the curtains and sending beams splintering down. A hole opened up above us, and without a word, Mother leaped into the sky.

As fast as we had taken off, my fears fell away. We were soaring through the air, and the joy on my mother's face spread to me. I didn't realize that my clothes had burned in the fire. I only knew that my mother was happier than I'd ever seen her before, and we were flying.

When we heard the screams below, I looked down to see the house in flames. Father and my sisters were screaming my name and Mother's name, and people were rushing into the streets. Someone shouted and pointed up, and then we were flying toward the woods.

Mother laid me down in a nest of ferns and kissed my brow. "I'm so sorry, dear girl. I love you so very much, but I have to go."

"Why?" I asked. I was very sleepy and warm, and the fact

that my mother could fly was so wonderful I just wanted to curl around it and dream.

She smiled and stroked my hair. Her cheeks were damp. "Go to sleep, little one. Everything will be all right." In a heartbeat, she was gone.

I took a deep breath, and when I exhaled, a bit of the weight I'd been carrying on my chest evaporated. "Our mother could fly." I smiled through my tears and turned to Father. "And she didn't die in that fire. Our mother is still alive."

Father wept silently as Adelle and Mina stared at me, incredulous.

"What do you mean?" Adelle asked. "How can you possibly know that?"

I told them about my repressed memory and how it had come back to me when Evran attacked Darius. By the time I finished, we were all crying.

"How could you?" Mina said to Father, her face contorted with grief.

"I'm so sorry." Something about the sight of my father sobbing made me want to turn away. I loved him, but I was so mad at him for what he'd done to us. "I thought it would be worse if you knew she'd chosen to leave. It was easier to pretend she was dead."

"Easier for you," Mina spat. "How could you do that to us?"

An ache was building in my chest, similar to how it had felt when I thought Evran didn't love me. It was heartbreak, I realized. Deep, wrenching heartbreak.

"And that's why you kept us ignorant about magic?" I asked Father. "Because you resented Mother? You resented magic? What was it?" I was angry and hurt, yes, but I wanted to understand. Because Father must also have been so angry and in so much pain. And he'd been left to take care of us as best he could, without the woman he loved, with only half his heart.

"Your mother left because I made her hide her magic, and I knew if you didn't, Darius would come for you. If you never knew any better, it would be easier. That's what I told myself. I know now that I was wrong. I shouldn't have lied to you. I only wanted to protect you. All of you."

"This is all your fault!" Mina cried. "If you hadn't made her deny who she was, she wouldn't have left. I would have had a mother."

Adelle stroked her hair. "Darius might have come and taken Mother *and* Liora if not for Father."

"Besides, we don't know that's why she left," I said gently. "Maybe she was afraid. Maybe she was ashamed." Or maybe she just wanted to be herself and still be free.

We were all quiet for a while, lost in our own thoughts. I was about to get up to check on Evran when Mina wiped her eyes on her sleeve.

"Do you think…?" she started.

"What?"

"Do you think Mother really is still alive?"

Adelle and I shared a long look before I answered. "She's a mage. We have no reason to think she isn't."

Mina's eyes, still wet with tears, lit up. "Do you think she could be in Belasava?"

"Yes," I said, and I believed it with all my heart. "I think that's exactly where she went. And I think it's time for us to go find her."

Evran and I agreed to travel to Belasava just before the first snow. There was plenty to take care of at home, and there was no longer any rush to leave. He slept in Adelle's old room, because she and Kylian had married almost immediately after we returned. It was strange not having her at home, but Mina was back in our shared room, and Adelle was just in town. Cyril had moved into Margana's house with Evran's blessing.

It had only taken a few weeks to get Helen officially seated on the throne. Thanks to Father's meticulous accounting ledgers, he had been able to dig up an old inventory from the palace that included Helen's amulet, which a visiting mage dignitary had given to Queen Salome before she was exiled. It was proof that Helen was who she said she was. And now, with Darius locked away in the dungeon until someone decided what to do with him, Helen was the Queen of Antalla. She was the first mage ruler in over a century, and I had no doubt she would be one of the best. Jean and her family had moved back to Corone, where Jean's powers made her a particularly good adviser to the queen.

With everyone seemingly settled and happy, I lost some of my desire to leave Sylvan. I had just gotten my family back and was dreading saying goodbye to them again. Life was finally peaceful.

But going to Belasava was something I had to do.

It wasn't just about finding my mother, though now that I remembered her, I couldn't stop thinking about her. Maybe Father was right and she had chosen to leave us behind. I had no way of knowing with any certainty that she wanted to be found. But I was done living in ignorance and allowing fear to hold me back. There was no invisible beast in the forest waiting to eat me. Even if there was, I knew the one inside of me was stronger.

Finally, when the threat of snow in the air was impossible to ignore, Evran and I packed our belongings and loaded the cart that would take us to the port city of Tremelle.

Adelle had been dreading this goodbye as much as I was, but she wore a brave face as she handed me a freshly baked loaf of honey bread. It was wrapped in a tea towel edged in colorful embroidered cosmos, my favorite flower.

Despite the simplicity of her new preferred clothing—a cotton blouse and checked wool skirt, the first ready-made she'd ever purchased—she was still so beautiful that I knew she wouldn't escape the notice of the townspeople, no matter how badly she wanted to blend in. She hadn't sought the attention our family received, but she had always borne it stoically, never complaining about the sacrifices she'd had to make to keep me safe.

"Thank you for this," I said, tucking the bread in a basket, along with the tea and lavender soap she seemed certain I couldn't get in Belasava. "For everything. You've been more than a sister to Mina and me. We're so lucky to have you."

"I'm the lucky one," she whispered as we embraced, her tears cool against my cheeks. "Be careful out there."

"I will." I wiped my eyes and turned to Mina, who was valiantly fighting back tears of her own. Her chin quivered slightly, and I pretended not to notice. "I'm going to miss you, Mina."

She nodded. "Of course you are. Be sure to bring me a souvenir." I laughed and she lurched forward suddenly, pulling me into one of her fierce embraces. "I love you, Ora."

"I love you, too." I kissed the top of her head, inhaling the scent of her rosewater shampoo. "And I promise I'll bring something back for you."

"Something shiny," she murmured.

I laughed again as I released her and turned to my father. We said goodbye silently, because while we had both struggled recently to find the right words to say to each other, we would always be family.

I finally climbed into the back of Kylian's wagon, waving as we started down the road. Kylian had agreed to take us as far east as he could, and from there, we would travel on foot. Evran and I sat in the back together, our legs dangling over the end of the cart, watching our homes grow smaller in the distance.

I brought his hand to my lips, brushing them over his knuckles. "We're really leaving. I never believed I'd go beyond Sylvan, and now we're going to another kingdom."

"Are you afraid?"

I shook my head. "For the first time in my life, I can honestly say I'm not afraid of anything."

He was quiet for a moment.

"If you're worried about your shadow magic," I said, "you shouldn't be. It just so happens that you're traveling with an inextinguishable light."

He sighed and leaned his head against mine. "I'm afraid the shadows are a bigger part of me than I want to admit. What if I'm no different than Darius? What if I'm just as capable of using my magic for evil as I am for good?"

"I think we all are. And I suppose we could try to live without our magic, like my mother. But we both had the chance to lose ourselves to our powers, and we didn't. I think we're going to be just fine."

I wasn't sure if he believed me, but a few minutes later, he squeezed my hand, and I decided that would have to do for now. I snuggled closer to him to ward off the winter chill. I could have summoned my own heat, but it was a sorry substitute for Evran.

He wrapped his arm around me. "I love you, Liora."

"I love you, too." I smiled to think that those words had once felt impossible to say, when nothing could be easier now.

It had taken facing the emptiness inside of Darius—and inside of myself—to appreciate how full my heart was.

In the fading light, our legs cast long shadows onto the road, reminding me of Darius's hounds. I shivered and nudged my way farther under Evran's arm.

"Everything okay?" he asked.

I was about to nod when I saw the first star twinkle overhead. *Keep watch, my dear, for the Evening Star, she warns when night is falling...* I hummed the tune quietly to myself, remembering that night on the road when Margana had discovered me and all our careful plans had unraveled. How different everything had felt then.

"It seems unfair that someone like Belle Sabine should have a lullaby," Evran said, "when no one will even know my mother existed. She saved us all, and what's left of her to be remembered by? She created so many beautiful things, and now all of them are gone."

"Not all of them." I kissed him, willing him to see the answer: that Margana's most magnificent creation, the one she had always been the proudest of, was right here.

"She deserves to be remembered, Liora."

I rested my head against his shoulder and we watched the rest of the stars appear, like diamonds scattered across the universe's own black tapestry. "She will be, Evran. We'll make sure of it, together."

★ ★ ★ ★ ★

ACKNOWLEDGMENTS

✴ ✴ ✴ ✴ ✴

There are so many people I need to thank for their contributions to this book, but if you'll indulge me just a little longer, I want to give a quick explanation of how this particular story came to be.

I started writing *Luminous* in the fall of 2016, almost immediately after finishing *Crown of Coral and Pearl*. I had stumbled upon an article about a substance lauded as the blackest material on earth, and it got me thinking about darkness as a place. With the genesis of the Shadow Tapestry, I needed something—or as it turned out, someone—capable of illuminating that kind of darkness. Enter my star girl, Liora, and her glowing skin.

I'm not a particularly religious person, but my Jewish upbringing forms a large part of my cultural and spiritual identity. In Judaism, light is a symbol of creation. The Hebrew word for light, *ohr*, has the same numerical value as the word for secret, *raz*. These elements certainly played a part in developing *Luminous*. But I also wanted to be clear that darkness does not represent evil (in Judaism, or in this book). I have dealt with depression for most of my life, and while I tend to view the most difficult periods as gray and dim, I would not be who I am without them.

Most important, I wanted to tell the story of a girl who believes she has to hide who she is in order to feel safe and valued. I think many of us have felt this way at some point in our lives—I know I have. It takes a lot of bravery to accept the parts of ourselves we fear the most. But only in doing so can we become who we were truly meant to be. (In my case, a quirky, outspoken, fortysomething writer with a small fluffy dog inching ever closer to my lap.)

Finally, I have to give credit to three dark-haired sisters who helped inspire this story. Lola, Clementine, and Delilah: you are all magical.

And now, without further ado, the thank-yous:

As always, thank you to my wonderful agent, Uwe Stender, and the entire team at Triada US. Uwe, you once told me this was one of your favorite books ever. At least I think you did; maybe I dreamed it. At any rate, I do know that you stuck with me through quite a few revisions of this novel, and I'm so grateful you did. I hope I made you proud.

Bess Braswell, I am eternally grateful for your support. You picked up Liora's story when I thought her journey was over and brought her to life in the best possible way. Thank you for seeing something in both of us.

To Connolly Bottum, the best editor a girl could ask for. Thank you for being so patient, understanding, and insightful. You know just how to phrase a critique (and a compliment!) so that I always feel encouraged and inspired. I've learned so much from you in our time together. Here's to many more books!

Endless thanks to the entire Inkyard team. Kathleen Oudit and Marisa Aragón Ware created a stunning cover that is truly luminous. Brittany Mitchell and Laura Gianino ensured that readers would see it! And Marisa Hopkins, mapmaker extraordinaire, not only read an early version of the manuscript, but then went on to create the most beautiful map ever.

Thank you to all the friends and critique partners who read one of the many iterations of this story: Nikki Roberti Miller, Elly Blake, Rosalyn Eves, Tracie Martin, RuthAnne Frost, Kristin Reynolds, Kip Wilson, Jenn Leonhard, Destiny Cole, and Vanessa Lillie. (I can't remember if my besties Kim Mestre and Lauren Bailey read this one at some point, but all signs point to yes.)

Special thanks to Erin Hagengruber, the Belgrade Book Club ladies, Marko and Jelisaveta, my quarantine pod squad (Sarah, Emily, Josh, Darcy, Griff; special shout-out to Cheddar Biscuit's ears), and the whole US Embassy Belgrade gang. You make my life infinitely brighter.

Thank you, as always, to my family: Mom, Dad, Patti, Aaron, Jennifer, Elizabeth, Amy, and my vast array of nieces and nephews. I love you all, and I miss you every day.

My twinsie, Sarah, deserves her own thank-you. Sarina: you write the best cards, sing the weirdest songs, and make me laugh harder than anyone. Someday we'll be together, two tiny old ladies with a herd of even tinier dogs underfoot. But for now, just know that I love you impossibly much from afar.

To my husband, John, for the unending love and support. Now that I've known you for more than half my life, I can say for certain that you're the better half. I love you so.

To Jack, for your imagination, sense of humor, and encouragement. Thank you for telling me I'm the best mom in the world. I'm definitely the luckiest.

To Will, thank you for always making sure I'm up to date on the latest memes and Minecraft hacks. You feel all the feels and live life to the fullest. Keep being you, and, kid, you'll move mountains.

And finally, to you, dear reader. Thank you for coming

on this journey with me. I hope Liora's story inspires you to embrace the parts of yourself you've kept hidden. The world needs your light.

Thank you for reading
Luminous!

Turn the page for a sneak peek at Mara Rutherford's next
captivating and atmospheric novel,
The Poison Season!

PROLOGUE

The wolf was not thinking of hunger as it chased its quarry through the dark woods, having feasted earlier that day on a large roe deer. It was driven by a sense of purpose, one that had infected its brain late last winter, when it had picked its way carefully across the ice to the wooded island that seemed so still and peaceful—and likely full of prey.

The wolf was not from this mountain. It had been born on another, not so far from here. The alpha had driven it from the pack, already aware that it would be competition in the near future. But the wolf hadn't known that; it had only known that it was alone for the first time in its life. Alone, and hungry, and wanting…

There were no other wolves on this mountain. It had searched everywhere, but something about this Forest was not welcoming to wolves, or any other large predators, for that matter. It wasn't a lack of prey; it was something in the Forest itself. A warning of some kind, that this place wasn't for the likes of the wolf. But it was tired and hungry and searching, and so it had found itself on the island, padding about on silent feet, past the sleeping cottages and their unwitting inhabitants, which would have made a lovely meal. But the Forest told it, "No, they're not for you, either." And it had found itself in a pine grove in the island's center.

The wolf had snuffled at the base of the trees for a long time, picking up the scent of old blood and new growth, deep below the Forest floor. The roots of the trees, which had been replenished in a ceremony not long before the first snowfall, were always alive, even when the rest of the island slept. Feeling safe and quiet for the first time in many months, the wolf lay down amid the roots and slept a long, dreamless sleep.

When the wolf awoke the next morning, it felt different. It was no longer hungry or tired or lonely. It was as if the Forest itself had sustained the wolf in the night, and now the Forest bid it farewell, told it to go away from the island, before the lake thawed and it would be trapped. The Forest only asked one thing in return: that the wolf nourish the Forest the way it had nourished the wolf. And now the wolf, which was still young and still learning, would finally fulfill its duty.

As the island finally came into view, the wolf released a long, doleful howl and drove its quarry onward.

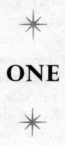

ONE

The Watchers stood on the lakeshore, peering through the heavy mist that hung low on the water this time of year, when winter was just thawing into spring. Across the lake, the outsiders' voices were as hollow and mournful as a loon's cry.

Sound had always traveled strangely on Endla.

"What do you think they're doing?" Sage whispered against Leelo's ear, sending a chill down her spine.

Leelo shook her head. It was impossible to tell through the fog. They'd only been Watchers for a few weeks, and so far they'd had no interaction with the villagers across the water. They shouldn't even be here. They *wouldn't* be here if it were spring. Winter had made them complacent.

She stretched and looked out at the few remaining ice floes, scattered like the reflections of clouds on the water's glassy surface. The majority of the lake was too deep to freeze, and only the rare fool was bold enough to attempt the crossing.

The carcasses of young migratory birds served as the occasional reminder—should anyone need it—of the lake's magic. They washed up on the shore with their feathers and flesh eaten away by a poison so strong it could sink a wooden boat long before it would ever make it across.

"Maybe we'll be lucky this year," Leelo murmured, more to herself than Sage. "Maybe no one will come."

Sage snorted. "They *always* come, cousin." She tugged on Leelo's blond braid and rose. "Come on. Our shift is over, and they're not going anywhere for now. Let's find Isola."

They hadn't seen their friend much over the winter, but Isola, who was a year older, had been finishing up her own mandatory year as Watcher. Now that Leelo had done it herself, she wouldn't blame Isola if she spent an entire month hibernating. Watching was both boring and exhausting all at once.

Leelo followed Sage into the trees, the soles of her shearling-lined boots quickly becoming mired in the mud and dead leaves left behind by the melting snow. She hated this time of year. Everything was dirty and drab, even their clothing. She wouldn't wear the bright, beautiful dresses her mother made until the spring festival.

Sage stopped to pluck a branch of red holly berries from a bush, quietly murmuring a prayer of thanks to the woods that provided so bountifully for Endla. As Watchers, it was their job to protect their home from the merciless outsiders who had destroyed all but this, the last of the Wandering Forests. "We have to finish making our crowns. You haven't even chosen a theme yet."

Leelo sighed. "I still have time."

She had always loved the spring festival, but now she clung to the days like a child at her mother's skirt. The sooner it was spring, the sooner her little brother, Tate, would be leaving, unless by some miracle his magic emerged before then. Whenever she thought of Tate out there among the outsiders, she wanted to cry. Because if she wouldn't be there to care for him, who would?

They left the main trail and made their way to Isola's cottage, where Sage knocked briskly on the door. Nearly a minute passed before it opened a few inches, revealing Isola's sleep-swollen face and tangled hair.

"What is it?" Her words came out as a croak, clearly the first she'd spoken this morning.

"We're sorry." Leelo ducked her head, already retreating. "We didn't realize how early it was."

"It isn't early," Sage said. "Isola is just lazy."

Leelo nudged her cousin with her elbow, though Sage had never been known for her tact.

The girl blinked a few times, trying to rouse herself. "I didn't sleep well, that's all. What are you doing here? Shouldn't you be Watching?"

Sage shrugged. "Our shift ended. Nothing was happening, anyway."

A shadow passed over Isola's gaze. "Nothing ever happens, until it does."

It was such a strange thing to say that Leelo wondered if something had occurred on Isola's Watch, something she and Sage had never heard about. It was entirely possible an outsider had attempted the crossing without all the younger islanders knowing. But any successful breach would have been announced. Outsiders caught by Watchers were always given a choice: the Forest or the lake. Either way, they were never heard from again.

A low voice called Isola's name from inside the cottage before Leelo could ask what she meant.

"Sorry, that's my father. I should go."

Sage rolled her eyes and turned back to the woods, not even bothering with a goodbye. Isola shrugged an apology at Leelo, and she smiled in sympathy, having borne the brunt of Sage's short temper for seventeen years.

Every rose has its thorn, her mother would remind Leelo after Sage had said or done something cruel. Her cousin *was* prickly, but she was also strong, intelligent, and fiercely loyal. If Leelo were ever in trouble, she knew Sage would come to her rescue, no questions asked.

They were almost back at their own cottage when movement in the bushes caught Leelo's eye. A flash of dark hair and pale skin. She stopped and looked around as if she'd just had an idea.

"You're right, I should get to work on my crown. Take my bow and tell Mama I'll be home soon?" Sage and her mother had moved in with Leelo's family when both of their fathers died in a hunting accident, when Tate was still a toddler. It wasn't unusual for several generations of one family to live together on Endla, but it was rare that two women would be widowed so young, especially sisters.

Fortunately, Leelo's mother, Fiona, and her aunt, Ketty, were resourceful women. Ketty had taken over tending to her family's small flock of sheep, which produced the wool Leelo's mother wove into clothing. Endlans traded for most of their possessions and food, so it was important to have a skill, something that few other people could provide. They weren't the only shepherds, but Leelo's mother made the finest woolen goods on the island. Together, the sisters were able to provide for their family, but winters were always lean.

"I can help," Sage offered, but Leelo shook her head.

"No, no. Aunt Ketty will be expecting you. I won't be long."

"Suit yourself." Sage hefted both bows and went into the house, the little string of bells they kept on the doorframe tinkling as she let the door fall shut behind her. It was several more minutes before Tate dared reveal himself, afraid he'd be caught shirking his duties by his strict aunt.

He had grown so much in the last year Leelo almost didn't recognize him as the same raven-haired baby she'd helped raise. He was so beautiful he was often mistaken for a girl, at least until he was old enough to walk and people saw him clad in trousers, not skirts.

Ketty had given him his name, calling him *as ugly as a potato* when he was born. She said it so often that "Tate" stuck, even though everyone knew it wasn't true. But sometimes, when Leelo's mother was nursing him to sleep in the middle of the night, Leelo heard her call him Ilu, "precious one," with a faraway look in her eyes that Leelo had never seen before.

"Come on, then," Leelo said, waving her brother closer. "You can help me make a crown for the festival."

He grinned, happy to be involved however he could. Islanders like Tate—*incantu*, they were called, or "voiceless"—weren't allowed to attend the festival, even though he wasn't quite old enough to be affected by the magic yet. Once an islander reached adolescence, generally around age twelve, they were susceptible. But even though she understood the reasoning behind it, Leelo hated the rule. As if the incantu didn't feel like outcasts already.

They walked in silence for a while, until the trail faded into the undergrowth and they were forced to forge their own path.

"What should I choose for my crown?" Leelo asked Tate. It was tradition for each young adult to decorate a crown honoring Endla's flora or fauna, a way of symbolizing that they were all an important part of its ecosystem. Sage had decided on a deer. Mostly, Leelo surmised, as an excuse to wear something sharp.

Tate chewed on his lower lip for a moment, eager to come up with the right answer. "What about a fox?"

"Hmm… A bit too cunning for me, perhaps."

He stared at his feet, thinking. "A squirrel?"

Leelo grinned and twitched her nose. "I was thinking of something a little less whiskery." They had wandered close to the lake, but they weren't in danger of encountering an outsider here, where the far shore was barely visible.

"A swan!" Tate said suddenly.

"Now, where would I get…" Leelo's voice trailed off as she saw the cygnet floundering in the shallows. She glanced around, making sure they were alone, before picking up a muddy stick and hurrying toward the water.

"Careful!" Tate called, shrinking back. They were taught from the time they could walk to never go near the water, but the poison was always weaker at this time of year. Leelo suspected it had something to do with the ice melting, diluting the poison somehow, but she didn't know for sure. All she knew was that the swan would die if she didn't help it.

"Foolish fellow," she said, trying to reach it with the stick. It had stopped struggling, its heart and lungs probably already damaged beyond repair. Finally, she managed to nudge the swan close enough that she could reach it.

Wrapping her hand in her cloak, she took a hold of the swan's long, graceful neck. It was so weak it didn't even struggle.

"Is it dead?" Tate asked, peering over her shoulder.

"Not yet, but I'm afraid it's too late to save it." Leelo's fingers itched to stroke the gray down giving way to snowy white feathers. The creature was so beautiful she felt her eyes fill with tears. "The poor thing. It didn't deserve to die this way."

Every year, young birds made the mistake of landing on what appeared to be a pristine mountain lake, not realizing no fish lived in its waters, no plants grew in its shallows. Within a day, the birds were reduced to nothing but their hollow bones. Given long enough, even those would eventually dissolve. Leelo had never encountered a bird that was still alive before.

Feeling the creature's life slip away in her hands was somehow worse than hunting, because this death was senseless. They couldn't eat the meat, as it was already tainted by the poison.

After a few minutes, Tate placed his hand gently on his sister's shoulder. "It's not suffering anymore, Lo."

She sniffed and dried her cheek on her shoulder. "I know."

"Maybe you can wash the feathers and use them for your crown. Then a small piece of it will live on, in a way."

Leelo turned to look into her brother's brown eyes, her heart swelling at his gentle earnestness. She rose and pulled him into an embrace. "That's a lovely idea," she whispered against his soft hair. "Will you help me?"

He nodded. "Of course."

Together, they rinsed the lifeless cygnet with fresh water from Leelo's waterskin, then wrapped it in Leelo's cloak before heading back toward the house. On the way, Tate gathered a few thin branches from the Forest floor, supple enough to bend into a crown. Leelo pointed out some brilliant blue berries that would make the perfect adornment. Tate plucked half a dozen, whispered a prayer, and placed them in his pocket for safekeeping.

When they were nearly at the house, Tate stopped to tie his bootlace and motioned for Leelo to kneel down next to him.

"What is it?" she asked.

He kept his voice low, though they were still alone. "Aunt Ketty is watching from the window." Leelo knew well enough not to look up. "She hates me."

"She doesn't hate you," Leelo assured him. "She's just Ketty."

He frowned. "She's going to wonder what we were doing."

"I'll tell her I asked for your help. Don't worry, little brother."

"I'm scared."

Leelo knew he wasn't talking about their aunt anymore. She reached out and cupped the dwindling roundness of his cheek for just a moment. "If it's any consolation, so am I."

They shared a small, sad smile before straightening. "I'll wash and pluck the swan," Tate said. "You should go and finish your chores."

"Be careful. Wear gloves."

He raised his chin as he took the bundled creature from her hands. "We look out for each other, don't we?"

Her chest ached with love, and with guilt for the lie she was about to tell. "Always."

Late that night, when everyone else in her house was asleep, Leelo sneaked out, taking a knife from the kitchen on her way. Guided by nothing but moonlight and her own sense of purpose, she made her way to the center of the island, to the heart of the Wandering Forest.

The trees here were special. Each belonged to one of Endla's families, serving as a kind of patron saint to which the
family prayed and left offerings. But winter was the one season that the islanders kept away from the grove. Offerings
required a song, and Endlans didn't sing in the winter. It
was the only way to ensure outsiders didn't come across the
ice inadvertently. After all, it was one thing for a Watcher to
stop an outsider intent on attacking the Forest or its inhabitants; accidentally luring an innocent with song, however,
was against their code.

But tonight, Leelo was prepared to violate the code. Prayers
hadn't worked, which could only mean the Forest wanted a
sacrifice. And while she wouldn't kill an animal—the killing
song, which lulled prey into a trancelike state, was too powerful to perform on her own, and there was too much of a
risk someone would hear—a small blood sacrifice might be
enough to wake Tate's dormant magic.

She hunched down below her family's tree, a tall, stately
pine that was hundreds of years old, as ancient as the Wandering Forest itself, according to Aunt Ketty. Even before she
dragged the knife across her palm, Leelo could feel the music
pressing at her throat, so eager to be released after months of
silence.

As the blade bit into her skin, the music poured out of her
along with the blood, and she almost believed she could hear
the trees sighing, though that was probably just the wind. And
the way the blood seeped into the ground so quickly, like the
roots were drinking it up, was probably just the moonlight
playing tricks on her.

And if somewhere across the water, an unwitting young
traveler was tossing in his sleep, unaware that the lake whose
shore he slept on was full of poison, or that the Forest on the

island in its center was just awakening after a long, hungry winter…

Well, then, he should have camped somewhere else tonight.

Copyright © 2022 by Mara Rutherford